# SEA OF LOVE

Hesther Quantock is loathed and feared by those who run the shipping lines between England and the Continent. With ruthless cruelty she has been involved in the sinking of many ships, with great loss of life, all to increase her own profit.

Captain Luke Calthan is resolved to avenge his many losses. He has hardened his heart against all women, until he discovers Gabrielle, Hesther's granddaughter – a stowaway on a mission to find her father.

The passion between Gabrielle and Luke is difficult to ignore, but will the hated name of Quantock come between them?

# SEA OF LOVE

# SEA OF LOVE

*by*

## Mary Minton

**Magna Large Print Books**
Long Preston, North Yorkshire,
BD23 4ND, England.

British Library Cataloguing in Publication Data.

Minton, Mary
    Sea of love.

    A catalogue record of this book is
    available from the British Library

    ISBN   0-7505-1523-6

First published in Great Britain by Severn House Publishers
Ltd., 1999. Originally published in 1981 by Macdonald Futura
under the title *Marriage of Revenge* and pseudonym of Jayne
Joyce

Copyright © 1981 by Ena Young

Cover illustration © Melvyn Warren-Smith by arrangement
with P.W.A. International Ltd.

The moral right of the author has been asserted

Published in Large Print 2000 by arrangement with Severn
House Publishers Limited

Magna Large Print is an imprint of Library Magna Books Ltd.

Printed and bound in Great Britain by
T.J. (International) Ltd., Cornwall, PL28 8RW

# CHAPTER ONE

## 1792

Every Christmas, after the midday meal, the family seated themselves round the oak-panelled room, their gaze on the cold-eyed woman who sat stiffly erect in the tall brocaded chair.

The room, although large, was warmed by the forest of logs in the huge stone fireplace. Dancing flames were reflected in copper jugs holding evergreens, there was a brightness of red berries in the garlands of holly placed round the room, bunches of mistletoe hung from oak beams.

In any other house all this would have given an air of festivity, but not in this one.

And how could it, thought seventeen-year-old Gabrielle Quantock. There was too much tension among those gathered here, too much fear. What would the next year hold? The well-being of all, their clothing, the roofs over their heads were dependent on her tyrannical grandmother who sat, a matriarch, surveying them all, contempt in her eyes. She knew she had only to point a bony finger at one of them, issue a command to come to her and the one concerned would jump up immediately.

Gabrielle felt a contempt for them too, apart from her much-loved father who would stand up to her grandmother from time to time. But even he was forced to give in to her on occasions for the sake of her mother, who had a mortal fear of losing the home that Hesther Quantock provided. Her father, during the year, spent some time away from home conducting business for her grandmother, and it was Gabrielle's great grief at this moment that he was not here to spend Christmas with them. He ought to have been, he was due back ten days ago. Even her mother, who no longer loved her father, was becoming anxious. To all enquiries, however, her grandmother informed them coldly that Christmas was unimportant, profit came first.

Stephen Lawford was not here this year either. He had gone on the Grand Tour. Stephen and his family were neighbours of her grandmother and Gabrielle had known them since she was a child.

'Your attention!' At the rapped words of command from Hesther Quantock there was a perceptible straightening of shoulders.

Gabrielle knew that soon a husband would be picked for her. The announcement *could* be made this evening. If so she would refuse the man chosen. It was time someone

10

other than her father rebelled.

'George–' Her grandmother's imperial finger was pointed at her third son. 'You have a daughter as yet unwed. She has been bespoken by Sebastian Harcourt. The wedding will take place a month today.'

There was a gasp from Elspeth, George's youngest daughter, who looked about her as though seeking some way of escape. She seemed about to say something when her mother, looking distressed, laid a hand on her arm. George bowed his head, 'Yes, Mama, we shall make the necessary arrangements.'

Gabrielle leapt to her feet and, head held high, her eyes tawny in her anger, defied her grandmother. 'I make a protest.'

The astonishment at this was so great that in the ensuing silence the sound of a log shifting in the grate seemed to be magnified a hundred times. Her mother shook her head at her in a desperate way, but Gabrielle was not deterred.

'How can you all sit there and allow this to happen? My cousin Elspeth is not yet fifteen years old, and is to be married to a man who is old enough to be her father. Sebastian Harcourt has lost four wives in childbirth – the man is – diseased.'

'Hold your tongue girl, and sit down!'

This almost hysterical outburst came from her mother whose thin, tight-lipped face

11

was suffused with blood.

'No, Mama, I will not hold my tongue. I will have my say.'

'How dare you!' This from her grandmother whose clawed fingers gripped the arms of the chair. 'Come here to me, girl. At once.'

'No.'

There was a murmur of disbelief at such open defiance and the gaze of the people went to Gabrielle's mother for her reaction. Although the woman's face worked with temper she could not get her words out. Then she too was ordered to stand in front of her mother-in-law.

'Your daughter will also be wed a month from today,' said the cold and penetrating voice of the old lady. 'She will be married to Gideon Walraven.'

Gideon Walraven? Gabrielle felt rage boil within her. Even her mother looked startled.

'I refuse to marry Mr Walraven, Ma'am. He is not only an ugly man but has a name for brutality.'

The thin tight lips of her grandmother tightened yet further.

'He will wield a whip to you and that is what you need. You have been ill brought up – and to teach you obedience you will be soundly whipped now – and in my presence.' The old lady turned to her eldest son. 'Edward, in the absence of the girl's

12

father you will do the beating.'

Edward, whom Gabrielle liked best of all her uncles, looked at her with eyes that held pain. He was a big, generous man, but had never been able to stand up to his mother. And then suddenly, to Gabrielle's surprise, he protested.

'I cannot do it, Mama. I cannot bear Gabrielle to suffer the indignity of a whipping at her age – especially in public.'

'You will do it or you and your family will be homeless.' There was a look of malicious triumph in Hesther Quantock's eyes.

When Gabrielle saw the trapped and despairing look on her uncle's face she went up to him and said gently, 'Do it, Uncle Edward, you have responsibilities, and any pain inflicted will soon pass.'

Then she turned to her grandmother. 'I will submit to the whipping, the spectacle of which I feel sure you will greatly enjoy, but I will not marry Mr Walraven. I would rather kill myself first.'

'You speak with the glibness of the young. You will be married a month today. I have means of making you.' To Gabrielle's mother she said, 'Bring the switch from the cupboard.'

There was distress in the eyes of the women who had daughters. It could have been one of their children in a similar position. In the eyes of some of the men there was a look of sensual anticipation.

Her uncle still refused to take the switch and her mother, eyes aflame, said, 'I will do it, and take pleasure in it.'

She pushed Gabrielle face down over a chair, threw her velvet gown over her head and then her petticoats.

Gabrielle had suffered whippings from her mother in the past, but the last one had been when she was twelve years old. The whippings then had been severe and in preparation for the pain Gabrielle gripped the legs of the chair and clenched her teeth.

But the strokes were so brutally dealt it took all her courage to refrain from crying out. She felt sure that each cut must have drawn blood. Then, just as she was beginning to wonder how she could endure the excruciating pain without making a sound, she heard her uncle shout, 'That is enough!' and he snatched the switch from her mother.

As Gabrielle struggled to her feet her mother tried desperately to wrest the switch from her uncle. 'Let me have it, let me have it,' she shouted.

'You will not get it, Ma'am. And if you persist in trying to get it from me you shall feel it across your face.'

All that had gone before in the room seemed as nothing to this defiance of the gentle Edward. The pleasure it gave to

Gabrielle made her momentarily forget her pain.

Her grandmother gave a bark of laughter. 'So my firstborn shows some spirit. I was beginning to think I had spawned a complete weakling. I shall let this pass, Edward, but never, and I repeat, *never* defy me again. Is that understood? If you do I shall destroy you.'

'Yes, Mama.'

Hesther Quantock turned to two of her other sons.

'Lock my granddaughter in her room. She shall stay there until the day of her marriage.'

Gabrielle was hustled upstairs, thrown into the room and the door quickly locked behind her. She had caught hold of one of the poles of the four-poster bed to catch her balance, now she clung to it. If only her father had been here this would never had happened. There was one thing certain, when he did return and hear what had happened he would have something to say to his mother, and would never allow her to marry the brutal Gideon Walraven.

The throbbing pain in Gabrielle's buttocks brought on a quick surge of tears, but she hurriedly brushed them away. There was no time for weeping, she must escape. She went over to the window.

The room she had shared with Elspeth for

the past four nights was on the second floor and there was no shed underneath on which she could drop if she got out. But perhaps with knotted sheets–? There were, of course, other obstacles. For one thing she had no money, for another where could she go and then of course how could she let her father know where she had gone?

Gabrielle's body took on a sudden chill as she recalled her grandmother's words when she ordered her to be locked up. She knew her father would never allow her to marry the hateful Gideon and yet she had said, 'She shall stay there until the day of her marriage.' It was as though she did not expect her father back. Had something happened to him? No, they would have heard. Bad news always travels fast.

In spite of this Gabrielle found it difficult to dismiss the fact that something *could* have happened to her father. She had no idea of what type of business he conducted. When she once asked him he dismissed it lightly as being a man's affair. Even her mother, she felt sure, knew nothing about it. Gabrielle only guessed that her father travelled to another country by something he had once let slip. He had mentioned the weather in France, then quickly moved on to some-thing else. And close as they were she would not question him.

Gabrielle moved away from the window

and kept on moving around the room. It was impossible to sit down with any comfort and she felt she needed to be active. Would young Ellen the skivvy bring her up some food? It would probably be only bread and water, but Ellen might know what was going on. Servants often overheard things.

But Ellen did not come. Gabrielle had no means of knowing the time but it seemed she had been waiting for hours, hoping the girl would put in an appearance and she could question her. The fire, which had been lit earlier, had now burned to dull embers and there was no fuel to replenish it. Gabrielle pulled the eiderdown from the bed and wrapped it round her. Once she had climbed on to the bed and lain on her stomach but with the pain of her buttocks seeming to go all over her body she soon slid to the floor again.

Gabrielle felt sure if Ellen was not allowed to come near her then none of the family would dare, and yet she had a feeling of waiting for something to happen, she felt certain something *was* going to happen.

When at last she heard low talking she stood listening, her heartbeat quickening, but the people passed her door and moments later she heard two bedroom doors closing further along the landing.

After a while there were all the mild creakings and whisperings of a house settling down for the night and the scuttling of mice in the wainscotting. Gabrielle closed her eyes and leaned her back against the bed post, feeling as though she could sleep standing up. Then suddenly she heard someone scrabbling outside her door. She hurried over and whispered, 'Who is it?'

In answer a piece of paper was pushed under the door.

She picked it up and took it over to the lamp. The handwriting was an unfamiliar scrawl. It said:

*'Soon your door will be unlocked. Be prepared to leave. Travel light. Open window before you leave and lock door after you. Then go to secret place you knew as a child and wait. Someone will come for you.'* The note was unsigned.

Gabrielle, with a shivery feeling of excitement, brought out a small valise and packed it with necessary garments, replaced her satin slippers for stout shoes and put on a warm cloak. She then went to the door to wait. The secret place was a barn about half a mile away.

It must have been ten minutes later when she heard the stealthy turning of the key. Gabrielle pulled up the hood of her cloak, took a quick breath and opened the door. No one was in sight.

A fitful moon showed the way to the main staircase. With her heart thumping against her ribs she crept along the landing, and down the stairs, every creak making her wince, and glance back fearfully. Once in the hall she sped to the back door where the bolts had been drawn. Outside she stood listening for several seconds then turned to her left where bushes and trees would cover her flight.

The road to the barn was familiar but snow and ice had made ruts difficult to negotiate and several times she stumbled. Now and again she thought she heard footsteps behind her, but she ran on. By the time she reached the narrow lane that led to the barn her breath was rasping in her throat.

She paused here to look back and saw to her relief the road was deserted. From that point she walked the rest of the way, trying to recover her breath.

The moon, partly obscuring the cloud, gave a ghostly feeling to the night, the derelict barn stood stark against the greyness of the countryside. Then the cloud moved away and the bright moonlight silvered the fields and the roof of the barn, chasing the hobgoblins away. At least for the time being.

When Gabrielle pulled open the creaking door and faced the inner blackness she wondered how she had ever dared to hide here as a child, especially as the hiding place was under a trap-door, a storeroom cut out of the earth.

At that time, of course, their games had been during daylight hours. On the other hand once the trap-door was closed she had been in blackness.

On this occasion Gabrielle had brought a candle and tinderbox from her bedroom, unsure whether she still had the fearlessness of childhood.

Once inside the barn Gabrielle trod carefully, not knowing what vermin she might disturb. She would have liked to light the candle but was afraid of anyone seeing the moving flame. There were cracks in the wooden laths of the barn.

She kicked aside the rotting straw covering the trap-door. Would the wood have rotted? Finding the ring she hooked her finger in it and tugged. The trapdoor took some moving but surprisingly it felt strong. The worst part would be going down the ladder. The treads could be rotted.

The mingled smell of the rotting straw and the earthy smell that had risen when the trap-door was raised gave her a queasy feeling. But then she had had nothing to eat or drink since the Christmas meal, and she had a healthy appetite.

After going down three treads and finding them firm Gabrielle closed the trap-door over her. She had thought that descending the ladder would be the worst part, but being entombed with the trap-door closed was quite definitely the worst. She had to fight down a sudden feeling of choking.

Gabrielle brought out the candle and the tinderbox and felt better when the candle was lit. How long would she have to wait? Was there a possibility of her being missed before morning? Who would come for her? Who could have managed to arrange her escape? They were all questions impossible to answer.

It had been bad enough waiting in her room for someone to come, but a hundred times worse waiting here in this underground storehouse. She tried to fix her mind on the family who had once lived here, the farmer perhaps hiding a portion of his grain from the searching eyes of the landowners who claimed a third of whatever he grew.

But whoever had owned the farm had gone from the district long ago. The barn had been empty from as far back as she could remember.

Gabrielle tensed as she heard a movement above her. There were footsteps, men's voices. Her heart began to thump. She blew out the candle. Had they found her hiding place? The voices came nearer, sounding as if the people were above the trap-door.

Then a man called, 'She ain't here–' and the footsteps moved away.

She let her body relax and prepared herself for a long wait. There would be no rescue while men were searching the countryside for her. She relit the candle.

Another movement came from above. Gabrielle tensed. The footsteps this time had a stealthy sound. Once more she extinguished the flame and moved as far as possible from the trap-door.

There came the creaking sound of it being opened. The palms of Gabrielle's hands began to sweat.

'Gabrielle?' The voice was a whisper.

'Who is it?'

There was no reply and to Gabrielle the following silence held a menace. She had noticed a stout piece of wood against the wall and her hand sought it and grasped it. If it was someone who had come to take her back to her grandmother then the man was going to have to put up a good fight.

Gabrielle gripped the piece of wood more firmly as a booted leg appeared on the first step of the ladder.

# CHAPTER TWO

The thin shaft of moonlight which filtered through the open trap-door showed the outline of the booted figure as he carefully negotiated the steps, but once he was past the first three he was lost in blackness.

Gabrielle was standing, breath held, the piece of wood in her hand upraised, when a voice low and musical said, 'Into what Stygian darkness am I descending?'

Relief and gladness flooded through her. There was only one person who would use such a phrase.

'Stephen – where on earth have *you* come from?' She dropped the piece of wood and went to him.

'Where are you?' His hands groped for her and pulled her to him. 'Gabrielle, my dear–'

'Oh, Stephen, I can hardly believe it. We thought you to be on the other side of the world. When did you arrive home?'

'Yesterday, but explanations must come later. We must leave at once.'

She drew back. 'How did you know where I was?'

'Later, Gabrielle, the important thing is to get you and Elspeth away from your dragon of a grandmother.'

'Elspeth?'

'She and her brother are waiting in the carriage outside. It was Harold who came to seek my help. He and Elspeth will go to good friends in Hounslow while I shall take you to my aunt in London. Come along.'

Until they reached the doorway of the barn Stephen's features had been just a pale blur. Now by the light of the moon she saw how thin his sensitive face had become in the year he had been away. Dear Stephen, so gentle, so kind, he was the brother she had never had.

He put a restraining hand on her arm and nodded towards the moon. They waited until it was obscured by a cloud then moved away, keeping close to the side of the barn. With his hand under her elbow Stephen guided Gabrielle over the rough ground, telling her that the carriage was well hidden in the forest.

Once in the forest every shadow seemed to become a lurking figure, and yet Gabrielle felt strangely excited by the drama of the situation. She prayed they would manage to escape.

A road, broad enough to take a carriage, ran the length of the forest. In summer the linked branches of the trees overhead made a cool green cavern. Now they looked like witches' brooms and skeleton arms, the bony fingers splayed. The carriage was so well hidden by massive oaks that Gabrielle started in surprise when they came to it.

Elspeth reached out a hand to Gabrielle and gave a relieved cry. 'Thank goodness you are safe, Gabrielle. Come and sit by me. I need your bold spirit to bolster me up.' Elspeth handed her a silken cushion. 'Stephen thought to bring this, thinking it might help to ease the trial of the journey.'

How like Stephen, so caring. The cushion was beautifully soft but when Gabrielle sat down she had to bite on her lower lip to stop herself from shouting out. How would she manage to suffer the agony of riding in a jolting vehicle? But she must, and she must make no fuss. She was lucky to have this opportunity of escaping from her grandmother's tyranny.

Harold said, taking a seat opposite, 'It must be very painful for you, Gabrielle, *very* painful indeed.'

He was three years older than his sister, a small pale young man with a slightly receding chin. Gabrielle had always thought him weak, but his voice was forceful enough as he went on, 'When I heard of Grandmother's plan to marry Elspeth to that odious Sebastian Harcourt, and I saw the indignity she made *you* suffer, Gabrielle, I made up my mind I must get you both away from her clutches.'

Stephen, who had been giving instructions to the driver said as he climbed in, 'And it was commendable of you, Harold. Thank heavens you came to me for help. We can only hope we will not be intercepted.'

They moved away, the horses at walking pace at first, but once they had turned right into a high-hedged lane they moved more quickly. There had been little traffic on this part and the snow which had fallen in light flurries during the afternoon was soft enough to muffle the sound of wheels and hooves.

When Harold, with some consternation, remarked they were surely going in the wrong direction for London, Stephen explained they were making a detour and would join the main road later, adding that anyone searching for Gabrielle would expect her to go to the village inn and board the London stage from there. In spite of this, all four were on edge until they accepted they were not being followed.

Now a little more relaxed Elspeth asked Stephen if he thought that she and her brother would have been missed yet. Stephen shook his head and smiled. 'I doubt it. Your grandmother would certainly not expect to have *three* rebels in the family. To her, this would be totally unbelievable.'

'*I* am a very frightened rebel,' Elspeth declared. She was pale like her brother and had the sweet prettiness of a child with her pale blue eyes and golden curls.

Some people in the family thought they saw a resemblance between Elspeth and Gabrielle, but although both were fair and slenderly built, the resemblance ended there. Gabrielle gave an impression of height in the way she held herself at times. She had big, widely-spaced eyes, eyes that would turn a soft warm golden when dealing with a sick animal, appear tawny and flash fire when angry or opposed, and be a lovely amber colour when shown affection. Men, on social occasions, had declared themselves willing to 'drown in their depths', but although Gabrielle had flirted a little, she had not allowed any man to take a liberty with her. Not that there would have been much opportunity with her mother constantly on the watch, wanting to know what this man or that one had said to her.

Gabrielle, who was suffering more and more agony with every sway and jolt of the coach, tried to ease her position, but this brought an added pain. Her mother had drawn blood with the severe whipping and now that it was drying and sticking to her clothes each movement was like the tearing open of a wound. She began to ask questions to take her mind from the pain.

'Harold, was it you who wrote the note?'

'Yes, I had managed to persuade Elspeth to leave so I decided to try and get you away as well. It helped tremendously when I heard that Stephen had come home.'

Stephen said, 'It was homesickness that brought me home, but I had no idea until I arrived that my parents would be away visiting. As it happened I was thankful to be there and able to help.'

Gabrielle gave a deep sigh. 'If only my father had been home all this would never have happened. It's the first time he has not been home for Christmas. I wish I knew where he was.'

She was aware of a sudden change of atmosphere in the carriage, a wariness, not with Stephen, he was sitting lost in thought as he so often was. No, the wariness came from Harold and Elspeth. Gabrielle looked from one to the other.

'What is it?' Alarm made her voice sharp. 'Harold, do you know anything about Papa? Has something happened?'

'No, no – not as far as I know.' He looked uneasy.

Elspeth sat up. 'I think Gabrielle should be told.'

Harold spread his hands. 'What is there to tell? After all, it's only surmise on our part. It was just a conversation I overheard. It would be foolish to worry Gabrielle over such a thing.'

Stephen was now alert. 'What conversation? Was it something to do with your Uncle Jonathan?'

'If it is for heaven's sake tell me, Harold,' Gabrielle said, 'no matter whether you think it important or not.'

He shrugged. 'Well, I shall tell you but it really is so little to go on. I don't really know why I told Elspeth. I didn't pay any attention when I first heard it. But, here it is.'

Harold told how he was looking for a cravat pin which he had lost in a field while out riding the day before, when he became aware of voices on the other side of the hedge.

'It was Grandmama and a man,' he said. 'I was curious and eavesdropped. From what I could see through a gap in the hedge the man appeared to be a seafaring type, perhaps a captain. He had an air of authority. What really captured my attention was the old lady saying her son had now found out too much and something had to be done about him. I was so busy wondering which son and what it was he had found out, that I missed the next piece of conversation. After that there was an argument about money and in the end the man agreed to the amount offered. Then Grandmama said that the important thing was not only to get the goods out of

29

England, but that they stayed where they were, which I thought an odd thing to say.'

'And–?' Gabrielle prompted when Harold stopped.

'Some sheep nearby started bleating and the only words I caught after that was the man mentioning Australia and the name of a ship.'

'And after that?'

Harold raised his shoulders. 'That was it, there was no more.'

'Yes, there was,' Elspeth said. 'You told me the emphasis on the word goods made you think she could have meant a person.'

Gabrielle's eyes went wide. 'Are you trying to say that the goods meant Papa and that he was being shipped to Australia?'

'Well, I – I thought so, but of course I could be quite wrong.' Harold was now beginning to look most uncomfortable.

Stephen began to probe, wanting to know when Harold had begun to attach some importance to the conversation, but it was Elspeth who answered.

'It was when Uncle Jonathan did not return. He said the night before he left he would see us all at Christmas, and how he was looking forward to it. He promised to bring me some ribbons. Uncle Jonathan was always so sweet and kind to me.'

Gabrielle looked at Stephen in an anguished way. 'And his last words to me were that nothing, not earthquake, flood or fire would keep him away at Christmas. Oh, Stephen, do you think that Grandmama could be so evil as to send Papa away forever?'

'No,' he leaned forward and touched her hand gently. 'I think as Harold has said, it was surmise. You were all worried that your father did not come home, and a worried mind imagines all sorts of dreadful things happening. Try and get a little sleep, Gabrielle.' He laid a fur rug over her knees, pulled it up over her and tucked it in.

What with the pain and the worry Gabrielle would have thought it impossible to sleep, but nature often helps and she did sleep. She roused briefly when they stopped for a change of horses, and then drifted off again until they reached Hounslow where Harold and Elspeth were to leave them. Before they left Gabrielle asked Harold the name of the ship the captain had mentioned.

'It was Spanish,' he said. 'The Pueblo – something like that.'

'What did the man look like?'

'Small, bushy eyebrows, a thick nose, and well spoken.'

They parted then with a promise to keep in touch and Harold begging Gabrielle not to worry.

When the carriage bumped over some

31

deep ruts in the road and Gabrielle cried out Stephen was all concern.

'Oh, Gabrielle, if only I had called at your grandmother's last night it might have saved you all this pain. I doubt she would have had you whipped with a guest there.'

'It would have made no difference,' she replied grimly. 'Knowing my grandmother the punishment would have been carried out even if the King himself had been there!'

Stephen looked thoughtful. 'I never quite understood why your grandfather left the estate to his wife and cut out his sons.'

'No doubt she bullied him into it. According to Papa she was the one who brought the money and property to the marriage, and was obviously determined to get it back if he died. She probably assured grandfather that their sons would be well taken care of. And of course they have been – but at what a humiliating cost.' Gabrielle clenched her hands. 'If she has had Papa hurt in any way I shall kill her, I vow it. Would you help me find out what has happened, Stephen?'

'I know someone who might. Luke Caltahn who owns the house my aunt lives in is a sea captain. He stays with her between voyages. He owns a fleet of ships and trades at various ports. His mother and my aunt were good friends. Luke is a

32

difficult person to get to know but my aunt will have nothing wrong said against him, and although I have reservations about him I think he would probably help if he could. That is, if he is not away at sea.'

Gabrielle suddenly realized she had been so caught up in her own worries and pain she had not thought how Stephen's aunt would react to having an unexpected visitor. Stephen had often mentioned his aunt Helen and said what a wonderful person she was, but Gabrielle had never met her. When she mentioned it to Stephen he said, 'She will love having you, she's a warm, generous person and will make you most welcome. I called when I returned to England the day before yesterday but she was out visiting. I left a message to say I would come again to see her.' Stephen smiled, 'I think she will be surprised at such an early return.'

It was very early morning when they drew up at the imposing-looking house. Gabrielle felt she would remember all her life the welcome she received from the stately looking woman, who in spite of having been roused from her slumbers, exuded warmth and hospitality.

After greeting Stephen with delighted surprise at his return, then hearing the reason for it, she turned to Gabrielle and took her hands. 'Oh, you poor child. How you must have suffered. That monster of a woman. How have you endured her gibes, her cruelty? Stephen has told me about her. And that long and uncomfortable ride. My maid Marie will attend to you.'

Gabrielle tried to protest she would be all right but Lady Helen insisted. She offered them refreshments but both Gabrielle and Stephen declined. Marie was summoned and after a few words from her mistress she glanced at Gabrielle with compassion then went out.

When she returned a short while later she bobbed a curtsy and said, 'Everything is prepared, m'lady.'

Helen said to Gabrielle, 'You will find the room warm, the bed aired. We were expecting guests who were unable to come. Sleep as long as you wish, my dear. Let Marie care for you, she really is a most understanding girl.'

Stephen kissed her gently on both cheeks and told her they would talk when she was rested.

Gabrielle followed Marie up a wide curving staircase. She was too exhausted to take in all the furnishings but was aware of an air of wealth, in the carpets, the drapes, the gilt of chairs, the fine furniture.

The room was lovely and warm and the fire had been recently replenished. Flames danced along a pile of logs. Gabrielle, whose stomach had trembled with cold since discarding the fur travelling rug, welcomed the luxury.

Marie, after asking Gabrielle's permission to get out her night clothes, said after she had done so, 'My mistress has explained the situation, Ma'am. Will you allow me to bathe your – wounds and put on some salve?'

Gabrielle felt the colour rising to her cheeks, but she agreed.

No one could have been more gentle than Marie. With Gabrielle's shift soaked with the warm water, the material eased away from the weals and a soothing salve rubbed on the wounds she felt herself halfway on the road to recovery.

Then Marie, after warming the nightgown in front of the fire slipped it over Gabrielle's head and tied the ribbons. 'There, Madam.'

Gabrielle was glad she had brought her best gown. It was of fine white lawn, embroidered and trimmed with ruffles of finest lace which had been made by her godmother. Gabrielle felt that anything less exquisite would be out of place in this beautiful room.

Marie turned back the bedcover. 'Shall I help you into bed, Ma'am?'

'No, I can manage, and thank you, Marie. Would you turn out the lamp, I can see by the firelight.' Marie silently left the room.

Gabrielle flopped on to the bed. And the

next moment gave a sigh of pure bliss. The deepest feather mattress she had ever lain on wrapped itself around her, giving her almost a sensuous feeling. She watched the flames flickering on the ceiling, and felt she was in another world. Would she wake up and find it was all a dream? Her eyelids closed. Would this man Luke Caltahn be able to find out what had happened to her father? If he happened to be away at sea then she would have to start making enquiries herself. Nothing must prevent her finding out the truth.

There were many things Gabrielle wanted to think about but her thoughts became incoherent. Warmth seeped into her. She floated away on a cloud into nothingness.

Gabrielle soon found that the heavenly bed was only the beginning of the attention she was to receive. Breakfast was brought up to her the following morning and an hour later a hot scented bath was prepared, with Marie waiting to wrap large fleecy warm towels around her when she stepped out.

Later when Gabrielle went downstairs and was greeted by Stephen and Helen she said, 'I am being utterly and thoroughly pampered.'

'And enjoying it, I hope?' Stephen teased.

Helen smiled. 'I think it is the right of all beautiful women to be pampered. This morning we shall be thoroughly lazy. We shall read the newsprint and gossip about all the people mentioned. Then this evening–' She paused. 'Oh, I was going to suggest that Stephen escort us to Almacks, but it would perhaps be foolish to draw attention to you, Gabrielle, for the time being at any rate. If it got to the ears of your grandmother that you were here–'

'Gabrielle could be introduced as your protégée, Aunt Helen.' Stephen smiled happily from one to the other as though this solved the problem. 'We can give her another name. Just think of the stir it would cause.'

Gabrielle protested he was embarrassing her then added, 'I would much prefer to stay in, and in any case I brought no ball gowns with me.' She turned to Helen. 'But please, Lady Norton, you and Stephen go, I would be upset if my being here altered your life in any way.'

Helen smiled and patted her hand. 'We can talk about it later. Tomorrow you must choose from the many materials I have and dresses shall be made for you. I have three excellent women who sew for me. And now, let us see what is going on in London.' She opened the news sheet.

Although Gabrielle was wanting to talk about her father and ask about Luke Caltahn she nevertheless found herself interested in the way Helen discussed her contemporaries, freely talking about them, but without any malice. At home when anyone was being discussed the women spoke in low voices as though someone might be waiting outside the door to pounce on them for the indiscretion of their gossip.

When Gabrielle glanced at Stephen he seemed to be once more deep in his own thoughts. And yet, it was he who, eventually, introduced the subject of her father when Helen laid down the newsprint.

No mention of her father had been made when they arrived, only the cruelty of her grandmother and now Helen eyed her with consternation. 'But, Gabrielle, this is too big a load for young shoulders to bear. Some enquiries must be made.'

'Stephen wondered if Mr Caltahn would help?'

'Luke?' Helen looked thoughtful. 'He might. It would depend on the mood he happens to be in. I have a great affection for him, and he treats me with a great deal of respect, but I never at any time invade his privacy. He has his own rooms, and although he will accompany me to balls and parties he has to be the one to offer to do so. I would never ask.'

'Is he at sea at the moment?'

'Yes, but I think he should be about due back. He said when he went away if all went well he would be here just after Christmas.' Helen spread her hands. 'But, of course, anything could delay him, storms, unable to get the price he wants for his cargo... If Luke is not home within the next week I shall approach someone else I know.'

During the afternoon when they were all drowsing in front of a glowing fire Gabrielle tried to persuade Helen to go to Almacks that evening with Stephen accompanying her. At first they both refused to leave her, but Gabrielle persisted, knowing that Helen enjoyed a social life. It was still the Christmas season, she said, and Stephen, who had been away a year, would be pleased to meet his many friends. And finally won the day by adding she intended to have an early night anyway, and would be going to bed at the time they would be setting out for Almacks.

Helen laughed. 'You have a most persuasive way, Gabrielle. I think you could twist any man round your finger with your arguments and the haunting way you look at one with those very beautiful eyes. I really must take you to a rout or a ball one evening. I feel sure you would have men swooning over you.'

Gabrielle murmured it was an exaggeration but she was nevertheless pleased at the compliment.

By the time Helen and Stephen were

ready to leave, Gabrielle, who had discovered a wealth of books in the library, was leafing through a novel. She looked up when they came in.

Helen was wearing a gown of deep blue satin that enhanced the colour of her eyes and there were diamonds in her tall blonde wig and at her throat. Stephen, who declared he had not known what his aunt would be wearing, had chosen a deep blue velvet jacket to wear with a silver brocaded waistcoat and white knee breeches.

'Oh, how elegant you both look,' Gabrielle exclaimed. 'You complement one another wonderfully.'

Stephen swept her a bow and Helen kissed her cheek. And after instructions for Gabrielle to ask Marie for anything she might need, they left.

Gabrielle picked up her book, but found it impossible to concentrate. Luke Caltahn intruded into her thoughts. He sounded a difficult man, but surely he could hardly refuse to make enquiries. He would know all the sea captains and all the ships. For money sailors would talk. Gabrielle had brought a bag of sovereigns with her, which had been given to her over the years by her godmother, who had once said they might buy her something close to her heart.

Well, nothing could be closer to her heart than her father's freedom. That was, if his freedom needed to be bought. Perhaps she was jumping to conclusions. Storms *could* have delayed him. No, Gabrielle had a feeling that the conversation her cousin Harold overheard had been to do with her father. There had been the day when her grandmother threatened him. 'Jonathan,' she said, 'if you continue to be a thorn in my flesh with your constant criticism of my actions, you will regret it, so be warned.'

Gabrielle had no idea in what her father had been opposing his mother but both had been angry, her grandmother more so. He was the youngest son and the most distinguished looking with his aristocratic features, his regal bearing and his thick dark hair. And yet he was such a warm, loving man. Gabrielle had wished many times that her parents could be as loving to one another as they had been when she was a child, but they had drifted apart because of her mother's shrewish tongue.

Her mind ranged over all the marriages in the family and she realized there was only one couple, apart from her parents, who had married for love. This was her cousin Janet and her husband Roger. But within six months of the marriage poor Janet was dead – after a miscarriage – and Roger was not there. Her grandmother had sent him to India to attend to some side of her affairs.

Gabrielle had sometimes wondered if the

sending away of Roger had been deliberate, her grandmother unable to see any of her family happy.

With so much tension Gabrielle had been grateful to her cousin Janet, who was like an older sister to her. It was she who had told her what duties were expected of a wife, and who assured her that being in love was the most wonderful thing in the world. Gabrielle had been shocked at first at hearing the intimate details of marriage, but later began to find the subject intriguing and become curious to know how she would react to such an experience. Sometimes when she tried to imagine herself lying with a man strange emotions would stir in her body, making her limbs go weak.

Gabrielle wondered if Lady Norton had been happy in her marriage. Stephen once told her that Helen had married a man much older than herself and that when he died several years ago he had left a string of debts. But she seemed to live well. Perhaps her family provided for her.

Feeling restless Gabrielle got up and moved round the room. She drew books from the shelves, glanced at them and put them back again. At any other time she would have been totally absorbed with such a large choice. With a sigh she returned to the high-backed sofa and picked up the book she had chosen earlier. And was about to open it when there was the sound of the front door being slammed. The next moment someone came into the library. Thinking it must be Stephen who had forgotten something she peered round the settee and was about to ask what he had forgotten when she drew back, her heartbeat quickening.

Although the man who had come in was younger than one she would imagine owning a fleet of ships, she felt sure it could only be Luke Caltahn. There was the clink of glass and she guessed he was pouring himself a drink. Then he came over to the fireplace and stood, his back to her, staring into the flames. One hand rested on the mantelshelf and the other held a crystal goblet containing an amber-coloured liquid.

Gabrielle had seen him in that first quick glimpse as a tall, broad-shouldered man in his mid-thirties. Now she saw that his dark hair curled at the ends and that his clothes and hessian boots were travel-stained.

Gabrielle wanted to speak, to let him know of her presence, but for some reason she felt tongue-tied. He took a drink, turned – and saw her. He stared.

'Who the devil are you?'

'I – I'm the guest of Lady Norton. She and Stephen – Mr Lawford, have gone to Almacks.'

'And why did they not take you with

43

them?' He made it sound as though having left *her* behind in *his* house was sheer effrontery.

She said, 'I had been travelling and was tired. My name is Gabrielle–' She paused, thinking it perhaps unwise to give her surname. After all, she knew nothing about him.

He gave her a quick bow. 'Luke Caltahn. I too have been travelling, and need to get changed. If you will excuse me.'

Gabrielle felt annoyed she had not attempted to keep him talking and asked his help over her father. But immediately realized the timing would have been wrong. A man like that would have given her a definite no, leaving no opening for further discussion. She got up and put another log on the fire, feeling his presence had brought a chill to the room. It was not only his manner but his eyes. Grey eyes could be warm. Janet's eyes had been a lovely grey. But Luke Caltahn's had been cold, like steel. Was this library his domain and had he resented her intrusion? She must enquire, and if so, take care not to intrude again.

All thoughts of reading had gone from Gabrielle's mind. Would Luke Caltahn come back into the room again? He had obviously cared that he was travel-stained and wanted to change. She had been uncaring about what she had worn – until now. He must have thought her a dowd in her simple grey dress. She could have changed into a more pleasing one, she had brought two with her. Then she thought heavens, fancy worrying about what impression she had made on a man like Luke Caltahn. No doubt he could have his pick of women. In spite of his coldness he was certainly an attractive man. She closed her eyes, trying to conjure an image of him, and saw a strong face, a straight nose, a well-shaped mouth, it was the kind of face she had seen in her dreams when she had thought about the kind of man she would like to marry.

Gabrielle smiled to herself. Luke Caltahn was probably already married, or had 'wives in every port' as some sailors had. Gabrielle decided that whoever she married she hoped the man would show some tenderness, such as her cousin Janet had described. It had been so lovely seeing Janet and Roger together.

Gabrielle thought of her parents who had been happy until her mother began to upbraid her father for not complying with all of her grandmother's orders. One day she had screamed at him, 'If you don't obey her we shall end up without a roof over our heads, and what then?'

'Then we could rent a small cottage and grow our own food and know complete freedom,' he had said quietly. But her mother would have none of this. She was not going to struggle when everything could be provided for them.

Only Gabrielle understood her father's need. They had become very close. She had inherited his love of books, of languages, and they would talk by the river bank, discussing what they had read, or find a quiet corner in the garden where they were free from her grandmother's imperious voice or her mother's sharp tongue.

What did the future hold? Gabrielle, staring into the glow of the fire, began to feel drowsy. But when Luke Caltahn stepped back into the room her drowsiness fled. He was now immaculate in dark green.

He came and stood before her. 'Did you say that Lady Norton had gone to Almacks?'

'Yes.' Gabrielle drew herself up.

Luke Caltahn stood eyeing her with some curiosity. 'Who are you, where are you from? You gave me the name Gabrielle. Who are your parents?'

'I would rather not say. I have run away from home, and have no wish to be traced.'

'Indeed. It sounds quite irresponsible to me, and you certainly show little thought for your parents who must be worried sick about you. In fact, I feel quite surprised that Lady Norton agreed to give you shelter.'

'Lady Norton knows the full story and is sympathetic towards me. You see, Mr Caltahn, my grandmother wanted me to marry a man who is not only old enough to be my father, but is known for his brutality.'

'Your *grandmother* wanted you to marry this man?'

'Yes. She rules the whole family. She sent my father away, supposedly on business, but I think she had him abducted and shipped to a foreign country.'

'Oh dear, how very dramatic.' There was no mistaking the amusement in Luke Caltahn's voice. 'I fear you are letting your imagination run away with you, Ma'am, and I am very much afraid I have no time to indulge it. I have someone to see, will you please excuse me.' He executed an exaggerated bow and walked away.

He was in the hall when Gabrielle, furious at his condescending manner, flung open the door and shouted, 'My surname is Quantock and my grandmother's name is Hesther Quantock. If you ever meet her you will learn the kind of woman she is.'

He stopped, and stood, his back rigid. Then he turned slowly. '*Your* grandmother is Hesther Quantock?'

'She is. Do you know her?'

'Oh, yes, I know her, I know her very well – much to my cost.'

Gabrielle was surprised to see a look of

cold hatred in his eyes. 'Where did you meet?' she asked.

He looked her up and down. 'I wish you had borne any other name, because the name Quantock makes my flesh crawl.' With that he strode away, pausing only for the butler to help him into his caped greatcoat. Then he left, leaving Gabrielle no alternative but to go back into the room, where she stood, hands clenched.

If only she had not been so impulsive. Now perhaps she had lost the chance of his ever helping her. Not unless she could persuade him that by helping her father he would be getting his own back on her grandmother, for whatever she had done to him. What could she have done? Perhaps with some probing she might be able to find out from Lady Norton. Tomorrow she would ask.

But even as Gabrielle thought it she had the distinct impression that Luke Caltahn was not a man who would be easily persuaded about anything.

# CHAPTER THREE

When Gabrielle made enquiries the next morning she was disappointed to find that Lady Norton knew nothing of Luke Caltahn's involvement with her grandmother.

'As I explained, Gabrielle,' she said, 'Luke does not confide any of his business to me. He is an island unto himself. I can only say it is a great pity he has so much hatred for your grandmother, because he would be unwilling to trust you. He might even think it was a ploy of hers to get you here to find out his movements.'

Stephen, who had been sitting quiet, listening to the conversation, spoke up. 'But that is ridiculous. Gabrielle had no idea I would be bringing her here.'

'Ah, but Luke does not know this. We must try and see it from his angle. Most men in business have enemies. Luke will be no exception. Cargoes are plundered by unscrupulous men, men who have spies. Hazarding a guess I would say your grandmother might have interests in a shipping line, and being the kind of woman she is, she might have been responsible for Luke losing a commission, or a cargo.'

'But why should I suffer because of what my grandmother does?' Gabrielle protested. 'I think he behaved most unfairly. I would have appreciated having a chance to defend myself.'

'Well, you may have a chance to do so. Luke will be here for a few days. He came to Almacks last night and while there we all had an invitation to a ball at Lord and Lady Daveney's.'

'Aunt Helen and I decided that you must come too,' Stephen said, smiling at Gabrielle. 'Aunt Helen will introduce you as her protégée and give you a temporary surname, just in case any of your grandmother's "spies" should be lurking. It would be foolish for you to be shut in the house like a nun. You need to enjoy yourself.'

Gabrielle did not feel it would be enjoyment being in the company of Luke Caltahn, knowing the way he felt about her, but if he was to provide the means of finding her father, she must take every opportunity to try to win the man over. She did, however, protest about the lack of a ball gown.

Helen got up. 'We can soon take care of that. Come upstairs with me and choose some material. Once you have made a choice I shall send for the sewing women to make it up.' From a carved oak chest Helen produced the most beautiful materials

Gabrielle had ever seen, rich velvets in jewel colours, fine brocades, satins, silks ..., which she draped over the bed explaining that Luke brought them for her from foreign countries.

She fingered a deep rose velvet. 'No son could have been kinder to me, but when I try and thank him, or show any affection, he withdraws into a shell.'

'Do you know why?'

'No, Gabrielle, and I never enquire. Now, which material shall it be. A virginal white perhaps?'

Gabrielle, wanting something that would make her seem older, picked up a diaphanous silk and held it against her. 'This sea-green, do you approve, Lady Norton?'

'The colouring is perfect for you, but you will need an undergown in the same shade, I feel sure there will be something here–'

With the material found Helen began saying how it should be made. The new Viennese style, she thought, with high waist and full skirt. There would be no trimmings. Simplicity was the key word, and with a necklace of garnets to emphasize the pale column of Gabrielle's throat – Helen smiled suddenly. 'And then what man could resist you?'

The ball was the following evening and Gabrielle was in a fever the dress would not be ready in time, but it was and she could not have been more pleased with it, even though she thought the neckline just a little too daring. When she whirled round the skirt floated about her.

Marie, an expert in hairdressing, dressed Gabrielle's hair in soft curls and when Helen and Stephen saw her they declared their admiration. Then Stephen pulled a face. 'I had better start claiming dances or I shall not get a chance once we arrive at the Daveney's.'

Gabrielle had not seen Luke since the evening she arrived, but as he had promised to escort them to the ball, and as Helen assured her he never broke a promise she looked forward to seeing him again. With luck and a little cajoling she might persuade him to make enquiries about her father.

Luke arrived an hour before they were due to leave. But again Gabrielle did not see him. She hoped to make an entrance to impress him. Helen had lent her a white fur-lined hooded cape and Gabrielle knew she looked well in it. But, as it happened, it was Luke who made the entrance.

Gabrielle was waiting with Helen and Stephen in the hall when Luke appeared at the top of the stairs. She drew in a quick breath.

She had thought him attractive. Now she found something compellingly magnificent and terribly masculine about him as he

52

came down the stairs, head high, in bronze velvet jacket and gold waistcoat patterned in muted shades of greens and browns. His greeting included them all yet Gabrielle felt he had not even glanced at her. He spoke with Helen and Stephen, making sure precautions had been taken against any possible attack by a highwayman. Gabrielle had already handed over the garnet necklace to be put with Helen's diamond one in a reticule until they arrived at Lord and Lady Daveney's. The reticule was placed in a secret compartment under the seat. Gabrielle, in spite of Luke's manner towards her, found it all oddly exciting, especially as pistols were produced and laid beside Stephen and Luke on the carriage seat.

As the carriage drew away with the two men appearing to be on the alert Gabrielle said, 'Do highwaymen still abound in any numbers?'

'They do,' Stephen answered grimly. 'We passed two hanging from gibbets two nights ago. But it isn't only from highwaymen we need protection at the moment, it is—'

Helen, who was sitting beside him laid a hand on his arm and Gabrielle took it as a gesture for him to say no more.

She was puzzling over the reason when she suddenly felt a thrill of fear. He could have meant her grandmother. If she had found out where she was she might send some ruffians to abduct her. But then, Stephen and Luke would not allow such a thing to happen.

Helen spoke in a lighthearted way about people she knew who had thwarted highwaymen and by the time they arrived at the Daveney's Gabrielle was excited again.

People were spilling from carriages and chairs, their clothes giving a rich kaleidoscope of colours. There was colour too in the blue and gold uniforms of the white-wigged flunkeys and in the flaming torches of the link boys.

All was laughter and bright chatter. Helen and Luke and Stephen were hailed from all sides and promises made to meet up again.

Gabrielle's one small disappointment was her dress. She had imagined herself to be outstanding in the lovely seagreen and felt instead like a single feather in the exotic plumage of a bird of paradise, a bird she had seen depicted in one of Stephen's paintings, an art in which he excelled. But not even this could take away her enjoyment of the scene.

When the party met their host and hostess the rest of the guests were kept waiting for some time while Lady Sylvia and Lord Hubert welcomed Stephen with affection after a year's absence, greeted Helen and Luke and showed interest in Gabrielle.

Especially Lady Sylvia, a tall thin woman with a kindly manner. 'Your protégée, you say, Helen? How do you do, my dear. We must talk later. And you must meet my nephew, Edmund.'

Helen discreetly moved Gabrielle forward with a promise they would look out for Lord Sharalon, adding in an undertone to Gabrielle that Luke could not abide the man. This made Gabrielle decide if she did meet Lord Sharalon she would give him special attention, seeing that Luke Caltahn had given *her* none.

The ballroom, in a delicate blue and gold, was lit by the hundreds of candles in the six massive chandeliers and wall sconces. No sooner were they in the ballroom than a thin sandy-haired young man came hurrying up and begged Helen to introduce Gabrielle.

He executed a bow, kissed Gabrielle's hand and looked soulfully into her eyes. 'A sea nymph from an underwater cavern, where have you been hiding all my life? How beautiful you are.'

Gabrielle, noticing that Luke was watching them, a pained expression on his face, said laughing, 'Why, sir, I am just an ordinary mortal.'

'No, no, Ma'am, never ordinary. May I beg a dance – two, three, five–'

Helen took charge. 'Now Edmund, Gabrielle has obligations.'

'Yes, she has.' Luke stepped forward. 'Give me your card, Gabrielle. I shall have the first.' He signed it, handed it back and took his leave. Gabrielle was watching him, in mild astonishment, when she was further astonished to find herself surrounded by a number of young beaux who all wanted to claim dances. In the end she had to say her card was full, just in case Luke should ask for a further dance. Lord Sharalon had managed to claim two. Stephen had signed for three when they arrived.

When Gabrielle had a chance to look around her she saw Luke talking with a voluptuous-looking girl with jet black hair. The girl, gazing up at him in a coy fashion, waved a fan under his nose. Luke although not exactly amiable, did not draw away. In fact Gabrielle thought he might be smiling. Was this the type of person he preferred? If so he was welcome to her.

Gabrielle realized then with a small shock she had actually experienced a pang of jealousy. How could she with a man as arrogant as Luke Caltahn? Was it his sheer masculinity that appealed to a sensuousness in her? But arrogance in anyone was something she detested.

The orchestra struck up for the first dance, which was to be a quadrille. Luke excused himself to the girl and the older woman she appeared to be with and came over. He held out an arm. 'Our dance, I think.'

His manner was so stiff Gabrielle knew if the circumstances had been different she would have found great pleasure in making the excuse of a headache. But she did have to talk with him.

He said as he led her on to the floor, 'How you can smile and jest with that ninny Sharalon beats me.'

Gabrielle's head went up. 'I like him, I found him amusing.'

'You mean you enjoyed his idle flattery.'

'Can you show me any woman who does not enjoy a little flattery?' she asked sweetly. Luke made no answer.

Helen and Stephen with two more couples made up the set. On the surface it was a happy combination. Pleasantries were exchanged during the five sequences, and even Luke praised Gabrielle for her lightness of step, which made her feel glad that her grandmother, for all her other faults, had insisted on every girl in the family being schooled in the social graces by the best tutors.

With the dance ended and bows and curtsies given, the men were escorting the ladies back to their seats. Luke said, 'Please do not get the idea because I asked you for a dance that I've changed my mind about you in any way. The name Quantock still makes my flesh crawl.'

After the enjoyment of the dance it was like a slap in the face to Gabrielle. She stopped. 'Why did you ask me? You were under no obligation to do so. In fact, it might have been more courteous had you asked Lady Norton for the first dance.'

His eyes suddenly blazed. 'Do not tell me Miss *Quantock* what I must or must not do.'

'I apologize,' she said stiffly and walked on.

He caught her up and placed a hand under her elbow, saying under his breath, 'I do not want a scene.'

Gabrielle stared straight ahead. 'Neither do I, Mr *Caltahn*, I can only wonder why you attacked me with so much venom. It was the kind of tactics a child or a foolish woman might have used.' He withdrew his hand quickly as though her elbow had become red hot and she knew she had touched him on the raw by comparing him to a child or a foolish woman. 'I cannot help my name,' she added. 'And for your information I hate my grandmother as much as you do!'

They had reached a line of chairs and Gabrielle sat down. When Luke did not excuse himself she looked up. 'Pray do not feel obliged to stay with me. There must be many women *clamouring* for your attention.'

Helen and Stephen came up then

58

laughing, and Luke, his face thunderous, excused himself. Helen raised her eyebrows. 'What's the matter with him?'

'I happen to be a Quantock and he finds it impossible to forget it.' Gabrielle forced herself to smile. 'Did you enjoy the dance? I did.'

The arrival of Edmund Sharalon helped to get them over an awkward moment.

Gabrielle had never had so much attention in her life as she had that evening, never had such compliments from men who danced with her. Her head was in a whirl, her cheeks flushed. She told herself she no longer cared what Luke Caltahn thought about her, but in spite of this she found herself looking for him from time to time. Once she saw him standing a short distance away, leaning over a fair-haired girl, his arm resting along the back of the seat. An older woman with two younger girls were sitting nearby, all looking at Luke with hope in their eyes. Other fond mamas with marriageable daughters also had their eyes on him.

Just before midnight Helen, Luke and Gabrielle were caught up in another party and when a gong began to boom out the midnight hour she was hugged and kissed by Stephen, greeted by other men and women and was about to greet Helen, when amidst the popping of champagne corks she was seized, spun round and Luke Caltahn's mouth came down over hers. She wanted to push him from her, but his lips, moving in a sensuous, demanding way, brought an unexpected throbbing response in her and for a moment she yielded. Then, horrified at her action, she drew back. His smile held an arrogance. 'I thought I would relent and give you some enjoyment to start you off in the new year.'

Gabrielle, although trembling, managed to say coolly, 'Enjoyable, Mr Caltahn? There is an art in kissing, and one you have obviously not yet mastered. I suggest you take some expert tuition.' With this she turned away from him, but not before she had the satisfaction of seeing the arrogant smile replaced by a black scowl.

Unfortunately, she suffered too for the incident. It was some time before she could put it from her mind and freely enjoy the rest of the evening.

It was four o'clock in the morning when the threesome left the revellers with the weary musicians still managing to play the beautiful melodies as though the evening had just begun. They came out to find bright moonlight and a few snowflakes drifting aimlessly.

Gabrielle, wide awake and still excited, said, 'I could have gone on dancing for another two hours.'

Helen stifled a yawn. 'Good heavens, my dear, I feel sure you must have danced *every* dance.'

'All but one Gavotte. I sat talking with Lord and Lady Daveney and their nephew. I know Lord Sharalon is considered to be a ninny, but I find him so amusing.'

Stephen said, 'I think there is much more to Edmund than people give him credit for. He can talk quite deeply at times. Where is Luke – he ought to be here? The carriage is coming.'

Luke came up as the coachmen brought the carriage to the door. Gabrielle wanted to avoid looking at him, but found it impossible. He was quite the most handsome man she had ever seen. His very arrogance gave him a regal air and she had noticed earlier how he seemed to dwarf other men as tall as himself. Gabrielle was wondering how she could avoid letting Helen and Stephen know there was animosity between them when Luke announced he would ride behind the carriage.

Gabrielle was thinking he had gone to a lot of trouble to avoid travelling with her when Helen explained that Luke would be more likely to spot any highwaymen preparing to attack than if he were riding in the carriage, adding that people were more vulnerable leaving a ball, being sleepy and having drunk during the evening.

They arrived back without incident. The carriage stopped at the front door. Luke rode straight into the stable yard.

Although Helen and Stephen and Gabrielle stood talking in front of the hall fire for several minutes he did not put in an appearance, and at last Helen said they must go up to bed.

Before they went upstairs Gabrielle said, 'Thank you for a lovely evening, Lady Norton. It was the most wonderful I have ever spent.' She gave an ecstatic sigh, 'If I die tomorrow it will have been worth it.'

Stephen teased her and quoted from one of Dryden's poems:

'He who, secure within, can say,

Tomorrow do thy worst, for I have liv'd today.'

'Oh, for goodness sake,' Helen exclaimed, 'all this talk about dying and being secure.'

Gabrielle sobered. 'Am *I* secure? My grandmother could come tomorrow and make me leave with her.'

'Forget your grandmother,' Helen begged. '*And* about dying. You have had a wonderful evening, now savour it.'

When Gabrielle was in bed she did savour it. She went over each phrase spoken, each dance and the men who had claimed her. She heard again their flattering remarks. She had never thought of herself as beautiful. Looking in mirrors was not encouraged by her grandmother, or her mother. Her mother had once said, bitterly, 'I used to study my reflection. At that time I was considered a catch. Look at me now. Your father has turned me into a shrew. At times I feel a hag. I dare not look in a mirror.'

Gabrielle had been determined not to let her mind dwell on Luke Caltahn, but with thoughts of her father Luke surfaced too.

She wished now she had put a curb on her tongue after he had kissed her. Considering she needed his help in tracing her father she was doing everything she could to alienate him. Well, there would surely be other men who could help her. Lady Norton had said she knew of someone else who might help.

Gabrielle, on the edge of sleep, felt herself caught in a number of whirlpools and when she fought her way out of them she found a thin sunlight streaming into the room, and Marie standing at her bedside with a breakfast tray.

'Good morning, Ma'am. Lady Norton asks to be excused today. She is indisposed. Mr Caltahn says he wishes to speak with you and will be in the library at eleven thirty.' Marie paused, then added, 'That is, if the time is convenient for you.'

Gabrielle had a feeling that the girl had added the last sentence herself. Luke Caltahn would issue an order and expect it to be carried out, as he would his men on his ship. But why should he want to see her? He was hardly likely to bring up her remarks on his ability – or non-ability – to kiss. Curiosity made her say to tell Mr Caltahn she would be in the library at the time stated.

Gabrielle had been waiting in the library five minutes when Luke came in. 'Ah, good morning Miss – *Quantock*.' He said her name as though he would have liked to spit it out. 'Lady Norton tells me you have a favour you would like to ask of me?'

His manner was so stiff, so forbidding she had to practically bite her tongue to stop herself from saying she wanted no favour from him.

'I do need help,' she said, 'help to trace my father. You thought I was being dramatic when I told you I felt he might have been abducted on my grandmother's orders. On looking back it may have sounded dramatic, but knowing who my grandmother is I think you might now understand my worry.'

'What made you think she might have had your father abducted?'

Gabrielle repeated what her cousin Harold had told her and at this Luke Caltahn began to show an interest.

'Have you any idea what your father may have found out about his mother?'

'None at all.' Gabrielle paused. '*You* seem

64

to know her very well, Mr Caltahn. Perhaps you can tell me what her business activities are.'

'There are many.' He spoke grimly. 'And many people have suffered because of her. She's an evil woman. Already she has plundered two of my ships and stolen cargoes from my warehouses–'

Gabrielle looked at him wide-eyed. 'Plundered ships – *my* grandmother?'

'The gang of ruffians she employs has.'

'But why–?'

'Why?' He shouted the word. 'For gain, for greed, for power! And may I say I refuse to believe you knew none of this.'

'This is the first I've heard of it,' she said earnestly. 'I had no inkling, you must believe me.' Gabrielle paused. 'Are you sure my grandmother *is* responsible? I know her to be a terrible woman but–'

'Oh, for God's sake!' Luke turned away from her with an impatient gesture and began moving round the room. 'You tell me your grandmother had her own son abducted and shipped abroad, from where he was not to return, and you suggest she's not capable of plundering ships!' Luke stopped and thumped a small table, making the ornaments jump. 'I say that Hesther Quantock is capable of murder and one of these days I feel sure I shall end up killing her.'

Gabrielle's head went up. 'I know my grandmother is cruel and dominating, but I refuse to believe her capable of murder.'

Luke stared at her. 'Then you are more thick-skulled than I thought, girl, and your family must be thick-skulled too if they know nothing of her activities.'

Gabrielle's face flushed. She said quietly, 'My father obviously knew something,' and was aware of a catch in her voice.

After a short silence Luke came over to her. 'I think you must be prepared for the fact that your father may not be – alive.' Luke's more kindly manner softened the harshness of the words.

Gabrielle met his gaze steadily. 'If my grandmother has been directly, or indirectly, responsible for my father's death, then *I* would have no qualms in killing her.'

'You must love your father very much.'

'Yes, I do. He's a wonderful man, and I do know he would never take part in anything that was underhand, even though my grandmother might have tried to blackmail him into doing so. She has the weapon, she controls our lives. Every member of the family is dependent on her for being educated, housed, clothed and fed.'

'And for finding husbands' Luke said wryly.

'That too.'

Luke eyed her thoughtfully for a few

moments then said, 'I shall make enquiries about your father, but naturally, it's impossible to promise any news. I shall let you know if I hear anything.' With that he left and did not return that day.

The following morning when he arrived he appeared to be in a hurry. He went straight upstairs. Helen, who had been about to go up to the drawing room said, 'When Luke is in a hurry he is due to sail. He may be taking the Priscilla out on the evening tide.'

Gabrielle, in a fever of impatience, waited for him to come down again. When he did he was carrying a valise. She went up to him.

'Mr Caltahn, did you find out anything about my father?'

Luke eyed her blankly for a moment then said, 'Oh, oh yes. Apparently he was put on a ship doing a short run to Marseilles.'

'Marseilles? Not Australia?'

The butler came forward with Luke's coat. Luke pushed his arms into it and shrugged it over his shoulders. 'No doubt once the ship reached port your father would be transferred to another ship bound for Australia. Or–'

When Luke hesitated Gabrielle prompted, 'Or what, Mr Caltahn?'

'Your father was ill when he was taken aboard.' Luke spoke quickly and seemed to avoid looking at her. 'He may be left at Marseilles.'

Gabrielle's heart began a quick beating. 'You mean he was – very ill.'

'No, no, I have no idea how ill he was.' Luke's expression was that of a man wanting to be finished with a subject.

'My ship makes a call at Marseilles. I shall make some enquiries. Now I must go.'

'Mr Caltahn–' Gabrielle took a quick breath. 'Will you take me with you?'

'Take you–?' He looked astonished as if she might have suggested they elope together. 'That is impossible, utterly impossible.'

'But don't you see,' she pleaded, 'if my father is ill he will need someone to look after him. I'm trying desperately not to think he could be – dead. I have money and could pay for my passage.'

'Miss *Quantock*,' Luke spoke with controlled patience, 'I have *no room* on my ship for a sick man, nor for a woman who wants to play nurse–'

'I am not wanting to *play* nurse, Mr Caltahn.'

'All right, all right. The answer remains the same. I promised to make enquiries about your father and I did. I shall also make enquiries at Marseilles, but there my obligation ends.' Luke picked up the valise.

Gabrielle's head went up. 'I shall book a

passage on another ship and search for my father myself.'

'Oh, God–' Luke dropped his bag, and ran a hand over his face. 'Have you any idea, any idea at all what you are suggesting? Do you know what kind of port Marseilles is? It's teeming with vagabonds and cut-throats. I guarantee that within five minutes of a woman alone stepping on the dockside she would not only be robbed of every penny she possessed but she could be subjected to all sorts of unspeakable things, I leave you to guess the indignities. And now I must leave, I have a thousand jobs to attend to. I bid you good-day.'

Gabrielle stood fuming after he had gone, then she ran upstairs and burst into the drawing room. Helen looked up.

'Oh, how I hate Luke Caltahn, the man has no sensitivity, no soul.'

Helen listened to Gabrielle's story of her confrontation with Luke, but although she commiserated with her over her father, she was very much on Luke's side, pointing out he had a ship to run, responsibilities towards his crew and that there was no space to spare for passengers on a trader, adding that Luke was quite right when he said it would be foolhardy for Gabrielle to attempt to travel alone.

'Then I shall ask Stephen to travel with me,' Gabrielle said, her mouth set in a mutinous line.

'Stephen is out riding at the moment–' Helen spoke quietly, 'and while he is gone I hope you will think it over. You must realize, Gabrielle, he has only just returned to his home after a year away.'

Helen's voice, which held a gentle rebuke, brought a flush to Gabrielle's face. 'I'm sorry,' she said, 'I was being utterly selfish, it's because I feel so worried about Papa.'

'And I can understand it. But you can rest assured, Gabrielle, that although Luke was abrupt with you he is a man of integrity, and if he can find your father he will. Luke never makes idle promises. It will not be easy in a place like Marseilles, but–' Helen paused and sat, her head inclined in a listening attitude. 'A carriage–?' She got up and went over to the window. The next moment Gabrielle saw her body go tense.

'What is it, Lady Norton–' Gabrielle made to go to the window but Helen, turning, took her by the shoulders. 'No, stay away from the window. It seems your grandmother has decided to pay us a visit.'

'Grandmama? But I must see her, I must find out about Papa!'

Helen gripped her shoulders. 'Now listen to me. Neither Stephen nor I have any jurisdiction over you. Your grandmother can demand to take you back. You are a runaway. I suggest you go to the stables and stay there until someone comes to fetch you. I can handle her, but not if you are in the house. Go out by the back way.'

When Gabrielle stood hesitant Helen gave her a gentle shake. 'Do you want to go back with your grandmother?'

'No.' Gabrielle left then. As she sped along the landing towards the stairs that led to the back door she heard the clanging of the house bell. How had her grandmother found out where she was?

Gabrielle was outside and making in the direction of the stables when she stopped, and stood, until the wetness of the snow penetrated the thin soles of her slippers. Then her mind was made up. She just had to know what was going on.

She raced back and up the stairs then stood again, to catch her breath. A murmur of voices came from the drawing room. Gabrielle crept along the landing, saw the door was ajar and peered through a gap in the hinged side. In her line of vision stood the black-clad ramrod figure of her grandmother, surveying Helen as though she were some recalcitrant minion.

'How dare you harbour my grand-daughter, knowing she ran away from home. I want her and I want her now.'

'Your granddaughter is *not* in this house, Madam.' Helen spoke calmly. 'I give you my word.'

Gabrielle winced at having made a liar of Lady Norton.

'She may not be in the house at the moment but she is staying here. She was seen in the company of Luke Caltahn who lives with you–'

'Mr Caltahn does not *live* with me, Madam. He has private rooms in the house.' Helen's voice was as ice-edged as Hesther Quantock's.

'Very well, who has *rooms* here. May I also point out my granddaughter was also seen in the company of Stephen Lawford, who is your nephew. He was responsible for helping my two granddaughters and my grandson to get to London. I have no knowledge yet of the whereabouts of Elspeth and Harold, but rest assured I shall do so, just as I learned the whereabouts of Gabrielle. What is more, I am not leaving until she is brought to me.'

'Then you will have a long wait, Madam. A fruitless wait. Your granddaughter will not come while you are here.'

'Then may I inform you I shall not return without her. I shall suffer the discomfort of an overnight stay at an inn and shall call again in the morning. If my granddaughter is not ready and waiting to leave with me I shall take action against you.'

'Action?' Helen queried, sounding in no way put out.

'I shall apply to the magistrates and inform them that my granddaughter has been removed from the care of her father, who is her legal guardian.'

'Then might it not be best for her father to come for Gabrielle?' Helen said sweetly.

There was a slight pause and Gabrielle saw a pulse beating in her grandmother's scrawny neck. 'My son is away on business abroad at the moment, but he did appoint me as his daughter's guardian.'

'Bring the document in the morning, Madam. My brother, who is an eminent lawyer, will be here to check that all is correct. I will ring for my maid to show you out.'

Gabrielle, for the first time, saw her grandmother look non-plussed for a moment, then she drew herself up.

'Until the morning.'

Gabrielle darted away, and sought sanctuary in a linen cupboard opposite until her grandmother had gone, her heart beating in suffocating thuds.

If the document was proved to be correct she would be forced to go back home. No, never, she would run away from here first. And in that moment she knew where she would go, to the docks ... to book passage to Marseilles.

# CHAPTER FOUR

Gabrielle made up her mind, before going back to the drawing room, she would not say anything about her decision, knowing Helen would do her best to prevent her carrying it out.

Helen was standing at the window. Gabrielle went up to her and they both stood watching the big black carriage move away.

Gabrielle said, 'I overheard the conversation. I had to know what my grandmother had to say.'

'A terrible woman.' Helen shuddered. 'I can understand now why you ran away, Gabrielle. Unhappily, you must leave here, and soon, but where to send you–?' Helen mentioned several people but each time shook her head, discarding them as being unsuitable. Then she looked up. 'Yes, of course, Lord and Lady Daveney. Why did I not think of them at first? They were both very taken with you last night, especially Sylvia. She said she would love to have you to stay with her for a while. You will be safe there. I shall send a message to ask if you can come right away.'

With this proposition upsetting her plans Gabrielle suggested it might be better for her to travel when it was dark, in case her grandmother had posted a man to watch the house.

This alarmed Helen who said she had never thought of such a thing. She must enlist the help of Stephen, adding it was a pity Luke had already left.

Gabrielle thought it was a good thing he had left or there would have been further complications. It was going to be difficult enough as it was to leave the house without arousing suspicion.

As it happened everything worked in Gabrielle's favour. When Stephen was told of her grandmother's visit and the plan to get her to the Daveney's, Stephen suggested leaving it until the morning. Then he and Helen would leave in the carriage, with Gabrielle crouching on the floor, covered by a rug. Gabrielle applauded it, so did Helen, and Stephen looked delighted they approved of his plan.

It helped yet further that Stephen was dining out that evening and Helen retired at nine-thirty with a headache. Gabrielle went upstairs straightaway to pack. She put in her valise all she had brought with her, then added the sea-green dress at the last minute, praying that Lady Norton would forgive her.

She had already written a note saying as she had no wish for Helen to have to lie to her grandmother about her whereabouts, she was going to a place where her grandmother could not possibly find her. She thanked Helen and Stephen for their many kindnesses and told them not to worry, she had money.

Gabrielle then propped the envelope on the mantelshelf, and with her cloak drawn around her opened the bedroom door. The only sound was the gentle tick-tock of the grandfather clock further along the landing. As she sped down the stairs it seemed a month ago since she had ran away from her grandmother's house. Gabrielle went out by the back door, which was never locked, and went along by the front of the house, screened by bushes. Once in the roadway she paused, looking around her a little fearfully in case her own story about someone watching the house might be true. But there was no one in sight and not even a branch stirred. She had no idea how far it was to get to the docks but she hoped to be able to hire some conveyance at the first inn she came to.

There was no moon to help her avoid the ruts in the road and she stumbled many times before she came to the brow of a hill where below she could see the lights of the city stretched before her. A new excitement engulfed her. This, it seemed, was yet another whole world opening up for her. A voyage across the sea, where she might be lucky enough to find her father.

Gabrielle had still a long walk before she came to an inn. But there she felt the fates were really on her side. Not only was she able to hire a carriage to take her to the docks but had the companionship of a woman, who claimed she was bound for the same place.

'I'm going to meet my husband,' she said. 'Arriving at midnight. He's bosun on a merchantman. I wouldn't wonder but he'll be able to get you on a ship going to Marseilles. Knows them all does Jack.'

The woman, although a little flashily dressed, with hair a brassy yellow, was so pleasant Gabrielle warmed to her.

'The name's Marston,' she said, 'But everyone calls me Belle at the inn. I work there while Jack's away at sea. He has long voyages and I need something to do, and to earn a bit of money for when he comes home. Nothing wrong in earning a bit of honest money my mother always used to say.'

'No,' Gabrielle said. 'Mrs Marston – Belle, how much do you think the voyage to Marseilles will cost?'

'Probably six or seven goldies.' Belle threw her head back and laughed. 'There I go again, picking up the men's talk. *Sovereigns* dear, do you have that much?'

'Oh, yes, yes, and – a bit more.'

'Then you keep it safe. Never keep it on you when you're on the ship. Oh dear me no, there's some as would have it from you in the twinkling of an eye. You'll be sharing with other women. Hide your money somewhere on the ship, but make sure no one sees where.'

'I keep it in an inside pocket of my cloak. I could wear the cloak when I go to bed.'

Belle raised her hands in horror. 'It would be gone before you knew it. Now take my advice and hide it where I told you. And look after it while you're on the dockside. A lot of rogues are roaming about there.'

Gabrielle was beginning to see the voyage as a little less glamorous than she had imagined. 'I shall find somewhere safe,' she said.

The carriage bumped and rocked its way over cobbled streets, where shops, even at this late hour, seemed to be doing good business.

Later, when through the open window of the carriage Gabrielle could smell the dampness of the river, and see in the distance a forest of masts, the streets were thronging with people. There was the sound of shouting and singing and men cursing the young boys who darted in and out of the crowd, playing their games, or so Gabrielle thought until Belle explained they were picking pockets. 'See how careful you have to be,' she said, with a knowing nod.

When they reached the docks Gabrielle was fascinated by the scene. There seemed to be hundreds of ships, hundreds of men, so much activity it was impossible to take it all in at once. There were sailors swarming up masts, edging their way along yard arms, running hither and thither to orders, there were derricks swinging crates on to decks, down holds, men with huge steel hooks were catching at other crates and swinging them ready to be lifted, and above all was the constant din of voices.

Belle offered to pay half the carriage fare but Gabrielle said she was only too pleased to pay in return for all her kindness. Belle then said, 'I'll go and find Jack and get him to make you a booking. Perhaps I'd better take the money with me. And I think it would be best if you waited over here by the wall, there's a chill wind coming off the river.' Gabrielle paid out seven sovereigns, then added another one – just in case. 'Oh, my dear, you look frozen,' Belle said. 'Fasten up your cloak. Here, let me do it... There, now you wait here, don't move, or I won't know where to find you. I won't be long.'

Then Belle was away and Gabrielle watched her darting between laden barrows and drays and wagons, and within seconds she was lost to view.

At first Gabrielle was too absorbed in what was going on around her to worry about having to wait. She found something quite breathtaking in the thought that all these ships would soon be in full sail, carrying goods and people across the world. She was not going across the world but the very name Marseilles had an exciting sound to it.

It was when Gabrielle's feet became numb with cold that she began to get worried. Belle might be having trouble finding her husband, but if she did not come soon the opportunity of leaving on the midnight tide would be lost. Then there would be a wait for the morning tide, and this would mean putting up at an inn.

Gabrielle began to stamp her feet to get her circulation going and put her hand inside her cloak and into the pocket for warmth – then stood, her whole body feeling frozen. The bag of sovereigns was no longer there. Oh, God – not Belle – surely not Belle...

It took only seconds more for Gabrielle to realize she had been duped. Fool, fool, she chided herself. How could she have been so stupid, so trusting? It was her first lesson not to take people at face value, but it had cost her dear, in fact, every penny she possessed. Now what?

If she could find Luke's ship would he take pity on her and allow her to travel with him? Her father, if they could find him, would reimburse Luke for her passage.

No – Gabrielle's shoulders slumped. Luke was more likely to regard her in his cold way and offer her enough money for a conveyance to get her back to Lady Norton's house.

She picked up her valise, and without any purpose in her mind moved away, keeping to the fringe of all the activity.

It would only need a drunken man to molest her for her to dissolve into tears.

But when a few minutes later a drunken man did approach her, anger at her loss came suddenly and she gave the man such a furious push he fell and sat staring at her, bewildered. Gabrielle started to run, the valise banging against her legs. Then suddenly she stopped– It was a voice, a familiar voice. It rose above all the others, shouting orders. Luke Caltahn... She would know his voice anywhere. But where was he? Gabrielle was distracted by seeing a horse in a sling being swung by a derrick over a deck. And was distressed at the terror in the animal's eyes and in its neighing. The horse was landed safely and she began searching the decks of other ships near.

Then she saw him, heard him shouting,

'Come along, come along, hurry it up!' Luke Caltahn was supervising the loading of his ship. In spite of being sombrely dressed in dark blue he looked a handsome, powerful figure against his men who were running to obey orders.

Gabrielle was not quite sure when the idea of stowing away on his ship was born, but it came quickly to fruition when several men on the dockside, in charge of crates, got into a knife fight. While the attention of crews and captains was momentarily distracted she hurried up the gangway, went to the stern of the ship and stood, heart pounding.

Now what? Where should she go? Wherever it was she would have to stay out of sight until the ship was well on its way. And, it would have to be now while blood-curdling yells from the dockside might still be holding the men's attention. Gabrielle moved forward cautiously, saw a companion-way and ran towards it. She negotiated the steep ladder, feeling her heart would jump out of her body at any moment and found herself in a dimly lit passageway. One door she opened led to a cabin, possibly Luke's. The next opened on to a rope locker and she was about to try the third door when footsteps and the murmur of men's voices made her squeeze into the locker and climb on to a coiled pile. She drew the door to and waited, praying she had not been detected.

After a while the smell of the tarred rope was so overpowering she wondered if she would ever be able to get the smell out of her nostrils. And yet, there must have been some ventilation, or she was sure she would have suffocated.

There was a constant movement overhead and even in the confines of the locker she could hear a continual shouting. There was a great deal of banging going on and once she wondered if they were battening down the hatches. She wanted to keep on the alert, but after a while the rise and fall of the boat began to make her feel drowsy. She had no worry about being seasick. She was a good sailor. Often, when they went to the sea for a holiday her father would take her out for a row with her cousins and the times when it was choppy she was the only one who had not even felt a little queasy. She was good at rowing too. 'You're a strong lassie for such a little 'un,' an old sea salt once told her. She loved rowing, loved the rhythm, *pull* – dip ... *pull* – dip. She had perfected her stroke until she could row without hardly making a splash. *Pull* – dip...

Gabrielle's eyelids flew open at the sound of men's voices and footsteps coming nearer. They stopped outside the locker. She sat tense. If they had come for a rope she was done for.

'It weren't my fault,' a rough voice grumbled. 'Bosun told me to put 'em on master's deck.'

'Well, get them afore 'ee gets any more mad.' The men moved on, and seconds later they passed the locker again and Gabrielle breathed more easily. Cramp in one leg made her change her position. She tried to imagine Luke Caltahn's anger when her presence became known, and wished she had brought some food with her, then she could perhaps have stayed here for much longer. He was going to be furious. He had already told her there was no room on the ship for a passenger. Perhaps he might make her sleep here, or in the bilges. Wasn't that where they kept prisoners? No, in the Brig – Gabrielle shuddered at the thought.

After being in the rope locker for what seemed hours she felt ready to throw herself on the mercy of Luke, promise to scrub the decks or cook the food. Anything to get out of this hell-hole. She knew now what her father meant when he said he suffered from a complaint called claustrophobia, which was a horror of being kept in a confined space. Gabrielle had to keep opening the door a fraction to get some air to her lungs, otherwise she was sure she *would* have suffocated.

After a while she drifted into sleep, and when she roused there was a different movement to the ship. They were on their way! How long would she have to wait before she could be sure Luke would not have her sent ashore? An hour – two hours? She was so stiff, every muscle screamed when she tried to move.

Gabrielle would not have thought she could possibly fall asleep again but she did. And when she roused the next time it was to be dragged from her hiding place by the scruff of the neck and flung in the passage. Not by a seaman, as she would have imagined, but Luke Caltahn, who stood over her, eyes blazing.

'What the devil do you think you–' She looked up at him and blinked and he stared at her. 'Good God – *you*!' Then he caught her by her elbows and stood her on her feet. 'How dare you stow away on *my* ship.'

'I can explain,' she said, and would have fallen had he not supported her. 'Pins and needles,' she explained feebly.

'Pins and needles! You scuttle-headed–' He urged her towards his cabin. 'If anyone comes along they will think I have a whore on board, and that is not my habit.'

She stumbled as she tried to face him, found support against the wall and glared at him. 'So I look like a whore?'

'I did not say that. The situation *implies* it. Now come along.' He all but dragged her into his cabin and there flung her on to the bunk. 'Now get this straight, you are not travelling on my ship. I told you I had no room for passengers.'

'*Please* let me explain. I had no intention of being a stowaway. I wanted to book a passage on another ship but I was robbed of my money.'

'Serves you right for behaving so irresponsibly.'

'Mr Caltahn, why do you condemn me as being irresponsible? My only fault was in trusting a woman who I thought was kind. We shared a carriage to the docks, then she robbed me.'

Luke's eyes narrowed. 'Who was this woman?'

'She said her name was Mrs Marston. She told me to call her Belle. She told me she worked in the inn where I hired the carriage and was travelling to the docks to meet her husband home from sea.'

'And you believed her story?' Luke gave a short bark of laughter. 'Ding Dong Belle, still at her old games! But in a different country this time. You should have seen the type of woman she was. Oh, lord, what a little simpleton you are.'

Gabrielle flared. '*You* might be acquainted with this type of woman in the sea-faring life you lead, Mr Caltahn, but for me it was the first time. And, I might add, the last. It was a hard lesson to learn, but a valuable one. I

86

shall never trust the word of another person again, man or woman.'

'Then you have not learned the right lesson. The one you should have learned was how to discriminate between the true and the false.' Luke suddenly flung up his hands. 'But what am I doing, standing here philosophizing when I have a boat under sail. Do you happen to know what the penalty is for stowing away?'

'No, I am not acquainted with the rules of shipping life.'

'A female becomes the property of the captain. You do as I tell you, I must be obeyed at all times.'

Gabrielle ran her tongue over her lower lip as she realized the implication of the remark. 'And if I refuse?'

'I shall wait until we are further out to sea then I shall put you in a boat and cast you adrift.'

Gabrielle looked for some teasing in Luke Caltahn's eyes, but found none. In fact, his expression was so formidable she felt a shiver go up and down her spine.

'You couldn't,' she whispered, 'you wouldn't.'

'I could and would, and I would be perfectly justified under Maritime law. What is more, I would have no qualms in casting a *Quantock* adrift.'

'Why should you want to drown me

because of what my grandmother did to you? Do you call that fair? You are as evil as she is.'

'You won't drown. Another ship would pick you up eventually, and you would, of course, be given a certain amount of food and water.'

Gabrielle was sure this time she detected a note of humour in his voice, but this was dispelled when he said, 'The alternative is that you get undressed and get into this bed, and be waiting for me when I come back in an hour. The choice is yours.'

He was at the door when he added, 'I shall lock you in, just in case you should try and appeal for help from any of my men. Not that they would give it, they are all most loyal to me, but it would save embarrassment.'

With that he left and the key scraped in the lock.

Gabrielle's body sagged. Oh, God, what a position to be in. Surely Luke Caltahn would not carry out such threats? It was not as if she were some low woman to be used for a man's needs. And if he cast her adrift there would be an outcry at such inhumanity. He had his reputation to consider. What could he say to defend such an action.

She knew very well what he would say, and felt trapped. She could even hear the case being heard in court, with Luke giving evidence – that he had already told her he had no room on his ship for a passenger. If the court was to delve into her background and learn she had not only run away from her grandmother's house, but from Lady Norton's, and then had stowed away on the ship of a man who had refused her a passage... Oh, heavens, she really was trapped. If she allowed herself to be cast adrift and was picked up she would be classed as a loose woman, and if she stayed here in Luke Caltahn's bed the same stigma would be attached to her. The only difference was ... no one but the crew would know she was Luke Caltahn's woman.

Luke Caltahn's woman – Gabrielle felt an unexpected tremor of excitement. She would learn about the wonderful thing that married people experienced. Immediately afterwards came the sobering thought that she would no longer be a virgin, and no decent man would marry a girl who had been sullied.

She got up, then tottered against the small desk in the centre of the cabin. The ship must be out of the harbour, there was a good swell on. There was no window in the cabin but she could imagine what it would be like to be cast adrift in a small boat, in the dark, in the cold, with a rough sea. Although she kept trying to tell herself that

Luke Caltahn would never stoop to such an action she felt no conviction.

Gabrielle stood looking at the bed. It *was* a bed, not a bunk, although it did have low wooden rails all round to prevent the sleeper from falling out when the boat was pitching and tossing. What would Luke Caltahn be like as a lover? Gabrielle felt a small shameful thrill at the thought of lying in bed with him, being caressed. His love-making could be as ruthless as his manner. She could hardly expect any tenderness from a man who would cast a woman adrift in a boat.

Gabrielle sat down on the bed again and looked about her, trying to assess the man from his cabin. There were a number of books, all placed in box-like shelves attached to one wall, with only the titles shown. They were all technical books. Apart from the bed and desk there was one chair, a brass bound oak chest, a low chest of drawers and on top of it facilities for washing. The small cabin offered little room for moving around.

With a deep sigh of resignation Gabrielle knew if she wanted to get to Marseilles in the hope of finding her father she had better start undressing. It took her a long time. With each garment discarded there was a great deal of heart-searching. But at last she donned her best nightgown, slid between the icy sheets and lay, her teeth chattering and her whole body trembling. Above her the lantern swung to and fro casting shadows on the walls.

She was still not warm when she heard the key turn in the lock. Her heart became a mad thing, pounding, missing a beat then jumping. Luke Caltahn came up to the bed. 'So you've decided.' Then in the next breath he added, 'You can get this off for a start,' and tugged at the cuff of her nightgown.

Gabrielle, who held the sheet up to her chin, looked at him wide-eyed. 'My – nightgown?'

'It's an encumbrance.'

'I'm freezing as it is,' she said, her tone aggrieved.

'You will be warm enough when I am in beside you.' There was no relaxing in his manner. He could have been discussing the ocean's chart with one of his men.

While Gabrielle fumbled with the tiny buttons on her nightgown Luke divested himself of his coat and vest. For some stupid reason she had not thought about *him* undressing. She pulled the sheet over her head and making herself into a hump she struggled to get out of the nightgown. When at last she emerged from under the sheet, the rolled-up nightgown in her hand, Luke was standing stark naked as he folded his clothes.

Gabrielle wanted to look away, but found herself staring. 'Oh,' she said, then 'Oh,' again. Laughter suddenly bubbled up inside her. She tried to control it, but at seeing the astonished look on Luke's face, she found it impossible to stop.

He snatched up a large towel and draped it round his waist, tucking in the ends. 'Might I ask what you find so amusing?' he asked, his words falling like splinters of ice.

'I'm – sorry–' Gabrielle sobered for a moment then was giggling helplessly again. 'It was seeing– Oh, really I am terribly sorry, it was just that–'

'Stop it! Do you hear!'

The harshness of his voice finally calmed her down. She wiped the tears away with the corner of the sheet and looked at him. He stood like a god, magnificent in his outrage, his skin golden as though he had spent the summer in the sun.

'If I can explain,' she said in a low voice. 'I was not laughing at yourself, I was laughing at my own ignorance. You see, Mr Caltahn, the only male I have ever seen – without clothes, was a cousin and that was when he was small. For the first time I was aware of the difference between a boy and a girl. Only I had not allowed for – well, for growth–' Gabrielle's face was burning in her embarrassment. 'Nor for– for it being so – so ugly.'

Luke gave a sudden shout of laughter. 'Heavens above, I can hardly believe it. Is it possible you really are *so* innocent. No, it's a ruse.' He sobered. 'You wanted to ridicule me. The typical trick of a Quantock. Well, I shall make you pay for laughing at me.'

He pulled the sheet away from her, but she immediately snatched it back and shouted at him, 'I would have given in to you, but not now! I refuse to take punishment for my grandmother's sins. It was the truth I told you. Have you never met a truthful woman? Are all the ones you make love to so depraved they would ridicule you? Well please do not put me in that class.'

Gabrielle slid from under the sheet to the other side of the bed and grabbed her cloak. She put it round her shoulders and stood up. 'I was a fool to have even contemplated allowing you to make love to me.'

'Allowing?' he jeered. 'You have no choice. I take what I want. By your own actions you've made yourself my prisoner and you obey me.'

'Oh, no, Mr Caltahn, I do have a choice. You can put me in a boat and cast me adrift.'

'You are not leaving this cabin. Now get back into bed. I shall deal with you as I think fit.'

'No! You are not going to deal with me as you think fit.'

Gabrielle drew herself up. 'I have made up my mind that no man shall touch me until I marry.'

'And you think you can stop me, *you?*'

'Yes, Mr Caltahn, after I warn you that should you attempt to take me by force I shall do my best to gouge out your eyes. And if I am not successful in this way, I promise you will get a knife in your back, or in your heart, at a moment when you least expect it.'

'Why you – vicious little wretch!' He laughed. 'I really believe you would. It might be interesting trying to tame you.'

'You would have no success. My grand-mother found it impossible to do so and you know the strength of *her* will.'

His laughter died. He nodded slowly. 'Yes, I do, *and* her evil and I find it sad that such a beautiful creature as you should have inherited this characteristic.'

'Is it evil for a girl to fight against being raped?' Gabrielle retorted.

'It was the methods you suggested using that astonished me. Gouging out my eyes – sticking a knife in my heart. You certainly have the Quantock blood in you. Did you think by sneaking on my ship to twist me round your little finger and learn my plans?'

'No, and I have already explained my reason for stowing away.'

'And how feeble it all sounds now. I was even tempted to believe your sob tale about being robbed of your money. I despise liars.'

'Oh, dear me,' Gabrielle said. 'All that philosophizing about being able to distinguish between the true and the false and you are unable to do so.'

She saw his hands clench. He turned away from her, reached for a robe from the back of the door, put it on, tied the cord then stood studying her through narrowed eyes.

'May I ask what plot you are hatching now?' Gabrielle enquired sweetly.

'Yes, you may. I've decided to marry you.'

She stared at him, unable to believe her ears.

'Did you say – *marry* me?'

'I did.'

'Why? Why this sudden decision? Less than a minute ago you told me you despised me.'

'I do, but I think it an excellent way to partly revenge myself on your grandmother. I can just picture her fury. Her arch-enemy married to the granddaughter she planned to marry to someone else.' Luke was smiling but there was a bitter twist to his lips.

Gabrielle shook her head as though trying to clear it. 'I find it hard to believe you would be willing to marry a woman you despise to revenge yourself on someone else. And what an ego you have to think I would agree.'

'You will.' Luke Caltahn looked so assured

it took Gabrielle all her time to refrain from slapping his face.

'Is that so? And what dastardly method had you in mind to force me to agree to such a thing?'

'The only weapon left to me. Your father. You love him and want to find him. Marry me and I shall give you my word I shall do all in my power to help.'

'Your word?' Gabrielle said, her voice scathing.

'Whatever else I may be, Miss *Quantock*, my word is respected in every port I visit. It is my bond, I can get credit on it, yes, even from my enemies.'

Gabrielle felt suddenly that her legs had been whipped from under her. She sank on to the bed. 'I need time to think about it.'

'Take all the time you need. I have work to do.'

Luke sat at the desk, opened a drawer and pulled out a ledger. And to the scratch of a quill Gabrielle tried to sort out her thoughts. Was ever a girl in such a dilemma? It would need the wisdom of Solomon to reach the right decision. Her father could be already dead and she would be tied to this man for the rest of her life, a man she hated.

The quill scratched on and the lamp went on swinging and Gabrielle, watching the strange shadows the light made, wondered if her life would ever have the sun in it again.

# CHAPTER FIVE

Gabrielle brought her gaze away from the moving shadows on the walls of the cabin and looked towards her captor. In profile Luke Caltahn's face seemed less hard. There was a deep cleft between lower lip and chin she had not noticed before. Her godmother once said that such a cleft denoted a gentleness in a person. Although Gabrielle could not imagine Luke Caltahn ever being gentle she did have great faith in her godmother's summing up of a character. Also Lady Norton would have nothing said against him.

Gabrielle's thoughts went flitting back and forth again, weighing up every possible angle. If her father *was* alive and she refused to marry Luke Caltahn she would be missing the one opportunity of finding him. Marriage to this cold-looking man who sat there so straight-backed might not be all she hoped for but it would be infinitely better than being wed to the elderly and brutal Gideon Walraven. If she got into her grandmother's clutches again, and her father *had* been blackmailed into surrendering his legal guardianship of her, this would definitely happen. Gabrielle shuddered. Anything was better than that.

Luke put down the quill, sanded the entries he had made in the ledger then looked across at her.

'Well, have you reached a decision?'

Gabrielle stood up and held her cloak tightly around her.

'Yes, I agree to the marriage – on condition that there will be no love-making until we are married.' She thought this would at least give her a respite until they reached Marseilles, but Luke's next words disillusioned her.

'That can easily be arranged. We shall be married now – or at least in half an hour or so. We have a priest on board.'

He shut the ledger and put it in the drawer.

'A priest – on board?' Gabrielle's voice was barely audible. 'I thought you had no room for passengers.'

'The Reverend John Ballant is not a passenger. He wished to go to Italy and as he had no money for the voyage I accepted him as crew. I only hope he turns out to be as energetic as he talks and looks. I shall send Mr Taylor to rouse him.'

'Could we not wait – until morning?'

'It is morning.'

'Then until it is light.'

'As you wish, but you realize you must

share my bed. There is no other place for you to sleep. Not unless you would prefer to spend the next few hours in the rope locker.' Although his expression was one of gravity there was quite definitely this time a hint of teasing in his voice.

'I shall get dressed,' Gabrielle said. 'Would you please turn your back.' She half-expected him to refuse but he did turn away. It took her as long to get dressed as it had to undress, and she was trembling so much she wondered how she would ever manage to get through a marriage cere-mony. She certainly felt anything but a prospective bride in her simple grey dress.

'Can I turn round now?' Luke was dressed too. He stood looking at her for a moment then he said, 'I'll see if I can find you something to put round your shoulders. There may be a shawl suitable in the chest.'

There was a pile of garments in the brass-bound chest. From them Luke pulled out a paisley shawl patterned in soft browns and golden colours. He draped it round her shoulders. 'There, you should find a little warmth from it. It matches your eyes.'

He smiled then and it transformed him. The fact that he had showed some caring gave Gabrielle hope their married life together might be bearable. She murmured her thanks and immediately Luke was brusque again.

'Wait here, do *not* leave this cabin. Is that understood?' She nodded and he left.

Gabrielle straightened the bedcovers then sat down once more, her hands clasped tightly. Her wedding day. It seemed impossible to believe.

What would the Reverend John Ballant think when he was roused from his bed at this hour to perform a marriage ceremony? He too must surely feel it could have waited until daylight. But no, Luke Caltahn must have his way immediately. A marriage of revenge. How hateful it sounded. And what a mockery it would be when Luke Caltahn made his vows 'to love and to cherish' - It would be mockery for her too, but very real when she promised to obey. This was something any husband expected, but having escaped the domination of her grandmother, only to be immediately dominated by a man like Luke Caltahn, made her rebellious just thinking of it.

Gabrielle fingered the paisley shawl and thought of all her wasted dreams, imagining herself on her wedding day, in virgin white, and seeing the love in the eyes of her prospective bridegroom as they stood at the altar. And yet, she had never been able to put a face to this man of her dreams. If only there had been love between Luke Caltahn and herself how proud she would have been to be the wife of such a handsome and virile-looking man.

'My husband, Captain Caltahn–' How other women would have envied her. Gabrielle at once chided herself for her thoughts. Envy was as bad a sin as wanting revenge.

She looked up as the door was flung open and Luke Caltahn came in, followed by a man in clerical garb.

'My bride to be, Miss Gabrielle Quantock – the Reverend John Ballant.'

The priest bowed low over Gabrielle's hand. After the stern-faced and pulpit-thumping vicar of the church at home, John Ballant was an unexpected and delightful surprise to Gabrielle. He was young, had merry blue eyes and a beaming smile.

'What a pleasure it is to meet you, Miss Quantock. This is my first marriage ceremony at sea. I find it most touching.'

Luke said sharply, 'I do not want the name Quantock mentioned during the ceremony, nor to the boatswain or surgeon when they come in.'

'I shall remember, Captain Caltahn – sir.'

John Ballant looked like a small boy about to embark on an exciting adventure.

There was a tap on the open door and to Luke's command to enter an elderly bony-faced man came in, followed by a fair-haired man with a melancholic expression.

Luke introduced the older man as his

boatswain Mr Taylor, and the other as Mr Delacote, his surgeon. They were to be witnesses to the ceremony. Gabrielle could not help thinking if it had not been for the presence of John Ballant they could all have been attending a funeral.

'Dearly beloved, we are gathered together in the sight of God–'

Gabrielle's hand accidentally touched Luke's. It felt warm, hers was icy. Luke twined his fingers in hers and the comfort of it brought tears to her eyes.

Luke's responses were clear, Gabrielle's low. They were part of the way through the ceremony when she suddenly thought of the ring, and glanced quickly at Luke. It was produced at the appropriate time by Mr Taylor, and Gabrielle found her voice clearer as she said the words, – 'to love and to cherish, and to obey–' Luke slid the ring on to her finger and she saw it was a broad band of chased gold. It fitted perfectly. She wondered where it had come from.

Luke produced a bottle of wine and glasses and the bride and groom were toasted and congratulations offered. Gabrielle managed to smile and thank the three men, but was aware of the hostility from the boatswain. She sipped the wine and was glad of the warmth it brought to her body. After a few more sips she drank the rest, hoping it might help her over the ordeal ahead.

The party was broken up by Luke with what Gabrielle thought was an indecent haste. John Ballant gave her another beaming smile before he left, no doubt thinking of the wedding in romantic terms of an elopement.

The moment the door closed behind the men Luke began unfastening his neckcloth. 'Well Mrs Caltahn, how does it feel to be a married woman?'

'I shall be able to tell you better in a month's time,' she answered quietly. She turned from him and took off the paisley shawl then stood, fingering the buttons on her dress.

'Do you need any help?'

'No, no—' Gabrielle quickly unfastened the buttons. But before she could slip the dress from her shoulders, Luke did it for her, and the next moment she felt warm lips pressed against her neck. An unexpected surge of emotion made her tremble, and when Luke turned her to face him and his mouth covered hers she found herself responding.

He drew away and said softly, 'So you are not so innocent as you would have me believe.'

Gabrielle, furious at herself for allowing her body to betray her, retorted. 'You may have had dozens of women, Mr Caltahn, but no man has ever touched me.'

He gave a short laugh. 'Well, we shall soon

find that out, won't we? Now get the rest of your clothes off and quickly, before I do it for you.'

Gabrielle, who was getting more and more angry, was determined if this husband of hers showed any brutality towards her she would fight him tooth and nail. With her last garment almost shed she reached for her nightgown, but Luke snatched it from her.

'I told you, a nightgown is an encumbrance.' She would still not relinquish her shift until she got into bed and did so under the sheet. Then, with it clutched in her hand she pushed the sheet back and glared at him.

'What a start to a honeymoon,' he said wryly, and climbed in beside her.

Gabrielle closed her eyes and lay rigid, waiting for what was to come– And waited – and waited– When at last she opened her eyes Luke's eyes were closed and, judging by his gentle breathing, he had fallen asleep.

'Well,' she declared, affronted, and flung herself over on to her side. Was he really asleep, or was this his way of punishing her. But would he not be punishing himself? Her cousin Janet had said that a man suffered terribly when he was passionate if he could not get his emotions satisfied. But then, Luke Caltahn, she felt sure, had an iron will, and if he thought he was making *her* suffer–

Gabrielle, feeling the warmth of his body,

knew a longing to curl up against him, and – yes, she had to admit it, to have him make love to her. There were all sorts of strange emotions stirring in her which brought a delicious throbbing to her limbs. Janet was right, this part of marriage could be exciting. Gabrielle knew a desire to know Luke's body. She raised her hand, felt his warm flesh, then quickly drew her hand away. This, of course, was what he was hoping for. He was experienced, knew women. Well, she would not give him the satisfaction of knowing she was longing for him to make love to her. *He* would be the one to approach *her* in the future.

And she gave a small smile of satisfaction that she had been able to play Luke Caltahn at his own game.

# CHAPTER SIX

When Gabrielle awoke Luke had gone from the bed. Judging by the sounds of activity on the ship another day had begun for the crew. She lay, enjoying the motion of the ship for a few moments then looked towards the door as she heard a sharp knock. It was Mr Taylor the boatswain, following a swarthy-skinned man carrying a tray.

'This is Tomaso, Ma'am,' Mr Taylor said. 'He's the captain's man. He'll see to the meals and the tidying of the cabin.'

'Oh, thank you.'

Mr Taylor stared at a point above her head, disapproval of her presence showing in every line of his seamed face. 'If there's anything you need, tell Tomaso. He'll bring you hot water to wash. Captain will be down in a while for his breakfast.' To Tomaso he added, 'Set the tray down on the table there.'

With the tray on the bedside table Tomaso gave Gabrielle a quick glance from lively dark eyes, then as quickly looked away.

Mr Taylor said, 'There's goat's milk in the tea, Ma'am, you may not like the taste.'

'Do you keep a goat on board?' Gabrielle

asked in surprise.

'We do, Captain likes milk in his tea and coffee.' With that he turned and left, without having once looked at her. Tomaso followed.

Gabrielle decided it would be difficult breaking through the boatswain's reserve. Perhaps with patience.

The mug was thick, the tea strange-tasting, but Gabrielle was grateful for the drink.

Within seconds of Luke coming into the cabin some twenty minutes later breakfast was brought in. There were cold meats, fruit, bread and cheese and coffee. Luke made no comment until Tomaso had gone then he said, 'I trust you slept well, *Mrs Caltahn?*'

'Excellently, Mr Caltahn.'

'You may call me Luke.'

'How very generous of you.'

'I see you are still in a bad mood,' he remarked in a conversational tone.

'Actually, I feel in quite a good mood. I only wish Mr Taylor would accept that I am your wife and not your mistress. Not that he has said so in so many words. His manner suggests it.'

'Mr Taylor's manner at times suggests many things, but I would not wish for a better man. If you will treat him with *respect* he will treat you the same.'

Gabrielle was immediately on the defensive. 'What exactly are you implying? If you are suggesting I used coquettish ways on the man—'

'I suggested nothing. Eat your breakfast. I can recommend the ham.'

'I have no appetite, thank you,' she replied coldly.

'Is the motion of the boat upsetting you?'

'No, I happen to be an excellent sailor.'

'Then you must eat. There is no place on board this ship for a woman with tantrums.'

Gabrielle clenched her hands. 'Mr Caltahn, I do not have tantrums. I am small but basically a strong person. I can walk miles without tiring, ride a horse for a whole day without feeling any undue strain, I am never ill and I eat well *when* I have an appetite. At the moment I have none. But by midday I shall probably be ready to eat a man's size portion. Does that satisfy you?'

Luke smiled and it brought a warmth to his stern features.

'You really are an extraordinary person, Mrs Caltahn. You have the coquettish ways of a woman and the strength and will power of a man.'

'Coquettish? I would not stoop to such feminine wiles.'

'Oh, but you do, I noticed you the night of the ball. You used your – "feminine wiles" with every man who spoke to you.'

Gabrielle was indignant. 'That is quite

untrue. I told you, I would never–'

'Perhaps you do it unconsciously, but it is there. You had men begging for your favours, begging to sign your dance card.'

'You exaggerate. Men did ask for dances but they asked other young ladies too. It is usual at a ball, or had you not noticed?'

Luke's expression changed, it took on a hardness.

'Listen, my *sweet*, do not use sarcasm on me. And I shall tell you now, and I have no wish to repeat it, you will not use your feminine wiles on my crew, or on any other men we may meet in the future. You are my wife and I expect you to use some decorum.'

Gabrielle jumped up. 'How dare you suggest I try to attract men! Jealousy is an evil thing–'

'Ha–! Are you suggesting I am jealous of you?'

'Jealous of what you think of as *your* possession. Well, no man shall ever wholly possess me.'

Luke got up and moving round the table he gripped her wrist. 'Last night I was lenient with you, I let you sleep instead of claiming my – conjugal rights. Tonight you shall fulfil your *wifely* duties, whether you feel like it or not. Is that understood?'

'Perfectly,' Gabrielle said calmly. 'I was prepared last night to fulfil my wifely duties, but you fell asleep.'

'I warn you now,' he said grimly, 'you shall have little sleep tonight.'

Gabrielle felt annoyed to find her pulses leaping at the thought of Luke making love to her. She said, however, 'If you want me to act the part of a whore in my wifely duties, do not expect me to respond. And I repeat, Mr Caltahn, no man shall ever wholly possess me.'

He released her wrist. 'You have beauty, an attractive figure, but when I see you standing there looking at me in that arrogant way I see your evil grandmother.' Luke's face was set as he went back to the table and sat down. He cut a piece of meat.

Gabrielle sat down facing him and said quietly, 'Mr Caltahn, if we are to make any sort of life together will you *please* stop comparing me to my grandmother.'

Luke speared the meat with his fork then looked up. 'You would be wise never to mention the name Quantock on this ship. Most members of the crew have good reason for hating it also.' With that he went on with his breakfast and the next time he spoke was when he was ready to leave.

'I have no right to ask you to spend your days cooped up in this cabin, but do not go up on deck unless I take you. I shall find time later in the morning.'

With the door closed behind him Gabrielle swallowed hard to get rid of the lump in her throat. What a fiasco of a marriage. How could it succeed with Luke wanting to take out his revenge on her for what her grandmother had done to him. It was so unfair. She had suffered enough at her grandmother's hands.

When Tomaso came in to clear away the breakfast dishes and Gabrielle asked him if the weather was fine he looked embarrassed.

'Excuse please, Ma'am, I am not to speak with you.'

Anger flared in Gabrielle. 'Is that an order from my husband?'

'Yes, Ma'am. He fine man, very good, very strong but he–' Tomaso sought for the right word then concluded with, 'He captain.'

'Yes indeed, Mr Caltahn *is* the captain. Well, Tomaso, I shall talk to my husband about it and find out the reason why you are not permitted to speak with me. And, have no worry, I shall make it clear you are not involved in any way.'

The man stood, trying to string the words together to get the meaning then he suddenly beamed at her. 'Yes, Ma'am, no trouble for Tomaso. Thank you, Ma'am, thank you.'

When he had gone with the laden tray Gabrielle sat fuming. Was she to be treated like a nun in silent orders? Luke Caltahn might be captain of this ship but she would speak to whom she liked. And she would tell him so in no uncertain terms when next she saw him.

The opportunity came minutes later. Before Luke had a chance to open his mouth she said. 'How dare you give orders to Tomaso not to speak to me. Am I to be treated as a leper?'

He looked slightly bewildered for a moment then he said. 'Oh – you mean Tomaso. The man is excellent at his job but his English is not good and when told anything he often gets the meaning twisted. I am not willing to risk anything you say to Tomaso being twisted when repeated to the crew.'

Gabrielle, although mollified by the explanation said, 'I would hardly be likely to say anything that could be misconstrued.'

'You are not acquainted with Tomaso, Madam.' Luke picked up Gabrielle's cloak. 'If you put this on I shall take you up on deck for a while for a breath of fresh air.'

The salt-laden air was a balm and a tonic to Gabrielle. She held her face to the wind. 'Oh, how heavenly.'

When she looked about her she saw that the ship was much larger than she had imagined. There was a complement of guns, ten or twelve. There seemed to be men on every part of the ship. Those nearest touched their caps to her. Luke said, 'They know you are my wife and you shall get respect from them. Any man who shows any disrespect shall be punished.'

'In what way?'

'Ten to fifteen lashes.'

Gabrielle looked at him in horror. 'Ten to fifteen lashes?'

He nodded. 'I think it will be enough as a lesson to others.'

Gabrielle felt she hated him at that moment. He was so arrogant, standing there, legs slightly apart, hands behind his back as though he were king of all he surveyed. She looked quickly aloft as the sails flapped with a sudden veering of the wind. Then immediately they billowed out once more and she felt a sudden sense of exhilaration and she remembered a gypsy's prophecy of a year before. The woman had said, 'When the sails are full, good things will come.' It was all the gypsy had told her. At the time it had meant nothing. Now Gabrielle took it to mean that her father would be found – and that her marriage would be successful.

A man came out of the galley, threw a bucket of swill overboard and the gulls wheeling overhead swooped on it, their shrill cries filling the morning.

Luke took her up to the quarter deck, but hardly had she acknowledged the helmsman, who touched his cap to her, when Luke said, 'You may stay for five minutes, then go below again.'

Gabrielle looked at him in dismay. 'Oh, must I? The hours will seem long in the cabin. Surely I can do no harm just standing here.'

'You will be a distraction to the men.' Luke's face was set.

'I see none distracted by my presence,' she answered in a low voice.

'Do not argue with me, Madam.' Luke spoke in low tones. 'You will accept my orders as do my men.'

'Yes, sir– Of course, sir.' Then, realizing if she incensed Luke he might keep her a prisoner below she added, 'I'm sorry, I was disappointed at not being able to stay longer.'

'You can come up again for a while this afternoon.'

'Thank you, I appreciate it.'

Luke glanced at her, no doubt wondering whether she was being sarcastic again. Gabrielle smiled and his face relaxed. They were on deck much longer than the five minutes, which made Gabrielle accept if she wanted favours she would have to earn them.

Air came into the cabin through wooden slats, but after being on deck in the wind the cabin felt stuffy. Gabrielle picked up one of

Luke's books, read about mizzen masts and sprit sails and methods of finding the depth of water, replaced it, and was about to turn away when a title caught her eye. She seized on the book with joy. *Tristram Shandy*. Oh, how lovely. It would be the third time of reading but how she would enjoy it.

She was lost in the book when Luke came in. He said, in an aggrieved tone, he had called her twice. Gabrielle held up the book. 'Blame this—'

'Oh, you found my copy of *Tristram*.'

'Papa first introduced it to me, he enriched my life with his knowledge of books.'

They discussed books they had read over a light meal and Gabrielle was pleased they did at least have this one thing in common. It was this fact, she felt sure, that made Luke allow her to spend an hour on deck that afternoon. A few of the men looked at her from time to time but even they were too busy to give her more than a glance. Gabrielle not only felt glowing from the fresh air but acquired a small knowledge of seamen's language, which she thought was picturesque. When she asked Luke the meaning of some of the words, however, he told her grimly she was not to repeat them, not in *any* company. 'Oh, those words,' she said, laughing. Luke laughed too and she was glad. If they were to celebrate their nuptials that evening it would be easier if they were on good terms with one another.

Luke went back up on deck and it was unfortunate that he said to Gabrielle before he left, 'I shall be below again at ten o'clock, see you are in bed by then.'

Ordered to bed like a child, she fumed after he had gone. Why had she thought they would be celebrating their marriage nuptials? For Luke Caltahn it would be simply an act of revenge. It was a wonder he had not told her to make sure she would not be wearing her nightgown. What had he called it? An encumbrance. Well, she would not be in bed, nor would she be undressed. She would be sitting here waiting for him, to tell him how she despised him. No, she would be reading. That would be better. Let him think he was unimportant. No doubt she would have to get into bed ultimately, she was his wife and had promised to obey him, but she would show no response whatsoever when he did make love to her. It occurred to Gabrielle a few moments later that some of the sting of her defiance would be lost as she had no means of knowing the time. Well, she would have to go on reading for a while, ignore his demands.

When Luke did come below he appeared to be in a foul mood. He flung his tricorne hat on to the bed. 'A fight on board and we are hardly out of port.' Then, becoming aware that Gabrielle was sitting in the chair, a book on her lap, he gave her a long cold stare and added, 'I thought I told you to be in bed when I came below.'

'You told me ten o'clock, Mr Caltahn, but as I had no means of knowing the time—' Gabrielle smiled sweetly.

Luke glared at her. 'That must be rectified. It is now half past ten. So—'

Gabrielle turned a page of her book. Luke thundered. 'Did you hear me. Bed—'

Gabrielle looked up. 'All in good time. I am nearly at the end of a chapter and want to finish it. Is that an unreasonable request?'

For answer he seized the book from her and flung it across the cabin. Gabrielle went over, picked it up, opened it at random and made a pretence of reading a few lines. 'There,' she said, 'now I know how the chapter ended.' She closed the book and replaced it in the rack. In spite of her defiance and what she hoped was an outward appearance of calmness the trembling inside her would not be stilled.

Aware that Luke was watching her she went over to the bed and reached for her nightgown. Then she decided against wearing it. Not because of Luke's objection to her wearing it but in this mood he would be quite likely to tear it from her, and her godmother had spent hours and hours in the making of it. It was something she treasured.

She started to undress, taking her time over it until Luke said, 'Would you like *me* to undress you?' then she fumbled hurriedly with bows and buttons. She discarded everything but her shift. That could be removed once she was in bed. The cold sheets added to her trembling. She kept on the shift, and with the sheet pulled up to her nose she closed her eyes. Moments later Luke got in beside her. His body felt so warm Gabrielle longed once again to curl up beside him. They lay in silence, she rigid, he stifling yawns. 'Pardon me,' he said. The silence continued. She became angry. Was this part of the punishment, to keep her waiting for the ordeal to come? She was about to turn on to her side when she felt his hand on her thigh. He tugged at the hem of her shift. 'Can we dispense with this?'

The touch of his hand had sent her pulses racing. She swallowed hard. 'I – need it for warmth.'

'*I* shall warm you ... once we are rid of this – garment. Here, let me help you.'

'N–o, no–' Gabrielle slid under the sheet, got on to her knees and struggled to get the shift over her head. When she surfaced Luke was laughing.

'What a performance,' he exclaimed. 'And how unnecessary. You will not be the first woman I have seen naked.'

'But you would be the first man to see *me*,' she retorted.

'I happen to be your husband and have that privilege. I *want* to see you.' He made to move away the bedclothes but Gabrielle grabbed them and held on to them.

'Not yet,' she pleaded. 'Give me time, *please.*'

Luke eased himself up and, leaning on his elbow, studied her. 'I wonder if you are as innocent as you look, Mrs Caltahn? How shall I behave towards you–? Shall I–?'

'Just get it over and done with,' Gabrielle said, through clenched teeth.

'Get it over and done with?' Luke echoed in horrified tones. 'You are speaking of the act of making love, which is one of the most beautiful, the most enjoyable–'

'It might be for two people in love,' she snapped, 'but as I detest *you* and you married me for revenge I doubt whether either of us will find beauty, or enjoyment, out of the – the act.'

Luke chuckled. 'Although you may not realize it you have issued a challenge, and I enjoy a challenge. I shall make you enjoy our *love-making.*'

'Never.'

'Oh, yes, my sweet. I have never yet failed to satisfy a woman.'

'Then be prepared for failure this time. A woman who is paid for her favours will cheat to please a man, or so I understand.'

'Ah, but the body does not cheat. I will know by your response whether I give you pleasure or not.' He paused then added softly, 'Shall we start?'

He leaned over her and touched his lips to hers. His movements were sensuous and although Gabrielle steeled herself not to respond she felt a stirring of emotion. This must be Luke Caltahn's way of revenge, she kept telling herself, as his lips moved down to her throat. She forced herself to remain rigid.

His hand cupped her breast then moved slowly down her body and his touch of her skin sent fire through her. Luke must have been aware of it because he drew in a quick breath.

'Put your arms around me,' he said softly.

She kept them stiffly at her side.

'Gabrielle, do as I tell you.' His voice had taken on a note of command.

'No–'

His hand moved down over her thigh and although his touch was featherlight it brought a tingling in her. Revenge – Revenge, she kept thinking. He would get no response, no help from her. But even as she thought it the hardness of his body excited her, and she wondered with despair how she could keep from responding to his caresses.

Her cousin Janet had mentioned the word love-play, but she had not described it. This must be it, the touching, the teasing. She had not expected gentleness from Luke, but everything he did had a gentleness about it, a teasing nibbling at her ear, butterfly kisses on her closed eyelids, the tracing of a finger round her breast – then his hand was on her thigh again, caressing her. It took her all her time to keep herself tense.

'Gabrielle, stop fighting me,' Luke coaxed. 'I want you to enjoy it too. Relax, I promise not to hurt you.'

'Why do you lie? You *will* hurt me. No man has ever touched me.'

'It will only be at first. Afterwards–' He drew the back of his fingertips over her cheek. 'It will be worthwhile, believe me.'

His hand was moving again. It moved to the inside of her thigh this time and her whole being leapt in response. It fired Luke's passion. There was a wildness in him that she was unprepared for. Annoyed at the betrayal of her own body she began to fight him. But it seemed to incense him further. She made claws of her fingers and drew her nails down his back, and he shouted, 'Will you stop fighting me, Gabrielle. It will be worse for you.'

'I could kill you,' she shouted back. 'And I–' Her words were lost as Luke's mouth covered hers.

She stopped fighting when she realized she stood no chance against his superior strength and expertise. Fury at him diminished the first pain of contact, and afterwards, surprise held her passive. She had imagined them lying together, Luke entering her and that would be it. How ignorant she had been. Even Janet had not mentioned movement, rhythm, a rhythm that was rousing emotions she had not experienced before. Gabrielle was on the brink of an ecstasy when Luke rolled away from her with a deep sigh of satisfaction. She felt she hated him, sure this was his way of punishing her.

He said in a lazy way, a few moments later, 'You behaved very foolishly, Gabrielle. You suffered because of a silly childish tantrum.'

'Tantrum?' she exclaimed. 'I was fighting against being raped.'

Luke turned on to his side and leaned up on his elbow once more. 'Raped? You don't know the meaning of the word, woman. I was gentle with you.'

'Gentle? Heaven protect me if you decide to be rough.'

'I will be,' he said grimly, 'if you go on fighting me, so be warned.'

Gabrielle felt she would rather die than let him get enjoyment through her body. She said, her voice prim, 'I promise you that from now on I shall be a docile wife, completely docile, Mr Caltahn.'

'Then heaven help *me*,' he exclaimed and dropping back on to the bed he turned over on to his side away from her.

It seemed to Gabrielle that within minutes he was asleep, while she lay wide awake, wishing she had never set eyes on Luke Caltahn.

# CHAPTER SEVEN

During the next few days Gabrielle had plenty of time for thinking about her life and her marriage. The weather was stormy and she hardly saw Luke. He would come down for meals, eat quickly and be away again. He came to bed but she never knew when, even though she forced herself to stay awake until late. She only knew he had been to bed by the dent in the pillow.

On the day following the consummation of their marriage when she had asked Luke if she could go up on deck for a breath of air, he told her shortly she would have to wait, he had more important things on his mind. Feeling angry she had made up her mind to risk going up on her own when Tomaso informed her the ship had been blown off course. Then Gabrielle simmered down. Luke would have plenty on his mind.

The next day, when there was a lull in the storm, he came for her. 'Five minutes,' he said, 'more trouble is brewing.' He picked up her cloak and put it round her shoulders, anxiety puckering his brow.

When they went up on deck there was a feeling of eeriness. Apart from the usual creakings of the ship everywhere was still, even the men had an air of waiting. The helmsman looked tense. The sea was uncannily calm. But as Gabrielle watched she saw what appeared to be powdered snow skimming across the surface. It took her several seconds to realize it was the wind making a spray of the surface water. And yet she felt no wind on her face. There was a greyness overall with green tinges in the turbulence of clouds. She turned to Luke. 'What is it? Is there a big storm building up?'

'I fear so. When you go below you must stay in the cabin. And that is an order.' His eyes, which looked a very dark grey at that moment, held hers in a compelling gaze. 'You must obey me in this, Gabrielle.'

'I have no wish to defy you,' she said quietly, 'but I would prefer to be in the open, even if it would mean tying me with a rope to a mast – or something. I feel a prisoner as it is in the confines of the cabin, and with a storm coming up, and being alone – surely you must understand how I feel.'

His face set. 'And you must understand my position. I am responsible for the ship, for every man on it and for you. You will be safer below. I promise you this, I shall not leave you to drown.'

'Well, thank you for that small consolation,' she said stiffly.

'You are being sarcastic again,' he chided. Then, as the head and shoulders of the boatswain appeared above the deck Luke excused himself and went over to the man. While they talked Gabrielle looked about her for a place where she could be secure should the storm be bad. She peered over the quarter-deck to the one below and saw chained casks and beside them a ring in the deck with a rope through it. If the worst came to the worst–

A sudden squall had Luke grabbing her by the elbow and urging her below. Before she reached the companion-way it was deluging down. Luke shouted after her, 'Keep the cabin door shut.'

'Yes,' she yelled back, feeling like a recalcitrant child banished to her room. She intended slamming the door shut but once inside the cabin a lurch of the ship threw her against the desk. And after that she was forced to climb on the bed to keep from being thrown about. A few minutes later Tomaso appeared at the open door, a mug in his hand. By the time he got the coffee to her a good half of it had been spilled. 'Big bad storm,' he said, his eyes round. 'You stay there, Ma'am, safest there. Tomaso look after you, Captain look after ship. Captain very good man.' Tomaso looked as if he needed to convince himself as well as

Gabrielle that all would be well. He staggered out, promising to come later with a meal.

It was many hours, however, before Gabrielle was to taste food.

Tomaso had shut the door when he left and she had the feeling of being imprisoned, especially with the rails of the bed holding her there. And yet she knew she would be foolish at the moment to climb out of the bed. The ship seemed to be tossing about all ways, and every now and again a wave would hit the ship with an unnerving thud, making the craft shudder. The ship would then rise, seem to hover on the crest of a wave then drop into a trough, leaving Gabrielle's stomach behind. She began to wonder if she had not boasted too prematurely about being an excellent sailor. There were thumps and banging from above, yelled orders and creakings. She had become accustomed to the half-hourly bell as routine, but now she felt there was an urgency in the sound. Another wave battering the ship had her holding on to the bedrail. The sea became a monster determined to break this craft. Was a watery grave to be her fate? Gabrielle, feeling the cabin closing in on her, climbed out of the bed and grabbed her cloak. If the ship was to be wrecked then she would be in the open when it happened.

When she came up on deck the wind momentarily took her breath away and made a balloon of her cloak. Even then she had a certain amount of protection where she stood in the lee of the quarter-deck. In contrast to the stillness of her earlier 'breather' on deck, all was now noise and activity. Pumps were being manned, men were clinging to the rigging, reefing sails, the top-gallants were already down, the officer of the watch was yelling orders to men hauling on the shrouds, and the boatswain was roundly cursing a man who had nearly bowled him over as he had slipped on deck. Of Luke there was no sign.

Gabrielle marvelled that the men aloft could manage to hold on in such a gale. With the ship pitching and tossing she herself felt she needed something stronger to hold on to than having her fingers hooked into a decorative piece of fretwork. With the sturdiness of the chained water casks in mind, she began to edge her way towards them. And was near when, to her horror the ship rose at an alarming angle, the bows pointing to the sky. For what seemed heart-stopping moments it hung suspended then plunged. Gabrielle grabbed the chain of the nearest barrel and clung on grimly. As the boat dropped into the void, water from the quarter-deck cascaded over her, its iciness leaving her shocked and gasping. She lay flat out, drenched and fighting to recover her breath. Oh, God, which was worst, to be trapped in the cabin, or to be perhaps carried overboard by a wave into the maelstrom of the sea? With a superhuman effort she pulled herself up and reached for the iron ring, in the deck. Then, during a few moments lull she tied the rope about her waist.

With the water wiped from her eyes she watched men coming down from the rigging, sure-footed but looking grim and wearied. How long would the storm last? Pump-rods at the foot of the main mast clanked rhythmically, the men manning them looking stone-faced as they worked automatically. The carpenter kept urging them in a monotonous voice to 'keep 'em going'.

Noise, noise, the frantic clapping of sails, the hissing of water washing over the decks, the surging of the sea–

Once when a wall of green water rose above them Gabrielle was sure this would be the end, but the ship fought valiantly against it and survived the onslaught. It was after this that she saw Luke, and with his appearance, and shouted words, the men seemed to come to life again. 'Sink or swim,' shouted one man, spitting on his hands and hauling on a rope, and the cheerful note in his voice seemed to encourage the others.

After that Luke seemed to be here there and everywhere, but to Gabrielle's relief he had not yet noticed her. The storm went on relentlessly, waves swamped the ship, men clung to rope ends, to stanchions, to rings, to hatches. And came up fighting again. Gabrielle began to have great admiration for the ship and for the men. She prayed for the survival of all.

Thunder claps vied for supremacy with the thunder of the sea, a sudden shower of hailstones had Gabrielle burying her face in the cloak against their sharpness. They pattered against the sails, on deck, on the casks. And the storm went on and on.

It was still at its height when Luke found Gabrielle. He hauled her to her feet and shook her.

'Have you gone completely mad? When will you learn to obey me? I told you to stay in your cabin.'

Moments before Gabrielle would have thought it impossible to raise her voice above a whisper, but she found strength to shout back at him.

'No! I am not going below. I want to stay here.'

'*You* are going below.'

Anger brought a heat to Gabrielle's chilled body. She identified herself with the ship and Luke with the sea, and was determined he was not going to break *her*. Another sudden squall had rain streaming down both their faces. There was fire in Luke's eyes. He struggled to get the rope knot undone and Gabrielle kicked out at him. 'If I have to die I shall die here in the open! Not you, nor any of your crew can get me away from here, so leave me alone.'

'Oh you, you – infuriating wench!' He gripped her by the shoulders and they stood glaring at one another. Luke gave her a quick shake. 'If you were one of my men I would get the bosun to take a rope's end to you.'

'And no doubt you would enjoy the spectacle,' she retorted.

'At this moment yes, I would. You disobey me, taunt me, defy me– And if I get you below I shall–'

His grip slackened and Gabrielle, her head up, said. 'You shall what, Mr Caltahn?'

'You will find out soon enough,' he said grimly. 'And I promise you shall pay for disobeying me.'

Gabrielle was both astonished and appalled that she thrilled to the mastery and savagery of his words. For seconds they stood with the wind shrieking in the rigging, the storm thundering around them, an atmosphere so primitive that it took all Gabrielle's self-control to stop her from shouting, 'Take me now, Luke.'

His hands had gone to her waist and this

time he got the knot undone. Roughly he took her by the arm. 'Come along, you must get out of those wet clothes. The last thing I want is a sick woman on board.'

All emotion left Gabrielle. He was just an animal. 'I am never ill,' she snapped.

Luke gave her a scathing look. 'Don't tempt fate.' She allowed him to take her below.

There was little comfort in the cabin. It had been awash and the boards were still wet. Everything Gabrielle touched felt damp. Luke said, 'Tomorrow I shall see about getting a stove brought in. In the meantime you must do the best you can. Get undressed and put on my robe.' He took it from the back of the door and handed it to her. It too felt cold and damp.

Gabrielle said, her teeth chattering, 'It surprises me you have not had a stove in your cabin before now. The weather is cold enough.'

'But *I* never feel the cold.'

'You lie in your teeth sir, your face is blue.'

'It may be, but my body is warm and soon you will have the pleasure of it warming you in bed.'

Gabrielle's body leapt in response to the sensuousness of his tone. She hated herself for it, and turned away, not wanting him to guess her feelings. She sought for a sharp reply.

'I would have thought the safety of your ship would be more important to you than having your sexual needs satisfied. I should imagine it would be with most – *responsible* captains.'

He swung her round to face him and his eyes were blazing. 'I would never sacrifice my ship for what you call my "sexual needs". I have good men in charge and the worst of the storm is over, or were you so concerned with thinking up sarcastic remarks you were not aware of it?'

It was only then that Gabrielle became aware of the smoother progress of the ship. The wind, however, was still blowing strongly, she could hear it, and there was an occasional thud of a wave against the ship.

'Now will you start getting undressed, please.' There was no fire in Luke's voice then, it was as cold as the cabin. Gabrielle unfastened the buttons on her cloak in a leisurely way, wanting to annoy him. She let the cloak drop to the floor and gave him a challenging stare. He stared back at her, his expression grim. Still watching him she undid the top button at the neck of her dress, then paused, and was about to undo the next one when Luke tugged at her bodice and said through clenched teeth, 'You little vixen, you've done your best to torment me.'

He tore the bodice apart. The buttons

sprang away and plopping on to the boards, rolled in all directions with a clackety sound. Furious she grabbed the bodice and made to hold it together but he slapped her hands away. 'I told you I would make you pay for disobeying me and I certainly shall.'

He dragged the dress from her shoulders, her shift followed and he then cupped her breasts. Every nerve in Gabrielle's body responded to his touch. Even then she tried to push away from him. But the ship lurched and she was thrown against him. His arms went around her and his mouth covered hers, not in the gentle way of the night of their wedding, but bruising her lips.

Weakly she tried to resist him but as he pushed her clothes down and she felt his hands on her skin her whole body throbbed. She could never have imagined that passion could be such a torment. Her arms, seemingly of their own volition, went round his neck and she pressed against him, wanting him.

'I knew there was a wildness in you,' he said, his voice soft but exultant. He carried her to the bed and after getting undressed himself he got in beside her.

But there was no love-play this time, he took her with an urgency that had her moaning, and carried her to an unbelievable ecstasy. Then, both spent, they lay back. Gabrielle longed for Luke to put his arms around her and draw her close, but he lay still, his hands behind his head. Where was the sweet aftermath of love-making that her cousin Janet had talked about?

The 'aftermath' for Gabrielle was Luke taking her again. This time she gave nothing of herself and he asked her coldly afterwards why she was crying.

'Because of your hatred for me,' she whispered. 'It was an act of revenge, not love.'

'Do you expect me to have love for a Quantock?'

'But I am no longer a Quantock,' she protested. 'My name is now Gabrielle Caltahn and I am your *wife!*'

'Yes, and I shall probably live to regret it,' he answered drily. 'I could never trust you.'

Anger rose in Gabrielle. 'Because of my grandmother? Whatever else you might be, I would have thought you to be a fair man, and not judge a person by their relations.' Luke made no answer and she watched the lamp swinging overhead.

After a while she said, 'Two months ago a man was hung for a brutal murder. The man's two eldest daughters were nuns. Would you consider these potential murderers because of their father?'

'They could well be, who is to say.'

'Oh – you are absolutely impossible.' Gabrielle climbed out of bed, looked round

135

for something to put on and picked up Luke's robe. It was seconds before she managed to get her arm into the right sleeves and in that time felt that Luke was staring at her back. She was fastening the tie about her waist, her fingers trembling when he said quietly, 'Who did that?'

She looked up. 'Did what?'

'Whipped you.' Gabrielle put a hand to her buttocks then moved away from the bed.

'My mother – at my grandmother's orders.'

'Is that the truth? It *was* your grandmother's orders?'

Gabrielle turned to face him. 'Mr Caltahn, I do not lie.'

He held up the bedclothes. 'Come here.' He spoke quietly, but when she made no move he said with impatience, 'Will you, for heavens sake, do as I ask you for once?'

'Not if you want to – do that–'

'I do not want to do – *that!* Now will you get back into bed before I drag you in.'

She kept the robe on and climbed in beside him.

'All right,' Luke said, 'tell me what happened.'

Gabrielle related the story then concluded, 'I am not altogether blaming my mother for meting out the punishment, she lives in constant fear of losing her home.

136

Her father was a gambler and although they lived in a big house their family existed – to quote my mother's words – in "genteel poverty". Mama never had new gowns or ribbons or all the pretty things a girl of her age craved for. She could never go to balls, or parties. She and papa were very much in love when they married, but once he started talking about breaking away from my grandmother, she became upset, became a nag. She was afraid that papa would be unable to support us.'

'And could he have done?'

'I have no idea. All I know is that Hesther Quantock has held the purse-strings, that the whole family is dependent on her for everything.'

'And your father obviously found out how she made her wealth and had to be got rid of.'

Gabrielle shivered. 'Got rid of? It sounds terrible.'

'Well, let us say despatched to another country.' Luke spoke kindly and Gabrielle longed for him to put his arms around her. She needed comfort. But no comfort was forthcoming. 'We had better get some sleep,' he said. Then he added, 'You must feel you were treated badly, but I can understand your mother wanting to punish you.'

Gabrielle flared. 'Oh, yes, *you* would. Most of the men in the room got sadistic enjoyment from watching me being punished.'

'You may be wronging them. Probably all they felt was satisfaction that you were getting your just deserts. You really are a most provoking person you know, always defying people–'

'Provoking? Would you have had me sit there meekly and agree to marry a man who was not only old enough to be my father, but who was brutal into the bargain? Is that what you would want for a daughter of *yours?*'

'I can tell you better when I have one.' Luke stifled a yawn. 'Although, of course, I would prefer to have a son first.'

Gabrielle drew herself up in the bed. 'And I suppose I would be severely punished should I *dare* to produce a girl for the first born?'

'Perhaps bread and water for a week. I would have to think about it.' The lightness of his tone did not appease her.

'Oh, yes, make a jest of it, let me tell you–'

'Nag, nag, be careful or you will turn out like your mother. Now lie down. I want to get some sleep.'

Gabrielle slid down the bed, dragged the bedclothes up to her nose and lay seething. Using her, that was all he was doing. 'You have no finer feelings,' she said. 'None at all.'

'Gabrielle, if you will not be quiet I shall

put you in the rope locker. *And* I mean it.'

She had no doubt he would. She lay still. Her thoughts, however, were in a turmoil, and she tried to sort them out and put them into compartments. The first she dealt with was children. It was stupid but such a thing had not occurred to her. She could be pregnant now. No, no, that must not happen. It would be terrible for a child to be conceived out of revenge. Then she wondered if Luke would be more tender towards her if she did have a baby.

It worried Gabrielle that she had felt such an ecstasy with him when there was no love between them. What they had felt, or what she had felt, was such a primitive thing she was sure it must be at least as old as time itself. She was fascinated by the thought that these feelings had lain dormant until Luke Caltahn had roused her. Why should he be the one? Was it God's will? Would there come a love between them eventually? Gabrielle suddenly needed comfort. Luke was breathing deeply as though in sleep. Dare she curl up against him? She turned carefully over on to her side, and when he made no sign of stirring she moved closer to him. She waited a few more moments then put her arm across him. He was so warm, his body so firm, so – virile. If only he would turn and take her in his arms and be tender towards her. There had to be tenderness for there to be real love. That was one thing of which Gabrielle was certain.

She willed him to turn towards her, but her husband slept on and Gabrielle, with a sigh, settled herself for sleep too.

# CHAPTER EIGHT

Gabrielle could lay wide awake thinking, but once she did fall asleep it was deep slumber. Her mother once said if the house collapsed around her she would still sleep, Gabrielle remembered this the next morning when she awoke and found herself naked. She felt colour rush to her face. It was not something new, she had awoken the past two mornings without her nightgown, but last night she had come back to bed wearing Luke's robe, and the fact that he had removed it was upsetting. She had not even come to partial consciousness. He could have been standing for ages studying her.

Gabrielle ran her hands over her body. Not that she had anything to be ashamed of, she was well shaped, but somehow nudity was not something to be stared at, not even by one's husband.

Her thoughts were interrupted by the arrival of Tomaso with the morning tea, and the information that the carpenter had come to fit the stove. Gabrielle slid further under the bedclothes. The wiry little man who came in kept glancing towards the bed

141

with an avid curiosity, but said nothing. There was already an iron base and fittings to take the stove and the job was done in minutes. Tomaso left with the man to fetch wood for the stove. When he returned he was not only carrying wood but Gabrielle's clothes, which he said the captain had brought to the galley to be dried. Her dress was on the top of the pile and it was not only Gabrielle's face that burned when she saw that the buttons had been stitched back on again but her whole body. Who had done it? Certainly not Luke. It could only have been Tomaso. Had he been asked by Luke, or had Tomaso, finding the buttons on the floor, undertaken the task of his own accord?

Oh, this was terrible. He would know she had had her clothes torn off by her husband. What must he be thinking? It was a shameful thing, indecent. Tomaso was whistling through his teeth as he struck the flint to light the wood and to Gabrielle there was something so self-conscious about it she felt she wanted to sink through the bed. Luke had said Tomaso gossiped. Every member of the crew would know. How could she ever appear on deck again?

'Soon have good fire, Ma'am,' Tomaso said brightly. 'Weather good too. No more storm, cold though. Tea getting cold, Ma'am.'

'Yes, yes, I shall have it in a moment.'

The larger pieces of wood soon caught alight from the burning shavings and Tomaso closed the stove door. 'There, cabin soon be warm, Ma'am. Captain come in a while for breakfast. I go now.'

Gabrielle could not fully enjoy the warmth of the stove for her agitation, and yet she had to admit it was more comfortable getting washed and dressed without shivering.

When Luke came in he greeted her then stood with his back to the stove. 'With this installed I doubt whether you will want to go on deck this morning. The wind is cutting.'

'After yesterday, I should imagine I could cope with arctic conditions. Was much damage done in the storm?'

Why was she not asking him about the buttons?

'Nothing that cannot be rectified. The men are working on the repairs now. I thought you would have heard them.'

'No, no – what cargo are you carrying?' Why was she asking about cargo?

'*That* is none of your business, Madam,' Luke snapped.

Gabrielle stared at him, surprised by his anger. 'I'm sorry, I asked – merely out of interest.'

'Why are you interested? Why is it important for you to know my cargo?'

She began to pour the coffee and found her hand was trembling. 'I have no need to know.' She put down the coffee pot, feeling annoyed with herself now. 'I asked a simple question and I expected a simple answer. I thought you would probably have said wool, or linen, or wheat or some such commodity. Judging by your attitude anyone would think you were carrying contraband.'

'I am not carrying contraband and I shall thank you not to question me about my cargo at any time, is that understood?'

'It is, Mr Caltahn,' she answered, calm now. 'And I promise not to mention any part of this ship, neither the hold, a sprit sail, or a—'

'Now, you are being utterly childish!'

'You are the one who is being childish,' she retorted. 'You accused me of having tantrums, but it is you who are displaying temper. And for what reason? Simply because I asked what cargo you are carrying. If you must know I was talking for talking's sake because I was agitated, I was hardly aware of what I was saying.'

'Oh, and what caused this – agitation?' His face had the cold expression she hated.

'The buttons,' she said. 'On my dress. The ones that were torn off last night.'

'What about them?'

'Someone has stitched them back on again.'

'Yes, I did.'

'You–?' Her eyes went wide. '*You* stitched the buttons back on to my dress?'

'Why the surprise? I am not entirely helpless. Even a captain owns a housewife.'

'A housewife?'

'A linen pouchette that holds everything required in case of emergency repairs being needed on a jacket or – well, on any article of apparel.' Luke was faintly smiling now. 'So why all the agitation?'

'Because I thought that Tomaso had stitched them on, and that he would know what had happened and he would tell the crew and I would not dare show my face on deck and–'

'Oh, Gabrielle–' Luke laughed and took her hands in his and drew her towards him. 'What a prim little soul you are. At least, on matters such as this.' He tilted her chin. 'I find you a strange mixture.'

'And so are you. A very strange mixture. You were thoughtful enough to stitch on the buttons to save me embarrassment yet scold me because I ask about your cargo. Why?'

His hands fell away. 'So we are back to that again, in spite of my having asked you not to question me.' He sat down at the table and attacked his breakfast.

'But it was such a simple question, one any captain's wife might ask her husband.'

'The difference is you are not any

145

captain's wife, you are *my* wife and you happen to be Hesther Quantock's granddaughter!'

Gabrielle was staring at him for the second time. Did he think she was spying for her grandmother? How could he, he knew how much she hated her. Then, reason took over. No, Luke would not know, he only knew what she had told him. He had proof by the weals on her buttocks she had been whipped, but no proof that her grandmother had been the one to order the whipping. And unfortunately she had no means of establishing that fact. She said:

'I should like to say one more thing. I can understand your suspicions of me, but I give you my word you shall have my loyalty in every way. I owe you that much as your wife, even though–'

'Even though–' he snapped. 'What a world of speculation those words evoke.' He got up and swept her a bow. 'But I shall do my best to believe you sincere in your *new* loyalties.'

Gabrielle refrained from replying to his mockery, knowing how much he had suffered at her grandmother's hands. They finished their breakfast in silence.

She had not expected Luke to take her on deck that morning but he did and his manner was surprisingly quite pleasant. The wind, as he had said, was cutting, but

Gabrielle found the air exhilarating. The waves were choppy and white-flecked, the sky a clear hard blue.

There seemed to be extra activity going on after the storm, men carrying planks of wood, sawing and hammering in a number of places, men repairing sails.

'Are we likely to encounter any more storms?' Gabrielle asked.

'Not at the moment, the wind is set fair, and with the Bay behind us–'

'When will we reach Marseilles?'

'Not for another two weeks at least, that is if all goes well. We make a stop at Lisbon first.'

'Two weeks?' Gabrielle said in dismay. 'I had no idea it would take so long. I know when an aunt and an uncle of mine travelled overland from Calais to Marseilles it took a very long time but–'

'It would, and think of all the discomfort, the rattling over rutted roads. On a ship – apart from storms, you travel in comfort, and remember a ship is still travelling while you are sleeping.'

'Yes, of course. It had not occurred to me. I find something intriguing in the fact that the ship is still moving while I am in bed.'

'And sleeping soundly. *You* are a very sound sleeper, Mrs Caltahn.' Luke who had been carrying a telescope put it to his eye. 'When I left our bed at five-thirty–'

'Oh – the robe–' Gabrielle used to the idea, felt less embarrassed about it now. 'I could hardly believe you could have taken it from me without my waking.'

'Do you know that you sleep with your thumb in your mouth?' Luke continued to scan the ocean.

'I do not!'

'Oh, but you do, and very appealing you looked, all curled up like a little girl – seeking solace. Am I such a ogre to you?'

There was a gentleness in his voice as he made the last remark and for a moment Gabrielle wanted to respond to it. But then she remembered the uncaring way he had taken her the night before and she replied stiffly, 'You are my husband and as I happen to come from Quantock stock I expect to be punished.'

'Thank you for reminding me.' Luke's voice was now curt. He snapped shut the telescope. 'If I am sensible I shall keep reminding myself of the fact.' He turned then added, 'Ah, here is our surgeon. I shall leave you in his care. Mr Delacote, will you entertain my wife? You are both avid readers so you should have a great deal in common. If you will excuse me.'

They both watched Luke go to the lower deck and Gabrielle thought again what a fine, handsome man he was, and wished that the perverse devil in her had not reminded him she was a Quantock.

The surgeon turned to her. 'How did you fare in the storm, Mrs Caltahn? I half expected to be called to attend to you. Even some of the crew were seasick. Evidently the motion of the ship did not upset you.'

'No, I am very lucky in that respect. I was, of course, afraid of the ship sinking and yet, I had a feeling of excitement. I suppose it was a case of man against the elements. From being a child I have had a spirit of adventure.'

'I was going to say you are at an advantage being the wife of a sea captain, but I imagine your husband will be like all seamen and look forward to getting home to a wife.'

'This voyage is an exceptional one,' Gabrielle said.

'Yes, indeed. A marriage and honeymoon at sea.' Mr Delacote's melancholic face lifted in a smile. 'Quite romantic.'

On the night of the wedding ceremony Gabrielle had thought the fair-haired surgeon to be in his late thirties. Now she saw that he might even be nearer fifty than forty; his hair was streaked with white and the skin around the mouth and under the eyes was deeply wrinkled. Gabrielle asked if any of the seamen had suffered injuries during the storm and Mr Delacote shrugged.

'A few cuts and bruises, a sprained ankle

and a broken collar bone, it could have been worse.'

Gabrielle began to talk about books and found that the surgeon's interest was in reading about other countries. But although he spoke knowledgeably he seemed to dwell most of the time on wars that had taken place, on famine and great storms. She asked if he had been to Lisbon before and he said yes he had, and his grandfather had been there at the time of the great earthquake.

'It happened on All Souls Day,' he said, 'when the churches were filled with people for the Mass. The river seemed to boil then the river bed dried up. A great wind came, it blew the candles over and there were many fires. Then a huge wave built up and crashed over the town. Tens of thousands of lives were lost.'

'How awful,' Gabrielle said.

'And how depressing,' interrupted Luke from behind them. 'Have you told my wife about the Sea of Straws, Mr Delacote? No. Then I shall tell her.' He turned to Gabrielle. 'When the sun is shining a certain part of the river looks as if there were a myriad golden straws on the water.'

'How lovely.'

The surgeon said in a flat voice, 'But when the day is dull the river looks muddy.'

Gabrielle found herself hard put not to

laugh at this. Luke, however, placed a hand on Mr Delacote's shoulder and said gently, 'Dear friend, you really must try and look on the bright side. The sun *could* be shining, and if not today then tomorrow–'

The surgeon nodded. 'Yes, you are right, I really must try and look on the bright side.'

Gabrielle, deciding to change the subject, asked about other ships. 'Why do I not see any? I have not seen even one since we left London. Is it that they pass when I'm below?'

'We passed four yesterday,' Luke said. 'Did you not hear the man atop hailing them?'

'I hear a lot of voices, much shouting, much bell ringing, but I have yet to sort them out into meaning. Perhaps if I were on deck more–'

'Impossible. How could I maintain discipline with a beautiful woman there all the time to distract my men! But there, I must leave you for a while longer in the capable hands of Mr Delacote.'

When Luke had gone the surgeon said, 'Your husband is a fine man, Mrs Caltahn. I owe him my life. Unfortunately–' He stopped abruptly once more, leaving Gabrielle wondering if he had been going to tell her something about Luke.

There was a long silence between them and Gabrielle, seeking in her mind for some

151

other source of common interest, began talking about London, and its social life. But Mr Delacote showed little interest and eventually he said that actually the sea was his whole life.

'Then I take it you are not married, sir,' she teased.

The interruption this time from Luke was to grip her arm and say, 'Come along, Gabrielle, the meal will be ready. Please excuse us, Mr Delacote.' Luke hustled her below and Gabrielle was furious.

'Your behaviour was unpardonable,' she exclaimed, 'so rude, and so embarrassing for me. How could you rush me away like that?'

'I rushed you away because you were probing into Mr Delacote's private life and you have no right to.'

'I was not probing! I simply said I took it he was not married because he had told me the sea was his life.'

'His wife died under tragic circumstances, now will you please leave it at that?'

'Yes, I will. I'm sorry about his wife, but you could have told me and saved me the embarrassment! The only other personal thing I asked was how long he had sailed with you. Otherwise we talked about books, foreign countries, war, famine, I did not mention cargo, crew or talk about *your* life. Not that I could, I know less about you than

I might know about a stranger asking me to partner him in the quadrilles. I just do *not* know how to please you.'

Luke sat back in his chair and a wicked gleam came into his eyes. 'There is one way.'

'Oh, *that*,' Gabrielle said with scorn.

'Yes, that.' Luke was laughing at her. 'You have no idea what you are missing. But – of course you do. You did once respond. Why not again?'

'To give *you* pleasure? I might, had your underlying motive not been revenge. When you took me last night what were your thoughts? Were you imagining the fury on my grandmother's face when she finds out we are married? That must give you great pleasure.'

'Believe me, my sweet, neither *your* grandmother nor anyone else was on my mind when I made love to you last night.' Luke's voice was lazy. 'And if my attentions offend I shall remain celibate. Oh, yes, you need not raise your eyebrows. I can do so even with an attractive and desirable wife beside me.'

'I consider that to be a vain boast, sir.'

'It is no boast, you shall find that out.'

Gabrielle did find out that evening, and was annoyed with herself for having goaded him into making such a statement. She longed for the touch of his fingers on her skin, to move them over her body in his

153

teasing, tantalizing way. She wanted to feel his lips on her, moving sensuously over her throat, her breasts – she ached for him, throbbed. What a torment such emotion provoked. Several times she reached out a hand to touch Luke, but each time withdrew it. If a man's feelings were stronger than a woman's and Luke was managing to resist his urges then she must.

Gabrielle managed to force her mind away from what their vicar at home once rousingly denounced as 'carnal thought' and concentrated on thinking about her father. She had purposely kept him from her thoughts, not wanting to admit that he could be dead. Dead? If he were she would want to die too. No, she must live to get her vengeance on her grandmother. Hesther Quantock *must* be made to suffer. Why, oh why, had her father not broken away from his mother when he first talked about it? 'It's your mama,' he had once said in explanation. 'She lives in fear of poverty. We would he hard-pressed but not poverty-stricken. I could make a living from the land, a cottage, several acres–'

He had told her this on a summer's day when the cornfields were waving in the breeze, when the river ambled and birds sang. The prospect then had seemed idyllic. It had not occurred to her that her father had never soiled his hands in manual work.

Now she was forced to wonder if her father, for all his strength in trying to defy his mother, was not a bit of a dreamer – and Mama knew it.

And yet, if a woman loved her husband surely she would be willing to put up with any discomfort, any hardship to live together in loving harmony.

In loving harmony? This was something that she and Luke would never enjoy. They were both too strong willed, there would always be conflict. But if there could be love, tenderness–

She was back to Luke again. Forget him, he had forgotten her, he was snoring lightly. What had happened to Mr Delacote's wife? In what way had her death been tragic? Gabrielle's question remained unanswered. She slept.

As before Luke had gone from the bed when she awoke. The days and nights after this followed the same pattern. Gabrielle had her outings on deck, and some of them were for quite long stretches, she and Luke had meals together and they slept together, but sleep was all they did. Gabrielle had managed to school herself not to let her emotions take charge, and apart from one night when she found herself curled up against his back, her hand on his body, she was sure she had kept away from him.

Then came a morning when she awoke

155

with a feeling of something about to happen, and found out what it was when Tomaso came in with her morning cup of tea and announced, beaming, that land had been sighted.

'Lisbon?' she said, and he nodded.

'Do you like Lisbon, Tomaso?'

He said he did, but he liked Marseilles better. Marseilles was bad good place.

Gabrielle laughed. 'How can a place be bad and good?'

'Men bad – gamble, kill–' Tomaso drew a finger cryptically across his throat. 'But much music, much singing.' He grinned. 'Women bad, but very happy, make men happy.' Immediately afterwards Tomaso clapped his hand to his mouth, knowing he had said too much. 'Sorry, sorry,' he said. 'No tell master. I go now.' He scuttled out.

When Luke came down for breakfast he appeared to be in a good mood. Gabrielle said, 'Tomaso told me that land has been sighted.'

'Yes, you would find very little to see at the moment but in another two hours–' Luke paused. 'Gabrielle, tomorrow is our surgeon's birthday. I thought we might have a celebration dinner in Lisbon.'

'Oh, how lovely. What shall I wear? I do have my sea-green dress–'

Luke nodded towards the brass bound trunk. 'You will find an assortment of dresses and shoes and cloaks and shawls in there. I feel sure you will find something to fit you.'

'An assortment? In sizes? Whose are they?'

Luke gave an impatient sigh. 'Why must you always be asking questions? They are not clothes discarded by my *many* mistresses, if that is what is in your mind.'

'Oh, so you admit to having had many women.'

'I have not been living in a monastery, although I could be now for all the marital enjoyment I am having. Yes, I have had women, but these clothes have not adorned any of them. Now I am not taking you out to dinner in what you are wearing at the moment so you either wear a dress you brought with you, or choose something from the chest, but do not ask me any more questions about my life.'

'What a pity,' she replied pertly. 'I had intended asking you this morning about your family, if you had parents living, brothers and sisters – it would be interesting to know the background of my husband. Or must that always remain a secret?'

'No, I shall tell you when I am ready, but that time is not now.' With this delivered Gabrielle knew she dare not ask any further questions.

Once Luke had gone back on deck she drew out the chest and began sorting through the clothes. There was an expensive simplicity about even the day dresses that made Gabrielle hazard a guess they had been made by Parisian couturiers. Most of the evening gowns were fashioned in the new Viennese style with the high waist and flowing skirts. The one that appealed to her was in white. It had loose panels at the back that would float when she walked. It was the sort of dress, Gabrielle felt, in which she could make an entrance. The only trimming was a narrow silver braid in a Greek design under the bust. The neck appeared to be very low cut. Would Luke disapprove?

Gabrielle tried on the dress and found it was more revealing than anything she had ever worn. Her breasts were small but firm and well rounded, and the design of the dress showed more of them than she felt was modest. And yet, was it not the right of a woman to look seductive? She would wear it.

The cloak she chose to wear with it was a midnight blue velvet, the hood edged with swansdown.

When she went up on deck that morning for her airing she had her first glimpse of the land, and felt disappointed to see only a vague outline through a fine mist. Luke said, 'You will see all the land you need when you wake up in the morning.'

'Luke, should we not have a gift for Mr Delacote?'

'I have one, you can present it to him tomorrow evening. I shall leave you now.' Luke called to the helmsman of the watch, 'Will you see that my wife does not fall overboard, Mr Strange.'

'Aye, aye, sir.'

Luke was smiling as he turned to Gabrielle. 'I know you are not likely to fall overboard but I just like to feel there is someone responsible to care for you, while I am not there.' He touched her lightly on the cheek. 'Enjoy the sea breezes.'

Gabrielle went to the rail. To care for her? Did he really?

She turned to smile at the sandy-haired Mr Strange. There were so many different helmsmen she had lost track of them. 'A lovely morning, Mr Strange.'

'Aye, aye, Ma'am.' He stared straight ahead. 'A pushing wind.'

Gabrielle turned her attention to the lower deck. She had not seen the Reverend John Ballant since the night of her marriage. Now she was surprised and delighted to see him running up the ratlines with the agility of a ten-year-old. He had still not lost his merry-eyed look. She wished she could talk with him, but that was impossible. In spite of his calling he was simply crew on this ship. He saw her and raised his hand with the briefest of greetings. Gabrielle acknowledged him, equally as briefly, but felt happy for having seen him.

Two men who had been busy hammering came across the deck towards the water casks. Gabrielle was thinking of the night of the storm and shuddering a little at the memory of the icy water washing over her, when she heard one of the men say, 'Never heard anything so stupid as carrying ballast only in that there hold. Coming all this way without cargo. What for?'

'The cap'n'll know what for. It ain't none of our business.'

The men checked the casks then left, leaving Gabrielle staring after them. Ballast? Only ballast in the hold? And Luke had been annoyed with her when she mentioned cargo. Why had he made the journey without one? It seemed senseless. Gabrielle shook her head. But as she could not ask Luke and, as he would not voluntarily offer the information, her curiosity would have to remain unsatisfied.

Gabrielle longed to have a bath, but as water was limited on the ship she had not wanted to ask. Now they were nearing land, however, she tentatively asked Luke if it were possible.

'Yes,' he said, 'I think it can be arranged. There is a hip bath I use. Tomaso will bring it in this evening.'

The hip bath that Tomaso struggled in

with was beautifully painted with horses and riders in a country scene. When Gabrielle admired it he said, 'Captain bought it in Italy. He has cold sea water bath every morning.' Tomaso gave a shiver at the thought. 'Captain very strong man.'

Yes, Gabrielle thought, he must be, then wondered suddenly if he expected *her* to take a cold bath. Tomaso's next words assured her the water would be hot. The water, he said, would be brought in soon.

Gabrielle could not see the men who brought it, but there must have been several because Tomaso would take a bucket of water from someone, tip it into the bath, and go for the next one.

He then triumphantly produced a large tablet of scented soap, which he declared was the captain's special. There were also fleecy towels which were placed near the stove to warm.

There was a big sponge in the water, the soap was perfumed with sandalwood and Gabrielle stepped in with a feeling of luxury. She washed her hair, soaping and rinsing again and again. She soaped all over her body and was letting the water from the dripping sponge trickle over her when the door opened and Luke came in.

'Oh,' he said, 'I'm sorry, I had forgotten–'

Gabrielle, with a gasp, grabbed a towel and held it in front of her. 'The door – I forgot to lock it.'

'Very foolish, my sweet, Tomaso might have walked in.'

'Tomaso *does* knock,' she retorted. Luke stood smiling down at her and she saw the wicked gleam come into his eyes.

'Shall I wash your back?'

'No, no, thank you, I can manage.'

'But *I* can do it much better,' he said softly. Taking the sponge from her he soaped it and began to rub her back. When Gabrielle had trickled the water over her skin it was enjoyable. When Luke did it she found it deliciously sensuous. She was still holding the towel over her breasts. Luke took it from her and she folded her arms over herself. He laughed and lifted her arms away and began to sponge round her breasts. Gabrielle was torn between saying, 'Please go on,' and 'No, no, stop,' when the decision was made for her by a knock on the door.

Luke, cursing softly said, 'Yes, what is it?'

It was Mr Delacote to say one of the men had had a heart attack. Luke dropped the sponge into the water with a splash, went to the door, turned and said to Gabrielle, 'One of these days, my sweet, I shall wash you all over, every little inch of you,' and with that he opened the door, and after a few words with the surgeon, he closed it and went with him.

Gabrielle sat motionless in the now cooling water, wondering if Luke would make love to her this evening.

But it was the next morning before she saw him and then he came down to tell her they were nearing the estuary of the River Tagus and asked if she would be interested in seeing the approach to Lisbon.

'Oh yes, I would. Will I see the golden straws on the water?'

'The day is dull, the river muddy-looking, but your hair is gleaming.' Luke wrapped a strand round his finger, withdrew his finger and left a dancing curl. 'Very pretty.' He was smiling.

Gabrielle bobbed a curtsy. 'Thank you, kind sir. The first compliment from my husband. This must surely turn out to be a good day.'

'Come along, wench.' He took her by the arm. 'You smell good enough to eat. If I stay I might attempt it, and I have no time to spare.'

'Was I not good enough to eat last night – after my bath?' she teased.

'I am quite certain you were not waiting in your bed frantic with longing for me, Madam. I was up all night.'

'Oh – I – do sleep heavily, as you so rightly pointed out. Perhaps this evening, after all the excitement of visiting a new port I shall not be so sleepy. And you know, sir, it is not impossible to rouse me.'

'I shall remember that. Shall we go?'

Gabrielle went happily on deck, sure now that good things were coming her way.

# CHAPTER NINE

It took some time to manoeuvre the ship over the bar and into the estuary. They passed green fields and on low hills beyond were windmills, the sails turning lazily. In between were two small villages of white fishermen's cottages, where at the river women washed clothes, slapping them on stones. A pair of bullocks, teamed by a lovely carved wooden yoke, dragged boats up the beach.

Then they came to the Bélem Tower, which stood in the centre of the river. Luke had told Gabrielle about it but she had not expected anything so beautiful. It was of white stone, a Moorish looking structure with its exquisite carvings, open-worked balconies, delicate windows and turreted sentry stands.

'Oh, how lovely,' she said to Mr Delacote, who was by her side. 'It reminds me of the sugar loaf castles in the stories of my childhood.'

'They keep prisoners below,' he replied in his melancholy way. 'When the tide is full the water comes up to their necks.'

'Mr Delacote!' Gabrielle wailed. 'How

165

could you? You've spoiled it all.'

'It's truth. You cannot cover the coarseness of truth with beauty.'

Luke said quietly from behind them, 'But might there not be times, Mr Delacote, when it might be kinder to do so?'

The surgeon glanced at Gabrielle then nodded. 'Yes, I think perhaps you are right, Captain. I do tend to be depressive.' He gave a slight smile. 'And I ought not to be on my birthday, especially when I have an invitation to a celebration dinner.'

'Which you must not forget, Mr Delacote,' Gabrielle said.

'How could I, Mrs Caltahn, when you are included in the invitation.' He gave her a gallant bow.

Lisbon and the river ahead were shrouded in mist but the river was alive with boats. There were Phoenician barges with their large triangular sails, narrow ones with lovely curved prows, fishing boats with painted sails, and several strange types which Luke said were trimarans and catamarans.

The men on the ship exchanged friendly greetings with those on the boats.

Then the mist cleared and Gabrielle had her first glimpse of Lisbon and was charmed by it. Built on seven hills it had the appearance of an amphitheatre with its tiers of houses, painted in pastel colours of pink and blue and yellow. Mr Delacote pointed out landmarks, churches, belfry towers, convents, monasteries, St. George's Church standing sentinel over the town, and the delightful oddity that all appeared to be linked together by garlands of greenery. He next drew her attention to the opposite bank where there were no buildings, just forests and green fields, which surprisingly for January were starred with wild flowers.

'Oh, I love it all,' she exclaimed, 'I cannot wait to explore.'

They were now nearing the larger ships which were anchored in mid-river, traders, brigantines, schooners, sloops. Their own ship was preparing to drop anchor. Men swarmed on decks, up shrouds, there was unloading and loading going on, the quayside was packed with merchant men haggling with buyers over prices, men shouting their wares – a thousand sounds, the creaking of masts, water lapping, the shouts of men in the small boats, a babel of voices from men of tongues unfamiliar to Gabrielle. The smell of the pine trees on the opposite bank mingled with that of tar and aromatic spices.

Gabrielle, on an impulse, slipped her arm through Luke's. 'Oh, isn't it exciting. It's the – foreignness of it all.'

He smiled at her, then disengaged himself. 'I shall be busy for several hours but Mr

Delacote has agreed to act as guide. He knows the town well. Be prepared when you get on shore to have "sea legs". It takes time to adjust. Terra firma will seem strange to you.'

It certainly did. For a time Gabrielle felt as though she had a rolling gait and, as on deck, there were times when a foot raised seemed to be suspended in mid-air for several seconds before touching ground. She laughed about it and Mr Delacote assured her that by the time she had climbed the steep narrow streets and the hundreds of steps she would have found her 'land legs'. Which she did.

Gabrielle was alarmed by the way children hurtled down the narrow steps, sure they would fall headlong, but they were as sure-footed as deer. She was intrigued by the shops of the money changers, the basket makers, the shoe makers, by all the haggling that went on. She was astonished at the ease and grace with which the women carried laden baskets and heavy jars on their heads. They were barefooted for the most part and she noticed what beautiful feet they had, slender, long-toed.

She loved the narrow alleyways with their tall houses, the balconies adorned with plants and flowers – and colourful washing!

Although the day was dull the air was warm and at last Gabrielle, dry-throated and breathless, begged for something to drink and somewhere to rest. Mr Delacote took her to a place where they drank wine under a canopy of vines, and where close by, in a kitchen, people sang a haunting melody.

'It's a love song,' Mr Delacote said, looking sad. 'It reminds me of the time when my wife and I– No,' he added quickly, 'I must not dwell on any unhappiness today.'

'But you were speaking of a romantic moment in your lives,' Gabrielle said gently. 'You must have been happy then. I think you ought to talk about it.'

'No, I would grow morbid. I think it's my nature. Let us talk about you, Mrs Caltahn. Where did you meet the captain?'

This was dangerous ground. Gabrielle ran a finger round the rim of her wine glass then looked up, smiling. 'Shall I confess that I pursued him? I stowed away on the ship. Then he *had* to marry me. I really am a dreadful person.'

Mr Delacote actually laughed. 'I think you are a delightful person, Mrs Caltahn. What a lovely story, so romantic.'

'It's true.'

'Yes, of course. You were a stowaway. Such courage. A most interesting thing for a woman to do.'

Gabrielle knew by the surgeon's tone he did not believe her but was indulging her 'whim'.

'You adjusted so easily, so readily to the seafaring life,' he said. 'I know the captain was very pleased about this.'

'He was?'

'Oh, indeed, yes, especially the time of the storm. He had a great admiration for the way you coped.'

'He did not give *me* that impression,' Gabrielle said with a wry smile. 'In fact he was angry with me for going on deck.'

'Yes, well, he would be, wouldn't he? He would be terribly worried about you. A man feels responsible for his wife, he–' The surgeon broke off and drained his glass. 'Some more wine, Mrs Caltahn?' Gabrielle saw his hands were trembling.

'No, I feel a little heady with one,' she tried to speak brightly. 'Shall we go? We have been away a long time.'

'Yes, we have.'

Gabrielle wished she knew what had happened to his wife, wished he would talk about her. She felt sure it would ease his unhappiness, but remembering Luke's annoyance with her for what he called her 'probing' she had to be content by asking questions about various things to keep his mind occupied. He seemed brighter by the time they were rowed back to the ship. Gabrielle was so full of impressions she was longing to tell Luke about them, but he was not there and it was another hour before he arrived. Then he was so concerned with a list he was checking; it was minutes before he noticed her. 'Oh, there you are, Gabrielle. Did you enjoy your sightseeing?'

'Oh, yes, I did–' She began to relate her experiences then stopped when she realized Luke's attention was on the list again. After a few moments he looked up. 'Sorry, what were you saying?'

'It's all right. I can tell you later. I see you are busy.'

'This is important. Supplies have to be checked. It would be no use checking after we've sailed.'

'No, of course not. You go ahead. I have plenty to watch.' Gabrielle paused. 'But we will have the evening with Mr Delacote?'

'Naturally. I promised. Now, if you will excuse me.'

Gabrielle stayed on deck, expecting to see supplies come aboard but none came. Eventually Luke went ashore and she went below.

It was late afternoon before he appeared. Then he thrust a parcel at her saying, 'For your shoulders. The evening could be chilly.'

It was a white silk shawl, exquisitely embroidered. There were minute birds, on branches, on the wing, butterflies, flowers, the whole a kaleidoscope of delicate colours.

'Oh, Luke, how beautiful, thank you a

thousand times. But this is not *my* birthday.'

'Let us say that this and the shawl are wedding presents.' He handed her a long velvet case. Inside was a gold locket and chain. 'The locket opens. Here, let me do it.' He pressed a catch and Gabrielle stared with astonishment at the tiny miniature of herself.

She looked up. 'What a wonderful likeness, but how, when–?'

'Our priest, the Reverend John Ballant did it for me. I knew he was talented and–' Luke raised his shoulders. 'He found pleasure in doing it. You must thank him later, I shall arrange it.'

'Oh, Luke, I feel so deeply touched, for the work and for your thought.'

'Now don't start weeping. You may kiss me.' His voice was teasing. Gabrielle stood on tiptoe and kissed him on the lips. Luke responded for a moment then drew away. 'You must start getting dressed.'

'Luke – the present for Mr Delacote. Did you remember it?'

'Of course, here it is.'

It was a cravat pin in chased gold, studded with a single emerald. This too was in a case. Luke closed it. 'Mr Delacote did say some time ago he fancied one. One set with an emerald.'

'How clever of you to have noticed and remembered.'

'But then I am a clever fellow.' Luke's voice was still teasing and Gabrielle was glad. In such a good mood the evening was more likely to be a success.

Luke said he had promised to have a drink with the surgeon in his cabin so he would get dressed first, and leave Gabrielle to her toilette. She found this arrangement most satisfactory, wanting to make an impression in the white dress.

Luke had chosen to wear dark grey, the jacket of patterned velvet. She thought the grey gave a hardness to his eyes, but the frills of his white shirt at front and cuffs had a softening effect.

She stood appraising him. 'You look very handsome, sir.'

'Thank you–' He walked round her and dropped a kiss on the back of her neck, which sent shivers of ecstasy down her spine.

'I shall expect you to be ready in half an hour.' He went to the door and, turning, gave her a grin. Gabrielle's pulses raced. There were times like this when he looked so gloriously wicked. She had to collect herself to start getting ready.

The time she needed most was in doing up her hair. It had a natural curl and twisted readily around her fingers. She piled the curls on top of her head, threaded a ribbon through them, loosened a few to hang at the back, and brought dancing tendrils over her ears. The finished result pleased her. After putting on the dress she clasped Luke's present at her throat, and was ready and waiting when her two escorts arrived.

She was well rewarded by Mr Delacote's gasp of admiration. 'A vision in white,' he enthused. 'An angel.'

Luke said, 'My wife is provocatrice, siren and rebel but she is quite definitely *not* an angel.'

To Gabrielle's surprise and dismay there was a coldness in his voice. He picked up the shawl and draped it over her shoulders, and she knew the reason then for his displeasure when he made sure it covered her breasts.

Gabrielle, trying desperately to overcome her choked feeling, said to Mr Delacote, 'This was a present from my husband, a wedding present.' She turned to let him see the full effect of the embroidery.

'It's a most beautiful shawl, Mrs Caltahn.'

'And this too is a present.' Gabrielle held out the locket. 'And see what it contains.' When the surgeon saw the miniature he also declared his astonishment at the likeness.

'How is it possible to capture such perfection on a surface tiny enough to go in a locket. May I know who the artist is?'

Luke explained and Gabrielle began to feel that the tension was easing. When they were ready to leave she asked if she would need her cloak.

Luke put it about her shoulders. 'Yes, you will need it for the boat.'

It was not easy to negotiate the ship's ladder with the flimsy dress, but Luke, who had gone first, reached up for her when she was so far down and lifted her into the waiting boat. The surgeon had gone back to his cabin for something and Gabrielle took the opportunity to apologize about the dress. Speaking in a low voice she said, 'I thought you would have liked it.'

'I would have done had we been dining in private. I dislike the idea of other men enjoying my wife's – décolletage.'

'But the style is fashionable.'

'In your case it is overdone. The subject is closed.'

Gabrielle touched his arm. 'Please let us not spoil Mr Delacote's birthday party.'

'No, here is the pin. Present it to him before dinner.'

The surgeon hailed them as he came down the ladder and said as he dropped into the boat, 'There we are, anchors away!'

Gabrielle was glad that at least one member of the party was in a good mood, but did wonder if Mr Delacote's joviality was due to over-partaking of wine.

The boat did not go in the direction of the Praca do Commercio, where Gabrielle and the surgeon had landed that morning, but up river. For a while the men rowing had several delays owing to the volume of traffic on the water, but soon it thinned out and they were going past a much less populated part of the town.

Eventually they landed at a place where a road led past a few fishermen's cottages. Luke said a conveyance would be waiting for them. This conveyance turned out to be a carriage drawn by a mule and only large enough for one passenger. Luke and the surgeon said they would walk by the side of it. Gabrielle wanted to laugh, feeling like royalty with an entourage, but did not dare.

They went past more cottages, some houses, then the road rose and twisted and turned and eventually they came into a courtyard where a fountain spilled water over strange-looking stone animals. All around the fountain were potted plants.

When Gabrielle looked questioningly at her two escorts Luke said, 'The house belongs to a friend of mine. He and his wife are away but the servants will be here to attend to us.'

A servant met them to lead them along a passage into a marble hall. From there he asked them to follow him up a curving staircase, where at intervals cupids balanced on wrought iron supports.

They came into a wide spacious room

where a log fire burned brightly in a huge stone fireplace. There was a lovely fragrance from the eucalyptus leaves used for kindling.

'Oh, how lovely,' she said, looking around her. There were delicate figures in porcelain on a shelf, oil paintings with intricately carved gold frames adorned the walls and, in an alcove a long highly polished table was laid with silver and crystal. Candles were lit in a many-branched candelabra.

Another servant came up to her. 'Your cloak, señora.'

'Oh, yes,' Gabrielle smiled at the elderly man who took it from her. 'And a balcony with a view.'

'Si, señora. You have a view of the river–'

Yet a third man came in with wine and asked their choice. Luke left the choice to the surgeon. 'This is your party Mr Delacote.'

When the wine was poured Luke gave Gabrielle a nod and she held out the velvet case. 'From us both, Mr Delacote, with every good wish for the coming year and many, many more.'

'An emerald-studded pin.' There was a glint of tears in his eyes. He looked from one to the other. 'How did you know I wanted to own such a one studded with an emerald?'

Luke raised his shoulders. 'A hazarded guess. I am glad the choice was right. Let us now drink to many happy hours of wearing the pin.'

Although Luke appeared to be nonchalant about his choice Gabrielle could see he was pleased the gift had given the surgeon so much pleasure.

They sat down to the meal and it was the most excellent food Gabrielle had ever tasted. They started with a pale green soup that tasted of cucumber and was ice cool. Tiny leaves with a flavour of cheese floated on top. The next course was lobster bouillabaisse followed by a dish of paper-thin slices of pork served with boiled eggs wrapped in greens soaked in oils and herbs. The last course was a work of culinary art. It was an almond based mixture in the form of a curved-prowed boat, with a 'cargo' of quartered sugar plums, 'sacks' of nuts and chocolate kegs, the sails being made of what Gabrielle thought to be paper, but which Luke assured her was edible. 'Delicious,' she said.

Luke and Mr Delacote agreed and the servant was asked to convey their pleasure to the cook.

The talk was lively during the meal, the two men relating incidents from their seafaring days. Mr Delacote told of the time a huge wave washed him from one end of the ship to the other and how, as the ship rose on the crest he was washed back to where he had started. Both men laughed, enjoying it. Luke had a deep, infectious laugh which had Gabrielle chuckling.

Luke then spoke of the time a man fell from the rigging and landed on a cork raft floating in the sea. 'The tale he told,' Luke said laughing, 'was that a whale had popped up and carried him back to the ship. I think he really believed it, and the men appeared to.' He shook his head. 'Strange all the things that happen and are put down to miracles.'

Several times Mr Delacote tried to draw Gabrielle out about her life but very quickly, after a reproving look from Luke at the first question, she said she would much rather hear about their ship life as it was so much more interesting and amusing.

Mr Delacote was only too ready to oblige. The more he talked the more he drank and the more merry he became. Gabrielle, afraid of drinking too much and becoming ill, drank sparingly. Luke, in spite of matching drink for drink with the surgeon, appeared completely sober.

An awkward moment came for Gabrielle when Mr Delacote gave her an indulgent smile and turned to Luke and said, 'Do you know what your dear little wife told me? She told me she was a stowaway on the ship.'

Luke stiffened for a moment then asked with a lazy smile, 'And did you believe her?'

'She told a very convincing story, *very* convincing. Do you know I kept picturing her as – as – what was I going to say? Oh, yes, as a little émigr–' The surgeon blinked. 'An émigré.'

Luke got up. 'Coffee is being served on the balcony, shall we go?'

'Coffee, now that is just what I can do with. Black and strong.' Mr Delacote gave a little giggle. 'I remember the time–' Luke took him by the arm.

'You can tell us your story when we are seated.'

With the coffee poured the surgeon went full spate into two more incidents at sea and the awkward moment was past. For a while they sat in silence.

They were higher up than Gabrielle would have imagined. To their right the mast lights of the anchored ships moved gently, looking like fireflies. Lights from the town spread a soft glow. All sounds were muted.

'How peaceful,' she said.

Mr Delacote, who was sitting slumped in his chair, his head sunk on his chest, mumbled, 'Émigré... Émigré...'

He looked up. 'Peaceful, did you say? Will there ever be peace for me again?'

He began to mumble again, this time in a truculent way, then suddenly he jumped up and shook a clenched fist in the direction of the ships. 'I shall have my vengeance one of these days!'

Gabrielle, alarmed, glanced at Luke. Luke caught hold of the surgeon's arm and begged him to sit down.

He shook himself free. 'No, I want my revenge!' He reeled, then steadied. 'I want to seek out Hesther Quantock and strangle her with my own two hands.' He twisted his hands together as though wringing a cockerel's neck.

Gabrielle sat, rigid with shock.

Luke got up, took Mr Delacote by the arm and led him inside, talking in soothing tones, 'Yes, we shall find her, all in good time.'

Hesther Quantock– Had she been responsible for the death of the surgeon's wife? The night to Gabrielle seemed suddenly full of menace. How many more times was she going to hear of the evil deeds of her grandmother?

Gabrielle put her hands to her face. Oh, God, was the name Quantock going to plague her for the rest of her life?

# CHAPTER TEN

It was a very subdued three who returned to the ship. Luke saw Gabrielle down to their cabin then said he would go and sit with Mr Delacote for a while. Gabrielle had been determined to ask about the death of the surgeon's wife but Luke forestalled her by saying, 'Go to bed, and don't start worrying about Mrs Delacote. We shall talk about her and your grandmother in the morning.'

Gabrielle sat huddled over the stove. Although there was still a considerable warmth to it she could not get rid of the dreadful chill of shock. Eventually she climbed into bed, but her whole body shook.

What an end to an evening. And it could have been so different. There had been such a happy, relaxed atmosphere. She had never seen Luke so happy. Gabrielle relived the evening hoping to blot out the awful part with the rest she had enjoyed. Then perhaps she could sleep. But no sleep came. After a while, however, the trembling ceased.

She was still wide awake when she heard footsteps coming along the passageway. If it was Luke he was being very quiet. Not wanting a confrontation with him at this hour she feigned sleep. The door opened, closed again after a few moments and footsteps receded. Gabrielle rolled on to her back. Why should Luke glance into the cabin and leave? Had he wanted to check she was all right before returning to Mr Delacote's cabin?

For some reason Gabrielle could not accept this explanation. And yet, what other reason could there be? It was some time later when she became aware of sounds above, different from the usual night sounds. It was as though things were being hauled over the side of the ship. There was a lot of padding of feet, to and fro. Could they be loading cargo?

Unable to contain her curiosity Gabrielle got up, put on her cloak and made her way to the door that led to the lower deck. Before she had a chance to push the door open she heard a strange sound, like an animal bleating. With the door opened a fraction she was astonished to see a nanny goat being lifted over the rail. The animal was looking about in a bewildered fashion, bleating in protest at such unusual transportation.

Why another nanny goat? They already had one on board. Then Gabrielle saw stores coming aboard, piles of what looked like blankets and long objects which she took to be palliasses. Boxes followed, of all shapes and sizes. She supposed it was usual to take supplies aboard during the early hours, but why the stealth? The movements of all *were* stealthy. Even Luke who was giving orders spoke quietly. There was the bump of boxes being lowered into the hold. A man had led the goat away. Then there came what appeared to be cooking pots and small iron cooking stoves. These too went into the hold.

When the unloading came to an end Gabrielle was puzzled. It was not a big enough load to be called cargo. They could, of course, be taking on more tomorrow.

She went back to bed and slept fitfully, and roused fully to sounds of activity which suggested they were preparing to sail.

Luke confirmed this when he came down before Tomaso had even brought her morning tea. When she asked why they were leaving he said, 'Because I have a schedule to keep, and please do not start asking questions now.'

'Mr Delacote, how is he?'

'He's sleeping. Stay in bed. It's still early. I shall be down later for breakfast.'

Gabrielle was waiting for Luke to come for the meal when he came down and said, 'The sun is shining. You can view the "Sea of Straw", there may not be another chance, clouds are coming over. Get your cloak, there's a surprising nip in the air.'

When Gabrielle went up on deck she stood entranced, wordless at the lovely scene before her. It really did appear as though there were thousands of golden straws on the water, which shimmered and danced with every undulation.

She turned to Luke. 'Thank you, a golden moment, I shall remember it always.'

'Yes, it is worth seeing. Now I'm afraid you must go below. You would be in the way. We shall be sailing soon.'

'Are you coming for breakfast?'

'No, ask Tomaso to bring me a mug of coffee.'

She did not see Luke again until the afternoon, then he undressed and flopped into bed without saying a word. Gabrielle knew by the motion of the ship they had left the estuary, and although she would have enjoyed being on deck knew she did not dare without Luke's permission.

He slept heavily, never stirring. Once as she stood watching him, she laid a finger lightly on the cleft between his lower lip and chin, wondering if her grandmother was right when she said such a cleft denoted a gentleness in a man. A man could be strong and also gentle. There was no weakness in Luke. How strongly defined his features were. She touched his thick dark hair and he frowned as a young boy might when receiving affectionate motherly attention. Luke would be the type of boy who would resent any fussing from a parent. If only she knew something of his background. It seemed strange to think she was married to him, yet knew nothing whatsoever about him.

It was supper time when Luke stretched and yawned. He opened his eyes, saw her and glared. 'What is it?' she asked.

'I had a nightmare.' He flung back the bedclothes. He was naked and Gabrielle handed him his robe without looking at him. He laughed, it was harsh. 'You have nothing to fear, my sweet, I am certainly not in the mood for love-making.'

'Nor I,' she retorted. 'I hope you were not thinking I was waiting with bated breath for you to awake.'

'I could never imagine *you* waiting to pleasure a man.' The venom in his voice took Gabrielle aback. Then anger rose in her.

'It's my wretched grandmother again, isn't it? When will you stop venting your spite on me?' She lowered her voice, knowing that anger would only make things worse between them.

'Luke, will you tell me what happened to Mrs Delacote and how my grandmother was involved in her death? I do have a right to know, seeing that I seem to be sharing the blame. Please tell me.'

'Very well, I shall tell you the story.'

But Luke did not tell it right away. As though to torment her he took the pan of water that was heating on top of the stove, and poured it into the bowl, stripped off his robe and began to wash.

Gabrielle turned her back, and not wanting to give him the satisfaction of letting him know she was annoyed with his method, she began tidying the cabin.

Then Luke began, 'We were bringing French émigrés to England when your grandmother's wreckers caused the ship to flounder.'

'Wreckers?'

'Surely you have heard of men on the coast who place a light in the wrong place to guide ships on to the rocks, and so collect the cargoes. In this instance three children were drowned and five adults, one of them being Mrs Delacote. And that, my dear Gabrielle, is only one of the reasons why I hate your grandmother and the name of Quantock.' Gabrielle saw his hands clench. 'When I see a man like my surgeon, broken in spirit and in health–' Luke began to towel his back, dragging the towel back and forth so vigorously it would seem he would take off his skin.

Gabrielle knew this was a time to stay silent.

By the time Luke had finished dressing Tomaso brought in the meal. Luke and Gabrielle ate without a word passing between them. He was ready to go back on deck when there was a knock on the door. It was John Ballant.

'You wanted to see me, sir?'

'Yes, come in, Mr Ballant. My wife wants to thank you for the miniature.'

Although John Ballant's manner was circumspect he could not quite control his effervescent nature. When Gabrielle thanked him his face was wreathed in smiles. 'It was my pleasure, Ma'am. It delights me that you liked it.'

'I thought it beautiful. I shall treasure it always. You are so talented. Are you enjoying the voyage, Reverend?'

Luke stepped in, speaking curtly. 'You must excuse Mr Ballant. He has duties.'

'Yes, of course.' Gabrielle, although knowing it was impossible to mix with crew, was, nevertheless, grieved that John Ballant should be dismissed in such a cursory manner, especially when Luke had asked for the miniature to be done. She would have enjoyed talking with him, finding out how a man with his calling could cope with a seaman's life.

When John Ballant had closed the door Gabrielle asked Luke if she could go up on deck for a while, pointing out she had been confined to the cabin all day. 'I shall send Mr Delacote for you,' he replied, his voice still curt. 'He wants to apologize to you for last night. But for heavens sake give no hint of your identity.'

'Is it likely,' Gabrielle replied quietly, 'since you consider me to be co-murderer of Mrs Delacote?'

Luke went out, slamming the door. Gabrielle sank on to the bed, so miserable she wished she was back in England. Anything would be better than living in this fashion. She perhaps could have found work as a governess. But then, not only would she be at the whim of other people, but she would not have had the chance of perhaps finding her father. This was the one recompense because life was going to be dreadful married to a man who hated her.

When the surgeon did arrive he looked so ill Gabrielle forgot her misery. 'Mr Delacote, you ought to be in bed.'

'No, no, I had a stomach disorder, but I feel quite all right now. I wanted to say how sorry I was for my stupid and unforgivable outburst last night. I spoilt our lovely party.'

'No, nothing could spoil it. I carry away very happy memories of Lisbon, and our evening.'

'You do?'

'Yes. Think of all the laughter you provoked. I had never heard my husband laugh so heartily. You told some lovely anecdotes, Mr Delacote, so please don't feel guilty in any way.'

'It only happened because I was in my cups, dear Mrs Caltahn. And that will never happen again, I promise. I gave my word to the captain.'

'Then shall we now go and enjoy some sea breezes,' Gabrielle said lightly.

It was a beautiful evening, the sky star-studded. Although there was no moon the sea shimmered in places as though the stars were reflected in it. For a few moments all sounds, all movements on the ship seemed to be suspended and there was only the swish of the water against the ship.

Mr Delacote said, 'Tomorrow night, no, in the early hours of the following morning, we should be passing through the Straits of Gibraltar.'

'We will? Oh, how exciting, I must stay awake to see it.'

'You might find it disappointing, it is only a lump of rock.'

'But it's so interesting to see places one has read about.'

As it happened Gabrielle did not see Gibraltar. During the afternoon she developed a headache. It was unusual for her to have a headache and this was a particularly violent one. Even Luke was concerned. He brought Mr Delacote, who

190

mixed Gabrielle a draught. It took about two hours to take effect and then she slept right through until late the following morning. She felt drained and there were dark hollows under her eyes. All she complained about, however, was missing Gibraltar. Luke, like the surgeon, declared it to be no more than a lump of rock and Gabrielle said, 'Men! You have no souls. Gibraltar has such history, it's changed hands so many times.'

Luke studied her. 'Are you all right, Gabrielle? What do you think caused the headache?'

There was a caring in his grey eyes and she felt a warmth towards him. 'I have no idea. The last time I had a headache must have been three years ago. I feel all right now.'

'Perhaps, but take care. Rest.' Gabrielle promised.

She was willing to rest, but by evening she needed air. It was again Mr Delacote who took her up on deck. He fussed over her, making sure her cloak was buttoned up. 'We cannot have you ill, dear lady, what would I do without your charming company.'

'How nice of you, Mr Delacote, I enjoy your company.' They went to the rail. It was another lovely evening. 'And now we are on our way to Marseilles. Do you know Marseilles, Mr Delacote?'

'Yes, quite well. I'm afraid you will find it

very different from Lisbon, Mrs Caltahn. I doubt whether your husband will take you ashore.'

'Oh, but he must, you see–' Gabrielle stopped abruptly. She had been about to mention her father, and mention of her father would let the surgeon know she was Hesther Quantock's granddaughter. She gave a little shiver. Her father and her grandmother were so different it seemed impossible to believe they were mother and son.

'And why must your husband take you ashore, Mrs Caltahn?' Mr Delacote spoke quietly and Gabrielle found something strange in the way he was looking at her.

'Why do you think he ought *not* to take me?' she parried.

'Because of the district near the docks. There are men who would cut your throat for a sou, there are houses of ill-repute, women who– Oh, look, Mrs Caltahn! Now there's a pretty sight for you.'

For a second Gabrielle knew fear when she saw strange moving lights on the water ahead. Then Mr Delacote explained it was phosphorous from the sea on the bodies of porpoises. There was a shoal of them and she watched with delight as they dipped and rose from the water.

'Papa once told me about them,' she said. 'But I never imagined I would ever see them. He also told me about natives diving from high rocks and how the phosphorous clinging to their bodies lit them up.' She laughed. 'That must have been a really awesome sight.'

'Yes, indeed. Was your father a seafaring man?'

'No. No, he travelled – on business.'

Gabrielle felt a momentary shock that she had used the past tense and said travelled, instead of travels, as though her father were dead.

'Where is your home, Mrs Caltahn?'

Gabrielle drew her cloak about herself. 'I find myself feeling chilled, Mr Delacote, I think I must go below.'

'Yes, of course, come along.'

Gabrielle thought if she could only have told the surgeon who she was there would be no need for all this subterfuge, also there would be no need to have had her outing on deck curtailed. But there would be too much of a risk. Although she was sure Mr Delacote liked her she could imagine his horror if she said her name was Quantock. There would be more than horror, she would see hatred in his eyes, as she did at times with Luke.

Fortunately for Gabrielle the surgeon asked no more personal questions in the days that followed because she came to rely on his company. She saw little of Luke. He was polite when he was with her, but no more than that. Each night followed the same pattern, Luke coming to bed when she was asleep and gone when she awoke. One time when she roused in the early hours his leg was across hers and his hand cupped her breast, showing his need of her. But although his close proximity aroused an emotion in her she lay perfectly still in case she should rouse him, not wanting him, because of his masculine need, to take her with this hatred in him.

Two days away from Marseilles the ship was becalmed and then Luke was in a constant temper, blaming everyone but the weather.

On the second night she got in his way when he was going back up on deck and he thrust her aside. Furious, Gabrielle slapped his face.

He raised his hand as thought to strike her back then let it fall, but his face was taut with anger when he said, 'Don't you ever dare do that again.'

'And don't you ever thrust me out of your way! I'm a person, not a chattel.'

Luke went out, slamming the door behind him. Gabrielle, in despair, wondered how long they could go on in this way. That evening she made up her mind she would go ashore when they reached Marseilles and make enquiries about her father. Luke would hardly be in the mood to do so.

But Gabrielle had no opportunity for going ashore at Marseilles. The ship anchored before they reached the port. It was during the early hours of the morning. Although she could sleep through many sounds the clanging of the anchor chains roused her. She got up and went up on deck. She could see the lights of Marseilles in the distance and could hear muted sounds of revelry but very little else. It was an exceptionally dark night and it seemed there was very little light on the ship.

Then she became aware that movements were stealthy, as they had been that night in Lisbon when stores were being brought aboard.

Luke and Mr Delacote came into view. They appeared to be talking earnestly. Then when they seemed to glance in Gabrielle's direction she drew back into the doorway that led to the cabin. But she did not go below. What was happening this time?

She waited a long while and eventually saw a number of men go to the side of the ship. Whispering voices reached her on the night breeze.

Then suddenly there was activity. Men were reaching over the sides and before long a cloaked figure appeared at the top of the ladder. Then another, and another. Gabrielle watched in astonishment as twenty or more people came on deck, and were then led towards the hold – where they descended.

Who on earth could they be? There had been women as well as men. Why such secrecy? There had been something strange about them. Although they had been shabbily dressed Gabrielle felt they were not poor people. They had all held themselves well, they had deportment. Could they be – émigrés escaping from Paris? Escaping from the dreaded guillotine? It was said that over a hundred of the French nobility were executed every day. There had been talk in London of brave men, in groups, arranging escapes. But surely all the émigrés had been brought from Calais to Dover, which was, the short crossing. From Paris to Marseilles would be a very long way to travel.

Boxes were being taken aboard. Although the night was not cold Gabrielle kept shivering. Mr Delacote had kept mentioning the word émigré. Had his wife been one, or had she been helping the émigrés to escape? Whichever it was – Gabrielle gave another shiver. Her grandmother had wrecked the ship carrying them. Was this why Luke had come this distance, to get away from such a risk?

If only he would confide in her she could help.

As Gabrielle stood watching, some rolled, canvas-wrapped packages came aboard. A

196

man hissed, 'Take care, them's valuable, they got to be kept separate. They're to go somewhere else. Cap'n'll tell us.'

Valuable? The rolls were not large enough to be material. Oil paintings? Perhaps the émigrés had brought their valuables with them to raise money. Snatches of conversation which Gabrielle had heard in London began to make sense. Women had spoken in low voices at social gatherings of the sale of jewellery – to help escapes.

The 'troubles' in France had seemed so remote to Gabrielle then. Her own troubles had been so much more important. Feeling chilled to the bone she turned and went below. And there was no more sleep for her that night. It was not only the thoughts of escaped French people that kept her awake but thoughts of her father. Now the émigrés were all safely on the ship Luke may not even go into port. They may return to London. Oh no, no, not without making enquiries about her father. If Luke would not listen to her she would appeal to Mr Delacote.

Gabrielle was dressed when Luke came down.

'*You* are up early' he said. His expression was wary.

'Yes, I have to talk with you. Will you be taking the ship into port or are you returning to London? And please do *not* say it is none of my business. You promised to make enquiries about my father.'

'And that I will do. I gave you my word.'

'Thank you. There is something else I must say. I saw the people coming on board during the early hours. Are they émigrés?'

A look of pure hatred came into Luke's eyes. 'How dare you spy on me? So you did come aboard for this reason. Well I shall tell you this, *Gabrielle Quantock*, you will not have an opportunity for getting this information to your grandmother, not even if it means locking you up.'

Gabrielle spread her hands in a weary gesture. 'Oh, for God's sake forget my name. All I want is to find my father. You can lock me up if you like, starve me, beat me, but only try to help me to find him.'

Tears welled and she clasped her hands tight in an effort to control them but they rolled down her cheeks, large tears that plopped on to her hands.

'I love Papa. I think he is the only person I have really and truly loved in my life. He is such a good man. And the only one in the family who tried to stand up to my grandmother.' Tears hung on Gabrielle's lashes. She blinked them away. 'Papa may be a little bit of a dreamer, but believe me he is a man well worth saving.'

Luke handed her a handkerchief and she wiped her eyes. After a moment he said,

'You are either a consummate actress or telling the truth. If it is true what you say about your father then I hope if ever I have a child he or she would give me the same affection. At this moment I can only repeat that I promised to make enquiries about your father and I shall do so this afternoon. But I ask something in return, that you do not leave this cabin while we are anchored.'

'I give you my word. If you have a Bible I shall swear on it.'

Luke's lips tightened. 'If you have in you the evil of your grandmother then your oath would be meaningless.'

Gabrielle made no reply. What was the use?

It was evening when she saw Luke again and then he stood looking at her, his expression grave. Gabrielle's heart began a dull pounding.

'Papa – is he-?'

'I found no trace of him, at least–'

'At least what?'

'I made extensive enquiries and know, if he had at one time been on the ship of the captain you mentioned, he is not there now. Nor has he been shipped to Australia.'

'How can you be certain? Who told you?'

'One can get any information in Marseilles for a price,' he said drily. He paused then added, 'Can you describe your father to me, Gabrielle?'

'He is tall, dark haired, carries himself well. An aristocratic looking man people say of him. Why? Has he been seen?'

Luke moved around the cabin for a few moments in silence then turned. 'Every day in Marseilles there are men found stabbed, beaten, knocked unconscious, having been robbed or in a fight. Many are buried unidentified. I made enquiries if such a man had been found and—'

'You found Papa.' Gabrielle spoke in a whisper.

'Please stop jumping to conclusions. I can only tell you that a man was washed ashore further along the coast and was found by people in a long boat. They were passengers from a schooner who had come ashore to picnic. The man, who had been stripped of everything, was more dead than alive and was unable to speak when they first found him. One, of the passengers swore he was an Italian nobleman who lived in Venice, and his wife excitedly verified it.

'Then why are you telling me this?'

'Because later the man was able to speak. The people spoke to him in Italian and he answered them in the same language. He said he had been abducted, taken on a ship and he had escaped.'

'Abducted?' Gabrielle felt a stirring of excitement. 'Was he not able to say who he was?'

'No, because after that his memory seemed to go. He could remember nothing else.' Luke paused then went on, 'Gabrielle, did your father have any distinguishing marks, visible ones?'

Gabrielle thought for a moment then shook her head. 'No, Papa had no birth-marks or scars of any kind.'

'Something other than a birthmark or a scar. This man had something that distinguished him but I want it to come from you.'

'No, nothing,' she began then looked up quickly, excited again. 'Yes of course, he did have one! Papa had dark hair, almost black, but in the centre is a thin silver streak. He used to jest about it, saying he must have used that particular part of his brain more than any other. Does this man–?'

'Yes, he does, a similar silver streak. This was the only thing that differed from the Italian the people knew, but as the couple so rightly pointed out, the streak might have developed with all the worry of being abducted and kept a prisoner.'

'This is Papa, I know it. Oh, please, when may I see him?'

'Well now–' Luke's expression became grave again. 'Here we have a problem. These people offered to care for him and take him with them to Venice, and, of course, the authorities were only too pleased to get rid of him. They left two days ago.'

'Oh, no–' Gabrielle sank on to the bed, despair sweeping over her. 'How could I possibly get to Venice?' She looked up slowly and searched Luke's face. 'Are you taking the ship to any other port – perhaps Venice?'

'No, we are returning to England. Remember I have a responsibility to my passengers.'

'If I had money I could perhaps book passage on another ship.' Gabrielle was pleading now. 'We are part of the way there, it will be terrible to leave without knowing whether Papa has recovered.'

'If he recovers I feel quite sure someone will see he gets passage back to England. I am not putting you on another ship. You are my wife and your place is by my side.' Luke spoke firmly. 'Your father is in the position he is in now because he allowed himself to be ruled by his mother. I am certainly not going to have my life altered by my wife. Is that understood?'

'Yes, I understand.' Gabrielle could not raise any anger at his tone, she was only too grieved by her father's position. 'I shall not mention Papa again.'

Luke made no move. 'I'm sorry, naturally, knowing the affection you have for your father, but as I explained I too have a responsibility. I must get these people to England. They have suffered a great deal.

They had a harrowing journey.'

'They must have done. My sympathies are with them. I would be glad to help in any way I can. They would perhaps be pleased to talk with an Englishwoman. I am quite fluent in French.'

Luke seemed non-plussed by Gabrielle's quiescent attitude.

'Yes, yes, we shall have to see. I must go.' He walked to the door, seemed about to say something, then changed his mind. The door closed quietly behind him.

Gabrielle got up and sat huddled over the stove, wondering if she would ever see her father again. It seemed terrible to be in sailing distance of him yet have to go in the opposite direction. And yet she could not blame Luke. She was his wife. Not only should he be the first consideration in her life but he was sailing the ship for business, not pleasure.

She wondered then if Luke was taking the émigrés to England from a philanthropic motive, or if it was for monetary gain. Monetary gain, she would imagine. He did run a shipping line and it would have to pay its way. He would also have to make up losses caused by her grandmother.

Luke did not come to bed at all that night and the next morning the ship was under sail. When Tomaso brought Gabrielle's tea he was despondent. 'No go to Marseilles.

No happy ladies, no music. We not even go back to England.'

She drew herself up the bed. 'Where *are* we going?'

Tomaso raised his shoulders. 'Only Captain know.'

Gabrielle's heartbeats quickened. Had Luke capitulated? Were they going to Venice? But what of the émigrés? She looked at Tomaso. 'Will my husband be down for breakfast, Tomaso?'

'In ten minutes, he said, Ma'am. Captain *not* in good mood.'

'Oh, dear, then I had better get up.'

It was late evening when Luke came below. Judging by his heavy frown he was still in a bad mood.

'You'll be pleased to know we are going to Venice, Madam. The French people are agreeable. Several of them have friends or relatives in Venice, or in the area. Their only concern seems to be in getting as far away from France as possible.'

'Thank you for changing your plans,' Gabrielle said quietly, but with mounting excitement as she thought of her father. 'I count myself in your debt.'

To her amazement Luke rounded on her. 'Don't think I changed my plans to please you. All *I'm* concerned about is getting as far away from Hesther Quantock's inter-ference as possible. I can get a good price for the valuables the émigrés managed to smuggle out. It will, of course, cost me extra money to keep them during the voyage.'

'Is the money all you care about?' Gabrielle felt disillusioned once more as to his good intentions.

Luke's eyes held ice. 'Let me point out to you, Madam, if money had not been involved in the transaction you would not have had the opportunity of perhaps finding your father, so do not speak to me in that contemptuous way!'

'You misinterpret my tone.'

'But not your expression. When you look at me in that holier-than-thou way I could – could–'

'You could what, Mr Caltahn?'

'There you go again, taunting me with your eyes!' He grabbed her by the wrist. Although she saw an almost ungovernable anger in his eyes Gabrielle tipped her chin disdainfully at him. He growled with rage. 'And *that* too, Madam, you shall pay for!' He dragged her to the door, locked it then dragged her back again with Gabrielle lashing out with her free hand and a foot.

'Why don't you admit you enjoy acting like an animal?' She found herself hissing the words, afraid someone might hear.

'Then stop fighting and submit.' Catching hold of her robe he forced it from her shoulders, but in the struggle her nightgown was torn. This infuriated Gabrielle still further. She clawed at his face. 'Who is the animal now?' he sneered. Luke pulled up her nightgown. 'You shall pay for that too.' He gave her two hard slaps on her buttocks,

'Fiend,' she yelled, no longer caring who heard her. Yet in spite of her fury she had felt a tremor go through her body at Luke's aggression.

Luke now had her nightgown off but she still retained her shift and was determined to keep it on. In the end Luke's superior strength won. He flung her on the bed. Gabrielle snatched at the pillow and held it in front of her.

Luke stood watching her for a moment then he said softly, 'I wait for the day, my lovely Gabrielle, when you will let me see your body of your own accord.'

'Never.'

Luke undressed quickly and getting on to the bed he pushed the pillow aside and rolled over on to her. Gabrielle was still determined to fight him, but when she felt the hardness of him against her flesh her body began to throb.

Even then she made a last effort to resist him. Luke became angry again. 'Stop fighting me, Gabrielle. You want me, you know you do.'

'I don't, I hate you.'

'Do you?' He had moved down and his

lips were teasing her nipples, pulling gently on them.

'Stop it,' she moaned, 'don't do that. You're hurting me.'

'I'm not, and you know it.' His lips moved up to her throat. 'You love it, you want me.'

Every word, every movement of his lips was a caress. His hand began to slide over her body, teasing the skin, tantalizing her, getting nearer and nearer to the part of her body she had thought of before her marriage as being secret and sacred. Now, here she was wanting Luke to penetrate and explore that secret part, longing for it. She was aching for him, wanting to know again the ecstasy, the heights to which he had once taken her.

When he did reach it her senses leapt in response.

'Touch *me*, Gabrielle,' he said. 'I want you to take part in the loveplay too.'

She reached out tentatively and encountered the fragile skin, then as her hand moved down and she felt Luke's immediate response she gave a shiver of excitement at her own power to make him respond. She guided him and gasped with pleasure as he entered her. Her arms went round him and held him close. Automatically her rhythm began to match his.

'Oh, Luke,' she whispered, 'I want this night to go on for ever and ever.'

'And so it shall my darling, so it shall.'

Luke's virility, his expertise, his caring she should share each moment of fulfilment, made her deliriously happy. Their marriage, she felt sure, had really begun at last.

It was not until next morning when Luke had gone from her side that she realized he had not said, in so many words, he loved her, but she consoled herself with the thought it would come later. She must not expect too much all at once.

# CHAPTER ELEVEN

When next Gabrielle saw Luke he said, 'The French people want to meet you. It will help to have an Englishwoman to talk with. Come with me now.'

There was no warmth in Luke, no hint of what they had shared the night before. Gabrielle felt dispirited. So much for her hopes of their marriage beginning at last.

Luke led the way to the hold in a direction she had never been before. He carried a lantern. There was a lot of scuffling noises and Gabrielle shuddered, guessing they were rats. When they came into the hold all the men in the party got to their feet. Daylight slanted from above. Some of the battens had been removed. The women sat round the iron stoves. One nursed a baby. When Luke introduced Gabrielle the men bowed, the women acknowledged her with gracious nods. An elderly man with a regal bearing came forward.

'Madam Caltahn, I speak for all of us when I say how happy we are to make your acquaintance. Do you speak French?'

'Yes, I do.' She smiled. 'Fortunately I had an excellent French tutor.'

'Then perhaps we can beg your help. Some of us wish to go to England. We would like to know how you live, about your food, your customs, and perhaps you would be kind enough to help those of us who do not speak English to learn a little of your language.'

Gabrielle said she would be very pleased to help and Luke left her then.

The first morning with the émigrés was the most exhausting and emotional Gabrielle could ever remember spending.

They were anything but a beaten people, they still retained a regal air, but their faces were drawn, their eyes pain-filled. This, Gabrielle learned, was not only because of what they had lost and suffered, but because they had been told in Marseilles that their beloved King Louis had been executed. The women wept when they spoke of him and there were tears in the eyes of the men.

The ages of the people were mixed. There were parents with sons and daughters, women whose husbands had been executed, elderly couples who had lost all their relatives, and a young woman with a baby, whose husband had been seized. It was all so tragic. Another young woman, Gabrielle noticed, was expecting a child. Her husband fortunately was by her side.

'But we must not dwell on what has gone,' said one woman. 'We must now look to the future.' She had two pretty daughters. The woman explained that none in the party had ever cooked, nor even boiled a pan of water until they came to Marseilles. They wanted to learn how to cook.

The youngest of the two girls said, with an air of distaste, 'Look at my hands, Madame, they are like the hands of a peasant.'

Her mother chided her. 'It was necessary to have them so to aid your escape. Your hands will get soft again, you have your life, are you not grateful for that, my daughter?' The mother turned to Gabrielle. 'We lived practically in holes in the ground before our escape was arranged. We had to scratch in the soil every day so that our hands would not look fine and white. Many of our people attempting to escape were captured because of their well-kept hands.'

Two hours later Luke came for her. Gabrielle promised to come again and Luke promised to arrange for the émigrés to come on deck in twos and threes for fresh air. When she tried to talk about the French people on their way back he cut her short. He was too busy for talk. She did not see him for the rest of that day, and he did not share her bed that night.

Nor did he on subsequent nights. Where he was sleeping she had no idea. Nor did she care. Every morning she visited the émigrés. Sometimes she went alone, other times Mr Delacote came with her.

Gabrielle had little chance of teaching English. They wanted to talk of their experiences. They praised the groups of Englishmen who arranged the escapes. Such courage! When Gabrielle asked if they were disguised one man said yes, as peasants, and they looked the part. He raised his hands. 'Mon Dieu, we were skin and bone. I never thought people could survive on a raw potato and a raw carrot for three days but we did. And we were grateful to survive.'

It upset Mr Delacote a little that the French people would accept no blame for the bloodshed. 'Not that they were wholly to blame,' he said one morning after a visit. 'Nor was it something that happened overnight.' He went on talking and for the first time Gabrielle really understood the reasons behind the bloodshed in Paris.

Mr Delacote quoted an instance where the hoarding of certain commodities caused violence. 'The people had become used to their bowl of *café au lait* in the morning, and were incensed when this was no longer available.'

He wagged a finger. 'Now it was not the aristocrats who were hoarding the sugar and coffee but the petit bourgeois, the grocers, the wholesalers, shopkeepers. Banks stored them in their vaults, even the churches were responsible.'

'The churches?' Gabrielle exclaimed in astonishment.

'Yes, indeed. Abbé Fauchet complained to the Legislature, naming three churches who were turning the buildings into food stores. Inns stored, in fact anyone with space. Even country people who came in with their produce hoarded in the cellars of relatives to get a higher price. How is it possible for people who had known poverty themselves, to deny their own kind food? This is the sadness of it. Windows were broken, doors smashed down, property burned, people were killed, injured.' Mr Delacote spread his hands. 'From small beginnings – the grumbling built into hysteria, and the hysteria into a war chant.'

Gabrielle longed to ask how far her husband was involved in the rescue of the émigrés, but kept silent, knowing Luke would be furious if he knew she had been discussing him.

At first it had puzzled her why he should so purposefully avoid her but eventually she came to the conclusion he was annoyed with himself for having given pleasure to a Quantock.

One morning when she awoke she was aware of the sound of torrential rain, but there was no wind, nor storm. Tomaso came with her morning tea, his face wreathed in smiles.

'Captain says not to come on deck. No ladies come on deck. Men will be having bath.'

'A bath? All of them?'

Tomaso nodded. 'Good rain, warm, we block the scuppers, rain fill deck. Good bath, men happy, much laughter. Clean to go ashore in Venice. Be there soon.'

In Venice soon? Neither Luke nor Mr Delacote had mentioned it. Later, when she heard the shouts of the men, the yells of glee, she found herself laughing too. It would be a sight to behold.

Half an hour after this, much to Gabrielle's surprise, Luke came to take her up on deck. He was in a good mood, and because she felt happier she appreciated the change in the climate. The sun was so warm steam rose from the drying decks. The sky was the cerulean blue that Stephen used in his canvasses. Stephen? How strange she should think of him now. He had been so much a part of her life when she was growing up and now he seemed so remote.

The young French couple with the baby came up on deck. Gabrielle had become quite fond of the five-month-old Henri with the infectious chuckle. She held out her arms and he came to her readily. She was talking to him in the way people do with babies, sweet silly talk, when Luke said, 'You present a most loving picture of mother-

214

hood, Mrs Caltahn. I hope to see you in that role with our child someday.'

There was nothing snide about the remark. Luke was smiling. In fact when he spoke to the child it was in the role of indulgent father. 'A fine little man, aren't you?' He touched the dimpled cheek. 'No smile for me this morning?'

Henri cooed and saliva dribbled down his chin. Luke pulled out his handkerchief and wiped it away. Gabrielle felt warmed and touched by his action. A man who could behave like this to someone else's child would surely be tender and loving to his own.

Henri's father laughed. 'You would make wonderful parents, I wish you many, many children.'

Gabrielle murmured her thanks. Luke acknowledged it with a brief, 'Some day, God willing.'

Everything seemed right with the world for Gabrielle at that moment. She closed her eyes and raised her face to the sun. 'What a heavenly day.'

'It is indeed,' said the voice of Mr Delacote. 'Wonderful sailing weather.'

The ship was full-masted this morning and it really was a magnificent sight. The small sky-sail looked as if it touched the blue of the heavens. She said to Luke, 'I understand we shall soon be reaching Venice.'

'Perhaps you are better informed than I, Madam.'

It was as though the sun had suddenly gone in. Luke was standing in his most arrogant way, back stiff, legs apart, hands behind his back.

Gabrielle walked to the rail, turned to face him and was about to say he looked as if he owned the whole ocean when she caught a look of utter misery in his eyes. She stared, shocked by it, and as she stood there Luke called something to his helmsman. When he turned to her again his face was expressionless.

'You were about to say something, Madam?'

'Only that I was perhaps misinformed about Venice.'

'We should be there in just over a week, that is if the wind remains fair. Now, if you will excuse me.'

Gabrielle and the surgeon stood for a few moments in silence then Gabrielle said, 'I think my husband is working too hard, I rarely see him nowadays.'

'Oh, my dear lady, blame me.' Mr Delacote offered abject apologies. 'I've been most depressed and the captain eats with me and talks, it helps. Sometime I've kept him late from his bed. Do forgive me.'

So Luke had not been sleeping in Mr Delacote's cabin. Where *did* he sleep?

Gabrielle assured the surgeon she was only too pleased that her husband was able to help, adding she understood depression was a dreadful complaint.

'Indeed it is, Ma'am. It saps one's will.'

'Perhaps your health will improve when we reach Venice. My father once told me the air has beneficial properties.'

Mr Delacote had been to Venice and talked at some length about it with a great deal of enthusiasm. Gabrielle absorbed it but deep down Venice meant only one thing at the moment, finding her father.

When Gabrielle returned to her cabin later in the day however she was surprised to find Luke asleep on the bed. She made to hang up her cloak then stood looking at his jacket on the back of the door. It was covered with dirt and pieces of straw. Where had he been to get it in that condition? And why had he not brushed the jacket when he had come in? Luke was so particular, always so immaculate.

She turned to look at him and saw then his cheeks were flushed and his skin was glistening with sweat. Gabrielle hurried to him and put her hand to his forehead. It was burning.

Fortunately, Tomaso arrived at that moment to lay the table and Gabrielle sent him to fetch Mr Delacote.

When the surgeon came he took Luke's temperature, examined him and seemed worried. 'He has a high fever. This morning three of the crew went down with the same thing.'

Gabrielle felt cold at the thought it might be the dreaded cholera, but when she asked Mr Delacote he shook his head. 'No, there are none of the symptoms.' She told him about the jacket and asked where Luke could have been to get it in such a condition.

'I can answer that. He called to see me after hearing about the crew's sickness. He promised to visit them and it was as he turned to leave that I noticed his jacket. In explanation he said he had slipped when he had gone below to see the émigrés. Then he left.'

'Could he have a chill, it seems to have come on so suddenly? He seemed quite well this morning.'

'Possibly, on the other hand he has the same symptoms as three members of the crew. We shall have to wait. I shall give you some pills for him to take. If the fever rises I will get Tomaso to sponge him with cold water.'

'I could do it,' Gabrielle said. 'I would want to.'

'Very well, but we shall, as I say, wait.'

By late afternoon Luke was tossing about the bed and muttering in delirium, although nothing he said made any sense. She brought a bowl of cold water and a sponge, started to draw away the bedclothes then stood, feeling embarrassed. She had seen him naked plenty of times, he seemed to flaunt it, but having him lying here helpless, vulnerable, it was somehow different. Then determinedly she set to her task, and even though he was ill and she acting as nurse she could not help but admire his magnificent body. The cold water seemed to soothe him and by the time, Mr Delacote came again Luke was more settled.

The surgeon said worriedly, however, that four more of the crew were down with the illness, including the cook. He looked harassed and appeared at a loss to know what to do. Then Gabrielle saw that his cheeks were flushed and that his skin had beads of sweat on it.

'You are ill, too, Mr Delacote,' Gabrielle said quietly. 'You must go to bed, and go now, before you get any worse. I shall see if any of our émigrés can help.'

He kept protesting and was still protesting when Gabrielle instructed Tomaso to see Mr Delacote to his cabin. By then the surgeon's legs were beginning to buckle under him. When Tomaso came back she left him with Luke and went to the hold.

To her horror six of the men were already stricken and five of the women. The men

219

left said they would do all they could to help and the women said they would take care of those sick.

Gabrielle tried not to think what would happen if all the émigrés and all the crew became ill.

Although only one more of the crew went down the following morning and two more women in the hold, the next few days were a nightmare to Gabrielle. She spent her time between caring for Luke and Mr Delacote and helping Tomaso in the galley to cook food for the seamen who were well. They were all doing double the work and were constantly hungry.

Luke threshed about in his fever day and night, and shouted at times, cursing Hesther Quantock and the ruffians who worked for her. Once in a more lucid moment when he realized he had been ill he tried to get up and Gabrielle thrust him back. 'Stay where you are. I've been nursing you day and night and you'll undo all the good.'

'But I have jobs to do,' he protested. 'I must get up. I will get up.'

Gabrielle, who was at the end of her tether, shouted at him. 'All right, get up, crawl on your hands and knees, do your jobs, but do not expect me to nurse you if you collapse.'

At this he stared at her. 'How long have I been ill?'

'I have no idea,' she said, with a weary gesture. 'Three, four days– *Please*, just rest for another day, if no more, give yourself a chance.'

His lucid moments were short-lived. Within ten minutes the fever was on him again.

The only good thing about it all was the weather. The days were sunny, the sea calm. Gabrielle had brief spells on deck and each time drew in great gulps of air.

Then one evening when she went below after her 'airing' she found tiny blisters on Luke's face. They were red, with a bluish tinge as though veins had broken. She flew to Mr Delacote's cabin, praying he would be conscious enough to tell her what they were. The surgeon was not only conscious but up. He too had developed the same blisters. Swaying a little in his weakness he said, 'I know now what the illness is. I saw the same blisters on the face of a seaman years ago who had been in the East. It's a rare disease, but I do know how to treat it. If you could help me, Mrs Caltahn–'

A few minutes later Gabrielle picked up the pestle and began pounding the herbs Mr Delacote had placed in the mortar, working with a strength she had not thought she possessed. And when the pills were ready she took some to Luke, found Tomaso to distribute some to the crew, then went to

221

the hold. And there collapsed to her knees, looking round her in surprise. 'I fell,' she said, and passed out.

When she roused she was surprised to find herself in bed and Luke up, shaving.

'How did I get here?' she asked.

'Tomaso carried you.'

'How long have you been out of bed, when did the fever go?'

'Yesterday morning.'

'Yester – that is impossible, it was last night when I–'

'It was the night before. Yes, you have slept for thirty hours, give or take five minutes. You needed it. And may I say how grateful I am for your excellent nursing.'

Luke did not look grateful. He looked annoyed. No doubt his pride would be hurt that he had to be nursed.

'The crew, the émigrés – have they recovered?'

'All except one man, he is still a little shaky.'

'You must still take care,' Gabrielle said, 'you look far from well.'

Luke bridled. 'I am perfectly well. It was a most unfortunate incident. One of the men must have picked up the germ from a sailor while we were anchored at Lisbon. I was weakened by having lain all night after a fall, and knocking my head while I was on the way to the hold. But for that I would never have had the fever.'

'I still say you ought to take care. If you start trying to get back into a normal routine too soon you could have a setback. You must still be weak after that terrible fever.'

Luke threw the towel on the bed. 'Oh, for God's sake, woman, stop nagging. I know when I am ill and when I am well.'

Gabrielle was silent. There was no reasoning with a stubborn man like Luke Caltahn.

# CHAPTER TWELVE

As the voyage progressed Gabrielle became aware there could be worse punishment than a whipping. There were days when Luke hardly addressed a word to her, and nights when he never came to bed. Where he slept she had no idea. The awful part was that she found herself longing for him, longing for contact with his body. She wanted to curl up beside him in bed, draw warmth from him. In spite of this she felt she managed to keep a coolness of manner towards him.

Recently she had been aware of Luke watching her from time to time and wondered if he was annoyed she made no effort to question him on his absences. After all, if he was wanting to punish her and she remained indifferent to him he could feel no sense of revenge. Gabrielle had come to think of their marriage as one of revenge.

Her salvation was her friendship with the émigrés and with Mr Delacote. She spent her mornings with the French women talking about England and giving them lessons, and they in turn talked about their lives before the bloodshed. Most of them found it impossible to understand the slaughter of the nobility. What had they done to deserve such terror, such horror? Gabrielle treated them with infinite care and patience, and learning daily of their terrible suffering, she suffered with them.

But when, two days later they sailed into the lagoon at Venice all Gabrielle's troubles magically evaporated for neither the surgeon's nor her father's descriptions, nor the painting she had seen, could have prepared her for its sheer beauty: the architectural grandeur; the incredible blue of the sky and sea; the harmony of light and colour; the cream and gold on buildings; the movement of gondolas; the anchored ships, so many different kinds, those with richly carved 'castles', the Dutch ships with their colour, pennants flying.

She had been entranced with Lisbon, with the Sea of Straw, with the Bélem Tower that reminded her of the sugar loaf castles in the stories of her childhood, but this was a fairy-tale world to live in *and* explore.

In those first magic moments Gabrielle completely forgot the reason for their being here. When she did remember she was swamped with shame and guilt. And it was in this state that Luke approached her.

'You look like a child who has been promised an apple and given only a core. I thought Venice would have appealed to your sense of beauty.'

'It does, but I was so lost in its beauty I quite forgot my father. It seems impossible.'

'Not to me. There are moments in our lives, such as these, when all agony is forgotten. It is only a temporary thing and I feel we can be forgiven for our lapses.' He gave her a reassuring smile.

Gabrielle said, 'Tell me, where did you sleep during the voyage?' She was astonished at her own question. It was out before she could stop it, and was annoyed she had asked it.

'In a hammock,' Luke said, but did not qualify where.

His attention was claimed and he left her, with another smile, this time she felt it was one of satisfaction that she had shown an interest in where he spent his nights. Gabrielle smothered her annoyance and concentrated on the scene ahead.

It was afternoon when Luke told her he was taking her ashore. She had had plenty to watch, as at Lisbon, the activity on the anchored ships, the colour and noise of the captains and merchants in their buying and selling of cargoes, but somehow she felt the noise to be a little more subdued.

The sun had come out at midday making dancing silver coins on the water instead of golden straws, but later when Luke came to tell Gabrielle to pack her valise the sun had gone in and the air was chilly.

'Pack a valise?' she said. 'Why, where are we going?'

'I have an apartment booked in a hotel, which was formerly a palace. I thought you might appreciate a more gracious way of living while we are here.'

'A palace?' Gabrielle echoed. 'Surely it must be very expensive?'

Luke dismissed it. 'There are many empty ones since the majority of the wealthy moved out. One can rent a whole palace for a song.' He paused then added, 'I shall be coming back to the ship to sleep. But you will not lack company, the French people will be there too.'

When Gabrielle made no reply he glanced at her, a coldness in his expression. 'I am not prepared to share your bed, Gabrielle. I am only human and the warmth of a woman's body, any woman's–'

'Any woman?' she demanded. 'I suppose by that you mean a whore. Do you enjoy tormenting me? Yes, of course you do, that has been proved many times. It continues to amaze me that a man who considers himself respected, even by his enemies as you do, should stoop so low as to marry for revenge. When we get back to England I trust you will give me my freedom.'

'Oh, no, sweet Gabrielle, you shall stay tied to me, at least while your grandmother

227

is alive. And before you start nagging me further let me remind you of our reason for being here. As soon as I have the opportunity I shall start making enquiries about your father.'

'Thank you for that,' she said stiffly.

Once they were in the longboat and being rowed ashore Gabrielle found herself watching every gondola that passed in the hope of perhaps seeing her father. He could be fully recovered and enjoying Venice. Pray heaven he was. But they reached the hotel without a glimpse of anyone faintly resembling her father.

The entrance to the hotel was in a side canal. The landing stage for boats, the steps and pillars were of green marble. Intricately wrought iron gates decorated with gold filigree opened into an impressive hall. The floor was mosaiced and so beautiful Gabrielle felt it was a sacrilege to walk on it. They were taken up white marble stairs to the first landing and ushered into the first of a suite of rooms. There was the large drawing room, two bedrooms, two dressing rooms and a bathroom. 'Oh!' Gabrielle exclaimed as she saw the sunken bath. 'How marvellous.' She turned to Luke, momentarily forgetting her animosity towards him. 'Have you ever seen such a bath? One walks down into it. I can almost feel myself soaking in it. Will there be hot water? Oh, do please say yes, I could hardly bear not to use it.'

'You will have hot water, plenty of it.' He was smiling. 'It's big enough for two. In fact, I feel sure it was meant as a bath to be shared. Have you seen the walls? Look at the cupids.'

The walls were tiled in a delicate shade of green. On one wall was a large inset of tiles that looked like an oil painting of a tangled garden in muted shades of green and rose coloured hues. Gabrielle saw the cupids in various poses. She wanted to say, 'Why not share the bath with me?' but instead found herself saying, 'I can see two little satyrs peering at us through the branches of a tree.'

'Ah well, if there were not little devils in each of us life would be most uninteresting. It's the devil in you that attracts me.' Luke spoke softly. He moved nearer. Gabrielle felt her pulses racing.

A knock on the outer door brought Luke to a halt. It was a maid who wanted to know if she could unpack for Gabrielle.

Gabrielle told her to come later, but the moment had passed. Luke moved to the door. 'I think you will find all you need, Gabrielle. If there is anything you want you have only to ring.' He indicated a bell pull. 'Mr Delacote and I will be here to dine with you at seven o'clock.'

One of the windows in the drawing room overlooked the landing stage. The men were waiting in the longboat to take him back.

If only the maid had not come to interrupt them, Gabrielle thought. She watched the boat until it rounded the corner into the main canal, and when it was out of sight she felt bereft. It was like being abandoned on a remote island with her only contact to the outside world gone forever.

She moved around the room. Although sparsely furnished and although brocades of chairs and the silk of the curtains were faded, there was yet an elegance.

A massive stone fireplace had an abandoned, cheerless look, as though no fire had been lit in it for years. Mr Delacote had talked about the temperate climate. 'It's always Spring or Summer in Venice,' he had said. Well, this was not warm enough even for Spring, Gabrielle went to get a shawl, longing to be back to the iron stove on the ship, round which she had huddled so many times, drawing comfort from its warmth. She got colder and colder. At last she rang for the maid and asked if she could have towels for the bathroom.

The girl's hand flew to her mouth. She had forgotten, the señora must forgive her. Then she said, 'The señora is cold. I shall bring heat.' The heat was a charcoal stove which emitted fumes that made Gabrielle cough. The girl assured her earnestly she would soon get used to it.

Gabrielle went to have her bath. The water gushed from massive gilt taps and the rising steam filled the bathroom with a most delicious scent. Oil must have been poured into the bath, it floated on the water in tiny globules.

With an ecstatic sigh Gabrielle lowered herself into the water. There were two sponges, a large and a small one.

She soaped herself with the small one and dripped water over her body with the other, feeling a sensuousness as she wondered what it would be like to make love in the bath. Perhaps tomorrow Luke might come and stay – Gabrielle shook her head vigorously. No, no, she must not allow herself to become weak over Luke because he suddenly decided his bodily needs had to be satisfied.

Then she remembered him saying he had been attracted to her because of the devil in her and she went weak again. Why, oh why, should she have to suffer this torment? Gabrielle, reluctant to leave the warmth of the bath to go into the chilly room, kept replenishing with hot water, but when she heard a loud chattering of voices coming from the canal and knowing it was the French people, she got out, towelled herself quickly, threw on a robe and rushed out on to the landing, with as much glee as though a rescue ship had landed on her island. She met them coming up the stairs.

The glad cries of the émigrés and their embraces put the magic of the morning back for Gabrielle. They must meet and celebrate. In an hour? Gabrielle nodded quickly. 'Oh, yes, yes.'

She decided to wear the white dress for the celebration, even if it meant changing into something more circumspect for when Luke and Mr Delacote came to dine. And Gabrielle was glad later she had done so when the elderly Monsieur Feyltaire came to escort her to the 'party' looking elegant in black velvet jacket, his grey hair deeply waved and his immaculate cravat adorned with a jewelled pin.

He threw open a door on the next landing and called, 'Voila!

Utter silence followed this. Gabrielle went into the room then stood transfixed at the tableau facing her. It reminded her of players she had once seen in a theatre, where the setting was a French château. Soft candlelight, the glow of jewels and the sparkle of diamonds were reflected in large gilt mirrors. On the beautifully coiffeured heads of the women were tiaras, round their throats necklaces of diamonds, rubies, emeralds, and on their fingers rings of immense value. The fingers of the men were also adorned with rings.

It was not until the tableau came to life that Gabrielle realized the people were carefully, but shabbily dressed. She was welcomed and embraced once more. She must have a glass of wine. Glasses from all sides were held out to her. Gabrielle laughed, enjoying their enjoyment. One woman said, 'We live again for one night but for this night only. Tomorrow our jewels must go. We shall have to live frugally. No one minds, every penny we can muster will go to help others of our compatriots to escape.' The woman's husband said, 'Tonight we forget penury, cherie. Yes?' He kissed her hand.

Although Gabrielle was in the mood to match every glass of wine with those of the émigrés she forced herself to drink moderately, imagining Luke's reaction should he find her unsteady on her legs.

Her dress was much admired and she had a wanton feeling when she saw men's eyes go to her decolletage. She longed to flirt with them, but was again careful, and saw that her shawl was ready to hand when Luke did arrive.

When Luke came, with Mr Delacote, Gabrielle could see it was costing him an effort to be pleasant. It cost him a greater effort when the French people insisted on the two men being their guests for the evening. Luke gave them a bow and said they were honoured.

To give Luke his due he did appear to be enjoying himself, but he said once to Gabrielle that it was not at all what he had planned. When she asked him what he *had* planned for the evening, however, he simply shrugged and gave no answer.

It was Mr Delacote who told her later that Luke had intended them dining at a small cafe along the canal. The surgeon smiled and added, the cafe had a romantic atmosphere.

Gabrielle's eyebrows went up. Was Luke intending to be romantic with her? Or – had he been planning a nostalgic evening? It might be a place where he had taken some other woman. If so she was glad they had missed visiting the cafe.

There were toasts given to Luke and his 'charming lady' for all their help, and toasts to just about everyone who had helped them in their escape. When the French people later began to get emotional Luke said it was time for them to go. He made the excuse that he had a great deal of business to attend to the next morning and wanted to make an early start.

Luke took Gabrielle back to her apartment and kissed her goodnight for the benefit of Mr Delacote. The surgeon seemed surprised the captain was leaving his wife and Luke said in explanation he had work to do in his cabin. Mr Delacote glanced from one to the other, said, yes, of course, then he took his leave of Gabrielle.

Luke paused to say in a low voice to her that he would begin his search early the next morning for her father, and would let her know as soon as he heard anything. Then he followed Mr Delacote.

Gabrielle watched them from the window hailing a passing gondola. And stood there for some time after it had gone from view, looking up and down the canal. The glow from torches in their sconces outside houses and buildings cast orange and gold patterns on the water. A gondolier, punting a couple in his boat, sang a love song and the man put his arm about the girl's waist and she looked up at him with so much love Gabrielle felt like weeping. What could be more romantic than reclining against the velvet cushions with the man you loved and having a gondolier sing a love song especially for you. Luke would decry such a thing.

Gabrielle turned away from the window with a sigh, and crossed the room to her bedroom. It was too big, like the bed. It would have slept six people. But she only wanted to sleep with one.

She undressed, slid into the vastness between the ice cold sheets and was back once more on the remote island. Tears of self-pity rose, hung on her lashes and slid slowly down her cheeks. She consoled herself that all this would be forgotten if Luke had word of her father the following morning. She prayed he would.

# CHAPTER THIRTEEN

Mr Delacote called for Gabrielle the next morning to take her on what he jestingly told her was his guided tour. She had been up an hour, breakfasted and was not only delighted to have an escort, but eager to be abroad in this city that somewhere held her father.

The morning had been dull when she was first up, but the sun came out and when they went on the landing to wait for a gondola the air was warm, the sun sparkling.

'How lovely to feel the sun,' Gabrielle said. 'I found the rooms quite cold.'

Mr Delacote assured her she would enjoy the best of weather that day, all indications pointed to it.

It was Gabrielle's first ride in a gondola, but although she could not help feeling excited she did, as the day before, search every boat that passed in the hope of seeing her father.

Then her attention was caught by the gondolier, who kept giving her bold, admiring glances. His supple figure had a grace as he wielded the pole. Gabrielle thought all the gondoliers attractive in their 'uniforms' of white with trimmings of red and blue and their flat black shiny hats. She knew she ought to ignore their young and attractive gondolier but could not resist giving him a fleeting smile.

When they came out into the main canal she likened it to the chaos of traffic in London at Piccadilly Circus, with the numerous carriages and phaetons and drays; only here it was craft – gondolas, fishing boats with attractive colourful sails, barges laden with fruit and vegetables, the whole a glorious summer garden of colours, reds, blues, pinks, yellow, orange, against the rich blue of sky and water.

The gondolier deposited them at St. Mark's Square and before he left he put his fingertips to his lips and blew Gabrielle a kiss. She found it impossible not to laugh at the merry-looking face, but Mr Delacote, who had witnessed it, was incensed at such effrontery. He swore to wreak vengeance on the man, but Gabrielle, still laughing, said, 'Oh, please, Mr Delacote, let me have my moment of romance, I get so little from my–' She stopped, aghast at what she had been about to say. To her surprise Mr Delacote patted her arm and said he understood.

'I sensed there was a rift between you and the captain, dear lady, but it will be only temporary. He adores you.'

Gabrielle thought what a relief it would be if she could unburden herself to the surgeon, but she nodded and said yes, she felt sure it would be, then added, 'And now, what are we going to view first?'

What indeed, she thought, it was all enchantment, the Doge's Palace, the clock tower where the bronze figures of the man and the youth struck the big bell on the hour, and St. Mark's; could anything be more beautiful? The arches, the cupolas, the exquisite half-moon mosaics, the elegant flourishes of the decorations with their mixture of Romanesque, Byzantine and Renaissance styles. Gabrielle was charmed by the four bronze horses which stood on the terrace, forelegs raised as though ready to step into space.

She was intrigued by the number of people walking in the Square, ladies and gentlemen, the ladies twirling parasols, Italian infantry, Turkish soldiers, Greek, Austrian, in their colourful uniforms, and overall the rise and fall of voices, the subdued laughter. Then a band began to play and Gabrielle, on an impulse, slipped her arm through Mr Delacote's and gave it a squeeze.

'Oh, how wonderful it all is. It's as though all these buildings and people have come to life from the pages of books I've read. I feel my mind can hardly absorb it all.'

She looked towards the Lagoon then suddenly tensed as she saw a man stepping into a gondola. It was her father! Without thought, without a word to Mr Delacote, Gabrielle rushed away, apologizing to people as she pushed forward among them. 'Papa,' she called, 'Papa!' The gondola drew away and she hailed the next one and indicated the one in front was to be followed. The gondolier shot the boat forward, soon came up alongside the other one and looked to Gabrielle for guidance.

To her disappointment and shame it was not her father but a stranger. With the little Italian Gabrielle knew she was able to apologize and ask the gondolier to take her back. It was fortunate that Mr Delacote, who was about to step in a boat to follow her, saw her, because Gabrielle had no money with her to pay for the short journey.

Once the man was paid the surgeon turned to her and his face was paper white. 'Mrs Caltahn, please never do such a thing again. If I had lost you how would I have explained to your husband? He put you in my care.'

Gabrielle, near to tears, apologized. 'Do forgive me, Mr Delacote, I rushed away on impulse, I thought the man was – was a relative of mine. I really am terribly sorry to have upset you so, and I give you my word I shall never do such a thing again. And may

I beg you not to tell my husband of my foolishness.'

Mr Delacote, whose colour was beginning to come back, managed a smile. 'That will be a secret between us. Now, I think we shall find somewhere quiet for a walk.'

He took her to where narrow streets lined with shops criss-crossed. There were prospective buyers in the shops, a few strolling along the streets, but there was a peace pervading the area.

'I like this "maze",' Mr Delacote said. 'But one can get lost, you must never venture alone, Mrs Caltahn. And never, never, at night. There are rogues and vagabonds in Venice as there are in any other town or city.'

Gabrielle said she thought it most unlikely she would want to shop when it was dark and added she would make sure she had an escort should she ever want to purchase anything during daylight hours.

There were some beautiful things in the shops but although Gabrielle stopped to look in the windows every now and then to admire, she did not linger. Without money there seemed no point.

They came eventually to a small quay where fishermen were mending their nets. There was a seat and Mr Delacote suggested they sit a while. Boats bobbed on the sunsparkled water and on a passing boat the gondolier sang.

Gabrielle felt a great rapport with Mr Delacote and knew an urge to tell him who she was, and about her life. He had been good to her, he was an understanding man, he had known trouble, grief. Gabrielle realized if she did tell her story she would have to miss out that Luke had married her for revenge. It would make him seem small and Mr Delacote, she knew, had a great respect for Luke.

As though Gabrielle had transmitted her thoughts the surgeon said, 'I still know nothing of your life, Mrs Caltahn. Not that I have any wish to pry, but I feel you must have led an interesting life, you are an interesting person.'

Gabrielle glanced at him. 'The only reason I refrained from telling you about myself, Mr Delacote, was that I might earn your hatred at the end of it.'

'Never,' he said firmly. 'Not for any reason you give.'

'Not even that I happen to be the granddaughter of – Hesther Quantock?'

Mr Delacote turned his head sharply. 'Hesther Quantock?' He paused. 'It seems impossible that you who are so open – so–'

He slewed round in his seat and gave her a direct glance. 'Even that information, Mrs Caltahn, would not make me hate you. I see no reason why a person should suffer for the sins of a parent or grandparent.'

Gabrielle wished that her husband had the same philosophy. She told Mr Delacote her story, keeping nothing back apart from the reason of Luke marrying her.

Mr Delacote was silent for a long time. When he spoke his voice was charged with hatred. 'No wonder there are many men who are willing to kill your grandmother, Mrs Caltahn. I would have no compunction in doing so.'

'Nor I, and I mean it. At one time such a thing would have been most abhorrent, just the thought of it, but not any longer.'

'Your husband, did he know you were a Quantock before he married you?'

'Yes, he married me to – protect me, so that if my father were dead my grandmother would have no jurisdiction over me.'

Mr Delacote gave a satisfied nod. 'Good thinking. Your father, have you–?

'My husband is making enquiries this morning.'

A gloominess had settled on them both and Mr Delacote, perhaps in an effort to lift it, suggested they go and see the merchants and captains haggling over cargoes. 'It's a colourful sight,' he said, 'and there are other traders with stalls.'

Even before they reached the quayside Gabrielle could smell the rich aroma of spices, just as she had done at Lisbon. She had thought the cargoes colourful at Lisbon, but here there were more exotic things.

Mr Delacote explained that although Venice was no longer an important port many ships still came with products from all over the world. There were handmade carpets from the East rich in colour and design, delicate porcelain, jade, ivory, silver, gold, pewter, copper. Gabrielle watched an elderly Jewish gentleman with a flowing white beard trying to sell his merchandise to a brawny-looking captain, and Gabrielle was so captivated by the elderly man's expressive gestures, his persuasive way, she felt sure if she had wanted to buy she could not have resisted him.

There was a stall nearby with trinkets, beads, necklaces of silver, bangles. She picked up a necklace and Mr Delacote offered to buy it for her. 'If the captain would allow it,' he said. Gabrielle thanked him but refused, not knowing how Luke would react to her accepting a gift from another man, even though it was his surgeon, who had no designs on her.

'No, well, perhaps not. If the captain was here, then I could have asked his permission.'

Gabrielle, who had been staring ahead, said, 'You can ask him now. My husband is over there.' She could hear the bitterness in her voice. Luke, who had said he was leaving early to make enquiries about her father, was now haggling with a merchant over the purchase of silks. So much for his promise.

Mr Delacote glanced at Gabrielle. 'He may have found your father and–' The sentence tailed off.

'Shall we go and see?' Before the surgeon could reply Gabrielle was way ahead.

'Good morning, Mr Caltahn,' she said coldly, 'I trust you have managed to find yourself a cargo at the right price.'

'Not yet, but I will.' He glanced beyond her. 'Will you wait with Mr Delacote? I need my wits about me and would not want to be distracted.'

'It takes little to distract you from your object,' she retorted. 'I thought you had gone on another errand.'

'And you were right. Will you please excuse me. We can talk about it later.'

Gabrielle went back to Mr Delacote, who had stopped a short distance away, and raised her shoulders with a helpless gesture. 'I have to wait to know about my father until his business is transacted.'

'Yes, well of course, it is important, Mrs Caltahn.'

'More important than my father?'

'It may be to the captain,' the surgeon said gently. 'This is human nature, he does have a shipping line to run, and that takes money.'

'Then if it is so important why did he travel from London to Marseilles with only ballast in the hold? I know he was picking up the émigrés and necessities for them, but he could have taken on cargo to sell at Lisbon.'

'It was the time factor, Mrs Caltahn. Word came to say the émigrés had left Paris and were on their way to Marseilles. One cannot buy a cargo and stick it in the hold in an hour, and it could have been dangerous to leave the French people in hiding at Marseilles for too long. The 'aristos' have many enemies.'

Although Gabrielle saw the reasoning, the sense in this, she still felt annoyed with Luke. And her patience was certainly tested when after waiting half an hour Luke had still not completed the transaction for the cargo. At least, he might have completed it business-wise but he was talking earnestly to the merchant and the man, after some thought, nodded and started giving directions.

At last Luke moved away and came over to where Gabrielle and the surgeon were waiting. Gabrielle said, 'Well! I thought you would never come.' Mr Delacote edged away and stood out of earshot.

'Straighten your face, Madam. It ill becomes you.'

Luke's words were clipped. 'How did you

246

expect me to start searching for your father? By boating all round the canals, knocking on doors? This morning I must have spoken to twenty or more people before I found one who had some knowledge of an Englishman who was being cared for after an illness.'

'I'm sorry, I had no idea.' Gabrielle looked down at her hands.

'No, you wouldn't, would you? Every one must jump to your command. You certainly are following in the footsteps of your grandmother.'

'Stop saying that! I have apologized. It was only natural I should be anxious about my father. I was disappointed and a little hurt when I thought you had not started to make any enquiries.'

'You were not hurt, Gabrielle, you were downright angry that your wishes should not be carried out at once. Now go back to the hotel with Mr Delacote, and no more protests or apologies.'

It was difficult for Gabrielle not to say something in reply. But for once she kept her mouth shut and walked over to where Mr Delacote was waiting, whistling tunelessly through his teeth and trying to look unconcerned, that there might have been more conflict between his captain and wife.

'Oh dear,' Gabrielle said, 'I seem to be in black books again. I always seem to say the

wrong thing. My husband is so – touchy.
Would you be so kind as to see me back to
the hotel. Orders.'

'Yes, of course.' Mr Delacote paused then
said as they walked away, 'You must make
allowances for your husband, Mrs Caltahn.
He does have a lot on his mind.'

Gabrielle smiled wryly. 'Including a
foolish and insensitive wife.'

'Oh, no, dear lady, you are neither of those
things. Just perhaps a little impatient.' The
surgeon's melancholy face lightened in a
smile. 'I think women of all ages are inclined
to be a little more impatient than men.'

'Perhaps. Anyway, thank you for a lovely
morning, Mr Delacote, nothing can take
away that pleasure. I hope you will be kind
enough to escort me another time, that is, of
course, depending on our stay here.'
Delacote declared he would be only too
happy to take her wherever she wanted to
go, adding it had done him good to get out
and about, normally he would have been
moping in his cabin.

The hotel seemed strangely quiet without
the voluble chatter of the French people and
the constant banging of doors. This
morning a number had gone to try and find
relatives and friends and the rest would be
sightseeing.

Gabrielle and Mr Delacote had a meal
together and afterwards, both restless, they

stood at the window watching the boats plying the canals. Gabrielle was about to turn away when she saw a gondola draw up at the landing stage. Luke stepped out. He glanced up at the window as though expecting her to be there and gave her a quick wave. He seemed to be in a pleasant mood.

His greeting when he came into the room was cheerful. 'Well, Gabrielle, you will be pleased to know I have managed to locate your father.'

'You have? Oh, thank God.' Gabrielle put her hands momentarily to her face then looked up. 'I can hardly believe it. How is he, where is he, can I see him? Are you sure it is Papa?'

Luke held up a hand. 'One thing at a time. He is your father, I have spoken with him. He's still weak, but recovering every day. I told him you were here, but not that we are married. I thought it wiser not to. It must come from you, and you must tell him gently. It will be quite a shock to him, seeing we had not met when you last saw one another.'

Gabrielle agreed with this. 'The people who befriended Papa, who are they?'

'English people actually, who have lived in Venice for fifteen years. Your father said Mr and Mrs Felstar have been unbelievably good to him. Nothing is any trouble. If you

get your cloak I shall take you there now.'
Gabrielle ran to get it.

Mr Felstar was an art dealer and the
couple had an apartment above their shop.
It was beautifully furnished with elegant
pieces. A maid showed them into the
drawing room, where a small woman with
auburn hair came forward to greet them.
Her smile was warm and friendly. 'And you
are Gabrielle. Oh, how your father has
talked about you since he knew you were
here. Before that he was so reticent. Even
when his memory returned he would not
tell us his surname, only his Christian
name. I think he was afraid the people who
abducted him might trace him and–'

'Oh, do you think that is possible?'
Gabrielle said in alarm, glancing at Luke.

He shook his head. 'I doubt that very
much.'

'No, of course not,' Mrs Felstar said. 'Your
father is quite safe here, but it was only
natural he would be afraid after all he had
suffered. My husband and I address him as
Mr Jonathan. Such a charming man. We
shall have some tea then I shall take you to
see him. He rests in the afternoon, the
surgeon insisted.'

'Oh, please, Mrs Felstar, may I see Papa
now, sit with him until he awakes?'

Luke laid a hand on her arm. 'Be patient,
Gabrielle. Let your father have his rest. If

your presence roused him, he might be startled, confused–'

'Yes yes, of course.'

They talked over tea, with Gabrielle asking Mrs Felstar to call her too by her Christian name. 'If it was Papa's wish to keep his identity secret, then I must respect his wishes. When someone is wanting to murder you–'

'I guessed it was something drastic, but I asked no questions in that respect. Murder, how dreadful.'

Gabrielle wondered what Mrs Felstar would say if she knew it was her father's own mother who was responsible.

When the maid came in to say that Mr Jonathan was awake Gabrielle found herself trembling. How would she find him?

He was propped up by many pillows in a four-poster bed. Although Gabrielle was prepared to find some change in her father she was unprepared for such a drastic change. It was not only that the thin silver streak in his thick dark hair had widened, but his strong features were pinched, his cheeks hollow, and there were dark circles under his eyes. Jonathan held out his arms and Gabrielle went into them, both weeping.

When they drew apart Jonathan wiped away a tear from Gabrielle's cheek and smiled. 'I'm so delighted to see you my darling Gabrielle, and here I am weeping over you. How are you? Captain Caltahn has told me of your exploits, your determination to find me. I love you for it, but you were very naughty, all sorts of dreadful things could have happened to you had you fallen into the hands of someone with less integrity than the good captain.'

'But I was well looked after, Papa, and I am here with you.' Gabrielle stroked the silver hair. 'I thought never to see you again after Luke found out what had happened.'

A look of pain came into her father's eyes. 'I still find it difficult to believe my own mother could have arranged for me to be—' He shuddered.

They spoke of the family, of Christmas Day, of her mother, then Jonathan brought the talk to Luke, and said what a capable man he seemed to be. It was then Gabrielle told him they were married.

At first Jonathan was delighted, saying she could not have chosen a finer man, but then he began to look worried. Would the marriage be legal, without his having given his consent? He said he must give them a document stating he had. He thought it might be better if they went through another marriage ceremony in England. He asked to see Luke and they discussed it. Luke assured him the marriage was legal but if it would make him feel any better, yes, they would have another ceremony.

Excitement and exhaustion were beginning to take their toll of Jonathan, his voice was growing weak and he was sliding down the pillows. Gabrielle got up and said they must go but promised to call the next day. She kissed her father gently, then stood a moment, reluctant to leave. When would he be fit to travel, and when he was fit how would she get him back to England? This question had worried her during the voyage. She was so dependent on Luke. She had no money and neither had her father. Would Luke lend her the fare for both of them, would he allow her to travel with her father?

As it happened the problem was taken out of her hands when they went back to the drawing room. Mr Felstar had come in and he said how pleased he was to meet them. He had as warm a personality as his wife. When Gabrielle mentioned about getting her father back to England he and his wife said it was unthinkable at the moment, and Gabrielle was not to worry. When her father was fit they would bring him home, they were due for a visit to their family in England.

Mrs Felstar said, 'Now you are not to worry, Gabrielle. I know how you will be longing to have him home, but it really is best he stays here to gather strength. He has gone through a great deal and he will be well looked after.'

Mr Felstar laughed. 'Your father gets better care than I do. No, I'm jesting. My wife enjoys looking after your father. She lost her favourite uncle a year ago. He lived with us and now your father is getting all the affection she lavished on Uncle Joseph.'

'I'm glad,' Gabrielle said softly. 'Papa thrives on affection. I can't tell you how grateful I am for all your kindness. I only hope I shall be able to repay it to you in some way.'

'You can repay it by putting your trust in us, and accept that your father will want for nothing. And now, will you do us the honour of staying for dinner? Then perhaps you can see your father again after he has rested.'

Luke said he regretted that he must refuse, he had a great deal of business to attend to. He hoped they would understand. Another time, perhaps—

Gabrielle was trying to hide her disappointment when Mr Felstar suggested that she be allowed to stay and followed it up by promising to see her safely back to her hotel. After a slight hesitation Luke agreed. It was so unexpected Gabrielle felt like flinging her arms around his neck and kissing him.

He left, saying that either he or Mr Delacote would call for her the next morning.

Gabrielle spent a whole hour with her father after the meal. He was much brighter and his voice stronger, but Gabrielle, afraid of tiring him, kept saying she had better go. Each time Jonathan begged her to stay. It was so wonderful to have her with him. Once he reached for her hand and said, looking wistful, 'Gabrielle, do you think your mother had any knowledge of what my mother planned for me?'

'Oh, no, no, not at all. I'm certain of it, she has her faults but would never be party to such a crime. This is wholly the plan of grandmama. She seems obsessed with acquiring wealth.'

'And power,' Jonathan said quietly. 'I have no idea why. She has never wanted for anything. She came from a wealthy family. I was shocked when I found out she had resorted to what can only be described as piracy. And she was very angry when she knew I had found out. When I accused her of being responsible for the drowning of some émigrés she did not deny it. She threatened if I made accusations about her in public you and your mother would suffer.'

'If you knew all this, Papa, why did you agree to go to Calais?'

'Because she assured me that this was a bona fide transaction.' Jonathan raised his shoulders. 'As you know I never reached Calais.'

Gabrielle asked him what he would do about her mother when he came back to England and he said, let her know exactly what had happened and try to persuade her to leave with him and start a new life together, adding that a simple life and peace were worth a king's ransom.

Gabrielle hoped he would achieve his aim, but had to admit to being doubtful. It would need a great deal of persuasion to get her mother to leave, especially while Hesther Quantock was there to dominate.

In spite of this Gabrielle felt happier knowing her father's health was improving. She had no idea how long the ship would be in Venice but Luke had not indicated any urgency to leave. Perhaps a few days?

For three days Gabrielle paid visits to her father, each time accompanied by Mr Delacote, who waited to escort her back to the hotel. Luke was frantically busy, he said.

Gabrielle was grateful for the company of the French people. The evenings would have been endless without them. Luke never came to see her nor did Mr Delacote come in the evenings. A number of the émigrés had already found homes with friends and relatives. Some of the others were still searching and the rest had decided to go to England.

On the fourth day it was Luke who came to take Gabrielle to see her father, but he did not arrive until the afternoon. 'This will be the last visit,' he said. 'We sail tomorrow morning, if the wind is fair.'

Gabrielle's heart gave a lurch. It would be terrible saying goodbye to her father. Her father, however, was philosophical about it. 'Just think how lucky we have been, Gabrielle, I to have had such wonderful people to care for me, and you to have a husband who was willing to bring you to Venice. If it had not been for his enquiries, and if I had not regained my memory we might never have met again.'

'Oh, Papa,' she wailed, 'you sound so cheerful.'

'I have reason to be. Look how strong I grow day by day. In a little while we shall be together again.' Then he said, a break in his voice, 'Oh, my darling child, no tears please, or I shall weep. I want you to give me a smile so that I shall keep remembering you like that.'

Gabrielle did manage a smile, but after they had held one another close and she had said goodbye to the Felstars she could not contain her tears any longer.

Luke consoled her when they came out into the street, but when she continued to weep he said, 'Now, Gabrielle, that is enough. People are looking at us. They will be thinking I am responsible for your tears.'

Gabrielle dried her tears, not wanting to

257

upset Luke. She was hoping to persuade him to spend part of the evening with her. Those of the émigrés who had not yet left had been invited to the homes where their compatriots were living, and she found the thought of being alone, after parting from her father, unbearable.

Before she could ask Luke, however, he said he would dine with her. She thanked him, trying not to show how pleased she was.

He glanced towards the bedroom and smiled and there was a wicked gleam in his eyes. 'It would be a shame to leave without sampling your very attractive bath. I shall come early. Would you perhaps – care to share it with me?'

Gabrielle's pulses leaped then her body began to throb.

'Why not?' she answered lightly. 'As you did say, it is big enough for two.'

'I shall be here at six o'clock. I shall expect you to be undressed, ready – and waiting.'

'Of course.' Thrill after thrill was running through her. How could she wait until six?

He tilted her chin, gave her a feather-light kiss and left, walking with quite a jaunty air.

At five minutes to six Gabrielle, naked under her robe, the water already drawn in the bath, the scent of the perfumed oil drifting into the drawing room, waited, her whole body aflame with the anticipation of stepping into the bath with Luke.

Seconds later the door was flung open and he stood facing her, his whole face taut with anger.

'After all I told you,' he declared. 'After all I did to impress on you the need to keep your name secret and you go shouting it all over the ship that *you* are a Quantock, or you as good as did so.'

Gabrielle stared at him in bewilderment. 'What do you mean? I told no one.'

'Do you call our *dear* surgeon *no one?*'

'Oh – yes, yes I did tell him but Mr Delacote happens to be a man of integrity and would not spread such a thing around.'

'Mr Delacote *happens* to drink to excess at times and when he's in his cups has no control over his tongue. This afternoon he's been bandying your name around, what a wonderful person you are, not at all like the evil Hesther Quantock, your *grandmother*. How do you think the men feel, how do you think I feel? I, who have been involved with émigrés, have an in-law who has been responsible for pirating our cargoes and drowning a number of escapees. How do you think I'm going to cope with that?'

'I'm sorry, I didn't realize–'

'Sorry, sorry, sorry. What good will that do?' Luke paced up and down the room. 'There is one thing certain, you are not travelling on my ship in the morning.' Luke

259

stopped his pacing.

'But I–' Gabrielle felt overwhelmed by the outcome of her confidences. 'Where can I go, what can I do?'

'I shall arrange for you to travel with the four French people who are returning to London.'

Gabrielle's heart was beating in painful thuds. 'What do you want me to do when I get back to England? Return to my grandmother's house?'

'Is that what you want to do?' His eyes held steel. 'Is it?'

'No!' Gabrielle shouted in her fear, her bewilderment. 'You know the way I feel about my grandmother.'

'No, I do *not* know how you feel. I only know what you tell me. When I saw you with your father today, so loving, I felt an affection for you. I wanted to care for you, I looked forward to making love to you, holding you in my arms. Now–' He gave her a scathing look. 'I feel nothing but contempt.'

Gabrielle clenched her fists. 'In other words you do not care where I go as long as I am out of your sight.'

'I married you and shall fulfil my obligations. You will go to Lady Norton, and sleep in my apartment.'

'And if I refuse?'

'You will not refuse, Gabrielle. You made a

bargain, I found your father for you, so you shall fulfill your part, as my wife. But, I might add, it will from now on be a marriage in name only.'

'How dramatic,' she said, to hide her hurt.

'It ill becomes you to add sarcasm to your faults,' he retorted, and with that Luke turned on his heel and left, slamming the door behind him.

Gabrielle stood motionless for some time, staring at the door. Then reaction set in and she began to tremble. How could she have guessed that dear, kind Mr Delacote would unconsciously condemn her to an empty, loveless life. But then, the fault was really hers. Luke had stressed the need for secrecy.

Draughts seemed to be coming at her from all angles. Gabrielle walked slowly towards the bathroom, hoping she might draw some comfort from the hot water, yet wondering at the same time if she would ever feel warm again.

# CHAPTER FOURTEEN

A message was delivered to Gabrielle that evening, telling her to be ready to leave by ten o'clock the following morning. It was signed 'Luke Caltahn'.

It was Luke who came for her and his expression was as cold as the message was worded. He told her he had managed to get a passage for her on a private schooner and that a Miss Mayland would chaperone her. Gabrielle thanked him but said no more. They left the hotel in silence. There was a gondola waiting for them, not as she had imagined the longboat. But then, Luke was not likely to expect his crew to transport the *evil* Gabrielle Quantock. Bitterness soured her tongue. She was being crucified for someone else's misdeeds. When they came out into the main canal Gabrielle was aware of Luke watching her. She sat staring straight ahead. At last he spoke.

'Mr Mayland owns the schooner. His two daughters were travelling with him but the elder decided to stay in Venice with an aunt. The younger daughter, Lavinia, felt the need for company during the voyage back to England. You will find her a most interesting person, she is well travelled. It will be a pleasure voyage for you.'

'Pleasure?' Gabrielle queried wryly. 'To be thrust into the company of a woman I have never met and may not like. But then, being such a criminal, I suppose I should count myself fortunate.'

'I had no choice. And when I said it would be a pleasure voyage I meant you would be living in a more luxurious surrounding. You will have your own, well-furnished cabin.' Luke's voice was edgy with anger. 'I was not the one who shouted your name around. If you had not made Mr Delacote your father confessor—'

'You need say no more, Mr Caltahn. I accept my punishment for the indiscretion. But there is one thing I must ask. How much does Miss Mayland know about me?'

'She knows that we are married, but not why. We are friends of long standing, she will be discreet. Do not attempt to question her about me because she will tell you nothing.'

Gabrielle flared. 'You need have no worry on that score, Mr Caltahn. I am no longer interested in your life, or your family, and in fact, would not care if I never saw you again.'

'Oh, you will see me again, Madam, rest assured on that.'

'Not if the ship goes down.'

'No doubt you would welcome my early demise.'

'I was thinking of the ship *I* shall be on, not yours.'

'You would survive. You're a fighter.'

Gabrielle, not sure whether it was meant as a compliment, kept silent.

She brought up a subject that had been bothering her since she knew she would not be travelling back with Luke. 'Lady Norton,' she said. 'I shall find it embarrassing to arrive and have to explain about our marriage and–'

'I wrote to her the first day we arrived in Venice. If you arrive first in England then you can say I am following. There is no need to make mountains out of simple problems.'

'I am not making mountains, I–' Gabrielle stopped then added with a helpless shrug, 'Oh, what is the use, you would never understand.'

No more was said until they boarded the schooner. Gabrielle, who had it firmly fixed in her mind that Lavinia Mayland would be a spoilt, rich girl who had been more than friendly with Luke, was surprised to find her a small, wiry woman who looked to be in her late thirties, with a lively face and a breezy manner. Gabrielle liked her on sight.

'You and I will get on splendidly, my dear,' Miss Mayland said. 'I knew the minute I set eyes on you. How lucky it is for me that your husband wants you to have a more comfortable voyage home. A thoughtful man, Luke.'

Gabrielle's eyebrows went up. Thoughtfulness was not something she would have attributed to her husband. She was introduced to Mr Mayland, a tall thin man with a vague manner, then was shown to her cabin. It was comfortably furnished and warm, with a rather elegant looking porcelain stove, or what appeared to be porcelain. Oddly enough, she would have given anything to be back in Luke's cabin with its old iron stove.

'It's most attractive,' she said to Miss Mayland. 'I shall be very comfortable here.'

Miss Mayland beamed at Luke. 'Now you are not to worry, dear boy, Gabrielle will be well taken care of. And when we arrive in England I shall see she is safely delivered to your door. I know you are due to sail soon so I shall leave you both to say goodbye.'

There was no ease between Gabrielle and Luke. She said, simply for the sake of saying something, 'I thought I was to travel with the French people.'

'They decided to stay for a while. They have accommodation. Many people, learning of their plight, seemed willing to help.' Luke paused then he said, 'I called to see your father before I called for you. He's very much improved. I feel sure you will be seeing him soon. He sends his love.'

Gabrielle felt a great ache inside her. Luke had bothered to go and see her father, yet he was casting her off in this cold way. She wanted to beg him to let her come with him but knew he would refuse.

'It had to be this way,' he said, as though aware of her thoughts. 'I confess to – well, to exaggerating that Mr Delacote had shouted your name aloud to the whole ship. Actually as far as I knew none of the crew heard–'

'No one. And yet you–'

'I dare not take the risk, Gabrielle, of letting you stay. I shall try and keep drink away from our surgeon. But if he should happen to get some and you were there your name would be on his lips. You must understand.'

For a moment there was pain in Luke's eyes and Gabrielle suddenly thought, I love this man who has caused me so much unhappiness. She reached out a hand to him but Luke drew back, and when he spoke again the coldness was back in his voice.

'I make no apologies for putting you on this ship. I have an excellent rapport with my men and I'm not going to have it destroyed because of you. I shall see you in England. Have a good voyage.'

'May I come up on deck and see you leave?' Gabrielle all but choked on the words. 'Miss Mayland would expect it.'

'Yes, of course.'

Luke played the part of the departing husband on deck. He teased her about behaving herself and even kissed her in a dutiful way on each cheek. Gabrielle felt as though her heart were breaking when she watched him walking away. He kept up his role, looked back and gave a brief wave before disappearing from view.

Gabrielle was unable to speak. Miss Mayland said in commiseration, 'I know how you feel, my dear, goodbyes are always terrible, but it will not be too long before you will be meeting again. Luke is so very fond of you and wanted you to have the best.' She put her arm about Gabrielle. 'And I shall see you get it. Come along, we shall have a nice cup of my favourite tea.'

Gabrielle tormented herself that night, thinking how different everything might have been had she not confided in Mr Delacote. She relived the moments when Luke had been talking about sharing the bath with her, she could see the wicked gleam in his eyes, a delightful wicked gleam, she felt a stirring of her senses just imagining it. Oh, if only, if only...

It was fortunate that Luke was right when he said Miss Mayland was an interesting person. She had a fund of stories of her travels and kept Gabrielle regaled with them. Mr Mayland was constantly lost in a world of his own.

Miss Mayland said, 'Papa and my sister Estelle are two of a kind, both wrapped up in archaeological finds, and art treasures. I like adventurous things, poking about in all sorts of out of the way places. You are a very good listener, Gabrielle.'

'I enjoy hearing all about your adventures. I enjoyed listening to my father, he had always so many things to talk about.'

'Luke told me about your father.' Miss Mayland spoke gently. 'A terrible thing, but then all that is behind him and soon you will be home together. We must always look on the bright side. Look forward, never back. Luke was saying how different the French people were once they reached Venice, they came alive again.'

'Yes, they did, Miss Mayland, how long have you known Luke?'

'Oh, we are old friends. We first met in Paris. We were there when the people thought the bloodshed had ended and the famine over. They brought the King back from Versailles and there was such a show of affection and loyalty for the Royal Family. They crowded into the Tuilleries, the humble folk, the bourgeois, holding out their hands, begging from the Queen a flower from her corsage, a ribbon from her hat, and she gave them with such delight. Poor Marie Antoinette. How could she think that anyone was in need when they showed such affection.'

'I can understand that,' Gabrielle said, 'but–'

'There was a new feeling.' Miss Mayland spoke with enthusiasm. 'It was wonderful. All classes became enchanted with the new idea of liberty. Funds were needed to make work for all. The nobility brought their jewels to the National Assembly, the King and Queen gave their plate, a town gave a wagon-load of buckles, some studded with precious stones. The deputies tore theirs from their shoes and handed them in. Charity workshops were set up to put men working on the roads. *Thousands* applied. Emigrants from all over had poured into the city, many of them were rabble, useless, but work had been promised to all.'

'And was there work for all?'

'Oh, yes. A Fête de la Fédération was planned and men were set to level the Champs de Mar and to build an amphitheatre for three hundred thousand spectators. Unfortunately, the rabble were undisciplined and work looked like coming to a stop. But no, help was at hand! People from all walks of life rushed to take over, gravediggers, butchers, gardeners, housewives, heroes of the Bastille, several contingents of monks; well-dressed women cheerfully pushed barrows, the staff of the

Royal Household brought spades and were wildly cheered. Deputies worked side by side with cobblers, bands played, drums beat; all was laughter and song. And do you know, in one week only, an embankment a mile and a half long with tiers had been raised, and in the centre of the arena stood the patriotic temple over twenty feet high.'

Miss Mayland paused and when she spoke again her face was alight, remembering. 'And when the day came for the Fête, what an unforgettable time it was. There were contingents of all kinds, massed bands, the Corporations, children's battalions, a hundred thousand *fédérés* who had marched from the Bastille – and in a deluge of rain. But who cared? The Royal Family were in a stand decorated with blue and gold in front of the Ecole Militaire. Louis took the oath and the Queen held up the Dauphin, and the cheers! It rained and it stopped and rained again and many were drenched, but for all it seemed a bright sunny day. The people danced a farandole, there was dancing at the Place de la Bastille and people shouted with heart and soul, 'Vive, vive, la Nation'. It was all so wonderful. That night I met Luke and his friends. We had known one another for some time, but had not seen each other for months. We were all a little wild that night, we danced and we sang and Luke was 'wilder than any of them.'

'He was? I find that difficult to imagine. Luke is so – so–'

Miss Mayland chuckled. 'I know this, he swung *me* off my feet.

Then she suddenly became serious and a look of sadness came into her eyes. 'The tragedy of it all was that a year later the Altar of the Nation became the scene of demonstration against the King. Martial Law was proclaimed, the red flag hoisted and the protestors shot. The Champs de Mar, where a united people had worked so joyously together, was strewn with bodies... And now, a hundred heads a day roll in the gutter. Oh, Gabrielle, where will it all end?'

They fell silent after that.

There were times in the days that followed when Gabrielle felt guilty because she was no longer enjoying the voyage. All she wanted to do was to get back to England and to see Luke, and to feel his arms around her. She would be so different, she thought, she would win his love.

The schooner was faster than Luke's but Mr Mayland was talking about them making a stop at Sicily and Gabrielle feeling frustrated, became tense. When they were becalmed for a day she walked around moaning about the delay. Miss Mayland spoke to her about it.

'Wishing, and getting irritated, Gabrielle,

will not make the wind spring up. You must learn to accept delays. I know you are anxious to get back to Luke, but I doubt whether he will arrive before us. We shall probably get there about the same time. Luke is making only a short stop at Marseilles.'

'To take on more émigrés?'

A solemn look came over Miss Mayland's face. 'I would rather not discuss Luke's affairs, if you don't mind.' The next moment she was smiling. 'Did I tell you about my strange experience with an elephant while we were in India. The animal caught me in his trunk, lifted me and let me down gently on to its back. I was so astonished–'

Gabrielle decided she would not question Miss Mayland again about Luke's activities.

There was excitement one day when they were chased by a privateer. The schooner outran them but it took them off their course and Mr Mayland said they would not make a stop at Sicily, especially as another vessel had warned them about a band of brigands being on the rampage the previous week.

Gabrielle silently thanked the privateer and the band of brigands for shortening the voyage.

They had many changes of weather. They were becalmed some days, had good head winds the next, and had to tack a number of times. They sailed through four minor storms, had three days of torrential rain after a thunderstorm and arrived in England at the end of March to find the countryside covered in white.

'Snow!' Miss Mayland declared with delight. 'I adore snow.'

Gabrielle's heart sank, expecting delays because of the weather.

There were so many ships in the Pool of London it was impossible to see if Luke's was among them. Gabrielle would have liked to search for it but Mr Mayland had been indisposed for the past few days and was anxious to get to his home.

The snow, as it turned out, was no more than a thin layer and inclined to thaw. Miss Mayland hired a carriage with outriders to accompany them. When Gabrielle questioned if they were necessary she said, 'I promised to deliver you safely to Luke and I am not taking any chances, especially as Papa is no hand with a pistol. We could encounter footpads, highwaymen—'

Mr Mayland offered little in the way of conversation. He sat in the corner, his chin sunk on to his chest. When he did speak it was to ask how much further they had to go.

The thing that struck Gabrielle forcibly during the ride to Lady Norton's was the fact she had travelled hundreds of miles, seen many lovely things, experienced happiness and unhappiness, yet knew little more about Luke's life than when she had set out on the journey.

Would he be there when she arrived? Gabrielle hoped so. Although he had written to Lady Norton she might not have received the letter. Then there would be a great deal of explaining to do; turning up on the doorstep with strangers, announcing she was married to Luke ... not something to relish considering she had run away to find her father, leaving only a brief note to the woman who had so kindly befriended her. Still, it was no use anticipating problems.

When the carriage stopped outside the house, Miss Mayland asked to be excused coming in to meet Lady Norton. 'Papa–' she said, nodding towards him. 'I must get him home.' Mr Mayland's cheeks were flushed and he was snoring lightly. 'A chill,' she added.

Gabrielle thanked her for all her kindness and told her she hoped they would meet again soon. Miss Mayland said, 'I feel sure we will. It was so good having you with us. Goodbye my dear. Take care of yourself and give our kindest regards to dear Luke.'

Gabrielle waited and waved until the carriage had moved away then turned towards the house. And saw Lady Norton fluttering a handkerchief at her from a first floor window.

By the time a maid had opened the door Lady Norton was there to greet Gabrielle, her welcome as warm and rapturous as she might have afforded a long-lost daughter.

'How wonderful to see you, Gabrielle.' She held her at arms' length. 'And looking so well. Congratulations on your marriage. What an exciting surprise. I could hardly believe it when I had Luke's letter. You were so naughty for running away, but it could not have turned out better. Luke needs a wife. Come along in by the fire, we shall have so much to talk about, I want to know everything.'

Gabrielle said, 'Have you had word from Luke? Has he arrived in England? We travelled separately, but I shall explain why later.'

'Oh, Luke explained. The ship docked yesterday. A messenger brought a note from him this morning. He should be here sometime this evening. Sit down, I shall ring for refreshments.'

Gabrielle was trying to think what excuse Luke had made for her not travelling with him when Helen explained it. 'How lucky you are to have a husband so caring. Not many would allow a practically new bride to travel on another ship. But of course, I can understand you wanting to be here to meet your father should he arrive. Luke could have been delayed, having to stop at various ports to pick up cargo. And how wonderful that you found your father, Gabrielle. Luke said he had had a bad time, how dreadful. But there, you will not want to go into details now.'

Helen gave orders to the maid who came in for the meal and Gabrielle walked to the fire and held out her hands to the blazing logs. She was beginning to think her husband quite adept at making excuses for his abandonment of her.

Helen came over and stood with her by the fire. 'Oh, Gabrielle, I still can't believe that you and Luke are married. It's *so* romantic. Luke said he fell in love with you the minute you stepped on his ship. I never imagined him to be the kind of man to fall head over heels in love, which just shows one never knows a person.'

'No, indeed.' Gabrielle wondered what Lady Norton would say if she knew the real reason for the marriage. She began to talk about the countries they had visited, about all the lovely things she had seen, and then, without intending to, mentioned the émigrés.

At the end of it Helen gave an ecstatic sigh. 'Could a girl have had a more wonderful honeymoon, not only did you have all the romance of a shipboard wedding and so many lovely places, but the reward of knowing your husband saved so many people from a violent death. You should be proud of Luke.'

'Oh, I am, I am.'

Helen smiled indulgently. 'And Luke must be very proud of you. How lucky he is to have a beautiful and warm and loving girl for a wife.'

Loving? No. She had not been loving towards Luke, but she could be now – if given a chance.

There was the sound of hoofbeats on the road and they both looked up. But the horseman passed. They looked up several times during the evening, but still Luke did not come.

Gabrielle had told Helen over the meal about her father, and Helen was shocked that any woman could do such a thing to her son. She kept bringing it up. Hesther Quantock was dangerous. Who knows but that she might try and get at Gabrielle. The next moment she was contrite. 'Forgive me, for being so alarmist. I got carried away, I just can't imagine there being a woman in the world who would arrange to have her own son killed.'

'It is hard to believe.'

Helen began talking about Luke again, saying she felt she could have fallen in love with him had she been younger. Then she added, 'But there, I would not have suited him. I don't think I could ever give myself wholly to a man. I never could to my husband. I think, deep down, I am too dominant a personality.'

Gabrielle said, 'Luke tells me I nag.'

Helen laughed. 'I feel quite sure when he said it he was teasing. You could never be a nagging woman.'

'I think I could be, I do have a temper.'

'It would make for a very dull married life if you never had a difference of opinion, but there is a difference between flaring up in temper and being bad-tempered.'

Gabrielle smiled. 'My father would enjoy your philosophy.'

'Will he be staying with you and Luke when he does arrive?'

'It was understood he would. Luke invited him, gave him this address. It would be impossible for him to go home. Will the apartment be large enough? I have no idea of the size. How many rooms are there?'

'Oh, Gabrielle forgive me, I must take you up. There are four bedrooms, dressing room, study, drawing room – large enough for the two of you, but of course Luke might want to have the whole house when you start a family.'

That day would be far distant, Gabrielle thought. If ever. She was not pregnant now and would never be unless Luke could overcome his aversion to the name of Quantock. Or unless he was unable to

278

control his physical need and make demands on her. She said:

'I do want children, and I think Luke does, but I feel sure he would never want to turn you out of the house. The apartment will be big enough for us for quite a time.'

It was a bachelor apartment. Although furniture and furnishings and carpets were of good quality there was an overall air of austerity. If fires had not been lit in all the rooms Gabrielle knew she would have wanted to run away from the chill. Fortunately, the drawing room and the main bedroom were not too large. In the main bedroom was a double bed. Leading from this room was a dressing room and on the opposite landing were the other bedrooms, all with single beds. Gabrielle noticed that all had been made up. Would Luke share the double bed, or–?

Nowhere in the apartment was there anything to show it was lived in, no knick-knacks, no miniatures or portraits. Helen had put flowers in the drawing room and master bedroom and that was the only sign of life.

Gabrielle wished Luke would come and she would know what kind of life he intended them to live together.

But Luke did not come. The grandfather clock in the hall had taken to striking only on the half hour since Gabrielle had been here last, and it reminded her of the half-hourly bell on the ship.

At midnight, Helen, who had kept stifling yawns and apologizing, said she must seek her bed. Gabrielle said she would go up too. After all Luke might not arrive until the next day.

'The bed has been warmed,' Helen said, 'so you should be comfortable. I do hope you sleep well. Are you sure you will not want Marie to help you undress?'

'No, really, I can manage, thank you.' They parted on the first landing.

Gabrielle undressed, put on a robe and sat by the fire, reluctant to go to bed in case Luke should arrive. It would be cheerless for him if there was no-one to greet him.

It could only have been ten minutes later when she was sitting upright, listening to the beat of horses hooves. They came nearer, slowed. And then there was the sound of steel striking the cobblestones of the yard to the left of the house that led to the stables. It could only be Luke.

How would he behave? Had he missed her, if so would he show it? Would he draw her to him, kiss her gently, touch her breasts – Gabrielle's hands went to her breasts, wanting his caresses. She would cling to him, let him know she loved him, wanted him, and was prepared to submit instead of fighting him. Their love-making could be beautiful, ecstatic– Her body began to throb.

She waited for sounds and the first she heard was a firm tread on the stairs. Then the door was flung open, and Luke was there, glaring at her. 'Oh, so you're here!'

Alarmed she said, 'Luke, what is it?'

He flung his tricorne on the bed, his face taut with anger. 'You might well ask. Your bitch of a grandmother has sunk yet another of my ships, and on the Calais to Dover run. I shall kill her, I shall fill her full of lead, slit her throat, strangle her with my own two hands!'

Gabrielle closed her eyes. More violence, more threats of murder ... she had expected love.

Without another word Luke went out. He closed the door quietly but when she heard him moving about in the next room he was venting his temper on the chest, pulling out the drawers and slamming them shut.

When at last all was silent Gabrielle climbed into bed and drew the covers over her trembling body.

Not until the day her grandmother died would she know any peace with Luke. If then...

# CHAPTER FIFTEEN

When Gabrielle came down for breakfast the next morning Luke and Helen were deep in conversation. They both looked grave. Gabrielle, after a bad night, was not in a good mood and was determined to ignore Luke. Catching sight of her he got up, came round the table and pulled out a chair.

'Good morning, Gabrielle. We were discussing you. Something urgent has come up. It will mean us moving from here. Sit down, please.'

'Moving?' She stared at him. 'Where, and for how long? What about Papa? You gave him an invitation to stay with us when he returned to England.'

'Yes, I know, but he will not be returning for about a month. The Felstars agreed with me he would need that time to recuperate before undertaking the journey. So that is one problem dispensed with.'

Gabrielle wanted to say to Luke that he was very good at dispensing with problems to suit him, but with Helen there she said instead, 'May I ask why this move has to take place?'

'Because your grandmother knows you are back in England, and I was told, from a reliable source, she has plans to abduct you.'

Gabrielle sank on to the chair. 'Abduct me? Have me shipped away somewhere – to die – as she did Papa?'

'I don't exactly know what she has in mind. I only know I am getting you right away from here. Helen has a house in Cornwall. We are packing and going there this evening. Helen is coming with us. The servants, at least some of them, will be coming too. No one will be told our destination. We are travelling by carriage. I am going out for a few hours, but shall be back in plenty of time to leave. We will not be setting out until it is dark.'

Luke paused. 'There is one thing I would ask, Gabrielle. Will you remove your wedding ring?' He gave her a fleeting smile. 'You can always wear it on a ribbon around your neck.'

Gabrielle twisted the thick embossed band of gold on her finger. 'Is it necessary to remove it?'

'I think it could be beneficial.'

'Am I then to revert to my maiden name of *Quantock?*'

'That is the last thing we want. Helen has agreed for you to play the role of her young ward. You will be Miss Norton, that is if the suggestion is agreeable to you.'

Suggestion? The decision had already been made.

'I agree if you think my new identity will give me immunity from abduction.'

'I feel it might help. Well, now that is settled–' He bid them au revoir and left. Gabrielle turned to Helen. 'I feel it is wrong for you to have to leave for Cornwall because of my troubles.'

'Please don't feel guilty, Gabrielle. I would have been paying a visit to Ninestones later in the year, so why not now? I need to see my agent about some repairs and a few alterations I'm planning. Have your breakfast, then we can decide what to take with us. We can buy food there but I think it might be wise to take some with us. We could encounter bad weather, gales–'

The staff were given orders, not only those in the house but in the stables. Trunks and chests were brought down from attics, boxes of groceries and whole hams and a barrel of flour came from the kitchens, so much food in fact, Gabrielle wondered if they were preparing for a siege.

Presses were emptied and clothes packed. Marie, who was helping Gabrielle, was full of excitement, wanting to know where they were going. Gabrielle, remembering Luke's caution about their destination said no one had mentioned the precise location – which was true. Marie then asked if she thought they would be going by the sea, and if so, how long would it take to get there?

Gabrielle was saved a reply by Helen coming in to say that warm clothes must be packed. And then Gabrielle told Marie she could manage the rest of the packing and Marie, reluctantly, left with her mistress.

It was seven o'clock that evening when Luke arrived and with him, to Gabrielle's surprise and delight, was Mr Delacote.

She seized the surgeon's hands. 'Why, Mr Delacote, how lovely to see you again. How are you?'

'How are *you*, dear lady?' In an undertone he added, 'I was so distressed I caused such an upset between you and the captain.'

Gabrielle gave him a warm smile, and shook her head, dismissing it. 'Are you by any chance coming to Cornwall with us?'

'Gabrielle–' Luke's stern tones made her jump. 'You were warned about giving our destination.'

'Oh, but I thought–'

'Mr Delacote will be travelling with us, but I do not want our destination to be shouted to all and sundry!'

Gabrielle wondered how she could ever be loving towards her husband while he made such extravagant statements. Where were these 'all and sundry'? She apologized and promised more caution in future.

The wagon containing the food and

luggage had left that morning, so had a groom on horseback to warn the house-keeper and her husband at Ninestones of the party's arrival.

Two carriages were brought to the door. Helen and Gabrielle got into the first, complete with footmuffs and plenty of rugs. In the second carriage was Marie, and three more of the servants. Marie was annoyed she had to travel with the 'lower order', but Helen said to Gabrielle that they might want to talk and Marie was an avid listener.

Luke and Mr Delacote were travelling horseback, but would take turns in riding in the carriage if the journey proved too tiring or the weather inclement. Gabrielle felt uneasy. If Luke and Mr Delacote were to act as outriders they must be expecting trouble from her grandmother's men.

Before the carriage moved away she looked back at the house. Some of the servants had been left in charge. In the downstairs room lamplight cast a warm glow on the garden. Gabrielle had felt at home in the house. Now she was being up-rooted once again.

Helen said, 'You will like Ninestones, Gabrielle. It stands on top of a cliff with wonderful views of the sea from the windows. And the air is so bracing.' She laughed. 'But, of course, I am forgetting all the sea breezes you have had.'

'I love the sea, I shall enjoy it.'

Luke had warned them their journey would be long and tedious but Gabrielle was unprepared for the endless days of travelling, of being tossed about on bad roads. And although most of the inns where they stayed overnight offered good food and reasonably comfortable beds, Gabrielle felt every morning when they set off once more on the next stage of their journey that she had never slept a wink.

The weather, fortunately, at first was good, dry and bright, but when they came to Dartmoor and Bodmin Moors they encountered appalling weather, heavy mists and torrential downpours. But at least the heavy rain had cleared away the last of the snow which had so often made the roads impassable earlier in the year.

There were evenings when they stopped at an inn where clouds of steam would rise from Luke and Mr Delacote's clothes the moment they were in front of a blazing fire. Both men were showing signs of strain and had little to say during meal times.

But at last came the day when Helen announced they were not far away from the house. She became animated, pointing out landmarks as they drove along a narrow lane.

The day was sunny, the air clear and fresh. The windows of the carriage were opened and Gabrielle could smell the sea and taste salt on her lips.

Then the vista opened and the sea was before them, the waves choppy and white-capped. 'Oh, how lovely,' Gabrielle exclaimed.

'And there is the house–' Helen pointed ahead.

It was large, stone built with steep roofs and high chimneys. Gabrielle felt a rise of excitement, feeling it was worth all the tedium of the long journey. The main windows of the house faced the sea. They were large and heavily mullioned. The entrance was like that of a church, with its massive oak doors. And when they were out of the carriage and a man and a woman came out, Gabrielle saw there was a porch with another door leading into the hall.

She had only time to notice that the bushes beneath the windows leaned away from the prevailing wind before Helen introduced her to Mr and Mrs Curnow, the housekeeper and her husband.

Mrs Curnow bobbed a curtsy. 'It's good to have you with us again, m'lady.' To Luke she added shyly, 'And you too, sir.' To Gabrielle she said, 'Welcome, Ma'am.' Gabrielle was captivated by the soft burr of the woman's voice.

There were stairs at either side of the spacious hall and in the centre a massive wooden chandelier was suspended from the ceiling by a chain that looked as thick as an anchor chain.

A fire blazed in the hall and there was one in each bedroom. Helen stood hesitant in the room she finally assigned to Gabrielle. She glanced at the double bed then said brightly, 'So, *Miss Norton,* what do we do? Give Mr Luke Caltahn another room? Unfortunately, none of them actually adjoin. I could have a bed put in the dressing room, but it is rather small–'

'No – give Luke this room. I shall be quite happy in a single bed.' Gabrielle paused then said quietly, 'Helen, I think it only right you should know there is a little rift between Luke and myself at the moment. It will make it easier for me than having to pretend everything is so lovely and romantic.'

Helen smiled in a consoling way and put a hand on Gabrielle's arm. 'It happens to every couple, but I feel sure the rift will be only temporary. Ah, there is the gong, the meal is ready. This air gives me a tremendous appetite.'

The long dining table, which was made out of solid oak, looked big enough to seat thirty people. Helen's servants had already settled in and were helping to wait on table. The fare was simple and excellently cooked. All did justice to it. Luke and Mr Delacote did offer conversation but most of the time were preoccupied. After the meal they excused themselves, and Helen suggested that Gabrielle might want to look at the garden and the surrounding land.

They started at the back of the house. There were a number of buildings that were separate from the house, then an archway which led into a cobbled courtyard. Here were stables and store houses. Gabrielle could hear voices and the next moment a door of one of the store houses opened and Luke and Mr Delacote came out.

Helen said to Luke, 'Would you and Mr Delacote care to join my conducted tour?' She spoke lightly.

'Why not?' Luke spoke in equally light vein, but he was frowning.

They came out of the courtyard and round to the front of the house. There was a high wall to the right and a low wall that ran all the way round. Stone steps led to a spacious lawn. The grass was a rich shade of emerald green and the borders were alive with purple and yellow crocuses and daffodils. At the end of the lawn more steps led to a grassy and gorselined path to the cove. Luke went first, holding out a hand and saying to Gabrielle, 'Careful.' Mr Delacote followed, holding out a hand to Helen. Luke's grip tightened as Gabrielle made one stumble. At the bottom he caught her by the waist and lifted her on to the sand. He held her to him for a moment and Gabrielle had a slightly breathless feeling knowing the touch of her had affected him.

The cove, a half moon of fine sand was interspersed with groups of rocks, some of them pinnacled. The wind, coming from the water, billowed out Gabrielle's cloak, blew her hood back and tossed her curls about her face. Exhilarated she stood, her head up, enjoying it. 'How marvellous,' she exclaimed.

Helen laughed. 'This lovely weather lends enchantment, but wait until a storm comes. Then the spray from the waves crashing on to the rocks can drench a person standing on the cliff top.'

She then mentioned there was another cove beyond the rocks and they made towards it.

Helen stopped at a rock pool and peered into it. 'Oh, look, what a beautiful shell. I must have it for my collection.'

Gabrielle rolled up her sleeve and plunged her hand into the water. She held out the shell. 'There, and it is beautiful.' The shell was a deep rose on the outside and the pearl inside a delicate green. 'You must show me your collection.'

Gabrielle was looking for more shells in the water when Luke picked up a piece of seaweed and drew it lightly over her bare arm. The effect it had on Gabrielle was startling. Her whole body responded to the sensuous action. And that it was intended to be sensuous showed in the darkness of Luke's grey eyes.

Helen said, 'There are caves in the next cove, I think smugglers must have used them at one time.'

Luke's expression quickly changed. 'Rubbish,' he said. 'They would be useless for smuggling. Not only are they small but they would be flooded at high tide.'

Mr Delacote pointed out a shell in another pool and the moment passed, but Gabrielle for some reason felt uneasy. Why should Luke be annoyed at the mention of smuggling? Was it because of her grandmother stealing his cargoes?

Luke led the way past the caves towards a path that rose to the headland. This path was well trodden and wound in parts, making it easier to climb. The top of the path brought them to the opposite side of the garden. As they approached it Gabrielle noticed a clump of bushes circling a number of stones. There were two tallish ones and seven of various sizes surrounding them.

'They look like a family,' she said.

Helen nodded. 'That is what they are supposed to represent. The legend goes that a couple and their seven children lived in the house and when they had to leave the husband placed the stones in the garden.'

'What a pity there are no names on them.'

'Perhaps he was unable to write.' This came from Mr Delacote, who examined the stones. He ran his fingers gently over the smaller of the two larger stones and Gabrielle, sensing he was thinking of his wife, was touched. 'I think it a lovely story,' he said. 'I feel they were a happy family, I wonder what their names were? Shall we give them names?' He addressed this to Gabrielle.

'Well, I can give you the names I planned for all of my children.'

'All?' Luke queried, his eyebrows raised.

'Yes, all ten of them.'

'Ten? Oh my, lucky me! I shall look forward to beginning this new dynasty. What a proud papa I shall be. A Romany once told me I would sire five sons and five daughters.'

'What a coincidence. That is exactly how I planned the names.'

'Splendid.'

When they walked on towards the house Luke cupped a hand under Gabrielle's elbow. His close proximity gave her a shivery feeling of excitement, especially as she sensed that Luke's emotions too were aroused. Perhaps this evening she would not be sleeping alone!

But Gabrielle did sleep alone that night. She undressed and climbed in to bed, and waited – knowing Luke had not come upstairs. The house was quiet and the only sound was the soft swish of the water against the rocks. Had Luke perhaps fallen asleep in a chair? She kept straining listening for footsteps, yet knew that Luke never crept about no matter what time he came to bed.

At last she got up. If there was a light on in the study, where no doubt he would be, she would go to him, tell him that she loved him. Gabrielle put on a robe, went to the door, opened it carefully and stepped out on to the landing. She froze. Luke and a strange man were crossing the hall, boxes in their arms. Their footsteps made no sound. A small pool of light lay on the hall floor from the open door of the study. The two men went in. The door closed.

Gabrielle, her heart thumping madly, came to a decision. She raced down the stairs on silent feet, slid into the open doorway of the drawing room opposite and waited. For a few moments she could hear nothing for the thumping of her heart, but as it steadied she was aware of voices, of the men speaking in low tones

She was not sure how long she had waited when the door opened and the stranger came out. Luke walked with him to the front door, said something to the man before he left and closed the heavy door silently after him. To Gabrielle's surprise when Luke went back into the study he spoke to someone else. Although Luke had not closed the door this time she found it impossible to see who it was. What she did see was an array of silver set out on the desk. Then a hand came into view, with a diamond necklace dangling from the forefinger. Luke nodded then he came over and closed the door. Gabrielle, afraid of being caught, took the opportunity to run back upstairs again.

Once inside her room she dropped to her knees in front of the dying fire, with a host of questions hammering at her.

Who was the stranger, who was the person in the study with Luke? Where had the silver come from, and the necklace? Was he involved in smuggling? Was this the real reason he had come to Cornwall knowing what spoils he could acquire?

When they had come up from the cove it had occurred to Gabrielle that Luke, having known about the caves and that they were flooded at high tide, had been to Ninestones before. Helen said yes, Luke had been several times, on his own, when he had felt the need to be isolated.

Which left Gabrielle wondering now if the hinted abduction by her grandmother had been a ruse of Luke's to get Helen to open up the house. The authorities may have become suspicious of Luke's activities and it was possible he thought it would give more credence to his innocence if Lady Norton and her ward were with him.

Gabrielle made up her mind to confront Luke with what she had witnessed, determined that neither she nor Helen were going to be involved in his nefarious pursuits.

# CHAPTER SIXTEEN

The next morning the whole area was blanketed in fog. Earlier Gabrielle had learned from Helen that Luke had gone out. She stood now at the big mullioned window on the landing. Not even a bush could be glimpsed in the garden. The lowing of cattle had as mournful a sound as the deep, hollow tones of the foghorn on the point.

Footsteps along the landing made Gabrielle turn. Mr Delacote greeted her. 'Good morning, Mrs – Miss Norton–' He smiled a little sheepishly at his near slip. 'I overslept. But judging by the weather I doubt that it matters.'

'Will the fog lift do you think?'

He raised his shoulders. 'I understand it can persist for days. I would advise you not to venture out while it lasts, but no doubt the captain, or Lady Norton has already warned you.'

'Helen did mention it, but Mr Caltahn has already ventured into the murk.' Gabrielle paused then looked at the surgeon with pleading. 'Mr Delacote, I must talk with you.' She looked about her. 'It would be more private in the study, would you–?'

'Yes, of course.'

Helen, pleading a headache, had gone to lie down for a while, so they were unlikely to be interrupted.

Mr Delacote drew chairs up to the fire. 'And now, what seems to be the trouble?' He smiled encouragingly, but for once his smile did not wholly dispel his habitual melancholic expression.

Gabrielle described what she had seen and begged Mr Delacote to clarify it for her. His face immediately took on a closed look.

'I'm sorry, but I know nothing of the captain's affairs – Miss Norton. You must ask him yourself.'

'But you must know if he is involved in smuggling?'

'Dear lady, I enjoy talking with you, enjoy your company, but I will not discuss the captain's affairs.'

'No, and I had no right to ask you to, Mr Delacote. I was being most unfair, forgive me.'

'There is nothing to forgive. If I may be so presumptuous, Miss Norton, do not question the captain. He is a man of integrity and it may cause an upset if you suggested that he – you do understand?'

'Yes, and I shall probably take your advice.'

But not, Gabrielle thought, about venturing into the fog.

When Mr Delacote said he thought he would go back to his room and read for a while Gabrielle got her cloak and went out.

The fog swirled about her, catching at her throat, and putting a film of dampness on her cloak. She trod carefully. At times the fog would clear in patches and she would see the way ahead clearly, but in seconds it would close in on her again.

Every sound was muffled. The seagulls must have gone inland because their cries seemed to come from quite a distance away. The only other sound apart from the gulls and the foghorn was the gentle swish of the water. The sea must be calm.

Gabrielle felt her way along the wall. When she reached the opening in the wall she hesitated. Would she be foolish to venture outside its protection? It was another clear patch that decided her. If the fog kept moving she could not get lost.

She had walked quite a way when during a lifting of the fog she saw a figure standing near the cliff edge, and knew it was Luke. It gave Gabrielle quite a turn to realise she had travelled in the direction of the cliff edge. She was so sure she had been walking away from it. She called Luke's name and he turned his head towards her. He came quickly to her.

'How foolhardy of you to venture out in this weather.'

'How foolhardy of you.'

'I know the area... Come along, you must go back.' He took hold of her arm, chiding her, declaring there were times when she behaved like a child.

'I'm not a child, I'm not a married woman, I'm nothing. I have no identity, I'm a nonentity!'

'Oh, be quiet.'

'I won't be quiet. I wanted to see you, wanted to tell you that I saw you last night, with all the silver and–'

His face changed. He was so angry Gabrielle felt a momentary fear. 'How dare you spy on me! How dare you?'

'I was not spying. I was waiting for you, thinking you might come to bed and when you didn't I went downstairs to look for you.'

'To come to *your* bed?"

'Yes.' She said it defiantly.

'So you were waiting for me, wanted me. Well, you can have me now.' He took her by the hand and started to walk quickly in the direction of the house. She had to take running steps to keep up with him.

'No,' she said, 'I don't want you like this, not in this rough way.'

'You are getting me,' he replied grimly.

'I shall scream.'

'If you do I shall gag you and take you right here and now.'

It was lack of breath that prevented Gabrielle from making any further protest. She was determined, however, when they did get to their room she would resist him.

But Luke did not take her to the house. He ran her in the direction of the outhouses outside the courtyard. There he opened one of the doors and lifting her up, dropped her on to a bale.

Gabrielle was incensed. 'In a shed! Like a whore! How *dare* you treat me in such fashion.'

'I'm treating you as my wife. I want you and you want me, so stop protesting and unbutton your cloak.' Luke was already taking off his greatcoat.

'I do *not* want you, not in this way.' Gabrielle's voice was less vehement. Against her will she was roused by Luke's demands. Thrill after thrill was running through her body. She fought against it. She would not 'pleasure' him, she would remain passive as she had done the last time when he took her without tenderness. She unbuttoned her cloak and the bodice of her dress, not wanting the buttons torn from them as Luke had done on the ship. Luke, obviously taking this as a sign she was 'panting' for him, came over to her with a quick intake of breath.

Gabrielle longed to put her arms around him, cling to him, but she resisted. She must get Luke to understand that as long as he wanted to take her in this way he would get no co-operation from her. She lay passive.

Luke wasted no time on the act, which made Gabrielle furious. 'You are no more than an animal, I hate you,' she said through clenched teeth.

'Hate is better than indifference,' he replied calmly, and began to dress. He lifted her from the bale and touched her cheek. 'You miss so much, my dear Gabrielle, by being stubborn. Come along, I shall take you back to the house.'

'I shall go alone. I would hate to be with you and meet one of the men, with you looking like a cat who has sampled the cream.'

'Up to now, my love, I've sampled only the whey,' Luke spoke softly. 'But there might come a time when I shall have the pleasure of sampling the cream. Now I'm taking you back to the house no matter who we might meet on the way, so say no more.'

They walked in silence with Gabrielle dragging her feet. Luke left her beside the hall fire, telling her he would be back for the midday meal.

I hate him, I hate him, she kept saying to herself as she let the heat of the fire seep into her chilled body. But as she said it she knew regret she had not responded to him, then perhaps they might begin to enjoy a marriage that at the moment was a travesty of one.

When Luke came in at midday he and Mr Delacote had an earnest conversation. During the meal the conversation centred on previous fogs and storms and afterwards the two men left, with Luke saying they may not be back that evening.

'Where are you going in this fog?' Helen asked. 'And where will you be staying?'

Luke gave a brief smile. 'I think we can manage to find a bed. I do have friends. Stay indoors and keep warm, ladies.'

Helen raised her shoulders. 'Really, men can be so infuriating. I know Luke has friends at Sennen, but to go so far in such weather— Well, we shall just have to try and amuse ourselves, Gabrielle. Would you like to start a piece of tapestry, I have one nearly completed and I need another for a pair of footstools.'

Gabrielle agreed and they sat by the fire. plying their needles with Helen chatting about social activities in London. Gabrielle looked up.

'How is Stephen, have you seen him recently? And Lord Sharalon?'

'I saw both about a week ago. Stephen is unable to get over the fact that you married Luke. It gave everyone a surprise. Edmund declared himself bereft, but then you know how dramatic the dear boy can be.'

Gabrielle smiled to herself, picturing Lord Sharalon's extravagant phrases. Helen laughed. 'He kept saying he deserved to be shot for not asking for your hand the moment you first met. Other men said they should have seized the opportunity of asking for your hand. The ego of them! All men think a woman is waiting to fall into their arms.' Helen sobered. 'Actually, the one most deeply affected was Stephen. He wanted only your happiness. He kept asking me over and over again if I thought it would be a good marriage.'

'And what did you tell him?'

'I told him I thought it would be a perfect union.'

Gabrielle eyed her with some curiosity. 'What makes you so sure? Luke can be – difficult, he needs understanding.'

'Luke is the kind of person who will have only one real love in his life and that woman will be everything to him. I think his arrogance is a veneer, that under it is a gentleness, which he is afraid to show because of being thought weak. He will always be master, but a woman with subtlety will be able to twist him round her finger.'

'And what subtlety would you suggest?' Gabrielle asked lightly.

Helen eyed her solemnly. 'Luke needs a lot of love. But then, I think you know that, Gabrielle.'

Gabrielle wondered if this talk was because Helen knew what was lacking in their marriage and wanted to put it right.

'Yes,' she said, 'I do know, but perhaps I am not – giving him enough. It takes time to – well, make a marriage work.'

'Oh yes, indeed.' Helen put down her work and leaning back closed her eyes. 'My headache is returning. Perhaps it was foolish to attempt working on my tapestry. A migraine, my mother suffered dreadfully from them.'

The pain became so bad Marie persuaded her mistress to take a few drops of laudanum and retire. Helen resisted at first, worrying at leaving Gabrielle on her own, but left with Gabrielle's assurance she had a book and could settle easily.

In spite of this assurance, however, Gabrielle was restless. The time dragged. What were Luke and Mr Delacote doing? Sitting at the fire of some inn? Had the fog lifted? Eventually, she went for her cloak. A short walk might settle her. If she went out by the back door she could walk as far as the stables without mishap. It would be impossible to get lost, the pathway was bush-lined and there were two thick-trunked trees at the end of it.

Gabrielle was near the end of the path when she heard a man speaking. There was something conspiratorial in the way he spoke and she stepped behind a tree trunk, her heartbeats quickening.

'I tell you, it's tonight. The ship's been laying off all day. Cap'n went to Sennen to muster a few more men.'

Another man murmured something about it being dangerous, but the first man dismissed it, saying that mules were sure-footed and could find their way up blindfolded. The footsteps moved away.

Gabrielle waited a few moments then stepped into the path. What ship, and what had mules to do with it? She walked slowly back towards the house. Smugglers used mules to transport cargoes–

Once this was firmly established in Gabrielle's mind the more convinced she was that Luke and Mr Delacote were involved in smuggling that evening.

At ten o'clock she went up to bed, but not with the intention of sleeping. She must try and find out what was going on. A wind was getting up. Would this dispel the fog?

Gabrielle paused on her way up to bed to look out of the big mullioned window at the end of the landing. The draught blew out the candle she was carrying. She set the holder on the floor and wrapped her arms about herself, trying to still a sudden trembling of her limbs. The scene from the window had an eeriness, with the fog shifting in patches and shadows conjuring up distorted shapes. Where were Luke and Mr Delacote? Standing on the cliff top, or in the cove below waiting for the small boats to bring the smuggled goods ashore?

She became aware of the acrid smell of candles being snuffed and glancing into the hall saw Mr Curnow putting out the candles in the massive chandelier. Gabrielle went along to her room.

She lay on the bed fully clothed, watching the firelight flickering on the ceiling. It would not be easy to venture out into the night when the time came, but it was something she had to do. If only it had been moonlight, but then moonlight was not something smugglers would want for their activities.

When Gabrielle felt her eyelids begin to droop she climbed from the bed and knelt in front of the fire. She must keep awake.

The house was full of creakings as it began to cool. The wind seemed to be stronger. She got up and went to the window. The fog was dispersing leaving much wider, clearer areas. The minutes were dragging so much she felt at one time like abandoning her plan to go and get into bed instead.

In the end, unable to contain herself any longer, she put on her cloak, a pair of stout shoes and tied a lacy scarf firmly over her head.

There were no other sounds when she

crept downstairs but the creakings and the low moaning of the wind. Neither the inner doors or the outer one was bolted, but both were heavy to open. The outer, as careful as she was in closing it, banged shut. She stood for a moment, her breath held, then released it. The mist was constantly shifting, in places it was like the smoke from a witch's cauldron, swirling then drifting away. Once her eyes had become accustomed to the darkness Gabrielle moved cautiously along in front of the house, wanting the protection of the wall before coming out into the open.

Her fear was less now she was actually doing something. In fact, there was a small tingling of excitement in her. What would she find? She started towards the path that led towards the cove then stopped abruptly as the mist cleared and she saw two figures standing at the top of the cliff. She drew back to the shelter of some bushes, her heart pounding. Before the mist closed in again she had seen they were two men, both short, both carrying guns. Guns–?

Taking advantage of the men being blotted out by the mist she raced to the edge of the cliff then dropped on to her stomach, hoping the furze would keep her from the men's view. A lurking fear kept her rigid. Was Luke involved in something in the cove and were they customs' men waiting to catch him? Would she be able to get down the path without being seen and warn him?

Gabrielle moved closer to the edge and peered into the cove – and gave a gasp of astonishment.

The cove was a hive of activity, men getting out of boats, others packing bundles on to the backs of mules. It was like being in a dream and seeing everything through a veil of mist. Two tall figures were standing at the water's edge waving lanterns aloft. Luke and Mr Delacote! As Gabrielle watched, two more rowing boats came out of the veil over the sea and beached. As parts of the cliff-path cleared she could see other men with guns. Obviously guards. It was a wholesale operation!

The wind began to strengthen. It blew the ends of her shawl across her face and she tied them at the back. She waited until the first of the mules was being led up the path then she made her way back to the house, in spurts, making a run, then dropping flat, depending always on the covering mist.

Back at the house she stood trying to regain her breath. There would be no going to bed until she knew where they were taking the contraband, then she could accuse Luke. She stood behind the opening in the high wall, keeping flat against it. Once the contingent had passed she could follow at a distance. Taking a peep out she saw the ghostly caravan of loaded mules, their hooves muffled. She had expected them to be taken out on to the road, but to her surprise they were led to the back of the house.

Surely Luke would not be so foolish as to stock the goods here.

After waiting a while she made her way cautiously to the back. If the men made any sound it was lost in the rising of the wind. The light of a single lantern from one of the outhouses cast a glow on the hard-packed ground. It was the only warmth in the blackness of the night. Gabrielle sought shelter in a shed opposite. With the door slightly ajar she watched until the last mule and man had gone then ventured out. She had not seen Luke and Mr Delacote leave so presumed they were in the outhouse.

Going across to it she hesitated a moment then opened the door, releasing a mingled smell of tar and wood and oiled canvas.

In the glow of the lantern she saw Luke's startled face. He was alone.

'In God's name, Gabrielle – what are *you* doing here?'

'You might ask! I saw you all in the cove. Smuggling! And to think when I first saw men on the cliff top with guns I was worried and wondered how I could warn you. I thought they were revenue men. All this–' Gabrielle waved a hand towards the bales and wooden kegs. 'Brought here under secrecy to avoid paying revenue. Do you know the penalty if you had been caught?'

'Oh, yes, I know the penalty.' Luke had recovered from his surprise and was regarding her in an amused way. It incensed her.

'If you have no care for your own skin then you should consider the families of the men helping you. How would wives and children live if husbands were hanged or transported? But I suppose that matters little to you.'

'That's enough, Gabrielle. Now get out of here.'

'You even brought Mr Delacote into your criminal activities. But then you have a very persuasive tongue.'

'Then perhaps I can persuade you to go to your bed and leave me to my checking.' His tone was icy.

'I have not finished what I want to say.'

Luke took a step towards her. 'If you do not leave here immediately I shall put you out bodily.' Although his voice was under control Gabrielle knew he meant it.

'Very well, I shall go, but this is not the end of it.'

Luke gripped her by the shoulders. 'Gabrielle, this is the end of it as far as you are concerned. You will say no more to me about it or anyone else. Is that understood?'

She tried to stare him out, but her gaze

dropped at the anger in his eyes. 'You will hear no more from me.'

'Good, now get to your bed.' He turned her, gave her a push, then opened the door. Gabrielle paused then asked where Mr Delacote was, and was told it was none of her business. The next moment she was out in the blackness and the wind, wishing now she had never interfered.

She made her way to the house.

# CHAPTER SEVENTEEN

Gabrielle breakfasted alone the following morning. Helen, although her headache had eased, looked drained and decided to stay in bed that morning. Of Luke and Mr Delacote there was no sign. Mrs Curnow said she thought the menfolk had gone out early, and clucked her tongue. It was to be hoped they had not gone far, a big storm was brewing. The wind had been 'teasy' all night.

Later, Gabrielle was standing by the fire in the hall when Luke came in. He rubbed his hands and came to the fire. 'Good morning, Gabrielle.' He paused. 'I think perhaps I owe you an explanation.' He glanced around him to see they were alone and turned to her and added, in a low voice, 'What you saw last night was a replacement of what your grandmother took from me. Wagons would have come this evening to remove the 'evidence', and may still do, but Mr Curnow tells me we are in for a bad storm.'

Gabrielle nodded. 'Yes, so Mrs Curnow told me.'

'Once the storm has passed the cargo will

be taken to Bodmin and sold, I have a buyer. Incidentally, it was Mr Delacote's own wish to be involved. If you remember he suffered too at Hesther Quantock's hands.' Luke could not mention her grandmother's name without his tone becoming bitter. Which was understandable.

'Thank you for telling me, Luke. I apologize for behaving the way I did.'

He touched her cheek gently. 'I think perhaps we are both behaving a little out of character with all the upset we have had. I must go out again, but if the wind isn't too strong perhaps we can have a walk to the cove later.'

'I would like that,' she said.

Gabrielle felt happier than she had been for some time. It had given her a taste of what their life could be together if both of them acted in a more amenable fashion.

Unfortunately they did not get their walk to the cove. The wind was so strong it took one's breath away to venture out of doors. By evening it was a howling gale. Helen and Mr Delacote and Luke and Gabrielle sat round the hall fire, which was the only chimney that was not belching down puffs of smoke.

When Mrs Curnow came in with bedtime drinks she said, 'I sent the girls to bed early, m'lady, we're in for a troublesome night. May I beg that no one opens doors or windows or we'll have the old wind rampaging like a mad thing. And it might be wise to turn out the lamps. If someone did happen to open a door and a lamp got knocked over—'

'I shall see to it,' Helen said. 'Later.'

Luke got up and turned them all out, saying it was better to be safe than sorry.

Seconds later the rain came. It lashed against the panes with the wind howling round the eaves. Gabrielle looked up at the ceiling. 'I hope the roof holds.'

'They do get carried away in gales like this,' Helen said, 'but this one will be all right. The house has withstood many storms for over a hundred years. I feel sure it will survive this one.'

They were silent as they sipped at their drinks. The wind by now was screaming round the house like a thousand demoniacal witches, and underlying it was the sound of the waves pounding against the cliff face. It was like thunder, rolling, crashing, booming – Gabrielle felt a thrill of fear. She had never known a storm like this. Every now and then there would be a tapping on the window as though someone was throwing a handful of tiny pebbles at it. Great gusts came battering at the house and as sturdily built as it was it seemed to shake to its foundations. Gabrielle's fear increased. Could the house withstand such violence?

Water from the gutters was a torrent, spilling over the already overflowing rain butts. Gabrielle looked around her and saw on the faces of all an anxiousness as to what would happen next. Helen's lips moved in silent prayer.

Luke said, 'God help the ships on a night like this. The coast will be scattered with their wrecks.'

'And women will lose sons,' Mr Delacote said quietly, 'and wives their husbands.'

Helen looked up. 'And children their fathers.'

There was a sudden lull in the storm and glances were exchanged. Was this the end? It was not the end but just a lull before a more vicious onslaught, like an army attacking an enemy stronghold.

The wind attacked the big mullioned window on the landing again and again, as though determined to gain entry. All eyes went to it. Then Helen sat up. 'Look, the window is bending, bowing in–!'

A great puff of smoke came down the chimney, they all jumped up and drew back, distracting them momentarily from the greater danger.

Suddenly there was a terrific crash, followed by another and a massive shattering of glass. And as the wind roared through the apertures people and chairs were sent helter-skelter to the far side of the hall, with tables and ornaments crashing around them.

Gabrielle, terror-stricken, spread-eagled against the wall, screamed, 'Luke–' but the word was lost in the fury of the wind.

All the candles but two on the massive chandelier had been extinguished, and she watched in horror as the chandelier began to swing, moving back and forth at first then swinging in circles on the heavy chain. Oh, God, if the ceiling came down.

She felt fingers touch her hand and saw Luke to her right straining to get a hold. She reached out and he held her hand tightly then signalled with his eyes to look to her left. Mr Delacote was trying to reach her. At last he caught hold of her other hand and Gabrielle saw he was holding on to Helen.

Luke signalled again to indicate the door to his right and began to edge towards it. At times the wind kept them captive against the wall and when they did manage to move it was inch by slow inch. At last they reached the door, only to find the force of the wind made it impossible to open it.

Gabrielle's gaze went to the chandelier and she watched with a horrified fascination as it still kept swinging madly, and unbelievably, with the two candles still burning. How long would the ceiling hold?

She had had to keep turning her head away from the force of the wind to catch her breath, and when she turned it this time she saw, as though in a nightmare, a head rising from the floor under the landing, followed by two arms. The arms began to wave. She tugged at Luke's hand urgently and nodded towards the head. He smiled briefly and Gabrielle realized then it was Mr Curnow. Relief flooded through her. She had thought she was going mad.

Mr Curnow, who was now further out of the trap-door, threw Luke a rope. Luke passed it back and with the aid of the rope they reached the stone steps that led to the cellars below. Mrs Curnow met them. 'Oh, goodness, what a terrible thing. When we heard the crash we guessed the landing window had gone.'

'And also the window in the hall,' Luke said.

Mr Curnow brought forward some wooden boxes, dusted them and placed them round an old iron wood burning stove he had lit. 'It'll give a bit of warmth,' he said.

Helen asked about the servants and Mrs Curnow told her they were all in the next cellar, she had brought them down when the storm got so bad.

Gabrielle turned anxiously to Mr Delacote. He looked deadly pale. To her query as to whether he was all right, he managed a wan smile. 'A little shaken, but otherwise fine. I kept thinking we might all have been killed.'

Helen said, 'Did you notice that two of the candles remained lit on the chandelier. It was a phenomenon. It meant that we were never in complete darkness. It seemed more than a glow from two candles. Could there have been a divine light to compensate us?'

'Perhaps,' Luke said quietly. 'The important thing is we are all safe, thanks to Mr Curnow. If that ceiling had come down...'

'It could still come down,' Mr Delacote said grimly.

'We are not going to think about it.' Helen turned to Mr Curnow. 'Mr Curnow, do you have the keys to the wine cellar?'

'Yes, M'lady.' He rattled them.

'Then bring a bottle of the best brandy ... and some glasses. I think we have good cause to drink a toast.'

Gabrielle pushed back her hair then gave a little shiver. When she looked up she met Luke's gaze. There was concern in his eyes.

'Are you all right, Gabrielle?'

'Yes, thank you, although I must admit I found it a terrifying experience.'

'We all did. I think we would be lying if any of us said otherwise.' Luke drew his box nearer. 'Are you sure you feel all right, Gabrielle? You look cold.' He took her hands in his. 'They feel like ice.'

Luke's hands were surprisingly warm. When she mentioned it he grinned. 'My hot blood.' Then soberly he added, 'I could have lost you.'

Mr Curnow came in with the brandy. Luke released her hands. 'The brandy will revive us all.'

Although Luke was no longer holding her, his warmth remained. Gabrielle waited to join the toast to their rescuer – and to hope this was a new beginning to their marriage.

After an hour some of the fury went out of the wind, but it was several hours more before the storm finally died away. They came out of the cellar, stiff and chilled, and eyed the chaos in the cold light of dawn.

The morning was so still had it not been for the littered floor and the gaping window frames one could imagine the storm had never happened.

'Thank heavens the ceiling held,' Luke said. 'Whoever hung that chandelier must have had faith in its strength.'

They talked about the chandelier and the ceiling as though they were the most important things in their lives at that moment, probably because they had survived against all odds. It gave a touch of stability in the devastation.

Mrs Curnow and the grey-faced servants began straightening the furniture, picking up pieces of wood, broken chair backs and legs and sweeping up fragments of china and glass. Mr Curnow said he would go and get the glaziers to attend to the windows.

They went outside to see what damage had been done. It was warmer out of doors than in the hall. The only damage to the house was, surprisingly, on the lee side where a number of tiles were missing. Mr Curnow said they must have been 'sucked' off by the wind. Unhappily a whole winter's stock of the hay had been scattered. Proof of it was in the clumps of straw clinging to drystone walls, to briars and bushes. In the courtyard lay several dead gulls, in seeking shelter they had been flung by the wind against the walls. All the sheds were miraculously intact, but through a gap in the roof of the hen-house rain had deluged, drowning some of the birds.

'I wonder how other people in the district have fared?' Helen said.

Luke and Mr Delacote rode off to investigate, and came back with news of damage to homes and barns, of fishing boats battered and farm wagons damaged.

Luke paused and looked around him. 'Where is Helen?'

'With her bailiff. He came to call about the repairs and the alterations she's planning.' Luke and Mr Delacote exchanged quick glances and Gabrielle said, 'It's all right. They only seemed interested in the damage to the henhouse. They never looked at – the shed.'

Luke said, 'Mr Delacote knows you saw us last night, Gabrielle. We are hoping to empty the shed tonight. I'm telling you because I do not want you anywhere near. That is an order, there will be no disobeying.'

'I thought you said farm wagons are damaged, so how?'

'The men are working on them. They should be ready in time. Will you tell Mrs Curnow we will not be in for any meals today. And remember, Gabrielle, what I said. No coming to investigate. Go to bed and stay there.' He ran a finger lightly down her cheek and added in an undertone, 'Keep the bed warm for me.'

He had a devilish look in his eyes which made Gabrielle's senses leap in response. 'Oh, I will,' she said softly.

The two men mounted and before the horses moved away Luke gave her a wave and a grin. Mr Delacote raised his hat, his expression melancholic.

Gabrielle was puzzled about Mr Delacote. They had been such good friends on the ship, but since coming to Cornwall it seemed he avoided her. Did he feel guilty for having caused the rift between Luke and herself?

But the rift was over. Gabrielle walked with a joyousness in the direction of the cove. Tonight ... tonight she would show

Luke how much she loved him.

As Gabrielle descended into the cove her joyousness died and she wished she had not come. The cove was strewn with debris, bits of timber, a piece of material that looked like part of a man's shirt, a sea boot, a woollen stocking and a tricorne hat. Near the waterlines gulls swooped with greedy cries on the dead fish that lay in small shoals.

Sickened, Gabrielle retraced her steps up the path then walked along the cliff top. But seeing more evidence of boats being wrecked she returned to the house. There Helen told her she would have to sleep in another room. 'You would catch your death of cold,' she said, 'come and see.

A fine spray had forced its way between the cracks of the window frames, not only laying a dampness on the carpet and bed and furniture but also soaking the wallpaper right to the far side.

Gabrielle was unwilling to change to another room, knowing Luke would be coming to her that night, but Helen was adamant. 'It would be foolish to sleep here. I'll show you a cosy room that is quite unaffected by the damp. It overlooks the courtyard.'

The courtyard? Well, at least she could watch for Luke, catch him as he came upstairs. The room *was* cosy, and although the bed was smaller than the double one Gabrielle thought it would be big enough if she curled up against Luke. 'Yes,' she said, 'this is quite nice.'

Gabrielle for the rest of the day had a feeling of waiting. Both she and Helen went to lie down after lunch to catch up on lost sleep, but Gabrielle found it impossible to sleep. Her mind shifted from one thing to another. Was her father now fully recovered? Would they be back in London for his return? They must be. He would feel utterly lost if he arrived at Helen's house and no one was there to welcome him. Was Stephen really upset by her marriage, had he really wanted to marry her himself? Dear Stephen. And then she thought of Mr Delacote. It seemed he was quite deeply involved with Luke in this 'smuggling'. It worried her that he was so distant. Perhaps Luke had objected to their friendship. There was certainly no reason for him to be jealous of her friendship with a man old enough to be her father. Gabrielle semi-dozed, and got up feeling worse than when she had lain down.

The rest of the day dragged. She and Helen played cards in the evening and went to bed at ten o'clock. Marie came in with some of Gabrielle's clothes from the other room. They too were damp, she said. She hung them in the press, stroking the sea-green dress and saying how she wished she was rich enough to wear such beautiful things. Then she said, 'I wouldn't mind marrying an old man if he were wealthy.'

Gabrielle scolded her gently. 'Marie, you are young, attractive, you must marry for love. Money is not important, it does not necessarily bring happiness.'

She grumbled that this was the cry of the people who had plenty of money. She gave Gabrielle a sly look. 'Will you marry for love, Madam?'

Gabrielle did not like Marie's expression. It made her feel the girl knew that she and Luke were married.

'Of course I shall,' she said lightly. And then dismissed Marie. The girl looked resentful as she left.

Gabrielle brought a chair to the window so she could watch the courtyard. There was a moon and although there was a haze over it everything in the courtyard was clearly visible. It was not the sort of night she would have expected men to move contraband.

There were a few clouds but when they obscured the moon it was only for seconds. She had let the fire die out and as she sat in the darkened room without logs sparking to keep her alert, and without even a sound from the courtyard, she found it difficult at times to keep awake. When Gabrielle had laid down during the afternoon she had purposely stopped herself from thinking about Luke. Wanting to save all her emotion for nearer the time when Luke would come to her. But now she kept experiencing sensual twinges. Oh, what a wonderful re-union she would make it. Luke would have no cause to accuse her of lack of response.

She stifled a yawn. Heavens, a sleepy wife was not what Luke would expect. Perhaps if she closed her eyes for a few moments she might get rid of the gritted feeling under her lids.

It was the sound of men shouting that roused her. She jumped up and looked about her in a bewildered way. What was it, what was happening? She peered out of the window then stood transfixed as she saw beyond the arch of the courtyard men waving wooden staves, fighting. Without thought of safety and totalling disregarding Luke's order not to attempt to come out to investigate, she grabbed her cloak and ran out and down the stairs.

She was halfway down when she heard Helen call from the landing. 'Gabrielle, Gabrielle, don't go out there! It could be dangerous.'

'I must – Luke–'

Mr Curnow came hurrying into the hall followed by his wife. Helen shouted, 'Mr Curnow, get the guns quickly.'

Gabrielle ran past him and made her way to the back of the house, her heart thudding wildly. Once outside she kept close to the sheds. From the hen-house and the stables came the mingled squawking of birds and a stomping and neighing of horses. From beyond the courtyard came angry shouts and groans of injured men in pain.

There was the clunk of stave on stave, the thud of the wood on bodies, and a snorting of terror from rearing horses. Reaching the archway Gabrielle stopped. There were three loaded wagons and the fight seemed to be to get charge of them. There must have been twenty or more men. The door of the shed was open and in the light of the lamp she could see Mr Delacote standing as though petrified. Without thought Gabrielle rushed to the shed, grabbed him by the hand and started pulling him. She got him through to the courtyard and ordered him to go into the house.

'No, no,' he protested, as though suddenly coming to life. 'I want to help.' His whole body was trembling.

Helen and Mr Curnow came rushing out of the house, both carrying guns. Servants followed with Mrs Curnow, but the housekeeper kept her flock huddled together. Gabrielle dragged Mr Delacote towards her and said, 'Please take care of him. I must know what has happened to Luke.'

Mrs Curnow called her back but Gabrielle ran on. This time she saw a man on horseback who was shouting, 'Get the wagons away, *now* and no killing, that is an order!'

As men tried to climb on to the driving seats they were dragged away. Several wooden staves knocked from hands lay on the ground. Gabrielle picked one up and looked frantically around her for Luke. It was impossible to pick out anyone. There was just a melee of grunting men punching, pummelling–

There was a sudden double flash of fire followed by two shots that exploded into the night. For seconds all was still and the smell of gunpowder hung in the air. Then the fighting began again with renewed violence. Suddenly she was grabbed from behind and given a push.

'Get away from here, Gabrielle, get back to the house.' It was Luke. When she resisted him he shouted '*GABRIELLE* – for God's sake obey me for once!' He released her and she spun round, and saw the flash of a blade as it sliced down Luke's face. She screamed and raised her stave to beat off Luke's attacker but she was seized by the waist and dragged away.

A coarse voice said, 'So *you* are the Quantock wench.'

She shouted and fought, tried to wield the

stave, but it was knocked from her hand. The last thing she saw before being thrown over the back of a horse was blood streaming down Luke's face as he slid slowly to the ground. 'Oh, Luke, Luke,' she moaned.

The man mounted the horse, pulled her up in front of him and called to someone, 'I've got her, I'm goin' on ahead,' and kicked at the horse's flank with his heel.

Gabrielle began to struggle again. 'Let me go!'

His arm tightened about her waist. 'Shut up, or else–'

She still struggled and he yelled, 'If you don't shut up I'll gag you!'

The man stank and the thought of having a piece of dirty rag stuffed into her mouth was sufficient to make her subside.

The shouts and the sounds of the fighting diminished as they rode away from the house. Gabrielle thought if she kept quiet she might get a chance to escape from him and get back to Luke and Mr Delacote. Before they moved into the roadway there was the sound of a shot and she wondered, in a torment, if it had been Helen or Mr Curnow shooting, or if their guns had been seized and if–

Gabrielle dared not let her mind dwell on the thought that all of them could be lying there dead.

In all the nightmare an image of Luke came into her mind when she had spun round to face him. There had been a concern in his eyes for her she had not seen before.

It was not until the man urged the horse into a canter that it occurred to Gabrielle to wonder where he was taking her. Were they ravishers of women as well as thieves, and would all the girls from the house be brought to some hideaway? Gabrielle shuddered at the thought and knew she must get away somehow and seek help.

She suddenly went rigid as she felt the man's hand moving up to her breast. All her instinct was to fight him but common sense told her if she let him caress her, lull him into a false sense of acquiescence, she might, once he was off his guard, have a chance of escape. There was a sharp corner ahead where the horse would have to slow, and near the corner was a pile of loose stones she had noticed that afternoon. If she dug her elbow hard into his fat stomach and winded him she could slide from the horse and use the stones as weapons. A well-aimed one might knock him out.

His hand was now inside her bodice and fondling her breast and although Gabrielle's flesh was crawling she kept her gaze steadily on the road ahead. Any minute now they would be at the corner. She had drawn her arm right back preparing to make her blow a telling one when there came the sound of galloping hooves behind them and shouting.

The man withdrew his hand with a muttered curse.

The horseman reined beside them and an authoritative voice, which she recognised from the courtyard, said, 'Hitchins, get down at once.'

'What for?' The voice was sullen.

'You know perfectly well it was my task to take the girl. I know what you are and the order was that she was not to be harmed.'

'I ain't harmed her,' came the mutinous reply.

'And you will not get the chance to do so. Now get down.'

The newcomer was older and in a different class to the one who had kidnapped her, but Gabrielle was aware of a resistance in her captor. Then the horseman snapped, 'Get down when I tell you or else–' and drew out a pistol.

'All right, all right.' The man dismounted, grumbling under his breath that some folks got too big for themselves.

'Some one will pick you up, Hitchins.' To Gabrielle her rescuer said, 'Can you ride, Ma'am?'

When she told him yes he nodded. 'Good, and please no trying to escape or I shall have to tie you up and sling you like a bundle over my horse. I have orders to deliver you safely.'

'Whose orders?'

'That you will find out soon enough. Ready?'

Because this man was older and seemed more reasonable Gabrielle begged to know what had happened at the house. 'My – my friends, was there anyone – killed?'

'I only know that two of my men were, they were both shot. I had orders not to take guns, now I wish I had.'

'Please tell me whose orders you were acting under.'

He glanced at her. 'I am not at liberty to tell, but you will know soon. We have about another mile to go.'

'May I ask one more thing? Will the other girls at the house be brought to – to the place where I am being taken?'

'No, only you.'

Why me? she wondered. Then, as though the clip-clop of the horses' hooves were beating in her head, she knew why. Knew there could only be one person who would want more than anything to hold her captive. Oh, God.

Gabrielle looked about her frantically for a way of escape but there was nowhere she could go, even if she could manage to outpace the man at her side. He rode as if he had been riding horses all his life. He also had a more powerful animal.

Gabrielle's lips tightened. She would not be held captive. She would get away, not now perhaps but some time later.

Round the next bend in the road stood a black carriage, a team of four horses in the shafts. When they reached it the man at her side ordered her to dismount.

He held her arm firmly as they walked up to the carriage. The stiff-backed figure inside moved slightly forward and Gabrielle saw once more the hated bony face, the parchment skin and the hooded lidded eyes.

'So – my *dear* granddaughter – you are back once more in my care.'

Gabrielle's head went up. 'Not for long, Ma'am, I assure you.'

'You will be tied up until the day you marry and then you will know what it means to be tamed.'

Although her grandmother had not raised her voice the venom in it sent a coldness creeping over Gabrielle's body. She wanted to shout that she was already married to Luke Caltahn but something held her back. Perhaps it was the thought that the marriage might not be legal. She had had no proof. She said, 'I told you on Christmas Day, Ma'am, if I was forced into marriage I would kill myself. I am still of the same mind.'

'One has to have the means. Without it

you would be powerless.'

'I have the means, my own mind. I would will myself to die. Many people have. My will is as strong, if not stronger, than yours, Ma'am. I could make myself resistant to torture if necessary.'

There was a small silence as though her grandmother was weighing up such a possibility then she said, 'I imagine if your *father* was being tortured you would agree very quickly to marriage.'

'But my father is dead, Ma'am, you had him murdered.'

This shook the old lady. But only momentarily. 'Nonsense, your father is alive and well. I can have him picked up any time I like. So be warned. And I can tell you this, when my son knows I have you in my power he will *crawl* to me and *beg* for your life.'

The viciousness in her grandmother's voice then made Gabrielle feel that icy worms were crawling up and down her spine.

'You there,' she called to the horseman, 'take my granddaughter and tie her up and lock her up and if you let her escape your own life will be forfeit.'

The man came up and putting his hand under Gabrielle's elbow led her to the horse. When they were both mounted she glanced back. Would she ever be able to beat this woman who must surely have been spawned by the devil?

It was easy to speak of resisting torture, but if it came to the actuality it would be a very different thing. Not unless it was to save her father or Luke from death.

Then she could suffer torture – for love.

# CHAPTER EIGHTEEN

They had ridden for about ten minutes in silence when Gabrielle asked her captor his name. 'Call me Culver,' he said briefly.

'Tell me, Mr Culver, if I had been inside the house instead of outside how would you have known where to find me?'

'I knew.'

Gabrielle glanced at him quickly, finding something quite frightening about this remark. It meant that someone in the house must have told him. Not Mr or Mrs Curnow, she was sure of that. One of the younger servants? Knowing he would not be likely to reveal his source of information Gabrielle asked if they would be travelling far that night.

'We turn left at the next bend in the road,' he said. 'And I'm not answering any more questions.'

The lane was deeply rutted, slowing the horses, but once they reached some open ground Culver gave Gabrielle's horse a slap on the rump and they set off at a canter. Under different circumstances Gabrielle would have enjoyed the ride, the easy rhythm of the horse, the speed, the air rushing past her face, but it only served to remind her of the distance she was putting between those she loved and an unknown destination.

They went down another lane, across more open ground, where once, between a massive outcrop of rock, she caught a glimpse of the sea, looking like a lake of silver tranquility. Then they veered inland again and when they finally stopped it was in front of a cottage where a dim light showed between a gap in the curtains. The cottage was in the middle of a lane with no other sign of habitation.

An old woman came to the door and a boy who brushed past her took charge of the horses. Without a word he led them away. Culver put his hand under Gabrielle's elbow. 'We're staying here for tonight. It's simple but clean. Will you want anything to eat?'

She shook her head. 'No, only somewhere where I can lie down. I could die of weariness.'

Culver spoke to the old woman and she got a candle and motioned to Gabrielle to follow her. They went up a narrow staircase that led from the living room. There were two straw palliasses on the floor. They looked clean and so did the blankets. The toothless old woman said something but her dialect was so strong she was unable to follow. Once the woman had gone Gabrielle lay down fully dressed. Where would it all end? Even if she did manage to escape would she ever be free from her grandmother's hounding? Gabrielle felt suddenly choked. If only she knew what had happened to them all at Ninestones. Mr Delacote felled by a blow, Luke with a slash down his face – had Helen been shot? And what of Mr and Mrs Curnow? Had they managed to– Gabrielle slept.

When she awoke it was daylight. At first she had difficulty in placing where she was. When she remembered she sat up and looked about her. The other palliasse had been slept on, but whether by the old woman or Culver she had no idea.

There was the sound of a key being turned in the lock and Culver's voice asking if he could come in. Gabrielle threw back the blankets and called, 'Yes.'

He brought in a bowl of hot water and a towel, which he placed on the chair. 'Soap is in the water,' he said. 'We must leave soon.'

Gabrielle had thought of Culver as elderly. Now, in the light of the day she saw he was no older than her father, not an unattractive man but one who, at that moment, had a grey look as if he had not slept for days. A smell of bacon cooking drifted upstairs.

Culver said, 'Breakfast is nearly ready, is there anything else you need?'

'I doubt I would get them if I asked. I could do with a change of clothes, a hairbrush or a comb, a carriage to take me where we are going. I feel bone-weary. And *you*, if I may say so, look it.'

'I can imagine.' Culver's expression held a wryness. 'I did no more than cat-nap last night. Tonight I may have to tie you up.' He walked to the door. 'Come down when you are ready.'

Gabrielle washed and tidied herself as much as she could. She had thought it would be impossible to touch food but she ate the thick slice of bacon and the hunk of dry bread with relish. And felt better for it.

The only furniture in the room was a wooden table and two wooden forms, roughly hewn from tree trunks, but the simplicity, the cleanliness and the fire blazing in the stone hearth made Gabrielle reluctant to leave.

Culver said in a low voice, 'Look, I'm sorry.' When Gabrielle made no reply he got up and pushed back the wooden form. 'I think we had better go.'

He gave money to the old woman and a coin to the boy. The boy's whole face lit up as he thanked him. Gabrielle did not look back.

The day was dry but there was no sun and it was much colder than it had been the day before. They rode for two hours and by then

Culver's eyes were red-rimmed and his chin kept touching his chest. At last he said, his head jerking up, 'I must have some sleep.'

They dismounted near an outcrop of rocks. Culver brought out some pieces of rope, and apologized to Gabrielle for having to tie her up. She sighed and submitted, there being no hope of getting away from such a barren place. He tied her hands behind her back, attached a rope from her ankles to his own and said, 'If you lean back against the rock you can rest too.'

Gabrielle gave a pettish tug at the rope. 'I detest being tied.'

'It would be foolhardy of me to give you the chance to escape. You heard your grandmother threaten me.'

'Yes, and I feel sure she would have no compunction in having you killed. What I cannot understand is her giving the order of no killing on the night of the raid.'

'She was probably afraid you might get shot in all the confusion.'

'And so deny her the pleasure of making me suffer.' Gabrielle said with bitterness. 'You know the kind of woman she is, Mr Culver, why do you work for her?'

'Because I have a family and an extravagant wife and as I want to keep her I have to supply the luxuries of life. I must add she knows nothing of how I earn my money.'

'She might hate you if she did.'

'I hate myself.' There was bleakness in his eyes. 'I've talked far too much. Now I must rest.'

Within seconds he was asleep. Gabrielle studied him. What a tragedy that such a well-bred man as Culver should sell his soul to the devil. And he was doing so by working for a woman like her grandmother. It was strange what men would do in the name of love.

She laid her head back against the rock. Although they were inland the wind brought the smell of seaweed. She could taste salt on her lips. How far did they intend going? All the way to London? Surely Culver would not expect her to travel horseback the whole way. She would refuse. They had made wide detours, keeping clear of the main road, making it almost impossible for anyone to follow. But then, who was there who could follow her? Gabrielle had made up her mind she would not give way to despair, but at this moment was finding it difficult not to burst into tears. If only she knew for sure that the others were all right.

The wind ruffled the grass and brought a rustling to the dry furze.

Gabrielle's shoulders began to ache. She changed her position. This situation could not go on. They would have to stop somewhere tonight and then she would make her bid to escape.

Culver, as though Gabrielle's thoughts had transferred themselves to him, opened his eyes and said, 'Still here?' There was, for the first time, a glint of humour in his eyes.

Gabrielle moved her shoulders. 'If I could have found a sharp edge on the rocks to saw at the rope I would have done so, but all the rock is so beautifully, annoyingly smooth.'

'I must remember how enterprising you are.' Culver was smiling at her and she returned his smile. Then as though remembering his mission his expression sobered. 'We must go on.'

They stopped again at midday to eat cold bacon and bread, washed down by home brewed ale, which the woman at the cottage had given them. Gabrielle tried to draw Culver out about his life but he made it quite clear it was not something open for discussion.

'Then tell me where you are taking me,' she said. 'To my grandmother?'

'Eventually.'

'What do you mean by eventually, a week, two weeks, a month? Mr Culver, I think I have a right to know. I am a person, not a chattel to be conveyed from place to place. I know my grandmother intends me to suffer but I have not ridden a horse for several months. My body is aching, if I have to ride for another two or three days I shall fall from the horse.'

'No, you will stay on, even if it means tying you on.'

Gabrielle stared at him. 'I knew you to be weak but I had not thought you to be a cruel man.'

Culver, who had been leaning up on his elbow, chewing on a blade of grass, threw it away and got up. His face was flushed. 'I am not weak, on the contrary–'

'You *are* weak, otherwise you would not work for a monster like my grandmother so you can bribe your wife to stay with you.'

'Leave my affairs alone.' His eyes were blazing. 'Now get on that horse.'

'Not before I have told you more of *my* life.' When he refused to listen and pushed her towards the horse she said, 'I just want to say one thing, Mr Culver, then I shall mount. You mentioned you have a family. If you have a daughter would you marry her to a man you know is brutal and who has beaten previous wives into submission, women who have died under his brutality?'

He was silent for a moment then said, 'Please get on the horse.' He cupped his hands to help her mount. 'We shall be staying at an inn this evening. The people work for your grandmother. We shall be there about four o'clock. It will give you the chance to have a long rest.'

There was no hope of escaping that night, and after that Gabrielle gave up the idea. From that day on they were hours in the saddle, stopping only briefly for meals. At night they slept at an inn or cottage and sleep was all Gabrielle wanted.

Then came the morning when Culver, after having been in earnest conversation outside with the woman at the cottage, came in looking worried and biting on his lower lip.

'What is it?' Gabrielle asked.

'Hitchins and two men are on our trail, no doubt seeking revenge on me and–' Culver stood looking at her for a few moments then he said, 'I'm going to let you escape. Thirza will take you, set you on your way, then we shall lead Hitchins in the other direction'

The woman came in. 'We have very little time. The horses are saddled. Will you get your cloak, Ma'am?'

When Gabrielle came downstairs she reached up and kissed Culver on the cheek. 'Thank you, thank you.'

'God protect you–'

Within minutes Gabrielle and the women were riding along a narrow lane, with Thirza giving Gabrielle instructions of landmarks to follow. Once she had passed an out-cropping of rock resembling a whale she would come to a derelict farmhouse. There she must rest, by then she would have done a hard day's riding. They left the lane and came to open moorland. Here the woman Thirza reined. She gave Gabrielle further landmarks she was to follow then pushed a piece of parchment in her hand. This was the position of a farmhouse of her friends who would help Gabrielle. 'There is food in the saddle bag,' she said. 'God's blessing go with you.'

Then Thirza was gone and Gabrielle was left alone with the vast expanse of sky overhead and miles and miles of open moorland ahead of her and knowing a desolation that made her feel it would be better if she were dead. She urged the horse forward.

It was the longest and loneliest day Gabrielle could ever remember. It was dusk before she saw the outcropping resembling a whale and she all but fell off the horse with exhaustion. After unsaddling the animal and tethering it she took the blanket, stumbled into the ruins, and finding a corner where part of the roof remained, she lay down and drew the blanket up to her chin.

It was the cold that woke her. Stiff and chilled she got to her feet. The first faint light was showing in the east. Her teeth were chattering so much the sound echoed in her head. Food. If she could bite on a piece of bread–

Gabrielle went to get the plaited straw bag the woman had given her, then paused, feeling there was something wrong. It was seconds before she realised what it was. The horse was missing. She had tethered it to the stump of a tree. And there was only one stump. She was sure she had tethered the horse securely. But then, she had been in a terribly exhausted state. The animal had probably wandered. When it was daylight she would no doubt see it grazing a short distance away.

A slow panic mounted in her with each change of light until it swamped her with the realization there was no horse in sight. Did people travel these moors? Gabrielle forced herself to think calmly. She had food, if she eked it out... She took out the bread and the small flagon of cider from the saddle bag, broke off a small piece of bread, and took a few sips of cider, and felt better. She did have a goal.

She picked up the blanket, weighed up the possibility of taking the saddle then decided against it. Its weight would impede her progress. If she did find the horse she could ride it bareback.

In the distance could be seen her next landmark, which Thirza had described as resembling a church steeple. It was a target to encourage her.

A quick flutter of wings as a bird rose from a clump of coarse grass startled her. Watching its flight she recognized the lovely brown plumage and the curved slender beak of a curlew. As it soared, its plaintive cry, in all the vastness, emphasized to Gabrielle her isolation. And yet, the bird was 'life'.

She walked with dogged steps in the direction of the 'church steeple'.

# CHAPTER NINETEEN

Gabrielle soon found that distances were deceptive. The landmark of the 'steeple' that she had thought to be an hour's walk away turned out to be nearer four, by what she could judge. It was here she rested and took more of the cider than she should. It was strong and made her feel heavy, and reluctant to continue her journey. She forced herself to her feet.

The next landmark was the rock formation resembling two men carrying a bucket. When Gabrielle caught her first glimpse she thought them to be real people and her spirits soared. Then she remembered.

During the afternoon rain came. It was light at first then it deluged down, driving at her with a piercing coldness. She drank the last of the cider, then cupping her hands caught the water and tipped it into the bottle. More went over the sides than into it. When the rain ceased she had a meagre store. The rain had soaked through the shoulders of her cloak and dress so that she had a feeling of being encaged in ice. And Gabrielle knew then she would not survive the night unless she found shelter.

It was getting dark when she saw it. A barn! She thought at first it might be a mirage, but hobbling to it, ignoring the pain of broken blisters on her heels, she touched the wood. Would there be a roof to it? There was not only a roof but hay in it. With a sob Gabrielle sank into the hay. This meant she was near some habitation. She would rest here tonight and in the morning – but first she must tend to her feet. With renewed strength, she went out, gathered grass and lichen, then finding a small scythe on the wall she cut strips of blanket, packed the grass and moss around her feet and bound them.

Gabrielle then sank into the hay, gathering it around her and marvelling she could find such luxury in such a simple thing. A sensuous warmth stole over her and she found herself thinking about Luke, imagining herself in his arms, his lips soft and exploring on her at first, then with more urgency. Her body was beginning to ache with longing for him when, into the sweet sensuousness came reality, an image of Luke, blood streaming down his face. He could be dead. They could all be dead.

A merciful sleep released her from her torment.

Hunger pains woke her. She ate the last of the bread and cheese, took a few sips of water and slept again.

She was between waking and sleeping when she heard it, the soft whinneying of a horse. She drew herself up. Was it possible? Yes, there it was again. She got to her feet. The horse was outside the barn. Shaking in every limb she opened the door – and the next moment she was staring at the man dismounting. She mouthed the word Luke, but no sound came. It was a mirage. She saw the scar from eye to cheek, which gave him a piratical look. Then he was coming towards her. He was no mirage.

'Oh, Luke, Luke, you are alive!' She took a step towards him, then stopped, appalled at the coldness in his eyes.

'No thanks to you,' he said, his voice hard.

Gabrielle put a hand to her throat. Did he think she had betrayed them? She shook her head. 'No, no, how could you? How could you think that I–' She swayed and Luke stepped forward and caught her. He laid her back in the hay. 'Stay here, I shall fetch a conveyance from the inn.'

After that Gabrielle had only a vague recollection of riding among straw in a wagon, of being carried upstairs and undressed and put into a bed that exuded warmth.

When she roused it was daylight and she was astonished to see Helen eyeing her anxiously. 'Helen, how did you–?'

'Oh, Gabrielle, how good it is to have you

back safe and sound. We searched every-where. It was a youth who told us he had seen a woman going into the barn.'

'Luke believes I betrayed you all,' Gabrielle said piteously. 'How could he?'

Helen soothed her. 'He was worried, upset– He not only lost his goods but Mr Delacote was knocked unconscious and–'

Gabrielle looked at Helen in surprise. 'But I took Mr Delacote to the house and asked Mrs Curnow to look after him, he seemed dazed.'

'He came back and joined in the fighting. But he's now fully recovered. Luke, though, also learned that another of his ships had been sunk, with the loss of two lives. He knows there is a traitor in the organization.'

'And he thinks *me* the culprit.' Gabrielle paused. 'Helen, when did you know about Luke's – activities?'

'Not until after the raid. Such slaughter needed an explanation. I just couldn't think why we should be attacked at Ninestones.'

'I was not responsible in any way,' Gabrielle said earnestly. 'I was abducted.' She told Helen about Mr Culver and Helen was shocked. She apparently knew Mr Culver, knew he had married for the second time and that his wife was young and ex-travagant.

'But not,' she said, 'that he would stoop so low as to supply her with all the luxuries she

351

craves. All his gifts will not hold a woman like that. Already there is gossip of other men in her life.' Helen drew the covers over Gabrielle. 'You must rest now. We can talk again. When you are well enough we shall hire a carriage. We are going to stay at Dover for a while. The servants and Mr Delacote have already gone ahead.'

'Dover?' Gabrielle queried and was told by Helen to rest.

Food and rest and sleep were all Gabrielle needed and the next day she declared herself ready to travel. Luke accepted it but Helen tried to insist on another day at least. It was Gabrielle who settled it, saying she wanted to get away from all she had suffered.

Luke said, 'Well, if you are sure you are well enough–?' and that was all the conversation they had together. Helen had tried to explain about Gabrielle's abduction but he refused to listen.

And so they set out in the carriage with Luke riding horseback.

Gabrielle said, bitterness in her voice, 'It surprises me that Luke wants me to go with him to Dover. Why does he not just abandon me if he thinks I acted as traitor?'

'He wants you with him, Gabrielle. I don't really believe he thinks you were responsible for the raid. I feel sure the traitor will be discovered in time and then–'

'Then it will have ceased to bother me. If a husband cannot trust his own wife– Oh, yes, I know I'm a Quantock. Why are we going to Dover, where are we staying?'

'Luke has business there and he was offered the loan of a house by Mr Mayland, the gentleman whose schooner you travelled on from Venice. He and his daughter have put to sea again. They are restless people.'

All Gabrielle longed for was to be back in London, to be there when her father arrived, to be needed, to be able to talk to someone who cared.

It was dark the night they eventually arrived at the house at Dover. It was out of the town and inland, but when Gabrielle stepped, stiff and weary, from the carriage she could hear the sea.

Framed in the lamplit doorway of the large house was a familiar figure. Mr Delacote. With a glad cry, he came forward and took Gabrielle's hand in his. 'Dear lady, thank God you are safe. We were nearly out of our minds with worry.' His voice was charged with emotion. 'Come into the warmth.'

Gabrielle was aware of only two things that evening, the comfort of the blazing fire and of Luke's ice-cold expression. After a snack and hot drinks she and Helen went up to bed.

The next day neither Luke nor Mr

Delacote put in an appearance. Helen said Luke had asked that she and Gabrielle stay indoors. Gabrielle was angry. 'I see no reason why he should expect *you* to be a prisoner too.'

To this Helen simply asked Gabrielle to be patient, that she was sure all would work out right. Gabrielle did not share this view, she could see her life ahead, living with a husband who hated her.

That evening Luke and Mr Delacote with three men, strangers, came in about eight o'clock and went to an upstairs room. Luke, after asking for food and drink to be sent up, gave orders they were not to be disturbed. It was midnight when the men left, and the next morning Gabrielle learned that Luke had gone with them.

Mr Delacote said a little unhappily to Gabrielle, he was unable to tell her their destination.

To this Gabrielle replied coldly, 'My husband believes I am a traitor, Mr Delacote. He refused to listen when Lady Norton tried to tell him my story that I was abducted. Therefore what he does, or where he goes no longer interests me. All I want to do is to get back to London to greet my father when he arrives, and if my husband does not give me permission then I shall leave without it.'

Mr Delacote laid a gentle hand on her arm

and gave her the same advice as Helen, to be patient, that all would turn out well.

Gabrielle spent most of the day standing at the window of the drawing room which was on the first floor. It overlooked the Channel but a light mist blotted out the French coast opposite. She had thought it would be a busy route but she saw few ships.

'Why?' she asked Mr Delacote when they met in the dining room at midday. 'Is it because of the trouble in France?'

'The crossing from Dover to Calais is as busy as it always was, the packet is full each day. Life goes on just the same. Businessmen travel. People leave for the Grand Tour. In Calais there is a chanting of 'Aristos' spoken in a derogatory way, but no one is molested. If I were walking alone in the streets of Calais at night, however, I would make sure I was wearing a tricolour cockade in my hat!'

Helen said, 'It seems impossible that life goes on just the same during all the bloodshed.'

'Away from the terror people make jests, the restaurants are full, the wine flows, the theatres are in full swing.'

Mr Delacote raised his shoulders. 'I find it difficult to understand but there it is—'

They played three-handed whist that evening and retired about half past nine.

Gabrielle, weary, but not sleepy, lay awake going over all that had happened since she had left her grandmother's house on Christmas night, and found it almost impossible to believe she had gone through so much.

She was thinking about Luke and wondering if in time he would soften towards her and listen to the story of her abduction, when there came an urgent knocking on her door. Gabrielle climbed out of bed, ran across the room and opened the door a fraction. It was Helen. She looked agitated. 'Gabrielle, something has happened, will you come downstairs? We know who the traitor is. Mr Delacote found her, it was Marie–'

'Marie–' Gabrielle rushed back and got her cloak, talking as she flung it around her. 'How did he find out–?' Helen caught hold of her arm and urged her along the landing.

'Mr Delacote will explain. Oh, Gabrielle, I trusted the girl, I sent money for her family, and this is how she repays me. Luke and the men are in great danger. But there, you will hear all about it in a moment.'

Mr Delacote was in the study. He was alone. 'I've locked Marie in the linen cupboard,' he said, 'and threatened I will shoot her if she makes a sound. She won't, she's thoroughly cowed. Now, Gabrielle–'

Mr Delacote told how he had been

outside for a breath of air when he had seen Marie come out. She ran down the narrow lane and he followed at a discreet distance. Then he saw her meet a man at the end of the lane. It wasn't a girl meeting her lover, there was something urgent in the way they talked for a few moments. Then Marie made to leave. Mr Delacote hurried back to the house and waited for her to come in. Marie was so shocked, so frightened he had no difficulty in getting a confession from her.

'The man is in the employ of your grandmother, Gabrielle, and he has been paying Marie for any information she could glean. She said she wanted pretty things. The other night when we had the meeting she had been listening at the door. So, of course, she knew all our plans.'

'Oh, God, what are we going to do?'

Mr Delacote stood thoughtful for a few moments then he said, 'I know where I can reach the men and there's a small boat in a cove at the foot of the cliffs. The wind is favourable at the moment for sailing, but I feel there will be a change in the weather, I might need to row. Unfortunately, I tire easily these days.'

'I can row,' Gabrielle said eagerly. 'My father taught me. An old sea captain once told him he never knew a girl who could row so strongly as I. I shall come with you.'

Mr Delacote shook his head. 'If any of the men happen to find out who you are they would think the information false, then Luke would be in more danger.'

Helen said, 'I wish I had learned to row, but I didn't. If only my young nephew had been here he could have gone with you.'

'Nephew?' Gabrielle looked up. 'Miss Mayland told me that her brother's son came to stay with them during his school holidays. She talked about their summer house by the sea. This must be it. If any of the boy's clothes were here– He is about sixteen. Yes, that is the answer, Mr Delacote, I could pass as *your* nephew.'

'Your hair,' he protested, 'it would have to be cut off.'

'Mr Delacote, this is a matter of life and death, what matter a few shorn locks.'

'Yes, you are right. Well – if there are youth's clothes here–'

Helen searched and produced a brown jacket, knee breeches, shirt, white ribbed woollen stockings, buckled shoes and a black broad brimmed felt hat. They fitted Gabrielle as though all had been made for her.

'Perfect,' Helen said. 'Now, with your permission, Mr Delacote, I would like to release Marie so she can cut Gabrielle's hair. She is adept at it.' He agreed.

Marie was in such a trembling state

Gabrielle could not help but feel sorry for the girl. Then Helen spoke quietly to her, told her what was required and some of the colour came back to Marie's face. 'Yes, M'lady, I shall do my best, M'lady–'

Gabrielle's hair curled naturally at the ends and she felt a pang as she saw strands drop to the floor. Then immediately consoled herself with the thought that her hair would soon grow again.

Marie made an excellent job of the cutting and when Gabrielle was handed a mirror she could hardly believe the change it made. Her hair was cut in a thick fringe across her forehead, the rest cut to reach just below her ears. And with the hat pulled on, the brim swept up at the front, Helen declared her to be a most attractive youth.

Mr Delacote also brought a caped coat belonging to Miss Mayland's nephew, saying with the briefest of smiles it would cover a multitude of 'sins'.

'Fortunately,' he said, 'we'll be going out on the tide, and with the wind set fair–'

This gave Gabrielle the impression of simply skimming across the channel to Dover. When they left the house with Helen's blessing, she had a shivery feeling of excitement. It was not only because of the adventure but because of this action she might prove to Luke she was no traitor.

The night was dark with heavy clouds. Mr

Delacote knew a short cut that took them to the cove. The boat was small but sturdy. They dragged the boat to the water, Gabrielle got in and Mr Delacote pushed it off then clambered in saying, 'Well, Master *Francis,* we are on our way!'

There was a smile in his voice. Gabrielle had seen several different sides to Mr Delacote that evening. She would never have imagined him to be the kind of man who would have been firm and ruthless with Marie... She would not have imagined him to have undertaken this journey and could smile about it, or to have been actually involved in the organization that rescued the French people from the dreaded guillotine.

Mr Delacote had unfurled the sail and the freshening breeze swelled it and the boat gathered speed.

When Gabrielle looked back she saw the lights of Dover, the castle dominating the town, the white cliffs. In the harbour were tall-masted ships preparing to sail, men swarming up the rigging unfurling the canvas. The muted sound of the men singing sea-shanties as they worked carried on the breeze.

Gabrielle suddenly found something dis-turbingly beautiful about the night, the sound of the singing, the movement of the boat, the water running along its side with only a gentle swishing sound, and the feeling of the wind on her face. It was like being in a different world, a mystic world.

Then Mr Delacote brought a reality to it by asking Gabrielle about Culver, if he had treated her with respect.

'Yes, he did, the utmost respect. I felt sorry that he found it necessary to work for my grandmother.'

'Yes, it's a tragedy. Rupert Culver used to be greatly respected at one time. I too feel sorry for him, and he has my sympathy. It's a terrible thing when a man becomes besotted with a woman. Culver was terribly lonely when his wife died. This girl played on it – and – well, the rest you know.' After a pause Mr Delacote said, 'But I have no right to condemn, who knows what I might do. Loneliness is a dreadful thing.'

Gabrielle said quietly, 'One can live with someone and still be lonely.'

Mr Delacote gave her a quick glance then remarked on a slight change in the weather.

There was a feeling of a storm, scudding clouds, the waves becoming choppy. When there was a gap in the clouds the foam-flecked waves were touched with a cold light from the moon. When the moon was obscured the night was black.

The boat chopped on a wave where currents converged and spray showered them. Gabrielle wiped her face.

They were to be showered many times

during the crossing.

Mr Delacote said he would have to start rowing and pulled down the sail. He rowed quite strongly for a while and Gabrielle saw the lights of Calais emerge, saw a number of church steeples rise starkly against the skyline. Then Mr Delacote rested on the oars, and he was breathing heavily. The boat rose and fell.

When Gabrielle begged to take over he refused, saying it was not only heavy going, but there was the danger of changing seats. It took Gabrielle some time to convince him that her father had taught her well about the handling of the boat and suggested if Mr Delacote became too exhausted they would never reach Calais. He gave in, and later expressed surprise at her strength and expertise.

They exchanged seats twice more then, when Mr Delacote took over the last time, he steered the boat further up the channel. They eventually landed on a strip of shingle. 'We have to walk back into town,' he said.

After pulling the boat up under an overhang of rock they climbed over rough ground and made their way to where a line of cottages showed the first sign of habitation. Mr Delacote stopped.

'We must put on our badges of *comradeship*.' There was a bitterness in his voice. 'I hate to wear them but it has to be done if we are to achieve our object.'

He pinned a tricolour cockade to Gabrielle's knitted cap and one on his own hat. 'There, now we are one of them.'

When they walked on Gabrielle said, 'Where are the men. Have we far to go?'

'Not too far, unfortunately we have to go through an unsavoury district.'

They came to the town and walked through narrow tortuous streets, where the smell of rotting fish mingled with the musty odours rising from damp cellars and ordure in the gutters. Everywhere was silent and dark until they came to a street with a tavern at the end. Here the light from the window showed a group of drunken men outside. They were singing lustily, their voices coarse. Mr Delacote told Gabrielle to leave any talking to him. All the men wore red caps and had the tricolour cockades pinned to them.

Seeing Gabrielle and Mr Delacote approaching they tried to bar their way, but Mr Delacote, edging past them, dragging Gabrielle with him, spoke to them in fluent French, making coarse jests then shouting, 'Vive la Republique!'

The men echoed his call and rolled along the walls of the houses, each laughing at the other's helplessness. Before Gabrielle and Mr Delacote were out of sight they were yelling out their bawdy songs again.

Gabrielle, who had taken the skin off her palms with rowing, was beginning to feel the pain when they stopped outside a house. Mr Delacote tapped once on the window followed by three more. Seconds later the front door opened and a low voice said, 'Identify yourself.'

'The sea is divided–' The door opened a little wider and Mr Delacote stepped inside. There was some talk then he beckoned Gabrielle to come in. 'Wait here,' he said. Whoever had been behind the door had gone. Mr Delacote closed it then went along the passage and Gabrielle had only a glimpse of a dimly lit room before the door closed.

Gabrielle had expected to hear the murmur of men's voices but there was nothing. The house was so silent it felt eerie standing in the dark passage. When she leaned back against the wall it felt damp, but any smell of mustiness there might have been was overlaid by the smell of onions coming from upstairs. Gabrielle tried to pierce the gloom as though it would tell her if Luke and Mr Delacote and the others were in the room. Then the door opened suddenly and Mr Delacote came hurrying out.

He took Gabrielle by the arm. 'The men have left. We must go to them. We'll have to go back to the boat. I'll talk later.'

Mr Delacote said no more until they were away from the town then he told Gabrielle the men were with the émigrés in a cave on the beach further along the coast.

'The schooner was not due to pick them up until tomorrow evening,' he said, 'but in view of what has happened Leon will try and get word to have it here before daybreak. Even then, he feels there may be danger. Some of Hesther Quantock's men have been seen in the town. If they've informed the authorities there's to be an escape the soldiers might be on the lookout quite soon.'

They went quite a distance along the coast before Mr Delacote indicated the place they were to beach. Once out of the boat he said, 'You will be questioned by the one in command. Answer briefly and keep your voice low. *You* must not ask any questions, be as self-effacing as possible.'

Gabrielle asked if Luke would be there and, when told yes, asked what would happen if he recognized her. To which Mr Delacote replied, 'The captain is too clever a man to give your identity away. Come along.'

They clambered over stones in the direction of the cliff face. Near it stood a large formation of rocks. Mr Delacote edged through what appeared to be no more than a crevice at the back and held out his hand to Gabrielle.

They stepped into a cave with sufficient light for Gabrielle to see there were a number of men with guns. Two stepped forward, their guns cocked at the ready.

Mr Delacote was asked to identify his companion. 'My nephew,' he said. 'We bring disturbing news. Take me to your second in command.'

They were taken to a second cave and Gabrielle's heart gave a leap as she saw Luke emerge from the back. He was unshaven and his eyes were red-rimmed from lack of sleep. Mr Delacote went foward and the two men stood talking for some moments. Luke glanced in Gabrielle's direction.

'Young Francis, he's changed, but it is some time since I saw him.' Not by a twitch of a muscle did Luke show he had recognized her.

Luke asked a question and Mr Delacote said, 'We shall be better prepared this time. Leon has not only managed to muster many more men, but has also acquired a cannon. This, with plenty of men on top of the cliff should deal effectively with any military and Hesther Quantock's men should they decide to attack. Those already here should deal with any trouble from the beach.'

Luke said, 'There will be no trouble, of course, if the schooner gets here soon.'

'We hope not.'

A young man came up to Gabrielle and held out a steaming mug. 'Here you are, nipper, coffee, it'll warm you up.

She thanked him, remembering to keep her voice gruff. When she looked for Luke and Mr Delacote they had gone. Gabrielle had a feeling of anticlimax. She had not expected to be welcomed after the story of Marie and crossing the channel had been unfolded but she thought that Luke might at least have said thanks.

Mr Delacote came back and said she was to come with him, the leader wanted to see her. Gabrielle put down her mug then wished she had kept it. It would have been something to do with her hands to help quieten her sudden attack of nerves.

They went through a short tunnel into, a third cave. Gabrielle had only time to notice some huddled figures sitting round a fire when Mr Delacote led her up to a big, bearded man. Luke, still expressionless, was beside him.

The bearded man said, 'You did well, Master Francis, to help your uncle with the boat, and we appreciate it.' He had a strong French accent. 'But our people are important to the organization and when the time comes for us to leave here you must be one of the last to leave.'

Luke, his manner stiff, said, 'The boy is very young.'

'Old enough apparently for his uncle to allow him to undertake the journey. I must point out that many of his age have given their lives for the cause, and that others, who have seemed bona fide, have betrayed us.' To Gabrielle he said, 'You must accept our decision'

'Yes, sir, I do.'

'Very well, sit over there, and speak to no one.'

Gabrielle went and sat close to the wall, trying to make herself as self-effacing as possible. Wood was crackling on a fire in the centre of the cave, surrounded by stones. Sitting round it, their bodies hunched, were the émigrés. They had a defeated look. Behind them stood six or seven men, all armed. They eyed Gabrielle with stony expressions. Their ages ranged from young to middle-aged.

Gabrielle stared at the fire. It was piled high with driftwood and even from where she was sitting she could feel some warmth. She felt suddenly exhausted and the cave took on an air of unreality. The women, their hair dishevelled, and who were stooped under the weight of blankets on their shoulders, looked like witches. The men, who were now moving round the cave, their faces distorted when seen through the flames, had an evil look about them. She watched the smoke rising to the roof and wondered where the outlet was for it. It worried her, niggled at her. Surely smoke rising could give away the hiding place. She tried to find reasons why the smoke would not show outside and could find none. She must tell someone of the danger they were in. Gabrielle tried to rise, but her body felt leaden. Her eyelids drooped.

# CHAPTER TWENTY

When Gabrielle roused the scene had changed. All the men had gone and there were only the women émigrés. The blankets were on the ground and they were pinning up their hair. There was an air of animation about them. No, not animation, hope, yes, that was it. Perhaps the schooner had arrived.

It had. A man came in to tell them they were to come to the front cave right away. One of the women came over to Gabrielle and said, 'We were told not to talk to you, Monsieur, but we wanted to thank you for getting the ship to fetch us. Thank you.'

Mr Delacote came in and went over to Gabrielle. 'You are to wait here, the captain will see to you.' He gripped her shoulder. 'You will be all right. I have to go with the émigrés, two of the women and one of the men are sick. God bless you.'

There was suddenly the sound of gunfire followed by a deep boom. Cannon? Mr Delacote said, 'We're discovered. Wait here, don't come out. The captain will come for you.' He left.

Gabrielle waited so long she began to feel

abandoned. She went hurrying to the front cave. It was empty. There was shouting, the sound of curses, another boom of the cannon, then another sound as though rocks were hurtling from the cliff top, followed by a pitter-patter of small stones. Gabrielle went to the opening and peeped out. Rain lashed against her face. Through the veil of rain she could see the schooner anchored, see the boat with the émigrés being rowed towards it. The boat was nearly there.

Another boom from the cannon seemed to shake the whole cliff face and fearing falling rock she drew back into the cave.

Luke came in and grabbed her by the arm. 'Can you never do as you are told? Come along.' He hurried her through into the cave she had left, stopped at the back of it and removed a heavy stone. 'Now listen to me and listen carefully, there is no time to repeat it. We dare not risk you getting away by boat. Some of the men think you are responsible for the attack. There are tunnels and caves through here that will eventually bring you to one as large as this. There you must wait. I will try and come for you this evening, if not someone else will.'

'Oh, Luke please let me come with you,' Gabrielle begged.

'No. Now do as I tell you, *please*. Feel your way along with your right hand. There is a tunnel, a small cave, a long tunnel then the

371

large cave. In it you will find everything you need, wood, tinderbox, food, blankets. If the worst comes to the worst there is a boat further up the coast, but pray heaven it will not come to that. Go along, bend your head. Go along.' Luke shouted it. Gabrielle went through the aperture and she was aware of the stone being put into place.

She stood in the pressing blackness fighting down blind panic. Had Luke, thinking she had betrayed them, decided to leave her to die. No, her grandmother might do such a thing, but not Luke.

Gabrielle forced herself to calmness and repeated Luke's instructions to herself, then began to feel her way along the walls. At times she felt the walls were closing in on her, then she would come to a part where she felt air on her face and was refreshed. Once she stopped alarmed when she thought she heard someone breathing heavily, and realized it was her own ragged breathing. She knew when she came to the first cave by the feeling of space around her. One more tunnel and then–

The tunnel curved then she was in the cave and after the darkness it seemed like coming into daylight. There was a ring of stones as in the other one where she could build a fire, a pile of driftwood, all the things Luke had mentioned. And a piece of dry bread and stale cheese. She walked round the cave seeking an opening, and found it at the end of a very short tunnel. The opening was narrow and sheltered by another outcrop of rocks.

Gabrielle went outside and held her face to the rain, savouring the freshness, then she walked to the edge of the cove and looked for the schooner. There was nothing to see. The land curved at this point, hiding the inlet from view. She listened intently and thought she could hear gunfire, but could not be certain for the wind and the rain and the waves pounding against the rocks. It was difficult to believe the weather could have been so calm when they left Dover. Dover ... it seemed a lifetime away. With her face streaming with rain she went back into the cave, and felt cold and lonely.

A fire would help. She found kindling and when she had it alight she put on pieces of wood. It was a long time before she felt any warmth from it but when she did she looked for water, found a pitcher and a pan, and made coffee. By then she was ready to enjoy the dry bread and cheese. When she had eaten she could collect more driftwood, she must keep the fire going until Luke came. She would not allow herself to think he might have been killed.

When she went out for driftwood she was surprised to find it was daylight. There was no shortage of driftwood, it was wedged between rocks, scattered on the shingle, and there were large pieces carried in by the waves. Gabrielle with the wind buffeting her, her fingers numb, gathered an armful, carried it in and went back for more. She carried in three loads then rested. There was all day to gather more. It was difficult to assess time, there was no sun to go by, she only knew it dragged unbearably. In between putting wood on the fire she went outside. But whenever a ship of any kind appeared she would take cover, terrified in case it was the 'enemy' seeking her. Eventually she lay down by the fire, pulled the blankets over her – and slept.

When she sat up the fire was almost out. She jumped up and dropped wood on to it. Had the fire died down more quickly or had she been asleep for a long time? When she went out she found it was dusk. Thank goodness! It would not be long before Luke would come for her. She felt an icy finger down her spine. He *had* to be alive, he *had* to be, God could not be so cruel–

The hours dragged by and the storm grew worse and Gabrielle knew despair as she listened to the pounding of the waves against the rocks. Would any small boat attempt to cross the channel on a night like this? But how could she stand being here for another day? It would drive her mad. It was not knowing what had happened which was the worst.

She had hope later when, standing outside in the darkness she saw quite a small boat battling its way up channel, disappearing in the troughs and rising again. A sturdy boat, it seemed, could ride the storm. Knowing Luke, who would tackle anything, Gabrielle felt sure he would be able to handle such a craft. She forced herself to think positively that he was alive and well.

She must have been in and out of the cave another ten times or more when her heart gave a great leap. A boat was coming in the direction of the inlet, not from across the channel, but coming down it, keeping close to the shore. A rowing boat with a single oarsman who rowed frantically to keep the boat on an even keel. Luke! There was no mistaking that virile figure.

Gabrielle ran to the waters edge, ignoring the iciness of the waves as they broke over her feet. She shouted and waved, but Luke was too intent on his task to acknowledge her. The boat chopped on waves and Gabrielle could almost feel the juddering of the craft. Luke was pulling madly on his right oar to get the boat directed towards the inlet but like a bucking horse it kept going everywhere but the way he wanted. Then suddenly, as though caught in a whirlpool it began to turn. It was now near to Gabrielle and she plunged into the water and grabbed the bow. Luke secured the oars then jumped into the water and between them they managed to get it beached.

Drenched and with rain streaming down their faces, they stood for seconds looking at one another then Gabrielle said, 'Oh, Luke, thank God you're safe.'

'And you,' he said. 'Come along.' He took her by the arm and they battled their way to the cave. The fire was blazing and they both went up to it and held out their hands.

During the long hours of waiting Gabrielle had pictured this meeting, pictured Luke sweeping her into his arms and murmuring glad cries that she was safe, and she weeping and clinging to him. And here they were, holding out cold hands to the blaze as though it were the most important thing in the world.

She said, 'I'll make coffee.'

She filled the pan from the pitcher and set it on the wood, poking the pieces to steady the pan. The she turned to face him. 'Luke, what happened this morning?'

'The émigrés got away all right, but it was the only boat-load that did. The men had to scatter. Fortunately we had only one casualty, but we managed to get him away. I hid with them. The soldiers are still on the look-out for us. I made my way up the coast to where the boat was hidden. I hesitated about coming when it was such a wild night, but I knew you would be worrying.'

'It was terrible waiting, not knowing anything.'

The caped coat Gabrielle was wearing was heavy with water, she took, it off. 'After you have had your coffee,' she said, 'you must rest, you look terrible.'

'So do you.'

Gabrielle's hand went to the knitted cap, feeling annoyed she had not taken this off too. Luke's gaze travelled down her body. 'But I must say, you have a shapely pair of legs.'

'That is not the remark one makes to a lady,' she snapped.

'No, Master Francis.' There was a glint of amusement in Luke's eyes. 'And may I suggest young sir, that you take off your wet clothes and get them dried. You can wrap yourself in a blanket.'

'Indeed I will not take them off,' she retorted.

'Oh, stop arguing. If this storm persists we could be here for days, and if there is anything I detest it's sitting with someone who has a snivelling cold.'

'Then you had better get *your* clothes dried too because if there is anything *I* detest it's a man who is constantly sneezing and blowing his nose and grumbling about his cold.'

'I am not prone to colds.' He picked up a

blanket and held it out to her. 'Here—'

She took it, then threw it at him. 'The stoic! The great Luke Caltahn! If you had been shot your blood would never have dared to flow!'

'If I had been shot you would have been weeping over me.'

'I would not,' she said, then after a pause added quietly, 'Yes, I would.'

The water began to boil. She scooped some coffee into it then drew the pan from the fire. They were both silent, staring into the flames. When the grounds settled she poured the coffee into two earthenware bowls and handed one to Luke. They sipped in silence but Gabrielle was aware of him watching her over the rim of the bowl.

She said, 'Why is it you bring out the worst in me?'

'You bring out the worst in me, because you always defy me or want to fight me, even when I suggest something for your own good.'

'It was not for my own good when you suggested I take off my clothes. All you wanted was to see me naked.'

'There you go again, being foolish! Putting a thought into my mind that was not there. The last thing I want to do is to make love to you, or anyone else. If I had a harem of beautiful women to choose from I could not find the energy. I've had no sleep for forty-eight hours and I'm weary unto death.'

Luke snatched up a blanket, crossed the cave and laying down, face to the wall, he pulled the blanket over him.

Gabrielle stared at him, sick with misery. What had made her say such a thing, especially after all he had gone through. It was sensible to take off her sodden clothes. She could catch cold. She got up to get more wood for the fire and her feet squelched in her wet shoes. Her thick stockings were sticking to her legs, the wet breeches were uncomfortable.

Gabrielle waited until she felt sure Luke was breathing regularly in sleep then she took off her shoes and peeled off her stockings. Then she wriggled her toes and ran her hands over her calves. Luke had said she had good legs. She had nice feet, narrow, long toed.

She had not intended taking off the rest of her clothes, or tried to convince herself she had not intended to, but now, drawing a blanket close in case of having to cover up quickly should Luke stir, she removed the breeches and slowly the rest of her clothes, savouring the removing of them in almost a sensuous way. She stood up and, still watching Luke, raised her hands above her head, stretching upwards, then she brought her hands down over her body, feeling delicious little tremors surge through her.

What a wonderful feeling of freedom.

She remembered once having a longing to run out naked in the rain. There had been no opportunity at the time, but now there was. She felt a sudden wildness. Why not go out, there was no one to see her, and Luke was dead to the world. It would be freezing cold but there was the fire to come back to. Gabrielle flung on some wood and before she could change her mind, ran out. Then feeling the cutting edge of the stones she darted back for her shoes, laughing to herself.

Outside again with the wind almost blowing her off her feet and with the rain driving at her she flung her arms wide and held her face to the elements, feeling a joyousness. This is how Eve must have felt in the garden of Eden, when she tempted Adam to bite into the forbidden fruit. This was nature, why should people be ashamed of their bodies, why had she always been unwilling to let Luke see her completely naked. She had always been grabbing her shift to hide her body from him. If he had not been so utterly weary she would have gone in – and tempted him-

The next moment she nearly died of shock when her hand was grabbed and a voice shouted close to her ear, 'Have you gone completely mad?'

Then she was being dragged over the

380

stones, stumbling over the bigger ones. In the cave Luke flung her a blanket. 'Put that round you and get over to the fire for God's sake! Do you want to die of pneumonia? You little fool.'

Gabrielle said in a small voice, 'I thought you were asleep.' It was all she could think of to say.

Luke gave her a push. 'Get nearer to the fire and stay there.' He picked up three pieces of wood, slotted them together, then picking up her clothes draped them over it. 'They won't dry lying on the ground, will they? But that is so like you, irresponsible, you go outside and flaunt your body. Did you hope a ship would pass and you could wave to the men?'

'Do you think they would have noticed me on a night like this?'

At any other time Gabrielle would have been shouting back at him, but she spoke quietly, sensing that all his talk was to cover an emotion in him. Any man, even one less passionate than Luke, could hardly fail to be roused at the sight of a naked girl. Only Luke would hate to admit it.

'Where is the pitcher of water?' He found it, poured some into a pan and set it on the fire. 'Even with a hot drink inside you I doubt whether it will do much good. No doubt you will end up with pneumonia, and–'

'And die,' she said. 'It might be a good thing, seeing you consider me so useless.' She could not resist that one retort.

This brought a further heated comment from Luke.

'That's right, be sorry for yourself, plead for pity. It would never occur to you that you would need to be nursed, that someone would have to sit up with you night and day–'

'Oh, Luke, *please* stop. You sound like my mother when she nags. I did behave foolishly, I realize that now, but I want you to know I have never done anything like that before. It was the storm, it roused something in me, something I find difficult to explain.'

He broke a twig from a branch and snapped it between his fingers.

'And what effect do you think the two things had on me, the storm and you standing there–' He paused then added, 'I wonder if you would have done what you did had you been alone? Answer me truthfully, Gabrielle.'

After hesitating a moment she said, 'I'm not sure. I once wanted to run out naked and there was no man in sight. I was younger. Tonight I felt a wildness in me, something primitive. I really did think you were asleep.'

Luke took a step forward. 'You certainly

roused something primitive in me.' There was a tremor in his voice.

The blanket slipped a little from Gabrielle's shoulders and instead of catching it up she let it stay. Luke was gazing at her bare flesh, but instead of the sensuous look she would have imagined there was tenderness in his eyes. He reached out and touched her shoulders, his fingers light.

'How soft your skin is, Gabrielle, how lovely you are.'

There was something between them at the moment, something so beautiful Gabrielle felt she wanted to cry. Luke eased the blanket away and looking up into his eyes she let it fall away.

'Oh, Gabrielle, Gabrielle.' His hands moved gently over her body, sending tingling shocks through her. He drew her to him and traced a finger down her spine. She arched her back and gave a small ecstatic moan. 'Oh, Luke–' His mouth came down on hers and his hands moved over her thighs.

With both, their passion rising, came yet another new feeling. There was none of the urgency with Luke there had been on two nights he had taken her and there was nothing passive about Gabrielle. This was a questing for knowledge of one another's bodies, and a desire to satisfy the needs of each other. Gabrielle, of her own volition, touched Luke. His response excited her, yet never once did their passion reach a savagery. Underlying it all the time was a tenderness, it was what Gabrielle had longed for, this was what she had expected marriage to be.

Afterwards they lay in the drowsy aftermath of love, Gabrielle curled up against Luke's strong firm body, drawing a warmth from him, and wanting the night to go on forever because this loving, she knew, would be repeated ... again and again...

# CHAPTER TWENTY ONE

Gabrielle awoke the next morning feeling chilled and disillusioned. It was unbelievable but they had quarrelled after their love-making, and all because she had asked Luke to tell her he loved her. He refused and when she begged him to say it just once he became angry, demanding to know why women expected men to swear undying love, could she not accept that he had wanted her.

'Wanted me!' she exclaimed. 'Is that all it meant to you? Was I just someone who could satisfy a need in you?'

'You felt the same need,' he answered shortly.

Gabrielle had shouted at him, and when she had gone on about his lust, the ruthlessness of his character, he left the warmth of the fire, and lay down by the wall. Within seconds he was snoring lightly. *That* was how much he thought of her.

After lying awake for what seemed hours she got up and dressed, hating the breeches, the thick woollen stockings, hating her body and the disillusionment it had brought. The fire was almost out. She broke off a few pieces of twigs, fed them to the embers, where they smouldered for a while then burst into flames. After putting on the few pieces of wood left she went out to collect some more, grumbling to herself that it seemed to be all she had done since coming to the cave, gathering wood and feeding the fire.

Before she was out of the cave she could smell the fog. Oh, no! If it was thick they could be stranded here until it lifted. And spending the day in a cave with Luke in the mood he was in – well, there was one thing certain she would quite definitely not satisfy a need in him this time, wife or no wife.

The fog was so thick Gabrielle had difficulty in finding wood. She managed to gather an armful. There were footsteps on the shingle and she heard Luke say, 'I can hear you, Gabrielle, but I can't see you. Say something.'

'How did you know it *was* me? It could have been the enemy! I could have been abducted and the boat gone–'

'Oh, no, I never sleep as heavily as that. I knew you were there.' He came up to her and held out the knitted hat. 'You forgot this, you could catch cold in this damp fog.'

'A lot you care! And anyway, I hate it. You left me in no doubt that I looked dreadful in it.'

'I did?' He sounded surprised. 'When?'

'Last night when you told me even if you were offered the choice of *beautiful* women in a harem, you could not summon up the energy to make love to one of them, implying that I was so dreadful I would not even be contemplated for your – *attentions.*'

'But you did qualify for my – attention,' he said softly.

'Because there was no one else!' she retorted. Gabrielle tugged the hat right down over her ears. 'I satisfied a need in you, nothing more.'

'Oh, Gabrielle, was I such an oaf?' He drew a finger down her cheek in the light way that made such chaos of her feelings. 'I like you in the hat. I really do. You look quite – quite fetching in it.'

When Luke tried to draw her to him, she pushed the armful of wood at him. 'Oh, no, you don't get round me with your fancy talk, if you want to make love to someone you had better try and find yourself a mermaid!'

He laughed. 'Oh, Gabrielle, my sweet, you really are quaint.'

She stalked ahead of him, stumbling twice and was furious when he laughed and told her that her lovely legs were not very steady that morning.

Once inside the cave Luke became serious. 'I have to leave you for a time, Gabrielle – no wait,' he added as she began to protest. 'I must know how the others have fared.'

'But it would mean you going into town. You could be captured.'

Gabrielle stood, her hands tightly clasped. 'Stay with me, Luke, *please*. The thought of spending another day alone, after yesterday, the unbearable waiting, not knowing what had happened. If you go now and find it impossible to get back soon I would go through all the agony again.'

Luke took hold of her hands. 'I may not need to go right into town, we have many friends in Calais who could give me word, but I have to know what is happening. I promise not to be long. I shall go through the tunnels and leave by the caves we were in yesterday.'

Gabrielle looked at him in alarm. 'But the men could be waiting there. They might expect you to come back to it.'

'I doubt it. And once I'm away from there they would hardly recognize me.' Luke crossed the cave, put his hand in an aperture and pulled out a leather jerkin. From the pocket he produced a red cap sporting the tricolour cockade. When he had donned both he rubbed the stubble on his chin and said, 'Vive la Republique! Will I pass?'

'Pray heaven you will,' she said with a note of despair. 'Otherwise—'

Luke tilted her face towards him. 'Try not

to worry, I never take foolish chances.'

She drew back. 'Not with your own life perhaps, but what about mine? You leave me without any protection. Even if no enemy invades how do I get away should you happen to be captured. I could, of course, leave by boat in the fog, where I would probably end up in the middle of the North Sea, where I would die of exposure. Alternatively, I could shoot myself, that is, if I had a gun.'

'Oh, Gabrielle, this is no laughing matter, but I have to smile. Such a tragedienne. You will not end up in the middle of the North Sea, nor will there be any need to shoot yourself. Should I not return, which is highly unlikely, some member of the group will come eventually. If not from Calais, from Dover. The cave is regularly checked. This is our life-line.' Luke kissed her. 'Try not to worry, Gabrielle, I give you my word I will not be long.'

When he had gone Gabrielle put a finger to her lips. What a complex character Luke was. He refused to say last night that he loved her, yet his kiss had been tender, he had been tender with her during their love-making. She felt then he did love her but was afraid to admit it. Was it because she was a Quantock and he was not able to trust her yet? Or was it because he had suffered at the hands of a woman, perhaps having been jilted?

With a sigh Gabrielle picked up some pieces of wood to replenish the fire. What a hungry maw it had.

Luke, as it happened, was back more quickly than she had thought possible. Judging by the gravity of his expression something was sadly wrong.

'The military are searching every house, every hovel and tavern in town,' he said. 'The men have already fled, thank God, and are safe. We must get away, Gabrielle, and lose ourselves in the fog. Soldiers are searching the cliffs. One of the women has given me food. Take the blankets to the boat, if there is any water left take that too.'

Gabrielle gathered up the blankets, picked up the flagon and went out, leaving Luke prowling round the cave looking for a gun that was hidden. The fog was so dense she had difficulty in groping her way to the boat. Luke came up as she put the blankets in. They both looked up as there came the muffled sound of gunfire. They dragged the boat to the water. Gabrielle tried to stifle the thought that one might already have been launched somewhere near and was waiting for them in this eerie world of fog. She would have wondered how Luke could ever have found direction had she not seen the compass in his hand. He laid it on the planks.

Fortunately the sea was calm. Luke rowed

with barely the sound of a splash, but Gabrielle could not still the panic in her. She asked about ships. They could be rammed and drowned.

'Ships will sail if they have a schedule to keep, but we would have warning, you would hear a man call their approach. Then we get hurriedly out of their way.'

'And if we should meet up with a – smaller boat?'

'I know what is in your mind, Gabrielle, and yes, there could be men seeking us, but that was a calculated risk I had to take.'

Gabrielle felt at times as though the fog were closing in, trapping them. She wanted to push it away. To take her mind from it she asked if she might take a turn at the oars, explaining she had rowed when she was with Mr Delacote. Luke refused. 'You just sit and listen,' he said.

He must have been rowing for a good half hour when he said they would anchor and have something to eat. 'Anchor?' she queried.

For answer Luke picked up a leather bucket attached to a long rope, put a big stone in it and dropped the bucket over the side, explaining it acted as a check. He then brought out a packet in which was a piece of dried meat, a piece of smoked bacon, a strip of cheese and some bread. 'A feast,' Luke said. He spoke low.

It was a feast to Gabrielle and she was enjoying the taste of the bacon when Luke straightened and put a finger to his lips.

At first Gabrielle could hear only silence, then she became aware of a faint splash, as of oars. The sound came nearer, there were men's voices. Her heart was thumping so madly she was sure they would be able to hear it. Then the sound moved away, faded to nothingness. Had Luke been aware of someone in the vicinity and that was why he had stopped? When she asked he said he had 'sensed' it. Gabrielle felt comforted. With such a sense of awareness, they would surely come to no harm.

Later, however, they were suddenly caught in a wash and they were tossed about and Luke cursed softly as he attempted to keep the boat under control. A big ship must have passed, but the fact there had been no warning was frightening.

'Some fool neglecting his duty,' Luke said, 'or a ship carrying illicit cargo and does not want its presence known.'

Not long after the waves had stopped chopping at the boat a wind sprang up. 'Good,' Luke said, and hoisted the sail. They seemed to skim over the water and Gabrielle felt heartened. But the wind was penetrating and before long she felt stiff with cold. The fog persisted, never shifting in patches, never lifting. Once they heard the muffled sound of a seaman shouting a warning of the ship's approach but the ship never came near and the man's voice was lost in the fog.

Then the wind dropped and they were becalmed for so long that Luke decided to start rowing again. They had eaten sparingly at their last meal and when they stopped to eat again Gabrielle kept some of the food back.

'Far better to eat just so much now to ease the pangs of hunger, and keep some for emergency. I remember when I was lost on the moors being grateful for crumbs of bread and a sip of water.'

Luke rolled a piece of bread between thumb and forefinger. 'As bad as that?'

'Worse, but best forgotten, especially at this moment.'

'Tell me what happened. Yes, I know I refused to listen before but now I want to know.'

Gabrielle told her story, omitting nothing. At the end of it Luke's face was drawn. 'I had no idea. And to think, after my behaviour towards you that you actually came to try and save me, and the men.'

'I love you,' she answered simply.

'Gabrielle, I don't deserve you. I have a lot to make up for, and I shall.'

She gave him a sudden impish grin. 'You did make a start last night. I liked the sample.'

'It will be more than a sample next time,' he said softly. The wicked gleam came into his eyes. 'You look cold, my darling, I could warm you–'

The next moment Luke was tense, listening.

'What is it?' Gabrielle asked in a whisper.

Luke shook his head. 'I'm not sure.'

Gabrielle could hear nothing.

Luke began rowing again.

There was a constant change in the wind, but the fog never lifted. Luke put the sail up, took it down, rowed, put up the sail, and after what seemed hours to Gabrielle he said suddenly, 'I can smell land.'

'Smell it?'

'Men who go to sea can, and having done this crossing so many times, I know we are near to Dover. I know the currents.'

Not long after this he said, 'I believe the fog is lifting.'

Gabrielle was about to exclaim, 'Yes, it is,' when Luke began pulling madly on one oar and was turning the boat around.

'Luke, what are you doing?'

'When the fog shifted I saw on the cliff top a big black carriage and a number of men on horseback. It may have been some entourage, but I dare not take that chance. We shall land further along the coast.'

A big black carriage. Gabrielle knew who Luke thought it might be, but could her grandmother possibly know they were crossing the channel, know they would arrive at this time and at this spot? No, impossible–

But yes, Gabrielle felt as though icy worms were crawling all over her. No use deluding herself. Where Hesther Quantock was concerned, anything was possible.

They had been closer to shore than Gabrielle realized. Luke had to pull hard to escape the strong current, the surf-crested waves, to avoid being carried in. He started to pull up channel when a booming voice startled them to alertness.

'You can't escape, Luke Caltahn, nor you, Gabrielle Quantock. Come in at once.'

Gabrielle stared at Luke with frightened eyes. He went on rowing, taking long strokes. The voice came again. 'If you don't come in, I shall shoot.' Luke said in a low voice that whoever it was would need all the luck of the devils to hit them in this fog. It had closed in on them again.

Then several things seemed to happen together, a sound, a squawking of birds, wings beating overhead and Luke all but toppling back in his seat, a look of surprise on his face. Then Gabrielle saw the hole in the shoulder of his jacket, a spreading stain, and her hands flew to her mouth. Oh, God, he had been shot.

Luke, recovering his balance, was now looking dazed, He swayed and Gabrielle sprang to action as she saw the left oar about to slip from his grasp. She seized it. 'We must get you ashore, Luke, lie in the bottom of the boat and I'll row.'

'No – no – we must get – up channel–' He shifted along the seat. 'I can manage one oar, if you can take–' She sat beside him and gripped the oar firmly.

Once they were in a rhythm they moved well. She kept glancing at him. Although deathly pale he kept nodding his head to assure her he was all right.

Gabrielle's heart, which had been thudding against her ribs, now began to steady with the task ahead. But questions began bombarding her. Even if she could get Luke ashore would there be habitation near where she could get help? And if they did get help would her grandmother's men find them? How bad was Luke's wound?

When next they heard the hailing voice it came muffled.

The boat was suddenly caught up in the inshore currents and although Gabrielle was willing to let it carry them in Luke began pulling strongly against it saying, 'Not yet – not yet–'

With the result the boat swung round. One moment they were being lifted on a wave and the next sliding into a trough with spray drenching them and the boat filling with water. Then they were in a seething cauldron being tossed about like a cork. Gabrielle, her eyes blinded by spray, could only cling to the oar and pray they would survive. Small waves chopped at the boat and larger ones battered it, then suddenly they rode on a long wave and Gabrielle was heaving a sigh of thankfulness when Luke suddenly slid from the seat to the bottom of the boat. He was, however, still clinging to the oar and Gabrielle leaned across, took it from him and prayed again.

She fought the sea to stop the boat from overturning and the fact that they kept afloat was not due to her expertise, she decided, but help from above. And with the Deity still on their side another long wave beached them in an inlet where an overhang of rock prevented the boat from being seen from the cliff top.

She thanked the Lord silently then turned to Luke, who was now trying to struggle up. She wiped the water from her face. 'Luke, stay still until I see to your wound.'

'I'm all right, we must get away from here.' He spoke thickly.

'In a little while,' she said. 'We do have some protection here. Now take your hand away from your shoulder. I must attend to your wound.' He gave in.

The material of the leather jerkin was

embedded in the hole and the blood had congealed over it.

She tried to persuade Luke to stay and rest while she went to get help, pointing out that any exertion could set the blood flowing again, but he would have none of it, saying he was all right now, it was the first numbing shock that had caught him.

He pointed to the left. 'There's a fisherman's hut up above, and a path leading to it, we shall get help there.' He shook his head, as though trying to clear it. 'On second thoughts it might be a rash move. They would expect us to seek help from such a place. It would be better if we made our way in the direction of Dover, using the cover of the fog, and go along by the cliff face. Yes, that is what we shall do. I would be unable to use the gun but I could handle a pistol.' He brought one from his waist band. 'Help me to prime it, Gabrielle.'

With the pistol ready they were about to leave the boat when a rattling of stones from above brought them both on the alert again. Gabrielle drew in her breath and held it for what seemed minutes, then had to release it. Luke put a finger to his lips, and they sat motionless.

The suspense was terrible, not knowing whether anyone was creeping towards them. Luke must have felt the same way because he motioned to her to get out of the boat.

She did so, trying desperately not to make a sound and give their hiding place away. Luke followed, his long legs making it easier to step over the side. He motioned for Gabrielle to go in front of him away from the direction of the scattering stones. She moved so cautiously, setting one foot down and balancing before putting down the other, she all but over-balanced several times. When she paused to look back and saw that Luke was not there she thought for one heart-stopping moment he had been grabbed and pulled out of sight. Then he appeared round a jutting piece of rock and the relief was so great she gave a small sob. A pebble came bouncing down. And then Gabrielle wondered if capture was inevitable, if those up above were following their every movement.

Earlier Gabrielle had longed for the mist to clear, now she was afraid it would and expose them to gunfire. It was Luke she worried about, his face was drawn with pain, another shot and–

A single pebble bounced on a rock close by. Gabrielle leaned against the cliff face, her blood pounding. She had been right, all their movements were being followed. She turned her head and saw that Luke had stopped. He came to her with barely a sound then motioned ahead where there was a deep overhang in the cliff face.

Gabrielle took off her shoes and walked in her stockinged feet, picking out flat stones that looked to be steady. When they reached the overhang she saw it was deeper than she had imagined. It was not exactly a cave but it gave plenty of protection from above. Luke whispered close to her ear they would stay here for a while, then after waiting a few moments he picked up a small pebble, took aim and threw it far ahead. 'It will keep them guessing,' he said. He waited another few moments, picked up a handful of pebbles and threw them in quick succession, but this time into the water. It was a sound, Gabrielle thought, that would confuse the watching people. Luke then motioned to her to sit well back and sat beside her.

Although they were both drenched Gabrielle did not at this stage feel cold, and sitting close to Luke she could feel the warmth of his body. She leaned over him and looked at his shoulder. There was no sign of bleeding. He gave her a wry smile. 'I shall survive.' He kept his voice to a whisper and Gabrielle did the same when she replied:

'Luke, is it wise to stay here? If the fog lifts we could be easy targets.'

'Not sitting here. I think we ought to wait about an hour. Some of our group will be on the look-out for us, they will see your grandmother's men and get a message to us. It's just a question of being patient.'

Luke was sitting, his head back, his eyes closed. He shifted his position and winced as he did so. Gabrielle said, 'Luke, do you think it wise to wait? Your shoulder needs attention. If the ball is not taken out the wound could fester.'

He opened his eyes, turned his head then ran his fingertips lightly over her cheek. She took hold of his hand and kissed it and he shook his head. 'No, it is my privilege to kiss your hand.' The next moment he was tense, listening.

Gabrielle queried his attention with her eyes.

'A bird call, our bird call.' Luke got up and moved forward. 'There it is again.'

Gabrielle heard it. It had the plaintive note of a curlew, but with chirruping notes in between. She got up and stood by Luke. He answered the call and it came again from above.

'Come along,' he said. 'A little further on there's a path, but still move cautiously.'

It was a long while before they came to the path. Luke had stopped several times to look back in case they had missed it. But then Gabrielle saw the beginning of a narrow track that led upwards. 'This is it,' he whispered.

Gabrielle suddenly became aware of a

change in sounds. She had become used to the surge of waves breaking over the pebbles, now there was only the gentle lap of the water running in and the gentle suck as it receded. There was a change too in the fog, it cleared in patches, closed in again then cleared.

For a way up the path was clear then it was obliterated. Gabrielle, who was ahead, glanced back and saw that Luke had stopped, saw his hand go to his shoulder and the blood seeping through his fingers. Oh, God– She went slipping and sliding back to him, sending down showers of stones. He looked up, then waved a hand motioning her to go on.

She came up to him. 'We must try and stop the bleeding. Have you a handkerchief? Mine is lost.' Luke said his was too, and Gabrielle started to unfasten his white linen neckcloth. She worked with nimble fingers. When it was unwound she made a pad of it, put it to the wound and Luke held it.

'Thanks,' he touched her cheek, 'for everything. We shall soon get help now. You go ahead, I shall follow to catch you in case you slip.'

The path widened at the top and Luke was beside her, giving her a helping hand when she stumbled. The fog was thick around them until they stepped on the cliff top then, as though a magic wand had been waved, it cleared – and they both stopped abruptly, Gabrielle giving a horrified gasp at the scene ahead.

Like a tableau in a theatre, stood the black-clad ramrod figure of her grandmother, the hated sallow face drawn in lines of cruelty. Behind her was her carriage, the breaths of the four coal-black horses hanging in the still air. To her grandmother's left stood Rupert Culver, his expression inscrutable, a pistol levelled at them. And to his left were six or seven men, two of them her grandmother's grooms, all with raised guns. Five other horses were in the background, grazing.

One of the men gave the peculiar bird call and grinned. 'Fooled you, didn't I?'

Gabrielle knew if she had had a gun she would have had no compunction in killing her grandmother there and then.

# CHAPTER TWENTY TWO

Hesther Quantock's gaze moved slowly from the top of Gabrielle's head to her shoes, then went as slowly up again.

'So – you've come to this,' she sneered. 'I hired the best tutors to educate you and to teach you deportment and you turn into a trollop, wearing youth's clothing, a camp follower, a whore–!'

Gabrielle made to take a step forward in protest but Luke gripped her shoulder.

'Your granddaughter is no camp follower, Ma'am. She risked her life over and over again to save the lives of men and women who were dedicated to saving the lives of others. *Decent* men and women, who expected no monetary gain. But then that is something you would know nothing about. You lust after money, after power, you dominate your family, make their lives a misery and get men to kill for you.'

'Be quiet!–' she blazed. 'How dare you even address me, Luke Caltahn, you who are responsible for my granddaughter's down-fall.'

'Downfall? *You* dare speak of such a thing, you would have condemned your granddaughter to a life of hell, married her to a man not only old enough to be her father, but who is known for his brutality. Oh, yes, and there was Elspeth, not yet fifteen years old, who you intended should marry a man whose five wives had died of a disease he transmitted to them through his depraved way of living. And beat them into submission.'

Luke put his arm around Gabrielle. 'And I can tell you now that Gabrielle and I are married.'

'Married?' There was such rage on her grandmother's face Gabrielle thought she would die of apoplexy. 'You may have gone through a ceremony but it would not be legal. My granddaughter would need her father's consent, and he is—'

'We have it,' Luke said calmly.

The old lady stared at him in unbelief, then she began to sneer again. 'Rubbish. My son is not in this country to give his consent, and while he is away I have jurisdiction over his daughter.'

'But we do have Papa's consent,' Gabrielle said quietly. 'Yes, we know where he is, where you cannot reach him. You ordered him to be murdered, but he escaped.'

'I did no such thing, I ordered him to be—' Hesther Quantock stopped, realizing she was about to trap herself. Then she said, 'The whole thing is fabrication.'

405

'It is no fabrication, Ma'am. My – wife and I can produce witnesses.'

'Impossible, impossible,' she screamed. She turned to Culver. 'Kill him! Kill them *both*, they lie about me.'

Luke's arm tightened around Gabrielle. He started to speak but Gabrielle interrupted.

'Go on, Mr Culver,' she said quietly. 'Kill us. Then with the money you get from my grandmother you can buy your wife a fancy ball gown. But when she wears it think of the cost in lives, and live with your conscience, if you can.'

Culver looked pale, and the skin over his cheekbones was taut. He lowered the pistol, raised it, then lowered it again.

This had Hesther Quantock screaming, but this time it was to the men she gave the order to kill. 'And *him* too!' She pointed a bony finger at Culver. '*He* is a traitor. He should be shot like a dog.'

The men shuffled their feet and some looked away.

Hesther stood raging, her hands clenching and unclenching. Then she strode over to one of the men, snatched his gun and levelled it at Gabrielle.

'You first, you filthy whore!'

Luke, who had stepped in front of Gabrielle, whipped the pistol from his waistband. 'Shoot, Ma'am, and you die too!'

There was a shot and Gabrielle, side-stepping, watched her grandmother, with a horrified fascination, recoil from the impact, recover her balance, then sink slowly to the ground. Then she saw it was Culver's gun that was smoking. She gave a strangled sob.

Culver had the pallor of death. He stood staring at the still figure on the ground, then he turned to the men and ordered them to mount their horses. When they hesitated he shouted, *'That* is an order!' To the two grooms he added, 'you will ride with us, you can double up.'

After a split second of hesitation the men ran for their horses, and within a few more seconds they were galloping away. Culver gave a brief glance at Gabrielle, then he too mounted and followed the men.

Gabrielle stood looking about her with a feeling of unreality. A minute ago there had been people, orders being given, shouted, screamed, to kill. Less than a minute ago she and Luke had faced death. Now her grandmother lay spread-eagled, a bullet in her heart. And the only sounds in the uncanny stillness were gentle ones, a soft sighing of the wind, the lapping of water, the muffled sounds of horses hooves as they receded into the distance. Not far away a bird hopped, stopping every now and again to peck at the earth. Life went on–

She went over to her grandmother and

knelt beside her. The eyes were wide open. Gabrielle thought that death would have brought a peace, but the sallow face still held a look of cruelty. She closed the eyes and Luke, who had come up to her said, 'Rest in Peace.'

Gabrielle stood up. 'I have no tears to shed for her. And now, Luke, we must get your wound attended to. I shall unhitch the horses.'

When they were ready to leave she brought a rug from the carriage and laid it over her grandmother. And then she saw a change in her. All the cruelty round the mouth had gone. It was not serenity she saw on the face but she felt that her grandmother had found ease at last from her tormented life.

Although Gabrielle felt no emotion at her grandmother's death a reaction at the violence of it set in before they had gone very far. She began to tremble violently. It was only the fact of getting Luke to a surgeon that kept her going. Fatigue and loss of blood, and no doubt reaction too, had Luke at times swaying in the saddle.

The fog still kept drifting around them but it kept clear long enough in between to find the way ahead. At least it did for a while then Gabrielle found it difficult to concentrate. Was she in Cornwall? Where was Ninestones? They were lost.

Some gulls came screaming over her head, flying so low she could feel the beat of their wings. The trembling ceased and she knew now where she was. Luke was riding, his chin sunk on his chest.

If Luke were to fall from the horse – Gabrielle tried not to panic. Should she leave him or rouse him? 'Luke–' she spoke softly. He raised his head and looked about him in a dazed way. 'Luke, are you all right?'

He turned to her but had difficulty in focusing. 'Yes – fine – fine.' He paused then said, listening, 'Is that the men – their call?'

Gabrielle was about to say no when she heard the peculiar bird call of Luke's group, but instead of bringing a feeling of relief she felt fear. It could be her grandmother's men waiting for them. They might have turned against Culver. She was about to tell Luke not to answer the call but before she could speak he had done so. And it was answered. She looked about frantically for cover, but even had there been any it was too late, several horsemen were rapidly approaching.

For seconds they were just forms in the mist, then they took shape and Gabrielle almost fainted with relief when she recognized Mr Delacote – and Helen. Gabrielle dismounted, tried to run towards them but her legs refused to move. Mr Delacote reached her first.

'Dear lady, are you all right – and the

captain. Oh – he's ill?'

'He needs help, he's been shot–'

Helen came running up and clasped Gabrielle in her arms. 'Oh, Gabrielle, thank God you are safe.'

'Luke–'

'Mr Delacote is attending to him.'

'Helen – my grandmother is dead. Mr Culver shot her.'

'We shall talk about it later.'

It was not until the ball had been removed from Luke's shoulder and Gabrielle had the assurance from Mr Delacote he would be all right that Helen imparted her news.

'It's good news this time, Gabrielle. Your father is back in England, in London.'

'Papa? In London? Oh, Helen, when, how is he?'

'In excellent health. "A new man" he said, a groom brought a letter this morning. Mr and Mrs Felstar are staying with him in the house until our return. Stephen and Lord Sharalon are also there. I wrote to Stephen before we left asking if he would stay in case your father did arrive. I had a feeling he might come sooner than we expected. At that time, of course, I felt your father might be in need of bodyguards. Now, with your grandmother–' Helen paused. 'Thank goodness there will be no need for protection.'

'Helen, I must go to Papa, but how can I leave Luke?'

'We shall discuss it in the morning, Gabrielle. You must go to bed. You look as if you could fall asleep standing up.'

Gabrielle realized then how under strain Helen looked. It must have been a great worry, not knowing if she or Luke or Mr Delacote would return. Gabrielle planned when she got to bed she would try and work out what to do for the best, but she had no chance to work out anything. She slept the moment her head touched the pillow and did not rouse for ten hours.

Her first thought was Luke. She put on a robe and hurried to his room. And there found him sitting propped up in bed, his arm in a sling. He greeted her with a smile. 'Good morning, Gabrielle.'

'How are you feeling?' She eyed him anxiously. 'You look pale.'

'Now stop fussing. I feel fit and shall be getting up soon.'

'Oh, no you won't.' This came from the doorway. It was Mr Delacote. He came into the room. 'You will stay in bed today, and that is an order you must take from me, Captain.'

Gabrielle nodded. 'Yes, you must, Luke. You must take every care.'

Luke groaned. 'Now I have two people nagging at me.'

411

Mr Delacote felt Luke's pulse, touched his brow and declared him to be on the road to recovery. He then left them together.

Luke reached out and ruffled Gabrielle's hair. 'You had it all cut off to help us. Where is your funny hat?'

'Must you remind me of it?' she wailed. 'I wonder you managed to recognize me that first day in the cave.'

'Faces remain the same,' he said softly. Then he added, the wicked gleam in his eyes, 'Mind you, I might not have recognized your shapely legs, but then I had not had the opportunity of seeing them so often.'

'It's easy to tell that *you* are on the mend, Luke Caltahn!' After a pause Gabrielle added, 'Luke, did you know that Papa is back?'

'Yes, Helen told me. You must go to him as soon as possible.'

'I want to, but at the same time I want to stay with you.'

'Your father needs you the most, Gabrielle. It will be better if news of his mother's death comes from you. Then there will be the funeral.'

'I shall not attend, of course, nor I imagine will Papa want to, not after all he suffered at my grandmother's hands.'

'Your father may want to go, Gabrielle. It is his mother when all is said and done.'

412

Gabrielle stared at Luke. 'I fail to understand you. How can you have sympathy for such a woman? *You*, of all people. You swore undying hatred, swore to kill her, to knife her, to strangle her with your bare hands.'

Luke lay back against the pillows. 'Yes, I know, but all my hatred is gone. It went when I saw your grandmother lying there dead yesterday. One minute she was screaming for our deaths and the next she was nothing.'

Gabrielle felt a sudden coldness. Luke was right. All the power she had had was gone. All the family were free.

Luke said, 'For years I've had hatred in me, long before I even knew of your grandmother. There was a girl – I was twenty and madly in love. We were betrothed. I thought it was impossible to know any greater happiness. Then ... she left me for another man, an older man who could offer her wealth. I wanted to die. Later the hatred began.'

Gabrielle laid a hand gently over his. 'Oh, Luke, I'm sorry.

'There was worse to come,' he said, pain in his voice. 'My mother, whom I worshipped, took a lover. There had apparently been others, but I knew nothing of these at the time. The terrible part was that my father, in trying to defend my mother's name, was embroiled in a duel, and while he was dying of his wounds my mother went off with her lover. And that was when the real hatred began in me. I felt sure that all women were the same. Hesther Quantock, with her evil, fanned the hatred until at times it consumed me.'

Luke turned his head towards Gabrielle. 'And you suffered because of it. I treated you badly, Gabrielle, and I'm sorry.'

'Is your mother – still alive?'

'No, she died of a fever in some God-forsaken spot at the other side of the world where she had gone with her lover. I felt at the time she deserved to die. Now I feel regret that she went out of my life, that perhaps if she had lived I would find a reason for her doing what she did.'

Gabrielle was silent for a few moments then she said, 'I used to love my mother when I was younger, but she led my father such a terrible life I felt I hated her at times. I realize, of course, she was under my grandmother's influence. Mama has a terrible fear of poverty. Her father was a gambler and her family suffered through it. Perhaps she will feel differently when she learns all Papa has suffered because of his mother. I would like to see them get together again.'

'I think perhaps you could have some influence on that, Gabrielle.'

'I? What could I do?'

'A great deal. You once told me I had a very persuasive way with me. I think *you* have a more persuasive way. For one thing I was a sworn bachelor and yet I married you.'

'Out of revenge,' Gabrielle said quietly.

At this point Helen knocked and apologized for interrupting them. 'There are two seats available on the stage leaving for London in an hour,' she said, 'Your father will be anxious to see you, Gabrielle. Do you think you could be ready?'

It was Luke who made the decision. 'Gabrielle will be ready.'

When she tried to make a small protest at leaving him he said, 'That is settled, Gabrielle. I shall follow in a day or two. Now go and get ready.'

Although Luke's manner was not exactly cold when she was ready their leave taking was anything but impassioned. He kissed her in a dutiful way and said, 'Take care of yourself. Give my regards to your father and Mr and Mrs Felstar and tell them I shall be greeting them soon myself.'

Gabrielle felt so choked she could only whisper, 'And you take care of yourself, Luke.' And then she was leaving with Helen.

Mr Delacote came out to the carriage with them, which was to take them to the inn to board the stage.

'Now you are not to worry, dear Mrs

Caltahn,' he said gently. 'The captain is on the road to recovery. He is a very strong man, but exhaustion, lack of sleep and loss of blood took its toll. And now he knows you are on your way to your father he will rest easily. I should not be surprised if he sleeps the clock round.' He smiled and patted her hand. 'So there you are, I promise I shall give him every care.'

'You have been a very good friend, Mr Delacote. I appreciate it.'

'You and the captain have been good friends to me, Mrs Caltahn. Perhaps it may seem a little presumptuous of me, but I regard you as – well, family.'

'I feel that to be an honour,' Gabrielle replied softly, and she reached up and kissed the surgeon on the cheek.

# CHAPTER TWENTY THREE

Gabrielle had little opportunity for quiet thought during the drive to the inn. Helen talked, in an almost feverish way, about household concerns, about her maid Marie, and how changed the girl had become after her treachery.

'She made so many promises to me of future good behaviour,' Helen said, 'that I began to feel like a tyrant.'

Leaving Dover on the stage was little better. They had talkative travelling companions who had been on the Grand Tour and were full of what they had seen and done.

It was not until they were nearing London and the other people in the coach had exhausted their repertoire that Gabrielle had a chance to think about Luke. In retrospect the change in him had come about when she mentioned he had married her for revenge. It had perhaps been a thoughtless remark, yet Luke had said he was rid of all hatred. So it could not be because she had reminded him he was married to a Quantock.

Could it be that he was starting to think of

the girl he first loved? Her father once said that first love was something very special in one's life, and not easily forgotten. Gabrielle had not asked him to qualify it at the time. Now she wondered if her father too had been in love with someone else, before he met her mother. Gabrielle felt suddenly sad. Luke was *her* first love, was she to be his second? She was sure he did have an affection for her, it showed when he teased her about the knitted woollen cap. Perhaps something good would eventually come out of their marriage. At this moment it was all she could hope for.

The nearer they came to London the more impatient she became to see her father. Was he in such excellent health as he stated in his note, or was it something he had said to keep her from worrying about him?'

Gabrielle was prepared to find him as frail as he was in Venice and to have a quiet meeting with him. But, to her surprise, he was not only the handsome, straight-backed Papa she had known before he went away, but there was a joyous group of people waiting to welcome them.

There were the Felstars, Lord and Lady Daveney, Lord Sharalon, and Stephen. There were glad cries and embraces, a tearful reunion between Gabrielle and her father, but then they were laughing through their tears, and Gabrielle knew this was no

418

time to tell him about his mother's death.

Lord Sharalon bemoaned the fact he had let Gabrielle 'slip through his fingers'. Stephen was indignant, declaring he would have been first in line, he and Gabrielle were childhood sweethearts.

To this Gabrielle replied with a smile, 'But neither of you gentlemen offered for my hand. Mr Caltahn did.'

Both men agreed they were complete fools for allowing such a thing to happen.

Later Stephen, more serious, asked Gabrielle if she was happy. 'I ask,' he said, 'Because you have a haunted look in those lovely eyes of yours.'

'My grandmother is dead, Stephen. I feel I ought to tell Papa yet how can I spoil the happiness of this reunion? There is so much to tell, at the moment I shall only tell you that my grandmother died a violent death, at the hands of one of her own employees.'

Stephen took her hands in his. 'Say nothing until you are alone with your father. I'm glad Hesther Quantock is dead. She was an evil woman. Why is your husband not with you, Gabrielle? You need his support.'

'Illness prevented him from travelling with us. He should be following in a day or two.'

'Then we can perhaps all celebrate your marriage.'

Stephen looked deeply into her eyes. 'Luke Caltahn is a very lucky man. It was not until I was told of your marriage that I realized just how much affection I had for you, Gabrielle. I only wish–' Stephen smiled suddenly. 'But there, I missed my chance, and I think you must love your husband very much to have, well, more or less eloped. I do wish you both every happiness.'

It was late evening before Gabrielle was at last alone with her father. He stood looking at her, a smile playing about his lips, then he drew her to him and gave her a quick hug.

'Oh, Gabrielle, my baby. How good it is to see you again, and to know you are safely and happily married to a man like Luke Caltahn. It was one of the main things to help me get well.' Jonathan's eyes clouded. 'Before you came to Venice I was nearly out of my mind worrying what had happened to you. I realized that once my mother thought she had me out of the way she could have married you to any monster she pleased.'

A worried frown puckered his brow. 'What do I do now? I feel I ought to confront her and let her know her dastardly plot failed, yet I have no wish to give her a second chance.'

'There will be no need of that, Papa – Grandmama – is dead.'

'Dead?' Jonathan stared at her. 'How did she die, when did it happen?'

'Sit down, Papa,' Gabrielle said gently. 'I have a great deal to tell you.' Gabrielle knelt

420

at his feet.

When the story was told Jonathan wept. 'I am not weeping for the loss of my mother, I just regret that a woman so strong, so clever, wasted her life on wanting to destroy. She never invited affection or gave it, never. Yet it hurts that she wanted me killed, without any feeling or compunction. And all because I learned of her activities.'

'Papa, now that your mother is dead do you think Mama will be willing to leave the family and live in a smaller house with you?'

'I hope so. I feel she might when she hears of your grandmother's plotting. Your Uncle Edward, being the eldest, will inherit. Edward is a generous man and I know he will not see any of the family wanting. If I can borrow a small capital I would like to start a business of my own, I have the knowledge, the contacts. With security your mother would be happy. We must make arrangements to travel home in the morning, Gabrielle. There will be the funeral.'

'May I stay here Papa? I feel I could not stand another hour of journeying. What is more I do want to be here when Luke arrives. He will need care.'

'Yes, Gabrielle, I think it is more important than an unpleasant duty. When the funeral is over and your husband home I shall bring your mother to visit. She will be surprised, but I feel sure very pleased to know you have made such an excellent marriage.'

An excellent marriage? Gabrielle could only hope when the time came for her parents to visit she could, with the help of Luke, put on a convincing act.

When her father left the next morning Gabrielle wondered, with a tremulous feeling, how many more times she would be parted from someone she loved. But she was not allowed to be lonely. During the next few days there was a constant stream of callers, wanting to meet the happy bride and bridegroom. 'News travels fast,' Gabrielle said.

Helen nodded and gave a wry smile. 'And many a fond mama and daughter have gone away disappointed to find out the news is true, and that the eligible and desirous Luke Caltahn is no longer available.'

'Oh, Helen, I wish now I had not come away from Dover in such a hurry, and I did seem to be rushed. If I could have had more time to talk with Luke – his manner seemed suddenly to have changed towards me that morning.'

'There was a reason, Gabrielle. There was a great deal of speculation in the town as to who had killed Hesther Quantock. Luke did not want you to be involved in any way. If, for instance, Rupert Culver were suspected and to save himself mentioned you were

Hesther's granddaughter and hated her–'

Gabrielle was indignant. 'Mr Culver would never do such a thing. Have you forgotten, he let me escape – no, I will never believe that of him.'

'Anyway, it was best you were out of the way.'

Gabrielle walked to the window and back. 'Why have I not heard how Luke is? If he was unable to pen a note Mr Delacote could have done it.'

'Perhaps tomorrow. You know what they say, no news is good news.'

'Luke could be dead.'

'Nonsense. Then you *would* have heard.' Helen smiled. 'You know what else is said–'

Gabrielle nodded. 'Yes, bad news travels fast. Who thinks up all these sayings?'

Three more days passed and Gabrielle was at her wits end to know what to do for the best when Luke arrived at midday. He was immaculate in silver grey, brimming over with good health and was so handsome Gabrielle felt her heart give a lurch.

She wanted to say, 'Oh, Luke how wonderful to see you again!' but instead found herself saying, 'How typical of you, Luke Caltahn! No word, not even a brief line to let me know how you were, and you arrive as though you never had a bullet in you, as though I had never been worried sick–'

'Stop!' Luke held up a hand and appealed

to Helen. 'What do I do with her? The moment I arrive she starts nagging–'

'I was doing no such thing, I was simply pointing out–'

'Quiet woman!'

Helen turned away laughing. 'I shall ring for refreshments.'

Gabrielle said, 'I was not nagging.' This time she spoke in a penitent way.

'I hope not, because I warn you, if you do start I shall have to punish you – severely–'

Seeing his look of mock severity Gabrielle asked, looking at him pertly, 'Punished in what way, sir?'

'You know in what way.' The devilish gleam was in his eyes.

'Well – if the punishment has a tenderness in it, as it had the night in the cave, I would welcome it. You could mete out that kind of punishment as often as you like.'

'Come here, Gabrielle Caltahn.'

'No, you come to me.'

'Disobedient again?' He took a step towards her and she took a step towards him, then Luke reached out and drew her to him, none too gently. 'I once said you were a provocatrice, witch, siren, a rebel, but never an angel, and I have not changed my mind about you. I think there will be a strong clash of wills in our life, but remember this, I am master.'

'I shall have to think about it,' she said.

424

'Think about it?' he roared. 'Stop looking at me like that.'

'Like what?'

'Tempting me.'

'Oh, no, I am not tempting you to do anything, and I shall be quite willing for you to command me if you tell me you love me.'

He put his hand at the back of her head and drew her fiercely to him. 'I love you when you fight with me, I love you in your funny little hat, I love your cropped hair and your courage, your loyalty. Oh, Gabrielle, there should be no need for me to have to tell you.'

'A wife likes to hear it.'

'Very well, if it will make you happy I shall say it at the appropriate times.'

'And what would you consider appropriate times?'

He drew his fingertips lightly down her cheeks. 'Such as the long night we have ahead of us.' Luke drew in a quick breath, then added softly, 'And I think that night starts now.'

'Luke it's midday, daylight–'

He swept her up into his arms. 'I shall make you forget what time of day it is, what week, what month, what year – my sweet Gabrielle–'

'I've already forgotten,' she whispered.

And forgotten she had ever thought of it as a marriage of revenge.

The publishers hope that this book has given you enjoyable reading. Large Print Books are especially designed to be as easy to see and hold as possible. If you wish a complete list of our books please ask at your local library or write directly to:

**Magna Large Print Books**
Magna House, Long Preston,
Skipton, North Yorkshire.
BD23 4ND

This Large Print Book for the partially sighted, who cannot read normal print, is published under the auspices of

**THE ULVERSCROFT FOUNDATION**

# Other MAGNA Titles
# In Large Print

LYN ANDREWS
Angels Of Mercy

HELEN CANNAM
Spy For Cromwell

EMMA DARCY
The Velvet Tiger

SUE DYSON
Fairfield Rose

J. M. GREGSON
To Kill A Wife

MEG HUTCHINSON
A Promise Given

TIM WILSON
A Singing Grave

RICHARD WOODMAN
The Cruise Of The Commissioner